LISTENER'S REMAINS

L. Julia

A NineStar Press Publication

Published by NineStar Press
P.O. Box 91792,
Albuquerque, New Mexico, 87199 USA.
www.ninestarpress.com

Listener's Remains

Printed in the USA
First Edition
October, 2018

Print ISBN: 978-1-949340-90-7

Also available in eBook, ISBN: 978-1-949340-84-6

Warning: This book contains sexually explicit content, which may only be suitable for mature readers, and depictions of abuse, dubious consent, graphic violence, and infidelity.

For my husband, the love of my life

Chapter One

GILLEN SHAVED HIS face with care, knowing it would be the last face his friend would ever see.

Therese snaked her arms around his shoulders and smiled at him in the mirror. She had an ugly smile, as usual. Her smile matched her soul.

"You look wonderful," she murmured into his ear. The warm metal of her wedding band pressed against his collarbone as she pulled him in close.

He forced his lips into a grin. "So do you."

"I always look wonderful," she said. "But I'm not the one changing our lives tonight."

His fingers twitched as he envisioned how they'd look wrapped around her throat. She had pale skin, the kind that would turn bright pink from a throttling. Twenty seconds and her cheeks would be the same shade of crimson as her lipstick. Thirty seconds and he'd never have to hear her poisoned voice again.

Before his dark musings could consume him, Gillen took a deep breath and visualized a flickering candle flame. Focusing on the fire helped to clear his head, making space for the benign thoughts he needed instead. He rehearsed one of his many lists of empty topics as practice for the night ahead. *What do I need to pick up at the grocery store? Eggs, bread, milk.* Emptying his mind helped to calm him down; it also helped him to survive. If he kept himself focused on eggs and milk, nobody who peered into his head would know what was actually inside.

He flicked off his razor and set it on the countertop. He'd done a good job cleaning himself up, but he'd never had much hair to take off. In his youth, he'd appreciated the simplicity his smooth cheeks gave to his morning routine, but he resented it now because it denied him the cover of a beard. Once his picture hit the news, a baby face like his would stick out. A beard wouldn't transform him completely, but it would go a long way toward giving him the anonymity he would need to escape.

Therese slid out of the bathroom and reclined on their sprawling bed. To call it 'theirs' was a bit of a misnomer, since they hadn't slept in the same room in years, but he didn't care to interrupt the charade. As long as she left him alone at night and didn't look on his computer, she could claim all the furniture she wanted. Losing a few chairs and couches bothered him a lot less than the inevitable line of questioning that would come if she saw the sort of things he looked at "after hours." He didn't give a damn what she thought of him or his browsing history, but he also didn't want to listen to her baseless assumptions about his sexual preferences. Those videos were just that: videos. They didn't know him any better than she did.

Therese's dark hair brushed the tops of her shoulders as she made circles on the comforter with her hand. "Do you want to go over things one more time?"

He checked the mirror to make sure she couldn't see the hatred on his face. His reflection beamed back at him, all sunshine and red hair. "I've got it under control, Therese."

"I'm not sure you do."

His fingers tensed again. He clenched his fists below the counter and glanced at her. "All right, how about you tell me what I'm supposed to do?"

A better woman would have taken umbrage with his remark, but Therese had been happy to tell him what to do for years. He'd swear she got off on it, except she never cared if he was there when she got off. In fairness to her, he felt the same way.

"It's about time you ask for my help," she said. "If you'd been smart enough, you would have let me make all the decisions from the get-go."

As Therese ran through her limited understanding of Gillen's job—get in, kill Eduardo, get out—Gillen closed his eyes and worked his way through his actual plan in his mind. While Therese had the basics down, she didn't know the key detail that guided every step he took.

Eduardo could read his mind.

For all Therese knew, killing Eduardo would be as simple as buying a new pair of shoes. Eduardo's ability to read Gillen's thoughts made the task much more difficult. Years of experience had taught Gillen that trying to keep a clear head made even the simplest task mind-bogglingly difficult. In spite of Therese's cavalier attitude, killing someone was no simple task. That was another thing he knew from experience.

Gillen tuned back in to Therese's lecture just as she was wrapping up. "—and by that point, your sister and I will have finished dinner, and we'll share a cab back and I'll get out first. Once I'm home, I'll text her, saying something about how you were there when I arrived, and then she'll get to her house and have a good cry over her husband's body and you and I will have both safely returned home." The red marks from Theresa's earlier eyebrow wax flared up as she scrunched up her nose. "You think you can handle that?"

"Getting home at an appropriate hour? Yes, I think I can handle that." He had no intention of coming home, but she didn't need to know that. If she knew that, she'd probably kill him. Therese had never been the kind of woman to do her own dirty work before—not when cleaning ladies existed—but a betrayal like that would be enough motivation. He almost wanted to tell her, just so he could see the look on her face, but he had nothing to gain from gloating before Eduardo was dead.

Therese glanced at his waistband. "Do you have the gun?"

"Is that why you're looking at my pants, or are you interested in what's underneath?"

She curled her lip and he resisted the urge to smile at her. If she was going to treat him like a moron, she shouldn't have been surprised by his moronic response.

"Yes, I have the gun." He patted the empty space at the small of his back. With his shirt bunched up under his belt, it resembled a weapon at a glance. Therese would figure out he was lying if she decided to look closely, but Therese never looked below the surface of anything.

"Do you have the wine?" she said.

He gestured to the green bottle on the nightstand. Not only did the midrange merlot serve as a good excuse for a visit, but it also gave him the advantage of dealing with Eduardo while he was drunk. Gillen was no expert on mind readers, but he couldn't imagine they functioned better under the influence.

Red lights reflected off the side of the wine bottle, drawing Gillen's attention to the clock. The bright lines flashed in a pattern forming 6:15. If he didn't get going, he was going to be late to his own crime.

"I'm ready to go," he said. "Try not to tip your hand during your dinner with Narcy." He cast Therese a sharp look out of the side of one eye as he snatched the bottle from the table. "You think you can handle that?"

"Don't be smarmy," she replied. "It doesn't suit you."

You don't know what suits me, he wanted to shoot back, but then he realized he'd let his inner monologue take control again and that kind of mistake could get him killed.

He strode past her and into the hall. The scattered shadows of trees waited in front of the windows, obscuring what little of the Chicago skyline they could see from their Lakeview home. Therese had always wanted to cut down the trees to improve their view, but Gillen had no interest in destroying the one thing that made their sterile mansion feel like a home.

His autumn coat waited for him on the rack in the foyer, acting as a dark sentinel in front of the door. With the first signs of snow spreading over the sky, a winter coat would have served him better, but that kind of bulk would only weigh him down once he was on the run.

Therese's sharp heels clicked against the tile floor. "Aren't you going to say goodbye to me?" she said behind him.

He closed his eyes and practiced his times tables. *Three times two is six, three times three is nine, three times four is twelve.* He'd been hoping to escape without ever seeing Therese's face again, but he couldn't risk upsetting her when he was so close to his goal.

"Goodbye, honey." He turned around and opened his arms. Therese's red lips formed a wicked crescent as she slid her hands around his waist and leaned against his chest. The sickening sweetness of her floral perfume wound through his nostrils, strangling him from within. *Poison*, the makers called it. Therese found the scent mysterious, but Gillen hated it with a passion. He couldn't argue with the name, though. It might not have been as venomous as its wearer, but it still smelled like seven different kinds of death.

She leaned in and adjusted his collar. "Just think. Once all this is over, we're finally going to be rich." Her hollow voice bounced off the walls of their six-bedroom house, creating a false harmony with the clinking of their crystal chandeliers. "It's everything we've been waiting for."

He faked his brightest smile, knowing it would be the last of him she would ever see.

Chapter Two

ANDREW'S HEART THUMPED in a persistent, panicked rhythm. He folded his arms over the countertop to make the pounding stop, but his nerves and his veins were dead set against allowing him to relax. They didn't need the help, though—not with Ed staring daggers at him from across the counter.

Deep shadows pooled around Ed's cheekbones as he leaned in close. "Do you have any idea why I asked you over here?" His narrowed eyes disappeared into the darkness.

The bones in Andrew's jaw ached with the effort it took him to keep his teeth from clacking. As he struggled to compose himself, he caught sight of a photo of Ed and Narcy holding hands on the beach. They were total opposites—dark and fair, tall and short, stoic and sweet—but the way they smiled at each other in the photograph made it look like they belonged together. Like she belonged with Ed.

Andrew reached for his drink and grappled with it in a clumsy gesture. Water sloshed over the side, sprinkling the marble countertops. He swore at himself for his clumsiness and swore twice more for his oversized hands. With fingers that resembled knuckled sausages, he should have been able to drink one-handed from a milk jug. Now he couldn't even grab his own glass.

Ed tapped the side of his bubbling glass of beer. "Relax." The edge in his voice made it clear it wasn't a request.

Andrew gulped down his water and wiped his lips. "I'm relaxed."

"Yeah, I can tell."

Ed pulled a stool up to the counter and sat across from Andrew. Though Andrew had a good three inches on Ed—not to mention a hundred pounds—the way Ed kept staring without blinking had Andrew feeling smaller by the second.

"Is Narcy here?" Andrew asked.

"No."

"Oh. Okay." *Damn.* Narcy's sunny attitude would have gone a long way toward cutting through some of the tension in the room. Then again, he'd have to stop himself from flirting with her, and he wasn't sure he'd be able to do that through his already crumbling nerves. "So, did you call me here to talk about work?"

"If I wanted to talk to you about work, we'd be talking in my office."

"Oh. Right." Andrew's fingers twitched against the countertop. "Is it about...uh...money?"

Ed furrowed his eyebrows and glanced around his palatial kitchen. Even with the lights dimmed, any idiot could have seen the proof that the owner of the house was rich. The crystal barware, the oriental rug, the opulent chandeliers; every object in the room proved that Ed was not a guy who would be calling for financial help. Especially not when the man he called depended on him for a salary.

"You can stop trying to guess. We both know why you're here." Ed took a swallow of his beer and set it down with a solid *thunk.* "You're just too chickenshit to admit it."

Andrew swallowed hard. *He knows. How can he know? Did I slip up and say something too obvious to her? No, I would have never done that. I haven't said anything to anybody! I only talked about it online!* His heart beat that much faster and goose bumps rippled up his arms. *Oh God, he knows what I've said on my computer! Did he go through my history, or is he using a key-logger? How much does he know?*

"You're stalling."

"I'm not stalling!"

"Then why don't you grow a pair and admit you're in love with my wife?"

The bitter truth struck in Andrew's face as stomach acid splashed the back of his throat. He clutched his waist and tried not to heave.

Ed's lip curled. "*Hijo de puta*, just look at you. You look like you're going to keel over and die."

Andrew snatched his glass of water and chugged it as fast as he could. It didn't help his stomach, but it did buy him time to think. *I look more pathetic than a dying fish, so there's no point in denying it. Do I have an excuse? Is there an excuse? "How could I not fall in love with her?" is a pretty good one—at least it's honest—but that probably won't make him any happier. Should I say she came on to me?* One quick glance down and Andrew dismissed the notion out of hand. *No, she'd never come on to me. People don't come on to me!*

Something soft settled on top of Andrew's shoe. He looked down to discover Ed's golden retriever, Hester, preparing to doze on Andrew's foot. The muscles in Andrew's back relaxed ever so slightly as Hester tilted his head back and yawned. *He sure doesn't seem to have a problem admitting what he wants, so why can't I?*

"All right," Andrew said, looking back at Ed. "You're right. I'm completely in love with Narcy."

Ed leaned in farther, crossing the battle line into Andrew's personal space. The little calm Andrew had collected from Hester's visit fell away as Ed said, "Give me one reason why I shouldn't fire you right now."

Andrew spit out the first desperate answer he could synthesize. "Because you'll never find somebody else who enjoys running HR?"

"I don't need someone to enjoy your job; I just need someone to do it."

"Um..." *Damn, that didn't work.* "Because you like me?"

"Not right now I don't."

Double damn! "Can I at least explain myself?"

Ed crossed his arms. A brief pause settled between them, stifling the air until at last Andrew dug his nails into the counter.

"Well?"

"I'm listening," Ed said.

"Good. Thank you." Andrew bit his cheek. *Now I actually have to explain myself.*

After buying himself ten more seconds by drinking the last drops of water in his cup, Andrew sat up straight in his chair and cleared his throat. "Look, I didn't have a lot of friends when I was a kid. Nobody ever wanted to talk to me. I was fat. I was stupid. I was weak—if the only person willing to talk to me was my mom, what luck was I supposed to have with other girls?"

"None that I can imagine."

A shiver ran down Andrew's back. *If looks could kill, I'd be dead on the floor.* "I never knew how to talk to girls when we were in high school. I didn't even lose my virginity until after college."

"It doesn't count when you lose it to a prostitute."

"She wasn't a prostitute!"

"Oh really?" Ed swirled his glass around in time with his rolling eyes. "Because the way I recall it, she sure took a lot of money from you when she left."

Andrew's cheeks flared. He hated thinking about his former fiancée, Julie, even more than he hated thinking about the debt she left him in with her desire for expensive gifts and dates. It was only in the past year that he'd gotten his finances back together, and he'd only been able to do it because he hadn't been in a relationship since. Just because he'd deserved to be suckered by Julie didn't mean he wanted to go through it again, especially now that he needed all his spare cash for his mom's caretakers.

He cleared his throat again and tried to keep going. "I didn't want to get caught up in another bad relationship, so I've always tried to stay out of people's way. I was doing a good job too...until Narcy started talking to me."

Even if he'd had the best speech writers in the world to help him, Andrew could have never described what Narcissa Sanchez's small acts of kindness meant to him. He'd been friends with Ed for over a decade, but it was Narcy who made the effort to get him out of his shell when his engagement ended. Just by being herself, she helped him pick himself up again. Her laughter made him want to try to make others laugh. Her smile made him want to give other people a chance. By making him feel human, she'd tapped into a desire for happiness he'd been suppressing since he was old enough to understand desires could be suppressed.

But Ed wouldn't understand any of that. Ed had never wanted something he couldn't have in his life. As long as Andrew had known him, Ed had possessed the uncanny ability to decide what he wanted and take it for himself. Women, money, power; no matter the prize, Ed could win it just by showing up.

"I swear I never wanted anything to happen between us," Andrew said, as much to Ed as to himself. "She's your wife! I would never do that to you! And come on, man." He sighed and gestured at his stomach. "Even if she wasn't, what are the odds that someone like her would end up with someone like me?"

"Jesus, spare the pity party."

Andrew screwed his lips into a knot. "I'm trying to explain things, okay?"

"What's to explain? You took your first successful attempt at communicating with another human being and twisted it into your own personal telenovela. You think some sob story about your wasted youth is gonna make me throw up my hands and say 'Okay, buddy, keep eye-fucking my wife!'"

"Hey! I have *never* eye-fucked your wife! I don't even use that term!" And even if he had, and that was the sort of thing he did, he never would have done it to Narcy. With the limited amount of friends he had, the thought of alienating her was—*Oh god.*

"Does she know?" Andrew whispered.

"Are you serious?" Ed tensed his hands against the countertop. "After everything you've done, that's what you're asking me?"

"Well, does she?"

"No."

A fraction of the weight on Andrew's shoulders lifted, and he sank into his chair. "Thank God."

"Yeah, thank God that I didn't want to put my wife through the ordeal of finding out her so-called friend is only being nice to her because he thinks he's in love with her." Ed chugged half his beer and slammed it down. "Gillen was right about you."

Alarm bells went off in Andrew's head. *Gillen's the one who sold me out!* It made perfect sense. Ed had no reason to spy on Andrew's online activities; if he'd discovered

Andrew's feelings for Narcy, he'd learned about it from another source. Andrew had never been stupid enough to share his feelings for Narcy with anyone—internet friends aside—but Gillen always found a way to get himself involved in Andrew's business. He'd probably been watching Andrew for months, waiting for him to make some slipup so he could run to Ed and say *"you have to fire him and put all your trust in me!"*

"Don't blame Gillen for your problems," said Ed. "This is your fault, not his."

"I never said anything about blaming him!"

"You were about to. It was written all over your face."

Andrew dragged his hand over his mouth. *Damn it, am I really that transparent?* "You've got to see what he's doing to you, Ed. He's been trying to mess with you for years. Can't you tell this is just part of his plan?"

"Oh, so now you're denying you're in love with my wife?"

"That's not what I'm saying!" His voice boomed around the kitchen, shaking the crystal champagne glasses in their delicate shelves. He winced and bowed his head. "Look, you're right about me. I'm an idiot. I fell in love with a married woman who—yeah, let me have my pity party—wouldn't want anything to do with me anyway. But I haven't said anything to her, and I never wanted to! The only reason we're even having this conversation is because Gillen's trying to get in your head!"

A barking laugh escaped Ed's throat. "*He's* trying to get in *my* head. That's rich." He leaned forward, so close that Andrew could smell the hint of alcohol on Ed's breath. "You must think I'm pretty dumb if you think I'd get played by someone that stupid."

Andrew cocked an eyebrow. There were a lot of not-so-nice words he'd used to describe Gillen in the past, but "stupid" had never been on the list. If anything, the guy was too smart for his own good. He'd only been working for Sanchez Commercial Real Estate for six years, and in that time, he'd gone from a do-nothing paper pusher in middle management to the head of finance and Ed's closest confidant. That had been Andrew once, not so long ago, but it hadn't taken much for Gillen to push him out. After all—as Gillen loved to remind him—who ever cared about an opinion when it came from HR?

"Listen, Andy, I'm going to level with you. We've been friends for a long time, so as a courtesy, I'm not going to throw you on your ass. After all," he added, lip twitching, "you've got action figures to feed."

Andrew gritted his teeth and let the insult pass. He really needed his job, even if he didn't need food for his action figures. He had to provide for people who could actually eat.

"I'm also not going to fire you because, in the time that I've known you, you've never had the balls to do a gutsy thing in your life. That's why when you say you never wanted to tell Narcy how you feel, I believe you."

"Thank you."

"I believe you," Ed went on, "but that doesn't mean I'm comfortable with brushing this aside. I'm also not happy with how obvious it is that you hate Gillen."

Andrew puffed up his cheeks. "It's not obvious!"

"Yeah, it kind of is, and it's been a real pain in the ass for me to navigate at the office. That's why I think it would be a good idea for you to take a break."

"What do you mean, a break?"

"I mean a vacation, Andy. The thing where you step away from your computer. You've heard of that, right?"

"I know what a vacation is. But I can't take time off now."

"Don't even try to tell me you don't have the days."

"It's not about the days! There's way too much work I need to do! There's a new hire orientation on Friday—and I'm leading a sexual harassment seminar next week!"

"And I'm sure everyone will be devastated when we have to cancel it."

"Oh come on!" Andrew knocked his fist against the counter. "You may not think it's important, but there are laws around this sort of thing! Do you want us to get sued because some idiot in sales thinks he can grab his secretary's ass as a compliment?"

Ed rolled his eyes. "Come on, everybody's known not to do that since the sixties."

"If you believe that, then you don't understand people as well as you think you do."

"And if you believe I don't understand people, you don't know *me* as well as you think you do." Ed jammed his finger into the countertop, turning his tan skin white above the knuckle. "We're not having a debate. Either you're taking the vacation, or you're putting in notice. Which do you want it to be?"

"I'm not putting in notice!"

"Great, enjoy your break."

"For how long?"

"I'll call you when I think I can stand to see you again without strangling you."

Andrew gnawed his lip. He badly wanted to cite some employment law in his favor, but there was none. Illinois was an at-will employment state, which meant Ed could fire him for just about any reason at any time. Really, giving Andrew the option to take an extended vacation was a gift Ed had no obligation to give. It just didn't feel that way.

"I'll need to go into the office tomorrow to grab my laptop so I can keep tabs on things while I'm home," Andrew said.

"You're not going back to the office tomorrow," Ed replied. "Your *vacation* starts now."

"*Now* now?" Andrew looked at his watch. "It's seven thirty-one!"

"I know, and Gillen was supposed to be here at seven thirty."

A burst of air shot from Andrew's nose. "You called him over to gloat?"

"No, he called me because he had a new merlot he wanted me to try out, and I told him to bring it over."

Oh good, so he's trying to turn you into an alcoholic. Now he just needs to screw you up enough to get you into rehab, and then he'll be the king of commercial real estate.

Ed's lip curled as if he'd had an ugly thought, but he didn't say anything out loud. It didn't matter; their conversation was completely over.

Andrew gently dislodged the sleeping Hester from his foot and stood. The drowsy dog looked up at Andrew with the eyes of someone whose heart had been broken in two.

"Sorry, buddy," Andrew whispered. "I've gotta go."

"You do," said Ed. He made a move to show Andrew to the door, but Andrew shook his head as he threw on his puffy coat.

"Don't bother," said Andrew. "I'll see myself out."

Chapter Three

A LONELY CANDLE lit up the darkness inside Gillen's mind. With his eyes closed, he could clearly see the different sections of the flame. Most people only ever noticed the orange edge, but he knew the fire inside and out. He'd seen the darkness underneath.

His eyelashes fluttered open, and he stared at Eduardo's house. The solid brick square had a good deal in common with Gillen's own home, but Eduardo's location a few blocks west meant he was the one with the higher property value. Gillen couldn't have given a damn about the difference, but Therese never let him forget it. To her, appearance was everything. She would never look beyond the edge of a candle flame.

Gillen's fingers twitched around his coffee cup as he approached Eduardo's front door. He'd gone to a coffee shop to kill an hour of time, as it didn't feel right to spend his last moments of freedom in his empty house. Holding a coffee cup also gave him something to think about that didn't involve his search for a murder weapon.

In an ideal world, he would have been able to bring something to help him. Unfortunately, having a weapon on his person led to having it in his mind. If he had it on his mind, Eduardo would know about it. Gillen couldn't risk being caught with a gun any more than he could risk being caught with his murderous intent, which was why he couldn't bring either inside. Lying to Therese had taken him all of a minute to accomplish. Masking the desire to kill Eduardo had taken Gillen almost a decade of practice.

He swallowed his fears and rang the bell. After a moment, warm light spilled onto the concrete steps as Eduardo opened the door. He was not alone.

"Andrew!" Gillen plastered a giant smile on his face, but he didn't bother hiding the hatred in his heart. Eduardo knew damn well how the two men felt about each other, so faking positivity would cause Gillen more problems than being open with his thoughts. "I didn't expect to see you here! How are you doing?"

Andrew's fat face wrinkled into a folded mess meant to resemble a frown. Gillen didn't need to be a mind reader to know what Andrew was thinking: *You know exactly how I'm doing, you smug jerk.* The emotion behind it would have been a lot worse than the word *jerk* implied, but Andrew had always been too much of a baby to swear.

Eduardo's narrow eyes locked onto the back of Andrew's skull. If Gillen had actually brought a gun, he might have offered it up to Eduardo then on the off chance he'd fire it through Andrew's head.

"Andrew was just leaving," Eduardo said.

"Ah, I see." Gillen glanced over Andrew's shoulder and into the sprawling house. "I take it Narcy already left to meet Therese?"

"She left about an hour ago, yeah." Eduardo nudged Andrew none-too-gently on the side. "Left right before he got here."

"Ah. Good timing on their part." Gillen winked at Andrew. "Means they didn't have to deal with you, right, buddy?"

"*Ha-ha-ha!*" Andrew blurted out. Eduardo winced like he'd cut himself. Gillen kept right on grinning.

"Well, I should probably let you get going." Gillen stepped aside and swept his arm wide. "I wouldn't want to keep you from your busy night."

"Yeah, real busy." Andrew eyed the bottle of wine in Gillen's hand and scowled. "Not as busy as yours."

"Well, you know what they say." Gillen hoisted the bottle up and beamed. "A good wine tastes best when you're drinking it."

"Nobody says that..." Andrew mumbled under his breath. Gillen pretended not to hear him. Instead, he simply held his smile and stepped aside as Andrew tightened his coat and trundled out into the snow.

"Be careful getting home," Gillen said as Andrew passed. "The snow's coming down hard."

"Yeah, because you really care if I make it home alive."

"Of course I care." He leaned in to Andrew's shoulder, obscuring his mouth so only the two of them could hear. "You've got a vacation to enjoy."

Andrew's mouth screwed up tight enough to double as a second asshole.

Gillen let out a triumphant laugh. "Go home, Andrew. I'll keep a close eye on the office for you."

"Screw you."

Gillen stepped back and let Andrew waddle off in steaming silence as the snow swirled around his bulk.

As Gillen smiled at the fruits of his labor, Eduardo stepped beside him and frowned at his departing friend. "You shouldn't keep getting under his skin."

"Oh, what's a little fun between friends?"

A burst of air shot from Eduardo's nose, a hint of a laugh he wouldn't actually permit. "I don't think he's having fun."

"What's he going to do, complain to HR? He deserves a little shit, anyway. What kind of man falls for another man's wife?"

The tight frown Eduardo had been wearing since Gillen arrived wavered on the sides. "He didn't do it on purpose. He's a shut-in, for God's sake. He would have fallen in love with a mailbox if it had paid enough attention to him."

"And if he'd fallen in love with a mailbox, he wouldn't have been risking his job." Gillen gestured toward the front door with the wine bottle. "Now are we going to spend all night in the snow, or are we going to go inside and polish this off?"

"Well, when you put it that way, it's hard to argue with you. Come on in."

As Eduardo guided Gillen into the house, decades of training took hold in Gillen's head. The scattered thoughts on the surface of his mind vanished like snuffed-out flames, leaving nothing but the still pool of his subconscious. Maintaining that stillness required deep concentration, however, and whoever saw it would wonder why it existed. For all Gillen knew, his mind was open to everyone. From what he could prove, only Eduardo could get inside.

Not wanting to keep his mind empty for long, he called up the greatest garbage he'd been storing up for months: the stories from Therese's tabloid magazines. Banal narratives about has-been celebrities flooded his head, smothering his desire to kill beneath torrents of botched plastic surgery photos and wild affairs involving the wives of rappers. He focused in on one he could remember—a story about some baseball player who'd crashed his car on a drinking binge—and held it as close as a man guarding a flame from the rain.

The low hum of a nearby television provided perfect background noise as the two men took their seats at the kitchen counter and uncorked Gillen's gift. Gillen studied the red liquid in the bottle with narrowed eyes. He had to get Eduardo drunk, get a weapon, and use it on him, all without giving himself away. Going for an immediate kill would be faster, but Gillen had waited for too long to botch things in a rush. Getting Eduardo drunk would be the easiest way to put his guard down. Until then, Gillen had to scout for a weapon with an innocent head.

"So where'd you hear about this stuff?" Eduardo said as he took two glasses from the cabinet. The smooth crystal had been etched with an icicle motif that trailed down to a delicate stem. *God, I bet all those rich athletes drink everything out of fancy glasses. I bet they don't even care if they break. Funny, since they break so easily.*

Gillen raised his glass and tapped the side. A delicate chime reverberated from the fragile rim. "I read about it online. Some wine enthusiast site one of Therese's friends got her into. I thought it was a little up-its-own-ass at first, but it really did turn me on to some good wines."

Eduardo took a small sip and let out a murmur of appreciation. "Damn, this is pretty good. Not as sweet as the stuff Narcy gets. Honestly, she'd be better off just getting grape juice and letting the shit ferment in the fridge."

Gillen laughed slightly. "She never did have good taste."

"Ouch." Eduardo chuckled and took another drink. "You know, you've never told me about how you ended up with Therese. There a story there?"

A chill ran down Gillen's spine. Like everything else in his adult life, his marriage to Therese was part of a carefully constructed lie meant to conceal his goal of driving a knife through Eduardo's back. Unlike with the rest of Gillen's lies, Gillen hadn't come up with an appropriate cover story. It had occurred to him in the past that he might need one, but he hated thinking about Therese any more than necessary. Unfortunately, that failure to think ahead meant he had to scramble to make up a lie on the spot. If he couldn't, the truth would bubble up to the top of his conscious mind and he'd be dead before he could finish his wine.

"We met on the set of a commercial she was in," Gillen blurted out.

Eduardo raised an eyebrow. "Therese was in commercials?"

The tabloid fiction shaped itself in Gillen's head faster than he could vet it. Some small part of him recognized it as the same story behind how the drunk-driving rapper met his wife, but he couldn't reel it back in now that the images had started to materialize in his mind. He had to go with it as best he could and trust that his training would finally pay dividends.

"Oh sure, she thought she could act for a while," he said with a short laugh. Even if it wasn't true, it sure fit with Therese's ego. She thought she was the greatest at everything from matchmaking to murder. "She got a few roles in basic cable commercials—you know, the kind where they care less if you can read lines and more if you're good looking."

"She's not bad looking, I'll give her that much." A slight smirk flickered across Eduardo's lips. "So that explains why *she* was there. How about you?"

"A friend of mine from high school had gotten a job on the camera crew. He told me to come by so he could show me a live set."

"Sounds like the beginning of a bad porno."

Gillen laughed without meaning to. Usually he had to force himself to enjoy Eduardo's company, but the commercial story was such bullshit that it had actually earned the jab. "Yeah, I guess it does."

"So you see Therese across the soundstage, and it's love at first sight, right?" Eduardo knocked back half his glass of wine and hissed as it hit his throat. "Is there more to the story, or is that all there is?"

Before he could check himself, Gillen stole a glance at Eduardo's half-empty glass. *He's really in the mood to drink tonight, isn't he?*

Eduardo's smile fell. He stared into his drink and sighed. "I know I shouldn't be drinking this much, but I really do feel bad about Andy."

As much as Gillen wanted to kick himself for allowing his real thoughts to surface, he couldn't let himself get off-balance while no real damage had been done. "Don't feel bad. He's a big boy. He can handle himself."

"He's a big boy alright," Eduardo muttered. "Still, I'm supposed to be his friend. What kind of friend am I if I let him turn his life into such a pathetic mess?"

"You're his friend, not his mother. His life is his own responsibility."

"I know, I know...but why did he have to fall in love with Narcy? *Hijo de puta*, this is not what I need in my life right now!" He buried his head in his hands. After years of observation, Gillen had determined that Eduardo only slipped into Spanish when he was angry, drunk, or sad. Given what Andrew had put him through, he could have been struggling with any one of the three. "Why does everything have to be so complicated?"

A thin whine rose from beneath Gillen's stool. Eduardo spread his fingertips and glanced at the floor, where his golden retriever sat with an expectant stare.

Gillen shifted back in his chair slightly. "Hello, Hester."

"I'll never understand how you can be afraid of him." Eduardo shook his head. "He's the friendliest dog in the universe."

"It's not that I'm afraid of him, I'm just...just not much of a dog person." His fingers twitched around the stem of his wineglass. "Say, do you have something to eat? I don't need anything fancy—I can live with a block of cheese and a knife."

"So that's where Narcy gets it from." After polishing off the rest of his wine, Eduardo hopped off his stool and went to the fridge. Gillen let out an audible sigh when Hester followed.

As Eduardo riffled through the fridge, Gillen steadied himself against the counter and focused on the black flecks in the granite surface. Devoting his attention to the small details in his environment always helped him to clear his head, especially when he was under stress. With the clock ticking down on Therese's dinner and the very-much-alive Eduardo walking around with his dog, Gillen was under about as much stress as he could handle.

Eduardo returned from the fridge with a cutting board and a block of cheese. He set the board on the counter and held out a massive knife. "I think the cheese knife is in the dishwasher. Steak knife okay?"

Gillen's gaze darted down the length of the sharpened blade. "Steak knife is perfect."

"I had a feeling you'd find a way to make it work." He handed the knife over with a laugh. "Narcy usually just tears off chunks of cheese and eats them like a bird."

The cool handle of the knife sank into Gillen's palm. He closed his fist around it and focused his mind. *If Eduardo keeps standing there, I can do the slicing myself and then give him the knife back. That's the way to keep things clean.*

He slid the cutting board over and went to work on the orange brick. He genuinely did love cheddar, which gave him easy memory fodder for piecing together his plan. *I wish I could eat the whole block, but Therese would murder me if I got fat. She always says I carry the weight in my ass, but she's never been right about that. What kills me is when it gets in my chest.*

A clipped bark broke up Gillen's thoughts. He jumped in his seat, dragging the stool legs back. Hester sat at Gillen's feet, his watchful eyes locked onto Gillen's hands.

"He's a scavenger." Eduardo rolled his eyes. "He'll never leave you alone as long as you have that cheese."

"I...ah..." What little focus Gillen could maintain slipped away as Hester opened his mouth, exposing his massive teeth. "Maybe if you could put him outside..."

Eduardo glanced out the window over the sink. A torrent of snowflakes formed a white sheet over the blackened sky. "I'm not sure he should be out there in this weather."

The knife slipped in Gillen's hand. He snatched it tight before it fell. "No, you're right. I'm fine, it was just—"

Hester jumped at Gillen's lap. A memory tumbled out of Gillen's head. A hated memory, something dark and draining, one he'd stamped into the corner of his mind so it could never escape. A memory of the life he led before his father was gone.

The stench of urine rose up from a flattened copy of the Hill City Prevailer. *Foul saliva sprayed across Gillen's cheeks as his father's dog gnashed his teeth in the air. Gillen scrambled back on his hands, but his head struck the wall and he couldn't escape.*

The floorboards groaned as Gillen's father shifted his weight. "He can smell when you're lying to me." The train whistled outside the window, blaring around and around in Gillen's head as his father leaned in and leered. "You wouldn't lie to me, would you, Gillen?"

A warm hand settled on Gillen's shoulder. "I'm gonna go put Hester upstairs. You don't need to worry about him anymore, okay?"

The past shattered around Gillen like so much broken glass. He clutched the side of his chair, wide-eyed and panting. Eduardo had seen inside Gillen's head. He'd witnessed a memory Gillen had never shared with anyone—not even Narcy, who'd been born after their father died. No one knew what he'd been through except him, and his one goal in life had been to keep it that way. Eduardo had taken that from him. Eduardo had to pay.

Footsteps echoed over Gillen's head as Eduardo ascended the stairs. Gillen clutched his knife in his fist. Blood pounded in his ears as he dropped from his stool. His thoughts swirled in a mirror of the snowflakes beyond the window, creating a haze even Eduardo couldn't penetrate.

Memories from Gillen's past floated up unbidden as he slunk up the carpeted stairs. Snippets of nights he'd spent cowering in the corner with his mother, holding her and trying to empty his mind so his father wouldn't know he'd thought anything bad.

The dim lights on the second floor cast a dull glow along the hall. Eduardo stood at the end, hand on his bedroom doorknob. Hester whined from the other side, out of Gillen's way.

Gillen approached Eduardo in silence. Eduardo heard him anyway. He turned around with about five feet left between them. His dark eyes narrowed as they passed over Gillen's knife.

"Gillen?" he said. "Everything okay?"

Seething hatred boiled the blood in Gillen's veins. He gritted his teeth and hefted his blade. "Get...out...of my... head!"

Eduardo's eyes snapped open. Gillen lunged at him, knife outstretched. He fell short of the soft flesh on Eduardo's chest, but he managed to land a blow on the left side of Eduardo's stomach.

Eduardo stumbled back. Unable to stop himself, Gillen fell with him. They tumbled to the floor in a heap, stained by the blood spurting from Eduardo's flannel shirt.

Fury raged across Eduardo's face. His lips pulled back, exposing his teeth. "*Pinche puto!*"

He snatched Gillen's wrist and yanked it forward, pulling the knife with it. Gillen tugged backward and broke the grip. Before Eduardo could try again, he scrambled backward on his hands and aimed a kick at Eduardo's face.

The blow hit home, cracking into Eduardo's jaw with a sickening *crunch*. Eduardo let out an animal scream.

Gillen seized his chance. Crying out, he pushed himself off his hands and drove his knife into Eduardo's chest. The serrated blade pushed through the gap between Eduardo's ribs with the ease of rain sinking through fresh snow.

Ribbons of red shot from Eduardo's chest. He tried to say something, but his voice had abandoned him. All he could do was gurgle as Gillen drove the knife through his neck again and again, screaming and stabbing until the man who'd invaded his mind had been reduced to an empty pile of flesh.

Chapter Four

ANDREW ALLOWED HIMSELF a small smile as his sensible snow boots sank into the powder lining the road. People always made fun of him for wearing snow boots before there was snow on the ground, but he hadn't spent thirty-five years in Chicago without learning that a storm could come on fast.

His smile faded when he looked over his shoulder for Ed's house. He'd only walked a block since leaving Ed behind, but Andrew still felt the shadow of his friend's presence lingering above him. Maybe it wasn't his presence that Andrew couldn't shake, though; maybe it was guilt.

With his own home still another half mile away and the snow blowing strong, Andrew decided to assuage both his guilt and his empty stomach by stopping off for a bite to eat at the local sandwich shop. His first thought upon entering the store was to get a hot cup of soup, but by the time he got to the register and warmed up a little, his appetite and his misery drove him toward a chocolate milkshake instead.

As he waited for the shake, he took the last empty seat in the house—a wooden booth next to the fogged-up window facing the street. He'd sat there once with Ed and Narcy, drinking shakes and talking about video games. Neither of them cared much about games in the present, but Narcy had loved her old Nintendo as a girl, so she and Andrew shared a few good laughs about the troubles they'd had with the game as kids. When Narcy asked Ed if he'd played games back then, he claimed that he didn't need to because "he was literate," to which Narcy replied by sticking her tongue out and telling him she read at a millionth-grade level so she could play whatever she wanted. It had been a stupid conversation, but it had always stayed with Andrew because it was one of the rare moments where someone had his back.

A sharp gust forced its way through the cracks in the window at Andrew's side. He glanced at the gaping hole in the seal around the glass and tightened his coat, giving him the luxury of warmth while he berated himself in silence.

I can't believe I was so stupid. He buried his face in his hands and let out a ragged sigh. *What kind of an idiot falls in love with his best friend's wife?* Calling Ed his best friend was a little much, granted—and more than a little one-sided—but seeing as Andrew didn't have any closer friends in the real world, Ed got to be the best by default.

One place Andrew did have friends was on the internet, and that was exactly where he went when he couldn't bear to keep sitting in shame. With a half an ear focused on any signs of his shake, he pulled out his phone and opened up the gaming chat room he'd been visiting for longer than he cared to admit.

A wall of white text popped up on a dark-gray screen. Andrew relaxed into his seat and typed in the first thing that popped into his head.

Broodlord: *well, my life is over*

A little melodramatic, true, but at least it fit his name. He'd picked his handle only halfway ironically, back when he had seen it in a video game and remembered how his mother used to complain about him "brooding" all the time. If she was going to accuse him of it, he'd figured at the time, he was better off owning it instead. On the upside, he sometimes had fun switching it to Dudelord or Brewedlord; on the downside, moderators had been known to switch it to Foodlord or Broodlard. Not his favorite names, but people who went out of their way to pick on him were still better than people who didn't notice him at all. Plus, if they ever really did hurt his feelings, he could escape them just by turning off his phone. Real-life friendships didn't offer that kind of luxury.

A new message flashed on Andrew's screen.

> KanyeEast: *so your boss found out you wanna bang his wife?*

Andrew winced hard enough to make his eyebrows ache. He'd told his gaming friends about his crush on Narcy about a month ago, and since then, they'd been giving him relentless grief. He hadn't given them any of the names or details—he wasn't that stupid—but he'd given them enough info for them to correctly judge him to be the dumbest man who'd ever lived.

> Broodlord: *yeah, he found out*

> MundeeMundy: *he mad?*

> KanyeEast: *did you ask for a threesome?*

Andrew's whole face fell. So much for hoping his friends would be able to talk about this seriously.

> Broodlord: *no, I didn't, and he didn't either*

> KanyeEast: *did the wifE?*

> Broodlord: *nobody asked for a threesome and nobodys having a threesome ever*

> Blue_María: *He didn't fire you, did he?*

The dying embers of hope for support flickered to life at the sight of Blue_María's name. As one of the few women in their group, Blue_María—whose picture he had never seen, but whose voice he'd at least heard—was one of the few people capable of holding a serious conversation without feeling the need to turn every line into a joke.

Broodlord: *he didn't fire me, no*

But he did put me on an 'extended vacation'

MundeeMundy: *paid?*

Broodlord: *I guess, I mean I've got the time*

MundeeMundy: *lmao then who gives a shit? Have fun on your vacay, play a shitload of games, smoke all the weed*

Broodlord: *I don't smoke weed*

KanyeEast: *seems like nows a good time to start*

Andrew's chocolate shake appeared on the counter. Tugging his coat close, he got up and grabbed the drink, then brought it back to the table. Once he sat back down and ate the tiny cookies off the top of the shake, he checked his phone again and saw a reply from Blue_María.

Blue_María: *So what are you going to do now? I mean, weed aside, obviously.*

Broodlord: *obviously*

Blue_María: *Seriously though. Are you going to look for a new job, or are you going to stay where you are?*

The thought of switching jobs hadn't even crossed Andrew's mind. It wouldn't have been difficult, given his desirable experience levels in an undesirable field, but he could tolerate the people he worked with and had never had any major problems outside of his issues with Gillen. Falling in love with Ed's wife had made a real mess of things, true, but Ed was giving Andrew a chance to make things right. Not taking it would just be rude.

> Broodlord: *i'm gonna stay with the company*

> Blue_María: *even if your boss never forgives you?*

> Broodlord: *God, I hope he forgives me*

> MundeeMundy: *I wouldn't forgive you if I found out you were into my wife*

> Blue_María: *you dont have a wife*

> MundeeMundy: *well I have a dog and I wouldn't forgive Broodlord if he was into my dog*

> Broodlord: *tbh I wouldn't forgive me either*

Someone new came in the shop and a gust of wind blew through the burgundy cover over the door. Andrew hugged his arms close to his chest and berated himself for getting a milkshake in the winter. Then he remembered how Ed used to bust on him for drinking shakes in the cold and he sank that much deeper into his chair.

In Andrew's thirty-two years of shambling around the earth, he'd had a fair amount of jobs. He'd had a far smaller amount of friends. Losing his job wouldn't have been the end of his life, but losing Ed meant losing one of the few tethers Andrew had to the outside world. If Ed didn't forgive him, Andrew would have nobody left except his gaming friends. As fun as they could be when it came to talking nonsense, they couldn't be there for him when life hit the fan.

Broodlord: *there's got to be something I can do to patch things up with him*

KanyeEast: *you can suck his dick*

Broodlord: *im being serious*

KanyeEast: *so am I*

Blue_María: *You did say you were sorry, right?*

Andrew drew a blank. *Did I?* He clawed through his memories of the discussion, hoping to find some glimpse of an apology, but the closest he'd come was when he apologized to Hester for having to go. Andrew didn't need a career in conflict mediation to know saying sorry to someone's dog didn't count.

Broodlord: *I don't think I did*

Blue_María: *Well that's your first step, smart guy*

María might have been an internet stranger, but good advice was good advice. Andrew had made a lot of mistakes in how he handled his interest in Narcy; this was one he could fix.

Broodlord: *I'm gonna go back and apologize to him. This whole stupid thing is my fault and he deserves an apology*

MundeeMundy: *Wait, you're gonna go apologize now? Won't that just make things worse?*

Broodlord: *probably.*

But I'm gonna do it anyway

Andrew slid his phone in his pocket and set his milkshake aside. Then he thought better of it and polished off the milkshake, then chucked the empty cup in the trash.

With that duty completed, he zipped up his coat and braced himself for the cold. As he did, his phone vibrated within his coat. For a moment, he considered leaving it be, then it occurred to him it might be Ed and he checked the front screen. Below the bold numbers displaying 7:45 p.m., a single message flashed in the center.

> Blue_María: *I'm proud of you, Brood. You're doing the right thing.*

Andrew's whole face burned. Had it been summer, he might have been embarrassed, but in the winter, he had one red face among many. Warm cheeks would also keep him warmer in the wind, so he couldn't be upset even if he wanted to be.

> Broodlord: *Thanks :)*

He plopped the phone back in his pocket and left the sandwich shop. As he trudged through the swirling snow, huffing his cheeks and rubbing his hands, he rehearsed a dozen different apologies in his head. Since none of them seemed to convey exactly how bad he felt, he decided he would wing it when he got there and hope for the best.

By the time he made it to Ed's house, his hands were freezing inside his gloves and the flush of embarrassment had long ago abandoned his face. He would have appreciated more time to stand outside and prepare himself, but with the cold air threatening to turn him into an Andrew-cube, he had no choice but to press on.

A flicker of movement in one of Ed's upstairs windows caught Andrew's attention. He knocked his snow-soaked hair off his face and peered upward.

Two shadows wrestled within a halo of orange light. One of them held a knife. Before Andrew could recognize either of them, they collided and fell from view. A second later, a line of blood sprayed across the windowpane.

"Ed!" Andrew tried to run forward, but his "sensible" boots weighed him down and he stumbled into the bushes. Sharp branches scraped his face as he pitched forward into the snow. His stomach heaved at the sudden change in elevation and all the wind flew from his lungs.

Damn it, why can't I just move like a normal person? He groaned, fighting back a mixture of nausea and shame. *I can't stay here in the snow, I need to help Ed!*

A voice echoed in Andrew's head. *¡No puedo creer que vaya a morir así!*

Pain lanced between his eyes. He tried to scream, but he couldn't hear his own voice over the pounding in his head. Spots flashed in front of his eyes and he buried his head between his knees, but the pain kept growing and the spots grew brighter until his body gave out on him and he fell forward into the snow.

Chapter Five

THERESE CLICKED HER acrylic nails against the inside of the cab door. Eduardo's garish mansion loomed over them from across the road. "We really don't need to stop here," she said. "We can just go back to my house."

Narcissa scooted toward the door, paying no heed to how the cheap beads from her thrift-store skirt scratched the fine leather on Therese's Fendi purse. "Come on. It'll just be a second! I just want to grab my phone!"

"I'm telling you, Narcy, you can live without it." Every time Therese said Narcissa's ridiculous nickname, a little piece of her died inside. Unfortunately, Therese didn't have the luxury of risking Narcissa's ire, so she swallowed her pride and spit out the stupid moniker. "Let's just go back to my house and enjoy the rest of the night. Eduardo knows you're with me; if he wants to get a hold of you, he knows he can give me a call."

"I know, I know, but I just feel so naked without it, you know?" Narcissa's big childish eyes went wide in a pathetic expression she must have thought would garner sympathy. Therese's lip curled. *If you think you're getting sympathy from me, you're barking up the wrong tree, missy.* Thanks to that stupid brat's inability to live without her phone, they'd had to leave the restaurant early and all of Therese's hard work was about to be thrown out the fucking window. If Therese couldn't keep Narcissa inside that cab, she was going to walk into the house and interrupt Gillen before he had time to finish the job. It would have been worse if she walked in on Gillen *during* the act, true, but Gillen had been taking his sweet time with "the Eduardo situation" for years. Why should he not be taking his sweet time now?

"Come on, Narcy." Therese put her hand on Narcissa's shoulder. "Just try going without your phone for one night. I know you young people are so attached to them, but it's good to be able to turn your electronics off."

Narcissa's coppery hair shone under the streetlight as she threw back her head and laughed. "Young people? Come on, sis, you're only thirty-four!"

Therese ground her teeth together. *If this little bitch calls me sis one more time, Gillen's going to be disposing of two bodies instead of one.*

Narcissa opened the cab door and stuck one foot out into the snow. "It'll just be a second. I'll just pop in, grab my phone, and then we'll head back to your house. Okay?"

"Oh come on. You really want to bother your husband and Gillen while they're trying to enjoy their quality time?"

The instant the words left her lips, Therese realized her mistake. Unfortunately, Narcissa had already heard her. "Gillen's in there? Why didn't you tell me that? We should go say 'hi!"

He's my fucking husband, I don't need to 'go say hi. I see him every goddamned day. She especially didn't want to say hi to him now, not after his lack of ambition was about to set their dreams back by years. Oh, sure, he'd been gung-ho about killing Eduardo when he pitched it in the beginning—*Do you want to live like a queen, Therese?*—but when push came to shove, he kept finding reasons to back out. *I need to be sure the partnership is structured so that the company assets will pass to Narcissa. I can't kill Eduardo until I'm sure Narcissa will give control of the company to me. I need to, I can't, blah blah blah.* All his need-tos and can'ts had taken him so long that Therese was starting to get gray hairs. What was the point of being rich if she couldn't enjoy it during her youth?

Narcissa wrapped her fingers around Therese's wrist. "Come on, sis! Let's just go inside!"

"But the cab!"

"Oh, the hell with the cab. We can always get another one. Sorry," she added, grinning at the cab driver. "It's nothing against you. I'm just trying to get this stick-in-the-mud off her feet."

Therese's nostrils flared. *Stick in the mud?* "Fine, you want to go in? Let's go in." She pushed past Narcissa and threw open the car door. "We'll go together." That way, she could find an excuse to get Gillen out of there as fast as possible, drag him home, and rip him a new asshole for being too simple to kill a single man.

As Narcissa started toward the house, the cab driver rolled down his window just enough for Therese to hear him say: "That's going to be twenty dollars, ma'am."

A burst of air shot from Therese's nose, forming steam in the cold air. She yanked her wallet out of her purse and shoved a twenty in the driver's outstretched hand. He stared at the bill as if she'd just handed him a dead rat.

"What, you want a tip?" she snapped. "Here's your tip: go back to Mexico!"

The driver's eyes snapped open. "I'm Puerto Rican!"

"Like there's a difference!" She slammed the car door hard enough to rattle the frame and stalked off to catch Narcissa before she could walk in the house alone.

Rainbow light flickered off the enormous chandelier at the foyer's center as Therese and Narcissa entered the house. Therese scowled at the opulent lighting. *Utterly tasteless.* Her lip curled. *Ours is much nicer.*

Narcissa peeked her head past the foyer into the kitchen. "Oh, they're not here."

Cold dread crawled up Therese's back. "What?"

She followed Narcissa into the kitchen, where two forgotten wineglasses sat next to a cutting board with a block of cheese. Therese picked up one of the glasses and sniffed the edge. It was the same cheap merlot Gillen had picked up hours before at the liquor store. She'd told him to buy something nicer since only an idiot would trust a friend who wanted to drink that swill, but he'd insisted it was fine and the quality of the wine wouldn't matter for long anyway. She had to admit he had a point there. *Not much point in spending money on a man who's about to be dead.*

A hard *thunk* shook the light fixtures over the island. Therese and Narcissa looked at the ceiling in unison. "What was that?" said Narcissa.

Eduardo's throaty voice echoed down the stairs. "Pinche puto!"

Primal fear gripped Therese by the throat, choking the breath from her lungs. *We didn't get here before Gillen had a chance to act—he's up there killing him right now!* That didn't make any sense, though. She hadn't heard a gunshot, yet Gillen had told her he brought a gun. *But if Gillen hasn't shot him yet, then what the hell is he screaming about?*

Narcissa gasped. "Ed? Ed, are you okay?"

Therese dug her nails into her palms. If Narcissa went up there and saw Gillen in the act, they'd lose any chance of calling the crime a home invasion. They'd be even more fucked than they would have been if they had to start from scratch.

"You shouldn't go up there!" Therese grabbed Narcissa's arm and yanked her back. "He sounds mad!"

Narcissa tugged at Therese's hand. "He doesn't sound mad. He needs help!"

"I'm telling you to stay here!"

"And I'm telling you to let go of me!"

Wine sloshed from Therese's glass as Narcissa jerked free from her grasp. Therese stumbled back into the counter. Pain split through her skull with the force of a hammer striking an anvil, and she clenched her teeth to bite back a scream.

Narcissa dashed for the stairs, but wrenching free from Therese had upset her balance and she twisted her foot on the polished floor and fell toward the ground.

Panic forced Therese into action. Heart pounding in her ears, she smashed her wineglass against the counter and kept hold of the splintered stem. As Narcissa scrambled for the stairs, Therese hurled herself forward and pinned Narcissa to the railing. Before Narcissa could cry out, Therese drove the stem of the wineglass into the side of her neck.

Narcissa's big blue eyes open wide enough to reflect the light from the chandelier. Her lips parted, but no sound emerged, and her bleeding body slid to the floor.

Therese backed away, blood dripping from her hands. "Oh fuck, oh fuck, oh fuck!" Her teeth clacked together and her heart slammed against her ribs, providing a horrific background track for the nightmarish scene that had become her life.

She didn't give me a choice. There was nothing else I could do. She'd done the right thing; there was no doubting it. They'd simply say Narcissa was killed by the same intruder that got Eduardo. It made sense, really; that sort of thing happened all the time. Over five hundred people were murdered in Chicago every year. The city was a cesspool of violent crime. Naturally, the occasional unfortunate, hardworking couple would be caught in the crossfire. And why wouldn't they be? Eduardo and Narcissa Sanchez had everything a person could want. They had the money for designer clothes, fine jewels, fancy cars, a mansion—why wouldn't someone kill them for that? Really, for all the good fortune they'd had, their deaths were inevitable. The universe had simply balanced their karma out. *Now I just need to make Gillen understand.*

Heavy footsteps descended the stairs. Therese gulped and backed away, biting her lip. *He's going to kill me,* she thought suddenly, and then an even darker thought occurred to her when she realized Gillen might not be the one left alive. If Eduardo had been the last voice she'd heard scream, then Eduardo could have been the one to survive. And if she had to take him on, she was going to lose.

Therese grabbed the second glass off the counter and pointed it toward the stairs. The crystal shook in her hand as two blood-soaked black shoes came into view on the steps. *I know those shoes.* Her teeth sunk deeper into her lip. *He's alive.*

Gillen appeared in full a second later, filling Therese with relief. Her relief didn't last long, as terror devoured it when Gillen's gaze drifted to the corpse of his sister.

His flat voice sent a chill up Therese's back. "I see you two had fun."

"She tried to kill me!" Therese raised the wineglass higher, only half-aware that it wouldn't be much good against a man who was holding a knife. Once she processed the knife's existence, she lowered the glass halfway and tilted her head. "What happened to the gun?"

"There was never a gun," he said, face as placid as a pond.

Therese lowered her weapon the rest of the way and studied her husband's empty expression. For a man who'd just discovered the body of his own sister, he was remarkably calm—far too calm for her liking.

Her fear turned into fury and she clenched her fist around her glass. "What the hell are you so calm about? You just fucked up our entire plan!"

"Did I?" He glanced down at the dripping knife and blinked. "Seems I accomplished what I came to do."

"You were supposed to make it look like a robbery, you idiot!" She gestured violently at the weapon. "This doesn't look like a robbery! This looks personal!"

"It was personal."

Twin bursts of air shot from her nose. "What were you, in love with him or something? Is that what this is about? You're gay?"

The veins in his neck tensed like he was clenching his jaw, but then he swallowed hard and smiled at her again. His eyes as dead as his sister on the floor. "Sorry, Therese, but the answer isn't as simple as you are."

Therese hurled her wineglass at the floor and screamed at him. "Why don't you care that your sister is dead?"

He glanced down at her body and frowned, as if considering it for the first time. "It wouldn't make a difference if I did."

"Wouldn't make a difference? Gillen, she was supposed to be our ticket to easy street! Now how are you going to get control of the company if she's not there to give it to you?"

"You know, I don't really care."

"What the hell do you mean, *you don't really care*?" She threw up her hands. "If you don't really care, then why did we do any of this?"

He descended the steps until he reached the bottom, then tossed his knife to the side. "It's like I said: it was personal."

She stared at the discarded weapon, then noticed the blood dripping from his uncovered fingertips. "You idiot!" she said. "Why aren't you wearing gloves? Now your fingerprints are all over the fucking knife!"

"That's not really my problem."

"Not your problem? Gillen, if they find out you did this, you're going to jail!"

He laughed again. "Not if they can't find me."

"What are you going to do, go on the lam?"

"Exactly."

A creeping horror grew in the pit of Therese's stomach, one that far surpassed the brief tingle she'd felt when she first saw Gillen's empty face. "You planned things like this, didn't you?"

He approached her like he wanted to talk to her up close, but at the last second, he reached past her and grabbed the block of cheese off the counter. With a smile that didn't affect his eyes, he broke off a corner of the block and tossed it in his mouth.

The blood spatter on his cheeks moved with the rhythm of his jaw as he chewed, swallowed, and said, "Absolutely."

The world dropped out from under Therese's feet. She'd been played. *She*, Therese DuCannes, smartest woman in every room she'd ever entered, had been played by an idiot like *Gillen*.

"You son of a bitch!"

"Yes, that's what Eduardo said to me. Or something like that." He popped another piece of cheese into his mouth and tilted his head. "Of all the things I did to prepare, I never did bother to learn any Spanish. Oh well," he added, "not like it matters now."

He brushed past her like he wanted to leave. She grabbed his arm and wrenched him back. "Where the hell do you think you're going?"

"On the lam, like I said. I'd ask you if you want to join me, but I can't imagine how you'd do without your creature comforts. Plus, I get the feeling you're not really in the mood for my company."

"Your *company* was the reason I agreed to all of this!" She dug her nails into the tender flesh beneath his wrist until the acrylic points sank into his veins. "You're not going to walk away from this!"

"I'm sorry. Would you prefer I stay and confess to my crimes? If I did, I'd have to name you as an accomplice."

"*Me?* How dare you rope me into this? This was all you!"

Gillen gestured to the bleeding pile of hair and skin that had once been his sister Narcissa. "With all due respect, Therese, I think that was you."

"I did it to help you, you asshole!"

"No, you did it to help yourself, and now you're backpedaling as fast as you can because your clever scheme is blowing up in your face." He twisted his wrist around so his hand was on top of hers. "Now the sooner you let me go, the sooner I can get out of your hair and let you start imagining how you're going to decorate your prison cell."

Whatever remained of her good judgment fled, and she drew back and slapped him in the face.

His empty smile warped into a twisted snarl and his nostrils flared. "You know, I always told myself I would never hit a woman."

She bared her teeth, readying a comeback, but then he stepped back and added, "but you're no woman," then cracked her cheek with the back of his hand.

Therese let out a howl of fury and clasped her palm over her stinging jaw. The cool flesh on her hands helped soothe the burn from the hit, but it did nothing to quench the flames of hatred in her heart.

He pushed her aside and strode toward the door. Her voice cracked as she tried to scream at him. "You won't get away with this!"

Gillen glanced over his shoulder, lips curved into the closest thing to a genuine smile she'd ever seen him make. "Actually, I just did."

A gust of wind tore through the house as he opened the front door. With one last wave, Gillen slipped on his coat, stepped into the snow, and slammed the door in her face.

Therese sank to her knees and screamed until her throat gave out. *How could he do this to me? That manipulative, traitorous, psychotic son of a bitch!* An hour ago, her life had been perfect. Now she had no husband, no money, and two corpses bleeding all over her favorite pair of Jimmy Choos, and all of it was Gillen's fault.

She had to make him pay.

Her breathing slowed as she reached into her purse for her phone. By the time she dialed 911, her heart rate had almost reached its usual speed.

A problem, really, since it made it that much harder to fake her terror when the operator picked up and Therese shouted, "Help me, please! My husband's just murdered his sister!"

Chapter Six

SEARING PAIN COURSED through Gillen's forehead, blinding him as he pushed his way through the falling snow. He'd been able to grit his teeth and hide it long enough to humiliate Therese—though he'd almost snapped when she made that 'gay' crack—but once he got outside, he couldn't keep up the facade any longer. He could barely pick his knees up high enough to trudge through the snow the short distance to his car. That distance gave his thoughts all the opening they needed to descend on him.

The image of his blood-soaked sister flickered inside of his head. *How could I have let her kill Narcy?* He gritted his teeth and shoved the memory aside. Narcy had led a charmed life, from the minute she was born until about ten seconds before she died. In a way, it was a mercy that she'd died without ever having to know what real misery looked like. *But she still shouldn't have had to die this way. I shouldn't have let her die!*

"Why did she have to die?"

Agony split Gillen's forehead in half. He cried out and crumpled forward into the snow. His breath shot from his mouth in short spurts as he clenched his eyes tight and tried not to scream. For the sake of his survival, he had to ignore both the pain and the unfamiliar voice of doubt in his head.

He pushed himself off the ground and ran the rest of the way to his car. The pounding slowed down when he finally caught sight of the vehicle. A few months prior, Gillen had gone online and found someone looking to sell one of the most common sedans on the market. Using the cash he'd been hoarding in his personal account, Gillen bought the car and parked it close enough to Eduardo's house to reach in a hurry. Sure enough, the beige sedan sat waiting for him on the corner, covered in snow but otherwise ready to go.

Gillen used the sleeve of his coat to wipe the powdery layer of snow off the windshield and ducked inside the car. Once inside, he peeked into the white shopping bag of supplies beneath the passenger's seat and sighed with relief. Everything he needed sat there, waiting to aid him in his brief life on the run.

I need to get moving. His own inner voice returned, full of conviction and drive. *If I know Therese as well as I think I do, she's already stabbed me in the back. The police will be on their way any minute.* The falling snow would cover his footprints and the police wouldn't be able to recognize his car, but there were only so many redheaded men in their thirties around, even in a city as Irish as Chicago. If he stuck around too long, he'd inevitably be caught.

He gritted his teeth and sat up straight, then threw the car into drive. The run-down sedan didn't start up with the same smoothness as the cars he'd had at home, but it got the job done without any unnecessary pretension. It also didn't stick out in traffic the way Therese's neon-blue Porsche did. His little sedan wouldn't fare nearly as well in a police chase, but he wouldn't have to worry about a chase if they couldn't recognize his car.

The orange streetlights sparkled off the falling snow as Gillen pulled away from the curb and made his way toward the expressway. He had a long drive ahead of him, but he didn't need a map. He'd been where he was going before. True, he'd never been the one to drive there, but he'd seen the route enough times as a child that it had been stamped into his brain. Perhaps if he'd lived somewhere that received frequent road reworking, he would have risked getting lost, but fortunately, the Midwest had never had the spare money to do a substantial overhaul of the roads.

The closer he got to the expressway, the more his headache lifted. Unfortunately, easing the fog in his brain made way for gut-clenching fear. *The police are going to catch me too soon. I didn't make it out in time. I should have never used Therese.*

"I should have never trusted that fucking pile of shit!"

The mental outburst caught Gillen so off guard that he almost blew a red light. He slammed on the brakes, bringing the car to a screeching halt. Had the roads not already been salted, he would have careened straight through the intersection.

What the hell is wrong with me? He clutched the steering wheel. He'd always had a lot of contempt for Therese, but "fucking pile of shit" was much stronger than his usual opinion of her. If anything, he preferred to pay her no regard. He'd never felt particularly bad about deceiving her, what with her toxic personality and utter disregard for human life, but he'd deceived her all the same. To write her off entirely would make him as big a monster as Eduardo.

The light turned green, casting emerald on the snow. Gillen stepped on the accelerator and rocketed forward. *Just a little bit farther and this city will be behind me and I'll never look back.*

Even with the weather acting against the cars on the road, the streets were still jam-packed with drivers trying to keep Gillen from his goal. In order to preserve the last vestiges of his sanity, Gillen grabbed a CD from his supply and slid it in the stereo.

The speakers jumped to life, blasting a Bob Dylan song off the soundtrack from one of his favorite films. He dialed the volume back a notch and smiled once the sound hit a reasonable level.

"This won't be so bad." He tapped his fingers against the steering wheel and focused on the music as he made his way to the expressway. Listening to old favorites was one of the few ways he knew how to relax. He could keep his mind clear without putting any effort into it, and he didn't have to worry about anyone discovering the man hidden beneath his surface thoughts.

"*¿Por qué chingados estoy dentro de la mente de Gillen?*"

Gillen grabbed the steering wheel so hard his fingernails cut the undersides of his palms. "What the hell is going on?" A runaway internal monologue was one thing; he'd been working on keeping a clear head for years, so it was only natural for his thoughts to rebel against him in moments of stress. But for him to have a thought in a language he didn't speak? To think something he couldn't even understand? It went beyond the "errant thought" category and into the insane.

His heart thudded against his ribs as he racked his brain for why he'd suddenly had a bilingual outburst in his head. *Was it what Eduardo said to me before he died?* No, that had been something else—one or two words, ones Gillen suspected were swears but ultimately couldn't place. That was true of most of the Spanish Gillen heard from Eduardo, though. For reasons Gillen had never fully been able to understand, Eduardo made a real effort to strictly speak English in front of his friends. The only times he slipped into Spanish were when he was tired, frustrated, or pissed. Those moods didn't lend themselves to full sentences—especially not ones Gillen could understand. *So if I can't understand Spanish, how did it get into my head?*

The current track on Gillen's CD faded out and segued into the next song: a Spanish cover of "Hotel California." Palpable relief flooded Gillen's body and he let out a hacking laugh.

"It's just the song!" He'd listened to that soundtrack a hundred times and knew it front to back. Obviously he would've remembered the next song coming up was in Spanish. Why else would he have a foreign language in his head?

He turned up the song and kept right on laughing as he approached the turn for the expressway, ready to leave the city behind him at last. With Eduardo gone, his sister dead, and Therese on her way to a ladies' supermax, he had nothing tying him back to the life he'd always hated. He was free.

With a smile on his face, he flipped on his blinker and glanced up at the rearview mirror. The reflection of Eduardo stared back at him, dark eyes narrowed and dead.

Chapter Seven

BRIGHT LIGHTS LIT up behind Andrew's eyelids, turning the darkness a blinding orange. He groaned and lifted his hand to swat at the air. A thin plastic cord smacked against the skin inside his elbow when he tried to move his arm. He furrowed his brow and cracked open one eye as much as he could handle.

Expensive equipment surrounded Andrew on all sides. Not computer equipment—not the type he was used to—but medical equipment, the kind that emitted all sorts of serious boops and beeps. The small noises mixed with the wail of a siren and blue and red lights flickering off the walls. Those lights didn't come from inside; they came from the other side of the squat door down by Andrew's feet. Andrew himself lay in the center of it all, with an IV in his arm and a white sheet beneath his legs.

"*Dios mio,* I was starting to think you'd never wake up."

Andrew whipped his head toward the voice. A short dark-haired woman with laughing eyes and a wide smile sat on the bench by his side. Andrew's first assessment of her would have been "friendly," except friendly people did not typically carry guns. This woman, on the other hand, had a big one right on her hip.

"Oh my God!" Andrew shrank against the hard cot beneath him. "Did you come here to shoot me?"

She cocked her head to the side. "Why? Did you do something I'm supposed to shoot you for?"

He clutched the sides of his cot and struggled to breathe. "Oh my God, did I?"

For just a moment, the woman held her expression perfectly still, and then she threw back her head and started laughing. "Relax, will you? I'm not here to shoot you. What do you think this is, a movie?"

His teeth chattered like his mother's old typewriter as he glanced from side to side. "I don't know what this is. Where the heck am I?"

"You're in an ambulance, *amigo*. We found you passed out in the snow."

Andrew propped himself up on his elbows so he could get a better look around. Sure enough, he *was* in an ambulance, and both he and it were rumbling down the road at a more than reasonable clip.

"Passed out in the snow..." he mumbled to himself. "Why would I have been passed out in the snow? I felt fine when I was at the sandwich place, and nothing changed when I was walking to Ed's house—"

His memories returned in a flash, bombarding him with the same force that had first laid him low. His eyes shot open and he jerked up straight. "Ed!"

"So you did see something." The strange woman's smile flattened into an uneasy frown. "I'm sorry you had to go through that."

"Go through what? What happened?" The murky shadows in Ed's window taunted Andrew from the edge of his memory. "Oh my God, is Ed okay?"

"I'm sorry, Andrew." She lowered her head. "Eduardo is dead."

Andrew parted his lips, but he found he had nothing to say. The oh-my-Gods he'd been stammering since he woke up weren't nearly enough to convey the whirlwind tearing through his head. *How can Ed be dead?*

Before Andrew could figure out what to say, the strange woman held out her hand. "I should introduce myself, by the way. I'm Detective Caroline Ramirez, with the Chicago PD."

He took her hand and offered a limp shake, which was the best he could do under the circumstances. "Hi, uh, I'm Andrew, Andrew Warner...but wait, did you call me Andrew already?"

"We got your identity from your wallet," she said. "But don't worry. We put it back in your pocket. We didn't take anything, I promise."

"We?"

"My partner and I. He's back at Eduardo's house, interviewing another potential witness."

"Another witness..." Andrew racked his brain, trying to think back. "Wait, are you talking about Gillen?"

She laughed again, but this laugh didn't match the others. This one had something cold in it. "Oh, he's definitely a witness."

A shiver ran down Andrew's back. "What happened?"

"How about you tell me what you remember first, and then I'll tell you what happened?"

"Oh, uh, I guess that makes sense." His tongue slipped between his lips as he concentrated on the hazy memories surrounding his evening. Had he been with a woman he cared about impressing, he might have worried about looking stupid, but sticking his tongue out helped him think, and right now, thinking was what mattered. "Well, I was over at Ed's house earlier tonight—it's still tonight, right?"

She smiled slightly. "Yes, it's still tonight."

"Right. Um, okay, so I was over at Ed's house, and we kind of had a falling out."

"Can I ask what you were fighting about?"

Fear dropped through Andrew's stomach like a heavy stone. "I swear to God I didn't kill him!"

Her eyes crinkled at the corners and she shook her head. "Andrew, if I thought you were the killer, do you think we'd be having such a casual conversation right now?"

He glanced around the ambulance with a cocked head. She *was* acting pretty familiar with him, but he'd also just taken a blow to the head. For all he could tell, he was completely misinterpreting the situation.

"This isn't what I would call casual…"

"Okay, maybe not—but if you were the one who killed Eduardo, then I'd love to know why you thought you could escape by running outside and passing out in the snow."

A hot blush consumed his cheeks. "I guess that would be pretty dumb, huh?"

"Not the dumbest thing I've seen, but up there. Now you were saying about your fight with Eduardo?"

"Er, yeah, that." Andrew rubbed his forehead and winced. "I, uh, kind of fell in love with Ed's wife." The realization that Narcy had just lost her husband hit Andrew hard enough to make his whole head throb. "Oh my God, Narcy must be devastated."

Detective Ramirez hesitated for just a second. That second was more than enough to stop Andrew's heart. "Did something happen to Narcy?"

"Look, Andrew, I…" She glanced away, brows furrowed. She probably wanted him to give his statement before she released any info that could alter his memory, but she must have known he had his limits. "She's on her way to the hospital too. She's not in good condition."

His eyes snapped open. The last time he'd seen Narcy hurt, it was because she'd tripped on the sidewalk while trying to text and walk. She'd torn a hole in her jeans and ripped up the skin on her knee, but she'd laughed it off and said the universe would have to try harder than that to get rid of her. Apparently, the universe just had.

"What happened to her?" said Andrew.

"That's what we're trying to figure out."

Andrew's heart sank in his chest. Detective Ramirez probably didn't want to have this conversation any more than he did. The least he could do was keep things moving forward.

"I had a fight with Ed about Narcy," he said, "and after the fight was over, I left his house. On the way out, I ran into Gillen."

"Gillen was coming to visit Eduardo?"

"Yeah, he had a bottle of wine for them to drink something. I'm not sure. After that, I went and got a milkshake about a block north of here—"

"You got a milkshake in this weather?"

His earlier blush returned with a vengeance. "I get milkshakes when I'm depressed, okay?"

"And you were depressed?"

"Because I'd just torched the only real friendship I had? Yeah, you could say that." He leaned back and rested his head on the pillow. "So that's why I decided to go back and apologize. Once I got there, things get a little hazy, but I definitely remember seeing something in Ed's window — I think it was two people fighting."

"Which window was this?"

He pointed upward, as if they were in front of Ed's house and not in the back of an ambulance. "Upstairs."

"The hallway. Right."

Andrew shot a quick glance at her empty hands. "Aren't you supposed to be writing this down?"

"I've got a good memory." She tapped the side of her head as if to prove her point. "So after that is when you passed out?"

"Right, and that's all I remember until I woke up here. So now that I've told you what I know, will you please tell me what you know about what happened?"

Detective Ramirez folded her hands behind her head and leaned back against the ambulance wall. Another person might have thought she was being flippant, but Andrew had been in Human Resources long enough to know that people dealt with uncomfortable conversations in a multitude of ways.

"Sometime between seven and eight o'clock, after Gillen arrived at Eduardo's house but before you came back from the sandwich shop, there was an altercation on the second floor that resulted in Eduardo's death. A few minutes later, Gillen's wife Therese arrived at the house with Narcissa—"

"Narcy," Andrew corrected.

"Therese arrived at the house with Narcy, and Narcy was wounded in a second assault."

Andrew had a dark suspicion that he knew who was behind both assaults, but he didn't have the guts to say it out loud. "Wounded by who?"

"According to Therese...that would be Gillen."

That son of a bitch! Andrew gritted his teeth with enough force to make his jaw tremble. *Why didn't Ed listen to me? Why couldn't he trust me as a friend?*

"I could ask you the same question!"

Andrew blinked. He'd heard another voice, but it didn't match the thoughts in his own head. "Did you say something?"

Detective Ramirez shook her head. "No, the last thing I said was that Therese said it was Gillen."

"Right." He scrunched up his lips. "That's what I thought." *Maybe I hit my head on something when I fell down in the snow.* "So what happens now? You've got Gillen in custody, right?"

Her smile twisted to the side. "We're looking for him."

"You mean he got away? How? Didn't all of this just happen? Can't you go follow his car or something?"

"He didn't use his car."

"So Therese's car!"

"He didn't use her car either."

"Then how did he get away?"

Detective Ramirez shrugged her hands and sighed. "*Sepa la bola.*"

God, am I the only person in this city who doesn't speak Spanish? "What is that," he asked, "the bus or something?"

"Not quite," she said with a laugh. "It means we don't know."

"Oh." The gravity of the expression finally sank in, and he stared at the floor. "He's not going to get away with this, is he?"

"We'll see."

The strange voice popped into his head again. *"What kind of fucking answer is that?"*

Andrew blinked, taken back. While he didn't know why his internal monologue had gotten so crass all of a sudden, he couldn't disagree with the sentiment. *We'll see* was barely an okay answer when the question was *Can we go out for ice cream after dinner?* It didn't help one bit when the question was about catching a runaway murderer.

"I just can't believe this..." He slumped over and buried his head in his hands. "I always knew Gillen was a slimeball, but for him to kill Ed—not to mention his own sister! It doesn't make any sense! I mean, did he want this all along, or did he just lose his mind?"

The voice whispered in his head. *"Hester."*

Andrew jolted upright. "Hester!"

Detective Ramirez raised her eyebrows. "The football player? What? You worried about your fantasy picks or something?"

"No, I'm not talking about the football player, I'm talking about the dog! Ed's dog, Hester!" He grabbed the hem of the detective's winter coat and clenched it in his fists. "Please tell me he's okay?"

"Oh, you mean the big goofy golden? Yeah, he's okay."

Andrew let out an audible sigh of relief. He could handle a lot of tragedy, but a dead dog would have pushed things well past his limit. "Thank God."

"He was locked in his crate upstairs when we got there. My partner took a real liking to him. Good, too," she added with a frown, "since that pup's going to need a place to say."

"I'll take him."

"You sure about that? You're sitting in the back of an ambulance, after all. We still don't know if you're okay."

"I'm fine," he said. "I'm just a big baby who got scared when he saw a fight and passed out in the snow. I'm sure the hospital's going to get mad at you for sending me there when they've got people with real problems to treat."

"Maybe they will, maybe they won't, but we're not going to take the risk just because you say you're okay." She flashed a grin. "Either way, your insurance company will be happy to bill you."

"Oh, good. That's something else I can look forward to." He pinched the bridge of his nose. "Maybe I can get Hester to eat the bills."

"If that dog knows how to eat bills, you can send him over to my house next."

"I'll do that."

A wave of fatigue came over him and he sank back against the cot again. "I just can't believe he's dead. And Narcy..."

"Narcissa could pull through. We need to have hope."

"Why? So she can wake up and find out her brother murdered her husband? She doesn't deserve that. She doesn't deserve any of this."

"And you're saying I did?"

Pain pierced the center of his forehead. He gasped and grabbed the sides of his head. When the agony finally subsided, he realized Detective Ramirez had her hand on his arm.

"Are you okay?" she murmured.

He swallowed hard and nodded. "I think I'm okay..." As he glanced around, trying to get his bearings again, it occurred to him that there was something majorly out of place. "Shouldn't there be an EMT back here with me or something?"

"They needed everyone they could spare for Narcy."

A pit opened up beneath Andrew's stomach. He'd never felt like such a baby. "Oh." Still, it seemed strange that he'd been left alone with someone without any medical training. Then again, maybe detectives did have medical training and he didn't know procedure. After everything that had happened that night, he wasn't sure he knew what was going on with anything.

"I'm going to rest until we get to the hospital," he mumbled. "I've got a lot to think about."

"Go ahead," said the detective. "You take as long as you need."

"Thanks."

He leaned his head against the stiff pillow and tried to calm himself down, but he couldn't stop thinking about Ed's death. *He didn't deserve this either. He was a good man. He just got manipulated. Gillen's the bad guy here, not Ed.*

"And when all this is over, I'm gonna make him pay."

Chapter Eight

THERESE SQUINTED AT the turquoise-painted brick, willing it to become less hideous. *I know they're trying to intimidate witnesses in this room, but there's only so much one person can take.*

The fact that she'd been waiting in the interrogation room for over three hours did nothing to improve her mood. On the plus side, the wait afforded her ample time to contact their family's lawyer. On the minus side, their lawyer had done more work for Gillen in the past than he had for Therese, which meant he could no longer be trusted. After Gillen's little stunt earlier that night, Therese had no idea just how many traps Gillen had laid for her as part of his escape. For all she knew, he'd paid their lawyer on the sly to put Therese in chains. Too bad for Gillen, though, because Therese was not a stupid woman. If Gillen wanted to trap her, he was going to have to work a hell of a lot harder than that.

The cheap wooden door in the corner opened with an agonizing creak. A tall man in an ill-fitting suit walked into the room and closed the door behind him. She'd seen the man briefly before; he'd been one of the detectives at the scene. While she hadn't had a chance to interact with him directly, she had overheard him long enough to pick out his accent: the Minnesota accent, perhaps the worst pattern of speech a person could possess. Had Gillen retained the accent he'd acquired there in his youth, she would never have married him. Fortunately, he'd worked hard enough to stamp it out, which until about four hours ago, she'd considered to be proof of his relentless drive. Now she saw it for what it was: just another part of the con.

The detective approached the desk and extended his hand. "Good evening, Mrs. Lynch. I'm Detective Jeremy Olson."

Therese sized him up in an instant. His pathetic attempt at a handshake—elbow dropped, wrist bent—marked him as a man of little worth and even less resolve. His cheap wristwatch did nothing to help matters. On the appearance front, he fared slightly better. He fell into the appropriate height range—above six feet, but not monstrously so—and had an acceptable physique for a man who appeared to have spent the first forty years of his life behind a desk. His hairline had clearly receded from its heyday, but he'd held onto the volume and styled it in a manner befitting both the quality of his hair and his age. On her most charitable day, she might have even called him handsome.

This was not her most charitable day.

"It's Ms. DuCannes," she replied, ignoring his hand, "and no, it's actually not a good evening. I just found out my husband is a psychopathic killer, and my sister-in-law and her husband are dead."

"And I'm awful sorry for your loss." His body language made him appear suitably chastened, but he had a twist to one side of his mouth that suggested he was amused. She flexed her fingers beneath the table and narrowed her eyes. *You may find me funny now, Detective, but you won't be laughing when I have your badge for mistreating a witness.*

The detective took his seat across from her—without being asked—and produced a pad of paper and a tape recorder. "There are a few procedural matters we need to go through before I can take your statement, Mrs. DuCannes. Are you ready to start, or do you need a few more minutes?"

Therese's back teeth ground together. *He's butchering my name on purpose. He's trying to get under my skin.* "I'm ready."

"Good." He picked up the tape recorder, then paused and put it down again. "Have you been in contact with your attorney?"

"He's unavailable at this late hour, as you can imagine."

"Do you want us to get you someone from the public defender's office?"

Therese bristled against her chair. *What kind of idiot does he think I am?* The last thing she needed was some snot-nosed little shit fresh out of law school talking to her like he knew best. If she wanted guaranteed bad advice, she had Gillen's lawyer right in her phone. At least she knew what that one would be billing ahead of time.

"I'm not worried about getting a lawyer, Detective. I have nothing to hide."

"I never said you did."

She hesitated for a moment, then flashed her brightest smile. "Let's get started."

He clicked on the tape recorder and rattled off a series of instructions and warnings she'd heard a thousand times before on dated reruns of police procedurals. Therese could barely handle it for five minutes before her patience hit its breaking point. *If this son of a bitch doesn't wrap this up soon, I swear to God I'll confess just to shut him up.*

"Would you?"

Therese snapped up straight. "What was that?"

"What was what?" said the detective.

"I thought I heard..." She stopped herself before she could say something that would potentially make her sound insane. "It was nothing. I'm sorry. It's been a very hard day."

"For sure, for sure. Luckily, I'm all finished dotting my Is and crossing my Ts, so now you and I can have a real conversation. Why don't you take me through what happened earlier tonight, in your own words."

"I think I can do that." She breathed through her nose and took a moment to collect herself. *The police want this case solved as quickly as I do. Even if they don't trust me, proving my involvement will take time. I just need to convince them that time would be wasted.*

She began by describing the evening with Narcissa, which gave her an opportunity to highlight how heartbroken she was over her sister-in-law's untimely death. "I'd been meaning to get together with Sis for some time, you know."

"Sis?"

"It's what I call her—or, rather, what I used to call her..." She sniffled and riffled through her purse as though she was looking for a tissue. Detective Olson offered a sad smile and retrieved a pack from his pocket. She took one and dabbed at the corners of her eyes. Not enough to be melodramatic, but enough to make it look like she really gave a damn. "She was always so fun, and such a joy to be around...one of those people who brought out the best in everyone, you know?"

"I do know," said the detective.

"Anyway," said Therese, with another sniffle for emphasis, "we'd been meaning to go out again for some time, and so, tonight was finally our chance to meet up for dinner. We had a wonderful time when we went out—to Alinea, down on Halsted."

"I've walked by it, yeah."

And I'll bet that's as close as you'll ever get to it because some pencil-pushing cop like you doesn't have the money to spend on quality food.

"Alinea is overrated."

"Excuse me?" said Therese.

The detective blinked. "I said I've heard of it."

A dark feeling came over Therese. She narrowed her eyes and leaned forward onto her elbows. *This hillbilly bastard is trying to mess with me.* Of course that's what he was doing. There was no other reason for her to be hearing something that wasn't there. She wasn't *insane.*

"Right. Well, after that, Narcy asked if we could go home early because she left her cell phone at the house." *Stupid Narcissa! If it weren't for her and her pointless insistence on her phone, I'd be home in bed with a book!* "I agreed that we should head back, so we went to her house, and she went inside first. And that's when...that's when it happened."

"When what happened?"

"I remember it so vividly—seeing Gillen's feet at the top of the stairs. He had on his favorite shoes, the ones with the peeling soles." She'd told him to throw those tattered shoes away ages ago, but he never had. He'd probably worn them just to piss her off. "That was when I saw the knife in his hand."

"Do you remember anything in particular about the knife?"

"There was blood on it—a lot of blood." That much was true, at least. Gillen would have fit right in on the set of a cheap horror movie, which made the fact that the police hadn't found him yet that much more ridiculous. *Honestly, how do you lose track of a person drenched in blood?* "It was a steak knife, I think."

Detective Olson jotted something down, as if she'd just said something incredibly groundbreaking and not an obvious restatement of a known fact. "Go on."

"At that point...that was when Narcy started screaming." This was where things got tricky. Without implicating herself, Therese had to explain why Gillen had stabbed his sister with the stem of a wineglass instead of the perfectly good knife in his hand. "She must have realized what had happened and gone mad. There was wine on the counter—a very good wine, one Gillen brought over—and Narcy grabbed a glass. Then she broke it on the counter and charged at him."

"She charged at Gillen, you mean?"

"Yes, that's right."

"Even though he was holding a knife?"

"I can't imagine she was thinking clearly. After all, her husband had just died."

"And how did she know that for sure?"

Therese cocked an eyebrow. "Because her brother was standing there looking like Bloody Mary in a bathroom mirror? What was she supposed to think?"

"It's still a pretty big leap to imagine your own brother killed your husband."

"Well, it was a pretty big leap for me to assume my husband had killed his partner, Detective, but I'm a big enough girl to add two and two in my head."

"Did Gillen say anything when you found him?"

She took a moment to consider the question before answering. Giving away the exact nature of their conversation would cause her all sorts of problems, but an admission of guilt had the potential to help put Gillen away.

"Yes," she said. "He said it was personal."

"Most stabbings are. Still, that raises a lot of questions." The detective pursed his lips and jotted something else down in his notepad.

Therese leaned forward to get a better look. "What exactly are you writing in there?"

"Oh, nothing much. Just a few notes to help with the ol' memory." He rapped his knuckles on the side of his head. "You know how the brain gets when you age."

Her nostrils flared. "I most assuredly do not."

"Give it a few years, then," he said with a laugh. "When you get to be my age, you'll be forgetting more than you remember. But enough about that—you were saying Narcy charged your husband?"

"Yes, that's right."

"And what were you doing during all of this?"

"I was in shock, obviously. I'd just found out my husband was a murderer. It was all I could do to keep standing."

"So you didn't try to get between Gillen and Narcy when they started to fight?"

"And risk getting stabbed myself? Don't be ridiculous."

"You wouldn't risk getting stabbed to save someone who needed help?"

Therese tapped her nails against the side of her chair. "If I had gotten stabbed as well, who would have been alive to call the police? Had I been able to get on the phone quickly enough, I might have even been able to save Eduardo's life. But I couldn't," she added, throwing in a sniff for good measure. "Gillen never gave me the chance. After he stabbed Narcy—"

"Hold on there. I think you missed a step. How did he stab her, exactly? After all, she was the one who ran at him. I mean, he was bigger than her, sure, but she could have caught him off guard."

"She could have." Therese hadn't been foolish enough to think the detective would let her get away without explaining the scuffle in detail, but glossing over it had still been worth a shot. "She did spook him a bit at first—that's why he dropped the knife. No, threw is more like it—it went flying out of his hand. Landed halfway across the room, I believe."

"You remember that pretty clearly, do you?"

"I remember seeing it on the floor after Gillen got away."

"So if he didn't have the knife, how did he stab Narcy?"

Therese crossed her arms. "You were there, Detective—you saw her body. Obviously, she didn't have as good a handle of the wineglass as she thought she did."

"So you're saying Gillen took the stem from her and used it against her."

"Correct."

The detective frowned. "Hmm."

"Hmm what?"

"It's just that..."

Therese leaned forward. "Just that what?"

"He can see right through you, Therese."

Goose bumps rippled along her arms. The last two times she'd heard a voice she couldn't place, she'd been looking in the opposite direction of the detective. This time, she'd been staring dead at his face. His mouth hadn't moved an inch.

"It's just that I'm surprised Gillen was able to get the stem of the glass out of her hand. They're thin little things, and the broken part was all splintered up. Seems it would've been a real tough thing to grab in a tussle."

"He grabbed it by the base. You know, the round part on the bottom?"

"Ah, that makes sense. I'm sure we'll find his prints all over the thing."

"Whoops."

A wave of horror washed over Therese. "He was wearing gloves! His prints aren't going to be on the glass because he was wearing gloves."

"He was wearing gloves inside the house?" The detective tilted his head. "Wouldn't Eduardo have found that a bit strange?"

"I don't know when Gillen put them on. Maybe he slipped them on right before we got there, to help him hide the evidence."

"Judging by the mess he left behind, he didn't seem too concerned with leaving evidence at the scene."

"Yes, well, I'd imagine our arrival threw a wrench in his scheme." That would have been her guess, too, except his little speech after Narcissa's death made it abundantly clear he'd never intended to conceal his role in the crime. Worse than that, he hadn't made any plans to conceal hers—as if Therese deserved the same treatment as someone as monstrous as him. *When they catch that son of a bitch,* she thought, gnashing her teeth, *they'd better give him the chair.*

"And once they find out what you did, you'll be sitting right next to him."

Agony pierced Therese's brain. She gasped and squeezed her eyes shut, but the pain kept right on coming.

The detective's chair scraped against the floor. "Ms. DuCannes, are you all right?"

"I'm...fine..." she hissed through her teeth. "It's just...a migraine..."

"Do you have a history of migraines? Is there any medication I can get you?"

She sucked in air through her nose and braced herself against the chair. *Leave me alone!*

And just like that, the tide of pain receded from her head, returning to whatever dark recesses of her mind had spawned it. She let out a grateful sigh and sank into her chair. "There. All better."

Detective Olson stared at her with half-lifted eyebrows and an unsteady frown. "You've got quite a will there, ma'am. It's not just anybody who can power through that kind of a headache."

"Yes, well, life is full of hardships," she replied. "Facing them head-on is all I know how to do."

"Words to live by." He picked up his recorder and tapped it against the table. "Look, it's getting late. Why don't we get you home so you can get some rest, and then we can talk to you in the morning."

"That sounds good to me." *Good Lord, finally.* "Will you give me a call if you find Gillen in the meantime?"

"You'll be the first to know. Oh, and we'll be sure to let you know if we get any good news about Narcy too."

Therese froze. A thin whine echoed in her ear, like a lightbulb dying in a nearby lamp. "Pardon?"

"Oh, I didn't mention it to you?" Detective Olsen flashed a warm smile. "The EMTs were able to get your sister-in-law to the hospital in time to save her. She's still in critical condition, but the doctors say she's got a fighting chance. Obviously we're all rooting for her to survive, but it'll also help us put Gillen away once we get her testimony. If she can corroborate everything you said, well..." He chuckled, though his smile didn't hold. "Gillen's gonna be going away for a long time."

With the ringing in her ears growing every second, Therese could barely hear her own reply. "Great."

Chapter Nine

BY THE TIME Andrew made it back home from the hospital, it was well past two in the morning. Just as he'd suspected, there was nothing wrong with him beyond a bad headache and some numbness in the tips of his fingers. They told him the headache was probably psychological—brought on by the trauma, maybe—and he didn't need a doctor to tell him that his fingertips were numb because he'd passed out in the snow. What he really needed a doctor to tell him about was Narcy. Unfortunately, nobody would let him get anywhere near her, and in the end they'd booted him right back out into the snow.

When he reached the front door of his family's old greystone, the first thing he noticed was that the living room light was on. All of his muscles seized up and he sucked in a gulp of air. His mother still had a key to the house, but she'd been in a home for almost six months, in large part because she could barely remember her own home. Since he hadn't gotten close enough to give keys to anyone else since Julie, that just left the one option: Gillen.

He must have broken into the house. Or, alternately, Andrew could have just left the lights on and forgotten about it. *But if I didn't leave the lights on, then it means Gillen's in there!*

Andrew grabbed a snow shovel off the front steps and held it in front of him like a rectangular-tipped spear. Even if Gillen hadn't come in with a weapon, there was a good chance he'd found the shotgun Andrew kept under his bed at his mom's insistence. He'd told her a thousand times that the odds of her needing a gun in Lakeview were a lot lower than the odds of her needing a gun on her family farm, but she'd refused to budge. Now that gun had a good chance of being turned against him and all he had to defend himself was a shovel with a rusty handle.

"I'm not gonna let him murder me too..." he murmured through his chattering teeth. "I'm gonna give him a piece of my mind."

With his shovel-spear wedged in the crook of his right elbow, Andrew slipped his right hand into his pocket and fished out his keys. He held his breath as he slid the key into the lock and turned it just far enough to hear it click.

The door creaked open. A shadow leaped through the air. Andrew dropped his shovel and screamed, then tumbled back when two paws took him in the chest.

"Hester!" Andrew sputtered up a lungful of air as the massive golden licked every inch of his face. "Hey, buddy, how did you get here?"

On the edge of Andrew's field of vision, he caught sight of a piece of paper flopping off the side of his coffee table. Andrew rolled out from beneath Hester and retrieved the paper.

Dear Andrew,

I called the hospital to check on you and they said you were on your way home, so I decided I'd spare you and Hester a trip to the pound. I brought you some dog food from the Sanchez place too.

Hope you are feeling better. Will be contacting you again in the morning.

—Detective Caroline Ramirez.

"Oh my God," said Andrew. "She broke into my house!" Then he noticed the postscript at the bottom of the letter and furrowed his brow.

PS: Try not to leave your door unlocked anymore, okay?

Andrew smacked his palm against his forehead. "I'm such an idiot."

After berating himself long enough to feel suitably guilty, he went in search of Hester's food. Sure enough, a bag of Hester's favorite sat in the corner, just as the note had said. With Hester on his heels, Andrew checked inside.

"Hmm, not a ton in here," he said to the dog. "How much do you eat, anyway?"

"One cup, twice a day."

Andrew jumped in place. "Oh my God, did you just talk?" Hester tilted his head to the side as though someone had blown a whistle a block away. Andrew sighed and patted Hester on the head. "I'm kidding, I know you didn't talk. It's just the voices in my head."

After a good deal of mental hand-wringing, Andrew had begrudgingly admitted to one of the nurses that he was hearing someone in his head. Thankfully, the nurse chose not to have him committed and instead told him it was probably a symptom of the shock and would pass. While it wasn't the most satisfying answer, it was as good as any answer he was liable to get.

"Well, I guess you're getting a cup of food in the morning," Andrew said. *Though I don't know how the voice in my head arrived at that amount...* Given that it was almost two in the morning, Andrew didn't intend to question it. "Not like you'll get mad at me, right, boy?"

Hester craned his neck back and let out a long yawn. Andrew patted him on the head with a laugh. "I hear you, buddy. Let's get up to bed."

After turning out the lights and triple-checking the locks on the windows and doors, Andrew guided Hester to his bedroom upstairs. Had Andrew been guiding a human around, he might have felt guiltier at the aging house's state of disrepair, but Hester wasn't going to complain about some water damage on the ceilings or a few crooked boards in the floor. He also couldn't judge Andrew for the plethora of action figures in Andrew's room either, and those were far more shameful. At least, that was what Julie had always told him, but then she'd made him get rid of his collection for the brief period of time they spent living together. He'd been a lot lonelier since breaking up with her, but at least he could decorate his own room the way he wanted.

When they got to Andrew's room, he opened the splintering door and let Hester go inside first. "Here we are, big guy. Welcome to Hotel Andrew. Sorry about the mess," he added with a chuckle. "I, uh, don't usually have company."

In true dog fashion, Hester ignored the surrounding elements in the room and hurled himself onto Andrew's bed. He landed dead in the center and flopped his head against the down blanket like he'd just worked an eighteen-hour shift.

Andrew sighed and sat down on the bed at Hester's side. "I guess you've had a pretty rough day, huh?" He scratched behind Hester's ear and grinned as the dog's giant tongue flopped out of his mouth. "I'm really sorry your dad is dead. And your mom..."

A stray tear formed on the edge of Andrew's eyelashes. He thought back to the way Narcy used to sit Hester up in her lap—all eighty pounds of him—and pretend to play drum solos with his floppy paws. Hester made it plain from his howls that he wanted no part of Narcy's impromptu rock band, but he never made a move to leave her. Even when she was picking on him, he loved her more than anything.

Andrew sniffed and wiped his eyes. "She's gonna be okay, just you wait. Pretty soon... you'll be back with your family again."

Even though no one could see Andrew except the dog, he still didn't want to break down crying on his bed. He couldn't help it, though, and the more he thought about what had happened to Narcy and his last conversation with Ed, the more his eyes spilled over.

"I'm such an idiot," he said between sobs. "Why did I have to fall in love with Narcy? Why couldn't I have made Ed's last moments be good?" But no, Ed's last hour had been devoted to fighting with a friend, and the blame rested squarely with Andrew.

A strong vibration shook the pocket of his slacks. Hester rolled over and smacked his paw against Andrew's leg.

"Hey, hey, easy on the phone, buddy." Andrew rubbed his eyes enough to clear his vision and turned on the screen. A notification from his gaming chat room flashed on and off in the center.

KanyeEast: *do you guys think @Broodlord is dead?*

Andrew sighed and rubbed his head. Part of him wanted to just turn off the phone and go to sleep, but he'd have to tell his friends about what happened sometime. It was bound to show up on the news sooner rather than later—if it hadn't already—and he'd given up enough identifying information in the past that his friends would see the story and know it had something to do with him. Even if they didn't recognize his relationship to the story, he'd want to talk to them about it anyway. He tried to keep the details of his offline life to himself—not that he had much of a life to tell about—but he needed to talk to someone who wasn't covered in fur.

He pulled up the chat room and started typing.

Broodlord: *no I'm alive*

KanyeEast: *did your boss accept your apology?*

Broodlord: *no but he kind of couldnt*

he's dead.

Android420: *Wait, he's dead? You mean the guy you were supposed to visit tonight?*

KanyeEast: *yeah android try to keep up*

he have a heart attack or something? tf happened?

dont tell me you murdered him

Andrew winced. It occurred to him that telling his chat buddies might not be in his best interest, on the off chance the police started to suspect him, but that seemed pretty doubtful. They'd found him outside of the house with no blood on his clothes, and he also had a credit card transaction proving he'd gotten a shake a half mile north only fifteen minutes before. Gillen being on the lam didn't hurt Andrew's chances of staying off the suspect list either.

Broodlord: *no, I didn't murder him*

his business partner did

Android420: *Wait, you're serious?*

KanyeEast: *holy shit dude*

Broodlord: *yeah.*

killed my boss and tried to kill his wife.

shes in the hospital now. Not sure if shes going to make it

Android420: *Jesus Christ*

Broodlord: *no kidding.*

Android420: *so what happened to the partner? He kill himself or the cops get him?*

Broodlord: *neither. he got away.*

Android420: *God Damn. That's fucking crazy.*

Remind me where you live again?

not trying to stalk you, just want to know where the runaway murderer is

Broodlord: *I'm in Chicago, but this was maybe six hours ago, so who knows where he is now.*

KanyeEast: *n e idea where he would go?*

Broodlord: *I have no clue. I didn't even know the guy that well.*

I mean, I knew him, I worked with him, but I didn't know him know him.

Android420: *so you didn't like like him*

Broodlord: *no I flat-out didn't like him at all*

But I still never thought he'd turn out to be a murderer

Andrew sighed and sank against the pillow. Saying he'd never thought Gillen would be a murderer might have been his life's greatest understatement. He'd never thought *anyone* he knew could be capable of committing murder. Sure, he'd thought about it in the abstract, like, *If this pizza guy takes one more minute to get here, I'm gonna murder everyone in Chicago,* but he'd never been serious about it. Apparently, he'd been naive to think everyone else was like him.

Hester shifted his head against Andrew's leg and let out another long yawn. Andrew smiled and scratched his head. "You're right, it's getting late. Well, I mean, I guess it is pretty late already, but I think you and I can finally fall asleep."

After saying a quick good night to his friends, Andrew switched off his phone and put it on his bedside table. The small array of colorful figures he kept on his nightstand stared back at him with vacant eyes. Normally, he enjoyed looking at them, but all he could think about when he looked into their dead expressions was how Ed must have looked as a corpse.

He rolled away from his figures and snuggled up against Hester's back. "I'm glad you're here, buddy. I know you'd rather be with your mom and dad... but it's nice to have a friend. Good night, Hester."

A drop of liquid ran from Hester's nose as his tired eyes rolled back into his head. Andrew chuckled, closing his eyes. "Guess that's the best good night I'm going to get."

Snowflakes danced around Andrew's head, but the bitter wind that carried them took no toll on his face. He felt none of the cold on his hands, nor could he smell the sharpness of the winter air that signaled a new storm on the way. His ears worked and his eyes worked, but they worked of their own accord, informing him only of the details they chose to perceive. He had no control of his body, and he moved as if life had become a dream.

Thick snow crunched beneath his feet, but he could not feel the weight of his boots as he walked. He could only see the street in front of him, bereft of signs of human life. His head tilted back, though not by his command, and his eyes scanned the empty sky in a fruitless search for stars.

His hands moved through his pockets. His fingers wrapped around his keys. The snow crunched behind him.

"A dónde vas, pocho?"

The shrill beep of an alarm clock split through Andrew's aching head. He jolted upright and came face-to-face with the massive tongue of a golden retriever.

"Hester? What are you doing here?" he said, and then the whole night came crashing down on him and he fell back against the bed. *Oh my God, Ed is dead!*

"Wake up, Andrew."

Andrew shot up a second time. With his eyes still fatigued from sleep, he could barely make out Hester's tongue in front of him, much less something ten feet across the room. What he didn't need sharp eyes to see was the outline of a man sitting in front of his desk.

His heart raced as he scrambled back against the headboard. "Oh my God!"

Hester bounded on top of him, ignoring the intruder entirely. Andrew shrieked and pushed him away. "Don't kill me, boy. Kill the bad guy!"

"He can't see me," said the man. *"Only you can."*

The air in Andrew's throat turned to vaporous ice. Teeth shaking, he blinked and rubbed his eyes until his vision regained its regular function.

Eduardo Sanchez sat before him, eyes narrowed and mouth tight. He looked like he wanted to kill someone, and he was very much alive.

"We need to talk."

Chapter Ten

GILLEN SPENT THE entire night driving, focused forward, not daring to look in the rearview mirror. Not an easy feat, considering how often trucks forced him to change lanes, but merging lanes without checking for impending traffic scared him far less than the chance of facing Eduardo's reflection.

When the sun's first rays appeared above the horizon, Gillen got off the main road and pulled into a run-down motel just north of Fairmont, Minnesota. He'd picked out the motel months ago, both for its remote location and its proximity to his ultimate destination. While Fairmont wasn't exactly far from where he intended to go, it wasn't next door either. On the off chance someone recognized him in the motel, just knowing the location wouldn't be enough for them to guess where he wanted to go.

Once Gillen reached his destination, he parked his car in the lot behind the building and pulled out his bag of supplies. He'd packed quite a lot into his supply kit, but he only needed three items for his trip into the hotel: a makeup kit, a thin brush, and a bottle of rigid collodion.

Back when Gillen was a child, he'd gone to church with his mother every Sunday. He'd always hated it, but it had mattered to her and so he'd gone without complaint. He mostly sat in silence, waiting for the hour to pass, but one thing that did alleviate his boredom was staring at a man with the terrible scar. He only came to mass once or twice a month, but every time, Gillen noticed him immediately—and so did everyone else. With a serpentine scar that ran from the outside of one eye to the edge of his mouth, he was a man who never had the luxury of disappearing into the crowd. That was what Gillen had thought as a child, anyway. As an adult, he'd realized that man could disappear better than anyone because the only thing people saw of him was his scar. With a disfigurement that obvious in the way, nobody ever bothered to look beyond.

Gillen clutched his makeup kit and glanced above the mirror out of one corner of his eye. "You'd better not be in there..."

He didn't get an answer, but he hadn't expected one. He hadn't had a single stray thought since he'd gotten on the route to Fairmont. As best he could figure, his mind had been playing tricks on him due to a combination of stress and fear. Once he got settled in his car and outside Chicago, his subconscious had relaxed enough to leave him alone.

With no time left to spare, Gillen screwed up his courage and looked straight into the mirror. His own eyes stared back at him, bloodshot and blue. He let out a sigh of relief and sank into his chair.

"Good," he said. "That's what I thought."

Using the thin brush and a red lip balm from his kit, Gillen sketched out a twisted scar along the left side of his face. He'd considered emulating the scar on the man he'd seen in his childhood, but that scar had skipped the border between terrifying and nauseating. Gillen wasn't trying to make anyone vomit; he just didn't want people noting the rest of the details of his face.

Once he laid down the foundation for the scar, he brushed a few layers of the rigid collodion over the outline. The clear tightening material helped emulate the texture of an authentic scar, allowing a makeup novice like Gillen to pull off an effect that wouldn't have looked out of place in Hollywood. He didn't have Hollywood to thank for the technique, however; for that, he had to thank Therese. She'd never cared much for Halloween when it came to celebrating herself, but she took invitations to other people's parties as a personal challenge. She would never wear anything hideous herself, of course—she insisted she was far too pretty for that—but she had no problem turning Gillen's face into a canvas of scars and blood. Ironic, perhaps, since Gillen had just done the same thing to her life.

Once the collodion dried, Gillen brushed over one or two layers of pale powder to tone down some of the excess shine. He then put the kit aside and took a moment to scrutinize the finished product. While Gillen's new scar didn't look anywhere near as realistic as it could have in a competent artist's hands, he'd done a fine job, given his tools and his nerves. With the faded scar stretching across his face, no polite Minnesota desk clerk would dare to give him a second glance.

He slipped on a baseball cap—a blank cap, as any team logo risked becoming a bridge for conversation—and entered the motel. The overwhelming scent of lemon cleaner emanated from the linoleum floor. While it wasn't Gillen's favorite smell, it certainly beat out the other potential smells that could have been seeping through the wood-paneled walls, and it also helped mask the lingering scent of his impromptu makeup job.

Gillen approached the counter and smiled at the clerk, a heavy-set woman with lipstick on her teeth. She took one look at Gillen's face and sucked in a breath. Thankfully, her Midwest sensibilities couldn't possibly allow her to stare, so it came as no surprise when she quickly tore her gaze away.

"Need a room, sweetheart?" she said to a space next to Gillen's head.

"Yes, just for the night."

"Not a problem. Just let me get you checked in."

He paid for the room with cash; part of a stockpile he'd been hoarding for years. Therese had always been a real hawk about their money, but she never questioned Gillen when he bought her expensive designer gifts. Doling out those gifts on a regular basis had been the key to buying her continued cooperation as his mission stretched out from months into years.

Once the clerk gave Gillen his key, he took the rest of his supplies from the car and got himself settled into his room. He didn't intend to stay the night—just until the sun went down—but while he had the space to himself, he had a good deal he needed to accomplish.

He started in the bathroom and set up his supplies: one box of hair-dye remover and one box of new dye. Dying his hair a new color would be easy, but that had to come later. For now, he needed to start with the most complicated task: stripping the red dye from his hair.

Unbeknownst to Therese, or anyone else in his life, Gillen had been going gray since the ripe old age of twenty-two. At first he'd hidden his grays out of a sense of embarrassment, but once it became clear to him that he would eventually be restarting his life on the run, he began maintaining his red as a method of self-preservation. For the majority of that time, he'd used a long-term dye and periodically touched up the roots, but he'd switched over to an easily removable dye once he made up his mind on the date Eduardo would die. From that point, it was just a simple matter of maintaining the red facade without Therese discovering the dye in the garbage, and Gillen was home free.

As he waited for the remover to set, he switched on the TV and found a channel airing Chicago's news. While the fearful part of Gillen's mind would have been much happier not knowing whether the police were on his tail, the logical part of him understood that working with upsetting information was better than working with no information at all. With that in mind, he steeled himself and sat on the edge of the bed, prepared for news of the worst.

The worst news never came. In fact, no news ever came. At least not any news Gillen could use. The Chicago anchors covered all manner of crimes from the previous night—and Christ knew there were a lot of crimes to cover—but they made no mention of the untimely deaths of Eduardo and Narcissa Sanchez. They also didn't mention that a wanted killer was on the run. Strange for a lot of reasons, not the least of which being the fact that manhunts were always a ratings boon. News stations loved those kinds of stories because they could spin them as a public threat—a herald of impending doom. This station had no doom for Gillen, however, and nor did any other. For all that he could tell, his crime had simply been forgotten.

"No..." he murmured, "that doesn't make any sense. There's got to be a reason they're not covering me." He wasn't so arrogant as to be upset that he wasn't getting any screen time—he wasn't Therese, for God's sake—but he couldn't ignore the fact that the coverage of his crime was inconsistent with similar crimes that had come before. Being forgotten worked better for him, true, but only if that was what was actually going on. If there was some other reason Eduardo's murder wasn't making the news, Gillen's situation had the potential to get a whole lot worse.

He switched off the television and returned to the bathroom to wash the dye remover from his hair. He hadn't quite waited long enough to maximize the remover's returns, but the lack of news about his escape had him spooked. Adequate dye removal was a luxury he could no longer afford.

The nauseating scent of bleach flooded the cramped bathroom as Gillen rinsed the remover from his hair. Red-orange dye ran down the drain in thin rivers that reminded him of Eduardo's blood. A day ago, the thought might have made him smile, but seeing it now filled him with a sense of disgust.

He shut off the water and toweled out the rest of his hair. Without the red dye in the way, his hair bore a much closer resemblance to his natural gray. Unfortunately, the remover left him with some yellow, so it took him another hour and another round of dye before the process was complete.

When he finally got the color the way he wanted, he rubbed his eyes and looked in the mirror. A gray-haired stranger stared back at him, frowning through a hideous scar.

"De pelos."

Gillen whirled around. Eduardo Sanchez sat on the edge of the tub, eyeing Gillen with the mocking grin of a man who didn't seem to realize he should be dead. It wasn't as if he *looked* dead, though, not with his laughing eyes and his clean shirt, opened just enough to expose his unbloodied throat and chest. He'd picked up some stubble since Gillen saw him last, but otherwise, he looked the same as he had before dying in a heap on his floor.

"Surprised to see me?" said Eduardo.

Gillen flailed his arm behind him until he caught something with a handle. He thrust it forward at Eduardo's face and screamed, "Stay away from me!"

Eduardo crossed his eyes and stared down the length of Gillen's trembling arm. *"Is that a toothbrush?"*

Gillen looked down. Sure enough, his weapon of choice was indeed a toothbrush—a cheap, soft-bristled model he'd thrown in his travel kit, something so inoffensive it couldn't even hurt the dead.

"Goddammit."

"Wanna put that down so we can talk?"

What little remained of Gillen's sanity wedged its way to the front of his head. *He's not actually sitting there; he's just a hallucination. You haven't slept in a day, remember?*

"Mostly true," said Eduardo, *"I'm not actually sitting here, and you really haven't slept in a day. Unfortunately, I'm not just a hallucination."*

"Was I talking to you?" Gillen snapped.

"No, but since I'm inside your head, I figured I'd answer."

With one simple sentence, Gillen's singular life goal exploded into a puff of ash. "No…"

"Yes."

"You can't mean it."

"I can."

Gillen hurled the toothbrush at Eduardo's head. The plastic chunk passed through Eduardo with all the ease of a raindrop passing through the air.

It hit the shower wall and Eduardo beamed. *"See?"*

"No, no, no, this can't be happening!" Gillen clutched his head and shut his eyes tight. When he opened them, Eduardo was still there.

He tried again, this time flicking his gaze to the other side of the room. Like a floater in the corner of his eye, the image of Eduardo moved automatically, repositioning itself on the edge of the sink.

"*Yo.*"

"Fuck off!" Gillen shouted. "Get the hell out of my head!"

"*You might want to dial down the volume a little bit,*" Eduardo said. "*You're supposed to be keeping a low profile, remember?*"

Gillen let out a howl of anguish and ran from the bathroom. When he emerged in the bedroom, Eduardo was waiting for him on the side of the bed.

"*Hola.*"

"Shut up, shut up, shut up!" Blood pounded in Gillen's ears as he clenched his jaw and tried to think. *This can't be happening; this isn't happening; this doesn't make any sense!*

"*I'm telling you, you can't escape from me inside your head. We're together here now, you understand?*"

"We are not together and you are not in my head!"

Eduardo rolled his eyes, something he should have never been able to do because he was supposed to be dead. "*The longer you fight it, the less time you'll have to sleep before you need to get on the road again.*"

"I don't need advice from you, you freak! I killed you for a reason!"

"*Oh, so you actually admit it, do you?*" He blew a lock of his messy hair off his face. He'd always had perpetual bedhead, but Gillen had never given it any thought until Eduardo's ghost appeared on Gillen's bed. "*Then you're a better person than I thought you were—though not by much. After all, you did kill your own sister.*"

Gillen sucked in air through his teeth. "That wasn't me!"

"*Oh, now you remember how to deny things.*" Eduardo clicked his tongue. "*So much for being a better person.*"

"What are you doing in my head?"

"That's a good question! What am I doing in your head? Let me think about it...hmm..." With his eyes crossed as if deep in thought, Eduardo drummed his fingertips along the edge of the mattress. *"Now, I'm not exactly sure, but I think it's because—and try to stay with me on this because it gets a little complicated—I think it's because I was a mind reader and you murdered me."*

"So?"

"So, Gillen—and again, just a guess, seeing as I've never been murdered before—but I'm thinking that in order to save myself, I jumped out of my brain and into yours instead."

A wave of bile rose in Gillen's throat. He clutched his stomach and bent over his knees. The damp skin on his palms clung to his shirt as he clenched his eyes shut and struggled to breathe.

"Ah, you're having a panic attack, huh?" Eduardo said. *"Hate those things. Used to smoke pot for 'em. Don't suppose you have any now, do you?"*

It took all of Gillen's strength to muster up a response. "Marijuana...is...illegal."

Eduardo burst out laughing. *"So is murder, pendejo! You're willing to do that, but you won't touch a little pot?"*

Had Gillen not been on the verge of passing out, the sheer ludicrousness of the conversation might have made him laugh. "I'm not...taking legal advice...from someone who goes through people's heads!"

"Oh, because I've really been doing that on purpose. You know I couldn't turn that shit off, right?"

Gillen opened his eyes. When he looked up, Eduardo was sitting above him, perched on the edge of the bed. His smile had vanished, as had the laughter in his eyes. If Gillen hadn't known better, he would have thought Eduardo cared about his answer.

When Gillen didn't say anything, Eduardo sighed and sat back on the bed. *"If that's how it's going to be, that's fine with me. You can keep ignoring me all you want. But keep in mind, I'm just getting settled in."*

"Meaning?"

"Meaning, pendejo—"

"I don't speak Spanish!"

Eduardo rolled his eyes. *"Meaning, idiot, that the more time I spend in here, the more I'm going to make this place my home. And when you make a place your home, it means exploring what's inside."*

Every cell in Gillen's body froze. "But you're already reading my mind."

"Oh, sure, I'm reading the surface thoughts—you know, the ones I could never turn off. That's not what I'm interested in, though. What I'm interested in is what's lurking down below."

"You have no right to dig through my head like that! My memories, my life!" He dug his nails into his palms. "You have no right!"

"And you had no right to kill me, but you went ahead and did it anyway. So now I'm going to get revenge, Gillen." Eduardo leaned forward, so close that Gillen swore he could smell the wine on his imaginary breath. *"I'm going to tear your mind apart until I figure out why you wanted me dead."*

Chapter Eleven

ANDREW'S TEETH CLACKED together as he hugged his knees to his chest. "Look, I don't know what you're doing here, but if you came to haunt me or something—"

From his seat at Andrew's desk, the ghost of Ed shot Andrew a patronizing look. *"You don't actually believe in ghosts, do you?"*

Andrew hesitated. On any other day, he would have said no, but the present circumstances had him second-guessing that. "Kind of?"

Ed dragged his hand down his face, obscuring his expression. Strange, since Andrew had always assumed ghosts would be a little transparent. Then again, Andrew hadn't exactly done much studying in the field of ghost-ology—or whatever people were calling undead studies these days—so he couldn't be sure if Ed's spectral hands were breaking the rules or not.

"Let's start over," said Ed. *"Back when I was alive, didn't you ever wonder how I was able to make so much money without putting in much effort?"*

Andrew rubbed the back of his head. "I, er...I mean, you inherited your dad's company. That's kind of how inheritance works."

"Nevermind the inheritance part. Focus on the part where I kept the business running and made it bigger than my father could have ever dreamed. I did it all through talking to people, but you know I've always hated talking to people. Doesn't that bother you?"

"Does it bother me personally, you mean? I wasn't jealous of you or anything, if that's what you're asking." Realization struck Andrew and his face went numb. "You do know I didn't murder you, right? You have to remember it was Gillen—I mean, it was Gillen, wasn't it?"

Ed let out a long sigh. *"It was definitely Gillen. Why he killed me, though—that's what I'm driving at. Just think for a minute, Andy. I was good at sales because I always knew what people wanted—like I always knew what they were thinking. Do you see what I'm asking?"*

Still rusted from sleep, the cogs in Andrew's head took their time in turning into place. Once they did, Andrew found himself even more confused than he'd been before. "You're saying you were a psychic?"

"If by psychic, you mean mind reader, then yes. That is what I am saying. Now doesn't that explain why I'm in your head?"

"Not really..."

Some of the life went out of Ed's posture and he sank into Andrew's desk chair. *"Yeah, it doesn't make any sense to me either."* He leaned back enough to clack his head against Andrew's chair. *"¡Maldita sea!"*

Andrew pursed his lips. "I'm guessing that means you're not happy?"

"No, Andrew, I'm not especially happy, because last night I thought my biggest problem in life was my best friend going crazy for my wife, and now I'm stuck inside his body and I don't know whether or not my wife is dead. Would you be happy?"

"I...um...I think I need a drink of water." He also desperately needed to pee, but he wasn't going to admit that to Ed's ghost. As for whether he actually was a ghost, that was still a technicality Andrew needed to decide. For now, peeing and clearing his head took priority. "Do you want to, uh, wait here?"

"*I can't wait here*, pendejo. *I'm living in your head.*"

"I'm still not sure I get it."

Ed sighed again. "*Just go piss and get your water. And while you're at it, make some coffee, too, yeah? Maybe if you drink enough, we'll both wake up from this nightmare.*"

"Um, sure. Sounds good."

It wasn't until Andrew had gotten halfway through urinating that he realized he'd never said to Ed that he needed to use the bathroom. He looked down at himself and twisted his mouth to the side. *How did he know what I needed to do in here?*

"*Would you stop looking at your dick and finish already? Dios mio, haven't I already been through enough?*"

Andrew jerked his head up and screamed. Ed stared back at him from the mirror, eyes blazing with fury.

"What the hell are you doing in here?" said Andrew.

"*Just finish already!*"

"How am I supposed to finish when you're watching me?"

"*How am I supposed to do anything else when you keep frowning at your dick?*"

"Oh my God, fine! What do you want me to do, close my eyes?"

"*Yes, that would be nice!*"

Andrew sucked in air through his nose. Praying that his thirty-some years of urination would help him, he closed his eyes and tried to pee again. Thankfully, he managed to hit his target on the first try, and he was finally able to relieve his aching bladder without any more of Ed's screams.

He didn't open his eyes again until he had his hands washed, teeth brushed, and his entire person outside of the bathroom. Once he was sure he'd gotten his whole body covered again, he cracked one eye open and glanced back around his bedroom. Ed sat on the edge of Andrew's bed, brows furrowed and lips pressed so tight they'd turned white. Hester sat at his side, panting and oblivious to his dead master's suffering.

"You wanna make that coffee now?" said Ed.

Andrew nodded dumbly. "Sure, I can do that."

WITH HESTER AT his heels, Andrew wandered downstairs and started up the coffeepot. He'd never been too picky about coffee himself, but Julie had always insisted he keep a few different types of beans around in case they had more discerning guests. Strangely enough, the fact that he never had guests of his own anymore hadn't done anything to help him break the habit.

Andrew looked over his shoulder to discover Ed leaning against the peeling kitchen wall. He didn't look uncomfortable, but it seemed weird for him to stand when he was in front of a table ringed by chairs.

"Do you want to sit down?" said Andrew.

Ed shot him another patronizing look. *"And how am I supposed to do that?"*

"Um, you were sitting down up in my room, right?"

"I was sitting down because that's how you're imagining me in your head. I'm not a ghost, no matter how much you keep thinking that. I'm literally inside your head. The only reason you can see me at all is because your idiot brain can't make sense of me talking to you any other way, so it's just putting an image of me wherever you think it makes the most sense for me to be."

"Really?"

"It's the best I can guess."

Andrew narrowed his eyes. "Wait a minute. If you're just guessing at all of this, then how can you be sure you're not a ghost?"

"Because I can hear what you're thinking, remember? And I used to be a mind reader? What makes more sense to you, Andrew: that some crazy god has sent me back to Earth to bother you as a way of cheating me out of my afterlife, or that I used the powers I already had to make a quick escape into your brain?"

"Neither of those really makes sense, honestly..." Between the rhythmic dripping of the coffeepot and the inane ramblings inside his head, Andrew was starting to wonder if anything he'd thought that morning made sense. "Oh my God, what if I'm going insane?"

"You're not going insane."

"Isn't that what an insane person's hallucination would say?"

Ed sighed and gestured at one of the padded chairs. *"Want to pull one of those out for me so your brain can let me sit down?"*

While Ed's request might have been the craziest thing Andrew had heard yet, he'd run out of energy to fight the insanity. "Sure, I'll get it."

He wandered over to the kitchen table and pulled out the chair closest to the back deck. Ed wouldn't exactly be able to feel the breeze, but Andrew didn't want to keep his back door open in January anyway.

"There," he said. "Now you can sit down."

"Thanks."

In the span of a blink, Ed switched positions from the far wall to the available chair. Andrew's eyebrows shot halfway up his head. "Holy crap, you really are in my head."

"Oh, so you didn't believe me when I was trying to talk some sense into you, but now you believe me because your brain pulled a party trick." Ed flicked his fingers over a broken peppercorn on the tabletop. The peppercorn stayed in place and Ed frowned at his hands. *"Great."*

Andrew bit his cheeks to keep his teeth from chattering. *There's a dead man living inside my head.* He'd played a lot of strange video games and read a lot of weird sci-fi books in his day, but none of them had prepared him for this. *What am I supposed to do now?*

"How about you pour us a coffee and sit down so we can figure that out?"

"Right...you heard that." He gulped and nodded. "Just give me a second."

His hands shaking, Andrew poured the coffee into a single mug. The rules of good hospitality had him ready to grab a second, but he'd finally figured out that a second mug would do Ed about as much good as a pushed-in chair.

"Here." Andrew raised his mug toward Ed in a joking toast. "Bottoms up."

The sharp aroma of a fresh brew filled his nose as he blew over the top and took a sip. With his mug covering most of his face, he could just barely make out Ed nodding in appreciation.

"That's better than I thought it would be. Do you always do a dark roast?"

The image of a ventriloquist's puppet popped into Andrew's head as he finished swallowing. It shouldn't have surprised him that Ed could talk while he was drinking, but somehow it did.

"Er, no, I usually don't pay much attention to what I make. I just thought I remembered you having a dark roast in your kitchen."

"You remembered right. I'm impressed." A strange look flashed across Ed's face, but Andrew didn't have time to interpret it before the not-ghost spoke again. *"So let's talk about where things are going to go from here."*

"Hold on, hold on." Andrew looked Ed in the eye, though he wasn't sure if Ed could sense the eye contact or not. If Ed's image really was just a trick of Andrew's brain, then the "Ed" in Andrew's head could only see what Andrew was looking at...but then Andrew was looking at Ed, which meant none of this made any sense. "I need to sit down first."

"Yeah, you should probably do that."

Coffee in hand, Andrew took the seat off to the right of Ed's chair. He made sure to give Ed his personal space, though he doubted it really mattered. "So, before we talk about Gillen, can we back up a little and go over you being a mind reader?"

Ed's gaze darted to the side. Dead as he was, he at least had the decency to look guilty—even if it didn't last. *"If you're expecting me to apologize, you can stop waiting. I couldn't go sharing the truth with everybody."*

"But I'm not everybody, Ed. I was your friend. I *am* your friend."

"Oh, is that right? Then how come you were too much of a coward to tell me how you felt about Narcy, huh? How come I had to fish that out of your head myself?"

"Because I...oh." The truth of how he'd been found out revealed itself to Andrew at last. "Gillen really didn't tell you about me, did he?"

"No, but let's not go throwing the asshole a parade. You were right about him—just not how you thought you were."

Andrew twisted his mouth to the side. "I'm not sure if that makes me feel better or not."

"Look, I'm sorry I didn't tell you about being a mind reader. For what it's worth, I'm really regretting it now—and not just because I need your help."

"What do you need my help for? I mean, you're already dead, right?" His eyebrows rose and he shot his hand into the air like a little boy in school. "Oh, I know, because you need me to help you cross over!"

Ed thunked the heel of his hand against his forehead. *"For the last time, I'm not a ghost!"*

"So wait, then how do you cross over?"

"I don't!"

A sinking feeling weighed down Andrew's stomach as the gravity of Ed's statement sank in. "You mean...are you going to be in my head forever?"

"Maybe. I don't know. This is all new shit for me, you know. For all I know, I could disappear from your head tomorrow—but as best I can tell, we're together for the long haul." Ed leaned forward, hands on his knees. *"And that's why I need you to help me."*

"Okay, so what do you need me to do?"

"First, you need to take me to the hospital so we can see Narcy."

Andrew frowned at his hands. "I tried to visit her last night, but they wouldn't let me."

"So you gave up?"

"What choice did I have? She was in surgery, Ed. What were they going to do, let me in the operating room? I'm not even family!" A hard lump formed in his throat. He shook his head and swallowed it down. "I'm just...some guy."

Some of the iron went out of Ed's posture, but his expression remained as hard as stone. *"They can't keep her in surgery forever."*

"They said they'd call me when she was ready for visitors." A dark thought occurred to Andrew and he bit his lip. *Unless something happens and—*

"Don't," Ed said. *"Don't even finish that thought."*

"I'm sorry."

"You should be. She's going to live." He narrowed his eyes and stared at Andrew through the dark slits. *"And once we've visited her, you're going to help me with the next thing on my list."*

"And that is?"

"Finding Gillen."

"Gillen? What good is finding him going to do now? What, you think he knows a way to get you out of my head or something?"

"Maybe he does, but that's not why I want to find him."

"Then why?"

He narrowed his eyes. *"Because you and I are going to kill him."*

Chapter Twelve

THE BACKS OF Therese's pumps cut into her ankles as she paced the length of her sunlit foyer. "I stabbed her in the neck!" She howled and threw up her hands. "How can she still be alive?"

"Because she's strong," said Eduardo's image, standing in the corner with his arms crossed over his chest. *"Stronger than some dried-up old bitch like you."*

Therese ignored him, just as she'd been doing for the last four hours. Hallucinations were nothing more than a weakness of the mind, one to be set aside and promptly forgotten. To acknowledge them would be to give them power; to succumb to them would be to admit defeat.

"I have to get into that hospital room. I can't let her live long enough to wake up."

"You're not going to be able to do that."

Therese ground her teeth together as Eduardo stared at her through his empty eyes. He looked horrific, but then that made sense for the hallucination of someone who was supposed to be dead. His stubble had grown into the beginnings of a beard and his blood-drenched shirt was covered in wrinkles. *Honestly, it's not like ironing would have killed him—the dumb bastard's already dead.*

"I heard that," he said.

She smacked her hand against the white banister surrounding the stairs. "I don't care what you heard!"

Eduardo's lips split into a skeletal grin. *"I thought you weren't acknowledging me."*

"I'm not acknowledging you! I'm acknowledging myself!"

"Is there a difference?"

She whirled on him, teeth bared. "Listen, you freak. I'm not a stupid woman—I've read *Macbeth*. I know you're just the manifestation of my own guilt over my role in your idiotic death. But you know what? I don't have any guilt over it! If you were stupid enough to get conned by someone as pathetic as Gillen, then you deserved everything you got. So quit standing there trying to make me feel bad because I don't give a damn if you're dead!"

"Well that makes two of us, puta, *because I don't give a damn if I'm dead either."* His smile spread, exposing black shadows inside his mouth. *"After all, what does it matter if I'm dead when I'm here inside your mind?"*

A shiver ran up Therese's back. She shoved the feeling aside and glared at him. "I'd tell you how scared I am, but I'm a little too busy." To emphasize her point, she tapped her toe against the floor, matching the rhythm of the grandfather clock in the corner. "I don't have time to stand here talking to myself anyway. I need to get to the hospital now."

She threw open the closet doors and snatched her cheapest coat out from the back. If she showed up overdressed to talk to a bunch of working-class hospital staff, they'd treat her like dirt as a way of compensating for the misery permeating their lives. Dressing to their level gave her a much better chance of getting what she wanted, even if it meant temporarily sacrificing her dignity.

Her lip curled on instinct as she tossed on her hideous coat. "This better not take long," she muttered. "The sooner I can get this done and get out of this jacket, the better."

The image of Eduardo reappeared in the doorway. *"You're going to fail."*

She swatted the air in front of him. "Please. You're nothing but a hallucination. You can antagonize me as much as you want, but that's all you'll ever be able to do to me."

"Why should I need to do anything to you? You're the one losing your mind."

"I promise you, hallucination, my mind is just fine." Therese pulled together her brightest smile and threw open the front door. Her smile fell to pieces when she found Detective Olson on the other side.

The halfway-handsome detective tipped his hat in a meek gesture he must have meant to be friendly. "Morning, Mrs. Lynch. I hope I didn't come knocking while you're in the middle of something."

A faint snickering tickled the back of Therese's ear. *"He really loves getting your name wrong, doesn't he?"*

Therese ground her teeth together and ignored the imaginary laughter. "Good morning, Detective—Olger, was it?"

"Olson, actually, but I can't say I blame you for not sticking it in your head. I've never been much of a memorable guy." He laughed to himself as if he'd said something funny, rather than something pathetic and sad.

"Yes, well, I hate to tell you this, but you caught me right as I was heading out the door to visit my sister-in-law. I hadn't heard back from you, you know, so I've been incredibly worried. It's important for me to visit her, especially now that I'm the only family she has."

"That sure is nice of you. Sorry to say, though—" His smile faltered. "—that's actually not going to be possible."

Hope swelled in Therese's heart. She masked it by making a show of clapping her hand to her chest. "She's not dead, is she?"

"No, she's still hanging in there. Still not awake, though."

The image of Eduardo flickered into existence at Detective Olson's side. He'd been scowling like he spent his whole life sucking on lemons, but the news lifted his nonexistent spirits enough to make him smile.

"She's still alive!"

Therese dug her nails into her palms. She wanted nothing more than to wring the hallucination's neck, but strangling an invisible person would buy her a one-way ride on the crazy train. Plus, she still had to settle the Narcissa situation, and that took far higher priority than getting in a one-sided fight with an apparition.

"Has her condition improved?" Therese said. There was still the off chance Narcissa was on the way out, which would save her a lot of trouble.

"Not out of the woods by a long shot, I'm afraid."

"Then that's all the more reason I need to be there for her!"

"Unfortunately, we can't risk letting her have visitors."

"What do you mean, you can't risk it? For Christ's sake, do you think I'm unsanitary or something? I'm not going to give her a disease!"

The detective shook his head. "It's not diseases we're worried about; it's her brother."

"My husband? He's gone. What's he got to do with it?"

"Well, that's just the issue, ma'am. As long as Gillen's out there where we can't find him, your sister-in-law is at risk. She's the only living witness to what happened—yourself excluded, if we're counting the aftermath—so we've got good reason to worry he might try to hurt her again so she can't sell him out."

Therese's nostrils flared. "What kind of monster would do that?"

Eduardo shot her a flat glare. *"You've got to be kidding me."*

"I know it seems pretty horrific, ma'am, but, well..." Detective Olson rubbed the back of his head. "You know what kind of man we're dealing with."

"Yes, I understand." Therese glanced at the ceiling to avoid Eduardo's judgmental gaze. *There's got to be a way I can get to Narcissa, even if the police are involved. I just need to find it.* "But how can you be sure Narcy will be properly protected just because you aren't allowing her visitors? I mean, my God, what's to stop Gillen from sneaking past the hospital staff?"

"Don't worry, we've thought about that. We've got officers posted at her door."

Shit! "Can you trust them?"

"A hundred percent."

"How can you be sure?"

"Because one of those officers is my partner, and she doesn't take guff from anyone."

Therese bit her tongue to keep from rolling her eyes. *Guff! Honestly, when was this man born? The eighteen hundreds?* "And you've been working with your partner a long time?"

"Oh, for years. She's a good woman. A bit strange at times—she's a lesbian, don't you know. Now, I don't know where that leaves her with the Lord, but she's been nothing but good to me, so I'm inclined to give her the benefit of the doubt."

"Hey, that's some useful information, right, Therese?" Eduardo flashed her a lascivious grin. *"If you care about getting to Narcy so much, why not go have sex with the partner? You strike me as the kind of woman who'd be into that."*

Therese's nostrils flared. She was absolutely not the kind of woman who would be into that, no matter what kind of debauchery her hallucinations imagined otherwise. "So you're telling me I'm not going to be able to see my sister until my husband is caught."

"'Fraid so, ma'am," said the detective.

She crossed her arms, not bothering to hide her scowl. *At least he saved me the trip to the hospital.*

"Yeah," said Eduardo, *"Probably because he knows you were headed over there to kill her."*

A flicker of doubt flashed through Therese's mind. *He couldn't possibly know that. He has no reason to suspect me.*

"Other than you being a disgusting bitch."

While Therese didn't much care for her hallucination's tone, it did raise an interesting question. Ignoring Eduardo once more, she eyed the detective and forced her bitter frown into something more sincere.

"You didn't have to come all this way just to tell me this, Detective. I can't imagine how busy you must be. I would have been fine if you'd gotten ahold of me via phone."

"That's actually not the whole reason I'm here—but it is related," he said. "We've determined that, because you were at the scene of the crime, you're still in danger as well."

"Well, obviously," she snapped. "How am I supposed to sleep at night knowing that psychopath could come barging through my front door at any moment?"

The detective nodded. "And that's exactly what my captain said when he assigned me to work your security detail."

"Say again?"

"As long as Gillen's out there, it's going to be my job to watch over you—just to make sure you're safe."

A miserable, sickening feeling crawled through Therese's bones as the image of Eduardo clapped his hands over his gut and burst out laughing. *"You walked right into that one, puta!"* he said between laughs. *"You sure you don't want to reconsider sleeping with the partner?"*

I wouldn't touch another woman if you put a gun to my head. Her fingers clenched. Then an idea popped into her head and she relaxed her aching hands. *But I'd have no problem sleeping with another man—especially one as easy to play as this.*

With the ruse decided, Therese's entire demeanor changed. She let the tension fall out of her posture and rested one of her hands on the doorframe, displaying the closest thing to vulnerability she could imagine. "Thank you, Detective. I know I've been short with you, but..." She chewed her lip and looked away. "I feel better knowing you're looking out for me."

Detective Olson smiled like she'd just handed him a birthday cake with his name on top. "I'm happy to help."

She glanced over his shoulder and noticed his police cruiser parked along the curb. *Perfect.* "I hope you don't have to sit in that car all day just to watch me." She threw in a little lip quaver at the end for flavor. "I can't imagine how tight it must be in there."

Eduardo shook his head. *"You just can't resist the low-hanging fruit, can you?"*

In truth, Therese despised resorting to such childish innuendos, but Detective Olson didn't strike her as the type who would respond well to subtlety. "You're more than welcome to come inside if you need a break." She ran her fingers through her hair in a gesture of feigned innocence. "I could make you a cup of coffee and give you a chance to stretch your legs."

Detective Olson rubbed the back of his head. "Well, I can't very well say no to a good cup of joe if you're offering."

Jesus Christ, a cup of joe? Am I going to have to gag him if I sleep with him? "It's the least I can do, Detective—and I could certainly use the company." She tilted her chin and gazed at the floor, emulating loneliness with enough pathos to show up a Hollywood actress. "It's been hard to handle all of this by myself. Especially with how worried I am about Narcy."

"A real tragedy, that—and so close to her birthday too." He crossed his eyes like he was trying to read a piece of paper in his head. "This Sunday, was it?"

Panic forced its way through the cracks in Therese's facade of sadness. *Is he testing me?* Birthdays were for children and twenty-somethings looking for an excuse to drink; no reasonable adult gave a damn about their birthday. She certainly wasn't going to waste the mental real estate to commit anyone else's birthday to memory. A "good" sister would remember that sort of thing, though, and that was exactly what Therese was pretending to be.

One of the veins on Eduardo's forehead stuck out from the others as he clenched his fists. *"It's this Tuesday!"*

Therese jerked her attention back to the detective and shook her head. "It's not Sunday. It's Tuesday."

"Ah, that's right—the thirteenth. I saw it on her license. That's why it sticks in my head." He tapped the side of his nose with a grin. "Should I come in for that cup of coffee?"

Therese plastered on her biggest smile. "Of course."

The illusion of Eduardo faded into nothingness as Detective Olson passed through the doorway. Once he entered the foyer, Eduardo reappeared beside the stairs. *"You'd better take off your ugly coat if you want any chance of fucking him. Not that you're going to have much,"* he added, *"considering you're losing your mind."*

Therese clenched her jaw. *I am not losing my mind!*

"*Oh no? Then how else do you explain a hallucination giving you a piece of information you didn't already know?*"

The world stopped cold around Therese as she halted midstride and blinked. *He told me Narcissa's birthday...*

A slow series of claps echoed around the foyer. Out of the corner of her eye, Therese spotted Eduardo with his hands together, eyebrows cocked to match his condescending grin. "*Congratulations, Therese. You're going insane.*"

Chapter Thirteen

AFTER TWENTY MINUTES back on the road, Gillen had already gotten used to seeing his gray-haired reflection in the mirror. What he hadn't gotten used to was seeing his murdered friend resting with his feet up in the passenger's seat.

"You know," said Eduardo, feet rocking back and forth to the radio's beat, *"at first, I thought you killed me because you found out I was cheating on Narcy."*

Gillen drummed his fingers against the steering wheel. "Are you telling me that to get a rise out of me?"

"Is it working?" Eduardo tilted his head. *"Or are you upset because it's not and you think it should be?"*

"What is that supposed to mean?"

"I'm asking if it bothers you that you don't feel any kind of connection to your own sister?"

With the sunlight bouncing off the remnants of the previous night's snowfall, Gillen had to squint to make out the sign for the on-ramp to St. Paul.

He flicked on his blinker and kept his gaze forward. "You don't know what I feel for her."

"I know you didn't seem too bothered when Therese shoved a wineglass in her neck."

Gillen tapped his fingers against the wheel that much harder. "Getting upset wouldn't have changed what happened."

"No, but it would have been human." Eduardo moved his feet far enough to the left for them to drift into Gillen's line of sight. They ticked back and forth, like a metronome that existed entirely in his head. *"You didn't care about her at all, did you?"*

"You've got nerve to grill me on this after you just admitted to cheating on her."

"Did I say I cheated on her?" One of his feet ticked faster than the other, wagging in disapproval. *"I just said you'd think I did."*

"And why would I think that?"

"Because I was fucking other people."

Gillen wrinkled his nose. "How is that not cheating?"

"Because she knew about it," he said, his grin apparent in his tone. *"And because she was fucking other people too."*

An instinctual ripple of disgust ran down Gillen's spine. The thought of his sister having sex at all was enough to turn his stomach; the thought of her out with strangers made him want to never eat again. "That's disgusting."

"Not really. It was a pretty good arrangement, actually. She had sex with whichever men she wanted, I had sex with whichever men I wanted—"

Gillen's eyes snapped open and his muscles froze. His foot dropped onto the accelerator, propelling the car forward. He jerked back and slammed down on the brakes just in time to avoid hitting the beer truck in front of him.

The second he regained control, he whipped around to look Eduardo in the eye. "Did you just say men?"

Eduardo laughed as though he'd just heard the best joke he'd been told in years. *"Oh don't look so shocked, Gillen! You've known me for years! You must have at least had an inkling that I was gay."*

"No, I did not have an *inkling!*" He threw up his hands, leaving the car free to drift left. Heart pounding, he grabbed the wheel and pulled the car straight before he could drift out of his lane.

"Oof, you really need to get your wheel alignment checked."

"Forget about my wheel alignment! You can't be gay—you were married! To a woman!"

"Yeah, and she was the best friend I ever had. I just wasn't attracted to her – but she knew that going in. Hell, I think that was half the reason she did it."

"What does that mean?"

Eduardo flashed a sharklike grin. *"I thought you didn't want to know about your sister's bedroom activities?"*

"Jesus, I don't! I don't even want to know about yours!"

"Really? Because you sure are asking a lot of questions for someone who says he's not interested. And judging by what I'm seeing in this head of yours, you're a lot more interested than you're letting on."

Gillen swallowed so fast that he closed his mouth wrong and bit his cheek. He swore and clapped his hand over his cheek to suppress the lancing pain.

"I've been rooting around in here for a few hours now," Eduardo continued, *"And I've got to tell you, I am fascinated by your sex life. But can you really call it a life, though?"* He clucked his tongue with the kind of disapproval that would make a priest proud. *"You certainly weren't doing much with it."*

A red sedan zipped into Gillen's lane. Gillen hit the brakes and dropped back for space. "Stay out of my head!"

"You had a nice little routine going with Therese there in the beginning. Once a week, just often enough to hit the amount you thought you should. Then, once you figured

out Therese was even less into it than you were—as if that were possible—you cut back to an even more impressive once or twice a year. And you know what the most outrageous thing is in there? I'm not finding a single example with oral, for either of you. How does that happen when you were married for four years?"

"Would you let Therese put her teeth anywhere near your dick?" Gillen snapped.

"Hell no! But I didn't marry her!"

"You're going to give me grief about not being attracted to the person I married?"

"Because at least I was fucking other people! You're not doing anything with anybody! And it's not even because of Therese! We're talking way before this!"

Gillen's eyes darted back and forth. *How far back is he able to go?*

"I can go as far as I want," said Eduardo, *"And you'd better prepare yourself because, eventually, I'm going to find everything. But for now, we need to talk about this."*

"We don't need to talk about anything I don't want to, okay?" Gillen thrust his finger at Eduardo's illusionary face. "I'm the driver, and you're the...whatever you are! So either go back to wherever you came from, or sit there and shut up!"

Eduardo blinked, stunned silent. Gillen pulled his attention back to the road and turned up the music. "There. That's better."

The album Gillen had been listening to as he left Chicago looped back around and the Spanish lyrics that had taunted him blasted through the speakers. Eduardo made a face like he'd just cracked open a treasure chest and began to laugh. *"Are you kidding me?"*

Gillen winced at the stereo. "Oh for God's sake..."

Eduardo's laughter grew until he was drowning out the music. *"Do you listen to this and pretend you speak Spanish?"* He pinched his fingers together like he had a puppet over his hand and pitched his voice up to a squeak. *"Hola, me llamo Gillen y me gusta apuñalar a mis amigos!"*

"Would you give it a rest? Christ, I'm not listening to something sacred! It's just 'Hotel California'!"

"Ooh, I see! With this, you can learn Spanish and have bad taste in music!"

"I don't need you critiquing my music preferences!"

"Oh really? Well, in that case, we can go back to the sex conversation—which I'm very interested in continuing because now I've got some questions about what you've been thinking about in your 'alone time'."

Gillen sucked in a breath through his nose. "Usually, I think about murdering you!"

"Yeah, I noticed, and it's nice to see you're so goal-oriented. You know what's funny, though? Most of the time—and by most of the time, I mean all of the time— you finish up before you get to the 'murdering' part. The way it looks here, just thinking about me is enough for you. Isn't that strange?" Eduardo tapped the side of his nose. *"I think there's something you're not telling me, cariño."*

Blood pounded in Gillen's ears. He tensed his fingers, curling them around the wheel like it was Eduardo's windpipe. "I don't know what kind of sick fantasies you're imagining—"

"Me imagining? They're your fantasies, not mine! I'm just calling a spade a spade!" He folded his hands behind his head and laughed. *"If I'd known what you really wanted from me, I'm sure we could have worked something out."* His gaze flicked up and down the length of Gillen's torso. *"After all, I could do a lot worse."*

"Don't fucking look at me like that! That's not why I killed you!" A truck moved to cut Gillen off and he pressed on the gas. The car lurched forward, leaving the truck in its wake. "I killed you to keep you out of my head!"

"But why, though? What did you have to hide in there that you didn't want me to see? I mean, I think I've already figured part of it out," he added with a smile of satisfaction, *"but I'm not going to quit searching until I get the entire story. Something to look forward to, yeah? Oh, and by the way, how many hours do we have before we get to your mystery destination?"*

Gillen checked the mile marker on the side of the road, then glanced at the clock embedded in the dash. "About ten hours," he murmured. Ten more hours until he'd be free.

"Ten hours?" Eduardo laughed and rubbed his hands together. *"Boy oh boy, are we going to have fun together."*

Bile rose in Gillen's throat. He clutched the wheel and tried to focus on the road ahead.

Chapter Fourteen

ANDREW'S COFFEE CUP wobbled in his hand. He set it down and did his best to look Ed in the eye, even though Ed wasn't actually there. "Look, Ed, I'm really sorry you got murdered, and I wish I could have done something to change that before it happened, but I can't kill Gillen for you. I mean, I wouldn't even know where to begin."

Ed furrowed his brows. *"It's not that hard to kill someone. Gillen did it twice."*

"Yeah, well, he's him and I'm me. I don't exactly have a killer instinct, and the thought of breaking the law makes me nauseous. I mean, come on." He clasped his hands together in a pathetic prayer. "I don't even jaywalk."

"So you'd rather let my killer go free than take some initiative and handle things yourself."

"He's not going to go free! The police—"

"The police aren't going to do shit. You think you can trust them? Did you trust that puta in the ambulance?"

Andrew pursed his lips. He thought about asking what a *puta* was, but then he decided he'd rather not know. "She was back there because she wanted to talk to me before I forgot anything important. She also brought over Hester."

"And you haven't even fed him breakfast yet!" Ed gestured at Andrew's feet. *"Look at him. He's dying!"*

Andrew looked down at his feet and jumped halfway out of his chair. Hester had been sitting right below him, waiting with his tongue out and his eyes wide like he wanted to cry. "Hester! Oh my God, I forgot about you! I'm so sorry! Let me get you something to eat."

"He needs to pee too!" Ed said as Andrew rose from his chair. *"First you won't help your murdered friend, and now you won't even let out his dog?"*

"All right, all right, just give me a minute!"

"I'll give you one minute, and then when you come back, we're going right back to talking about why we need Gillen dead!"

Andrew winced and nodded. He'd never thought of himself as capable of killing someone—not even someone as awful as Gillen—but it wasn't easy to argue with a dead man living in his head. It didn't help that Andrew had already done enough to make Ed's life difficult while he was still alive. The least he could do was to consider Ed's final request, even if he didn't intend to follow through with it.

Feeding Hester didn't take much effort, as the dog seemed all too happy to scarf his food down. Getting him to go to the bathroom was another story. Apparently, Hester cared about biting the snow a lot more than he cared about peeing in it, which meant Andrew had to chase him around and wear him out until his energy dropped enough to make emptying his bladder a priority.

As Hester searched for a suitable snow pile to desecrate, Andrew's phone vibrated in his pocket. He had it halfway out of his jacket when Ed reappeared in front of him. *"Is someone calling about Narcy?"*

Andrew's heart pounded in his ribs. He grabbed the phone and stared at the screen. "Oh." His shoulders sank and he shook his head. "Sorry, nobody's calling. It's just my chat channel." He held up the phone to face Ed. "See?"

Ed glanced at him over the top of the phone. *"You know I can only see things through your eyes, right? Remember, I'm not actually standing here?"*

It took Andrew a solid thirty seconds of frowning at the snow to work out the logic behind what Ed was saying. "So you're telling me...you and me both see things from the same perspective...which means you're looking at yourself?"

"Well, right now, I'm staring at the ground because, apparently, you can't hold your giant head up while you're thinking about something—but yes, I've spent my morning staring at myself."

"Oh wow, it's like you're playing a video game."

"No, because if I were playing a video game, I would be having fun."

"Er, right. Good point."

While Andrew had a lot more questions about the mechanics of Ed's dual perspective, the insistent buzzing of his phone reminded him that his name had just been mentioned. He opened his chat application and checked the message.

> Blue_María: *Has anyone seen @Broodlord this morning? Is he okay?*

Ed leaned forward to look at Andrew's phone—a gesture supplied entirely by Andrew's mind, as Ed actually shared Andrew's view of the screen. *"Who's Blue_María?"*

"She's nobody," Andrew murmured as he typed. "Just somebody I've been chatting with while playing video games."

He finished his message and sent it before Ed could ask any more probing questions.

> Broodlord: *Don't worry, I'm alive.*

Usually when Andrew said he was alive after an absence, he meant it as a joke. Typically his status of "living" was implied. Now, with a killer on the loose and a dead man in his head, reaffirming his existence carried a lot more weight than usual.

Blue_María: *Thank God you're ok. I just found out about what happened.*

KanyeEast: *we told her your boss got axe-murdered by his friend*

Ed frowned at Andrew. "*You went home and told the internet I was dead? That was your first priority?*"

Andrew's cheeks flushed and he pulled his phone closer to his chest. "They're my friends, okay? I just needed to talk to them."

"*These people are your friends? Do you even know them?*"

"I know enough."

Ed snorted. "*I doubt it.*"

As much as Andrew wanted to point out that Ed had no place to talk after hiding his mind reading, he didn't have the energy for the debate. Instead, he furrowed his brow and looked down at the screen.

MundeeMundy: *Hey you know what's weird about that murder?*

Broodlord: *uh that it happened?*

KanyeEast: *that they didn't kill brood for being a shitty healer?*

Blue_María: *shut up east*

KanyeEast: *make me mamacita*

MundeeMundy: *I checked the news this morning to see if they were saying anything about the murder, like if they caught the guy or whatever, but I didn't see anything about it at all*

Like, anything

Andrew scrunched up his nose. He didn't know much about Mundy's personal life, but one thing he did know was that Mundy lived close enough to Chicago that he got the local news channels. If Mundy hadn't seen anything on the news, that meant they weren't talking about it.

Broodlord: *Is there anything about it online?*

MundeeMundy: *I checked the crime blogs too. There's nothing.*

"That's weird," Andrew mumbled. "Why wouldn't there be any mention of it?" In a city with a murder rate as high as Chicago's, crime reporting had become a well-oiled machine. Someone could wake up on a Sunday morning and check online to see a list of every shooting from Englewood to Evanston—though the Evanston ones definitely get more coverage. Considering Ed's murder involved four wealthy people in one of the city's whitest neighborhoods, it should have been lighting up the screens.

Blue_María: *Maybe the police haven't released details because they don't want to compromise an ongoing investigation*

KanyeEast: *maybe you're living in the matrix*

u ever think of that?

Blue_María: *Don't let the news freak you out, Brood. The important thing is that you're safe.*

Broodlord: *I'd feel a lot safer if I knew where the killer was*

Blue_María: *you don't have any idea where he might have gone?*

Broodlord: *not a one*

> Blue_María: *You sure? I thought you worked with him. You sure he never said something to you that would be a good tip?*

"*I think she's overestimating your social skills,*" Ed said as he stared at the phone.

Andrew scowled and flicked the air by Ed's face. Still, he wasn't wrong. Andrew had never been much of a conversationalist, and that was with people he felt comfortable around. With someone he disliked as much as Gillen, he went out of his way to say as little as possible.

> Broodlord: *I really didn't talk to him much. But what does it matter?*

> *I mean, who could I really tell? The police?*

> Blue_María: *That's generally the first step, yes*

> MundeeMundy: *But what if the cops aren't putting stuff on the news because it's a conspiracy?*

> KanyeEast: *mundys is right, this whole thing is a trap*

> *its a trap and i blame maría*

> Blue_María: *Fine, you caught me. I admit it, Brood: I'm a member of an elite, top-secret organization that uses limitless wealth and power to cover up mysterious crimes. Because of my skill with video games, I was assigned to pretend to be your friend, all on the one in a million chance that you might be involved in a high profile case I'd need to sweep under the rug*

> *and also im gay*

> KanyeEast: *same*

MundeeMundy: *+1*

Andrew clunked his phone against his forehead. "This is not what I need right now."

"*No, it's not—but they're right about not trusting the cops.*"

"And why's that?"

"*It's part of the reason we need to talk about Gillen.*"

"You saw what I wrote to them, right?" He waved his phone at Ed. "I have no idea where Gillen is—and even if I did, I'm not sure I'm willing to kill him!"

"*He tried to kill Narcy!*"

"I know he did, but that doesn't necessarily mean he deserves to die! Do you really think one death makes another okay?"

A slight tug on Andrew's sleeve pulled him out of the conversation. He looked down to see Hester at his side, mouth around the cuff of his shirt.

Andrew sighed and patted him on the head. "I guess you've had your fun in the snow, yeah? Let's go back inside."

The chill of winter followed Andrew inside the house, even after he shut the door. The way Ed kept staring daggers at him didn't do much to help either.

"*He stole my life from me, Andrew,*" Ed said. "*Maybe that doesn't mean anything to you since I'm sitting right here, but he stole Narcy's life too.*"

Andrew's nostrils flared. "Don't talk about her like that! She could still live!"

"*You think everything will be okay for her just because she survives? When she wakes up, she's going to find out her brother tried to murder her!*"

"I know, but—"

"*And what about when she realizes her husband is dead! You may have been in love with her, but she was happy to be with me! We had a life together! We loved each other and shared everything we had with each other, and he ripped that all away! He stole our futures!"*

A distant memory popped into Andrew's head, one from the first time he and Narcy met. He'd been working in the Human Resources department of Ed's father's company for six months, and Narcy had come by to drop off lunch for a tired and cranky Ed. She didn't say a word to Andrew then, but he'd seen the smile on her face when she handed the sandwich off to Ed—as if her whole life had been leading up to that one little moment, a moment where she could turn someone's day around with the tiniest gesture. At that point, she had a whole lifetime of loving moments ahead of her. Thanks to Gillen, those moments might have come to an end.

"She's not going to be smiling anymore, is she...?" Andrew murmured.

"He tore her life apart, Andy. Her own brother. My fucking friend."

As some of Andrew's anger dissipated, he realized he hadn't sat back down since he entered the kitchen. He sighed and took his old seat across from Ed. "I'm really sorry about all of this, Ed."

"Thank you. I appreciate that." The sour look on Ed's face made it clear he was looking for more than sympathy, but he must have decided it was better than nothing.

"Can I ask you something?" Andrew said.

"What?"

"If you were a mind reader like you said, how come you never knew Gillen was going to do...this?"

Ed ran his fingers through his hair, tugging on the roots at the end. *"That's what I can't understand."*

"Did you just never read him or something? Was it because you trusted him?"

"No, that wasn't it. I mean, I did trust him, but I never had a choice with who I read—not on the surface, anyway. I heard everything everyone was thinking all of the time. He just never thought about anything worthwhile. Always stupid things like what he needed at the store or pointless movie trivia..." Eduardo stared at a point on the wall beyond Andrew's head. *"Back then, I always figured he thought about those things because he was an idiot. God knows I've seen enough of them. But now...now I'm starting to think he did it on purpose."*

"He knew about your powers?" A surge of jealousy jolted through Andrew. "Why would you tell him and not me?"

"Because I didn't tell him," Ed snapped. *"The only person I told who isn't dead is Narcy."*

"Dead? What, you're counting yourself in there?"

Ed waved his hand. *"It's not important now. What's important is that we get to him before anyone else does."*

"Why? Why can't we let the police handle it?"

"You see what your internet friends are saying, yeah? The news isn't talking about my death—which means the police are keeping it hidden. How can we trust them if they won't even tell people about it? How can we be sure they'll bring Gillen to justice if they aren't searching for him with everything they have?"

As Andrew shrank against his chair, Ed's voice echoed in the back of his mind. Not from their present conversation, though—in broken snippets, ones Andrew couldn't understand. Snippets of a conversation with the unfamiliar voice he could swear he'd heard before.

Ed's voice floated in first, loud and full of fury. "¡Mírame! ¡Soy un batido andante!!"

"Perfecto para ti, fresa," said the sarcastic stranger.

"¡Jódete!"

Andrew blinked, tuning into the present to hear Ed still rambling about Gillen. Raising his eyebrows, Andrew hesitantly lifted his hand. "Hey, what's a fresa?"

Ed jolted as if he'd been stung. *"Excuse me?"*

"While you were talking just now, I thought I remembered something..." Andrew wrinkled his nose as he ran through the memory again. When it first popped into his head, he couldn't make any sense of it. On the second run-through, the words started to make some sense. "But I feel like it was one of your memories, not mine."

"And?"

"And I think somebody called you a *fresa?*"

The skin around Ed's knuckles turned pale as he flexed his hands. *"Is that really what you want to talk about right now?"*

"Yeah, it is, because I just heard you talking to somebody else in my head. Who were you talking to?"

"It was nobody," he snapped. *"And all fresa means is strawberry."*

Andrew cocked an eyebrow. "You got mad because somebody called you strawberry?" While it wasn't the absolute nicest nickname on the planet, Ed had been called a lot worse in the time Andrew had known him. He'd also been murdered less than twenty-four hours ago. For him to be pissed off about getting compared to some fruit was some pretty weird timing. "Are you sure that's all it is?"

"It means spoiled, rich, piece-of-shit fake Mexican. Someone who's got more money than sense and has lost touch with the culture, and for all intents and purposes, might even be worse than a white boy." Ed threw up his hands. *"Okay? Is that what you wanted?"*

"Jeez, okay..." Andrew puffed up his cheeks. "When did somebody call you that? I mean, you look pretty pissed off about it, so it must have happened recently..."

His voice died in his throat as he remembered the previous night's dream. It had been so peaceful in his head: just him, the sky, and the snow, right outside his house. But he hadn't been alone. Someone had called to him. Someone he'd talked to; someone who'd come inside.

More snippets of conversation popped into Andrew's head, longer and more complicated than before. They phased in and out of Spanish, like his brain was translating on the fly.

Ed's fingers curled around a bottle of beer, but it was Andrew who felt the condensation against his skin. The voice belonged to him, too—but the words were not his own. "El sabía que yo podría arruinar su vida..." he said, "so he threw himself in the Chicago river."

"Qué lástima," said the stranger. "That's a disgusting place to die."

Ed narrowed Andrew's eyes. "That's what he deserved."

The memory faded, leaving Andrew behind with the nightmare that had become his life. His whole body shook as he glanced at the living room table, where an unknown visitor had left a half-empty bottle of beer.

He turned on Eduardo, quaking with rage. "You son of a bitch! You tried to steal my—"

Pain lanced through his mouth as his jaw clamped shut on his tongue. His limbs locked up like they'd been stopped with a remote control. He wanted to yell or swear or do *something* to take back control, but all he could do was scream inside his mind as Eduardo vanished from his vision and his body began moving on its own.

Eduardo's voice bounced around Andrew's head, echoing as if he were yelling in an empty room. *"I'm tired of hearing your excuses. If you won't help me, then I'll help myself."*

Chapter Fifteen

THERESE'S HANDS TREMBLED as she poured herself a glass of wine. She typically abhorred people who resorted to day-drinking to deal with their problems, but most people didn't have spies spilling secrets inside their heads.

"I'm not going to let you get to me!"

With her eyes on her drink, she couldn't see Eduardo. She could only hear him, laughing at her the same way he'd been doing since the detective left. Her hope had been that listening to the detective's silly problems would help restore her sanity, but Eduardo hadn't given her a moment's peace.

"*I've had fun chatting with you, Therese.*" His voice had a low rumbling quality that reminded her of a bass someone had turned up too loud. "*Are you having fun chatting with me too?*"

"Go to hell!"

"*Oh, that's not very nice.*" Eduardo made a *tsk* sound, as if he really cared. "*Did you enjoy talking to the detective, at least?*"

"Of course I didn't!" She banged her wine bottle down on the counter. "The man is an idiot! Why would I enjoy talking to him?"

Eduardo clicked his tongue. "*That's not a very nice thing to say about someone you're trying to sleep with. What if he's still outside and he can hear you being mean to him?*" He leaned in, close enough that Therese could swear she felt his breath on her cheek. "*What if he bugged your house and is listening right now?*"

Therese's eyes opened wide. She grabbed her glass and chugged half of it down in a swallow. "Quit trying to sell me your bullshit!"

She'd spent the last two hours ignoring Eduardo's taunting while she feigned interest in the tedious details of Detective Olson's entire life. He'd asked about her, of course—God forbid a Midwesterner not be polite—but she'd fabricated just enough backstory for herself to push the conversation back to him. She had no interest in sharing her real life with him; he was just a means to an end, a way to get into the hospital and handle the situation with Narcissa.

"Maybe she died while we were in there," Therese mumbled, wiping her lip. A warm tingle spread through her body as the wine took effect. She didn't have a drinking problem—not like all the other lushes in Lakeview—so it didn't take much for her to feel her drinks.

"*She won't die that easily,*" said Eduardo. "*She's not going to go without a fight.*"

"Oh please, she's not Wonder Woman. She can die the same as everybody else."

"*If that's what you think, then what are you worried about?*"

Therese narrowed her eyes, then snatched her cell phone out of her purse and called up the front desk at the hospital. Eduardo reappeared on the edge of her field of vision, lip curled, as a ragged-sounding older woman picked up.

"Yes, I'm calling to inquire about the status of a patient." Therese clicked her nails against the back of her cell phone, wishing she had a cord to wind around her finger to alleviate the tedium.

"*I wish you had a cord to wind around your neck,*" Eduardo said.

Therese flickered her fingers at him like he was a disobedient cat. He didn't even flinch; he just kept right on glaring at her, as though she was the one harassing him instead of the other way around.

"Do you have the patient's name?" said the clerk.

"Yes," Therese replied. "It's Narcissa Lynch."

"Narcissa Sanchez."

Therese tapped her middle finger against her cell phone case, making sure Eduardo could see it. "Excuse me," she said to the clerk. "Narcissa Sanchez. She's my sister—well, sister-in-law technically, but I've known her so long that we're closer than family and—"

"Please hold."

Eduardo snickered as Therese wrinkled her nose. *"Guess she's not buying your bullshit either, huh?"*

Soft strains of elevator music floated out of the phone. Therese's eyelid flickered as Eduardo hummed along. She made it all of forty-five seconds before gripping the phone and yelling, "Would you shut up!"

The music died on the line. "Excuse me, ma'am!"

Eduardo burst out laughing. Therese clenched her teeth and tried not to scream. "You'll have to excuse me. I wasn't talking to you. I have an obnoxious child who's testing my patience."

Without being able to see the clerk's face, Therese had no idea if she bought the lie or not. The way her raspy voice tightened suggested she didn't. "Narcissa Sanchez is still in critical condition."

Goddammit! "Has she woken up, at least?"

"I'm sorry, ma'am, but I'm not at liberty to disclose that information at this time."

"You can't tell me whether she's asleep or awake?"

"No, ma'am, I've shared everything I can."

Therese clutched the phone to her ear. "But I'm family!"

"I understand that, ma'am, but there are regulations in place that—"

"Oh, who cares about your stupid regulations!"

The clerk cleared her throat. "There's no need to be rude. If you want another update on your sister-in-law"—and oh, did she ever emphasize the *in-law*—"you'll have to call back at a later time. Goodbye."

A faint click popped in Therese's ear and the line went dead. Therese sucked in a lungful of air through her nose. "Did that barefoot hillbilly whore just hang up on me?"

Eduardo snickered slightly. *"Guess she didn't appreciate your attitude."*

"As if I care." Therese tossed her phone aside—it didn't matter if it broke, for all the good the damn thing was doing her—and chugged another mouthful of wine. "I'll just have to go down there myself."

"I'm afraid I can't let you do that, Therese."

Therese rolled her eyes. *I'm supposed to be impressed he can do a robot voice now?* "Just try and stop me."

Every muscle in Therese's hand clenched at once. It jerked down, smashing the wineglass against the counter. Red liquid and clear glass flew in all directions and Therese screamed as the shattered stem came rocketing toward her neck.

She twisted aside, dodging the thrust by a fraction of an inch. The remains of the glass slipped from her fingers and shattered against the floor. Seizing her chance, she thrust out her left hand and pinned her right to the counter, where it flopped uselessly like an upside-down crab.

Her chest rose and fell with the erratic rhythm of her breathing. The image of Eduardo reappeared on the other side of the kitchen. *"Nice dodge, Therese. A little slower and I might have had you."*

"Are you out of your mind?" she yelled.

"It's not your mind anymore. You've lost it, and now it belongs to me."

"That's not true!"

"Isn't it? You almost stabbed yourself in the neck. Who would do that but a crazy person? Wracked by guilt—that's what they'll say about you." Eduardo stuck out his lower lip in an exaggerated pout. *"Oh, pobrecita! She couldn't take her sad, pathetic life anymore, and so she snapped and killed her sister and herself. Maybe they'll even say that you killed me too. Wouldn't that be funny?"*

Flecks of saliva flew out of her mouth as she screamed at Eduardo's image. "I didn't kill you—and you're not real!"

"Maybe I am. Maybe I'm not." He leaned forward with a smile on his face. *"But whether I am or not, things aren't looking so good for you."*

Her right hand went limp against the counter. She jerked it back and pinned it to her side. *I can't lose control again. I can't let him take over my head!*

The elegant *bing-bong* of the doorbell cut their conversation in half. "Shit!" said Therese. "It's that stupid cop!"

"He probably heard you screaming at me." Eduardo shook his head. *"He's here to haul you off to the nuthouse right now."*

She tightened her jaw and hissed through her teeth. "He's not hauling me anywhere!"

With her right hand still stuck to her side, Therese marched toward the front door and threw it open. Detective Olson was nowhere to be found. In his place stood the cleaning lady, a full foot shorter and not a person to be feared.

The coiled spring that was Therese's body went slack all at once. "Juanita," she said. "You scared the hell out of me. What are you doing here?"

The little girl—how old was she, twenty-four?—stared up at Therese with a tilted head. "I always come on Fridays, Ms. DuCannes."

As much as Therese wanted to slam the door in Juanita's face, it felt good to hear someone get her name right for once. On top of that, someone had to clean up the broken wineglass on the floor.

"Yes, I know that." Therese opened the door all the way and stepped aside. "You can come in."

"Gracias, señora," said the girl.

Eduardo whispered in Therese's ear. "*Did you understand that much, or do you need me to translate it?*"

Therese had to bite her tongue to keep from answering out loud. *I know exactly what she said, you self-righteous prick!*

"*Just making sure. I didn't think you'd know much about anything when you're too stupid to leave your own house.*"

The thick vein in the center of Therese's forehead throbbed as Juanita carried her satchel of supplies into the house. She waited until the girl had her back to Therese before wrinkling her nose and thinking, *At least I'm not stupid enough to get myself killed!*

"*Are you sure about that, Therese?*" Eduardo—who had already reappeared in front of her, Goddamn him—wagged a finger at her, still wearing his mocking grin. "*I got close on my first shot. Who's to say I won't succeed when I try again?*"

Therese's fingers twitched against her thigh. She smacked the offending arm down with her opposite hand, eyes wide. *He's really going to kill me!*

Eduardo flashed his teeth. *"Now you're getting it."*

A whirlwind of details flew through Therese's head as she tried to make sense of the situation at hand. With so many conflicting facts, she could only say two things with any kind of certainty: there was a monster in her head, and letting her guard down meant death.

She waved at the cleaning girl to get her attention. "Could you start upstairs today, Juanita? I've got a headache, so I'd appreciate a few more minutes alone down here to recuperate. Do you understand?"

Juanita opened her mouth to reply, but then her gaze settled on the shattered glass on the floor and her eyes opened wide. Therese dug her nails into her palms and repeated herself through gritted teeth. "Upstairs."

That got her moving. "Yes, Ms. DuCannes," the girl said with a nod. She set her bag on the counter and started riffling through her supplies. After a solid thirty seconds of sorting through everything from lint rollers to pill bottles, she grabbed everything she needed and disappeared upstairs.

Once Juanita got to work, Therese abandoned the mess in the kitchen and retreated to the living room. She'd never particularly enjoyed how Gillen decorated the room—his taste was far too spartan for her liking—but he was oddly touchy about it and so she'd left it alone. In retrospect, she probably should have seen that as one of the many signs he was a serial killer. No real man would have given a damn about how she decorated the living room; his commitment to limiting "excesses" was an obvious sign that something was off.

Therese settled into their gray sofa, taking care to keep her arms locked against her sides. *I can't sit here all day with my hands folded in my lap,* she thought with a scowl. *I have to be proactive.*

With narrowed eyes and furrowed brows, Therese reconsidered the morning's events. *I started hearing the voice last night, but I didn't see Eduardo until the morning. I didn't lose control of my hand until the afternoon.*

The lower half of Eduardo's body appeared in her field of vision. She looked up to see him sitting across from her in Gillen's favorite chair, a leather recliner with a table sitting on the side.

"Maybe I'm getting stronger."

She made a point of not responding, but she couldn't ignore the hypothesis. Perhaps he *was* getting stronger. The problem with that theory was that it suggested Eduardo was an individual entity, which was a concept Therese still wasn't willing to accept. The only evidence she had to suggest he was anything other than a hallucination was his little trick with Narcissa's birthday, but even that fell apart under scrutiny. It was far more plausible that someone had told Therese when Narcy's birthday was at some point or another, and she'd committed it to memory without ever realizing it. Not a perfect answer, but a much more reasonable one considering the alternative.

So let's assume Eduardo is not, in fact, getting stronger, she continued, adding in a pointed gaze in his direction. *Let's keep assuming he's a hallucination.*

"A hallucination that took over your hand."

"That was a muscle spasm," Therese snapped.

"Careful talking to me out loud, puta," he said with a smile. *"If Juanita hears you talking to yourself, she's going to know you're losing it."*

One of Therese's eyelids flickered independent of the other. *I'm not losing it. I'm just hallucinating because I've forgotten how to focus.* The drinking, the lack of sleep, the detective's stupid questions: all of them were testing her willpower, and so far, she had failed. If she wanted to regain control over her sanity, she needed a helping hand.

A brilliant idea popped into Therese's head. Her lips curved into a celebratory smirk and she headed straight for the kitchen.

Juanita's overflowing bag of supplies sat on the counter, just where she'd left it. Therese took a quick glance up the steps to make sure Juanita wasn't watching, then tore the bag open and started rifling through its contents.

Eduardo appeared on the opposite side of the table. He leaned over to get a closer look as Therese tossed a box of cleaning sponges aside. *"What are you doing?"*

Funny, I thought you knew what I was thinking.

"Maybe I do, but I want to hear you say it."

Liar. With the sponges out of the way, Therese grabbed hold of her prize: the plastic bag of prescriptions Juanita had just picked up at the store. Eduardo's brows knitted together as Therese held up the bag with a triumphant grin.

"I get it now," he said. *"Still, I'm impressed you thought of this. I would have thought you would never believe a Hispanic woman could afford prescription drugs."*

Of course that's what I thought, Therese shot back. Normally she kept the majority of her less socially acceptable opinions to herself—not that they were wrong—but with Eduardo in her head, she saw no reason to censor things. *I would have never thought she could afford medication if I hadn't seen it in her bag earlier.* That, of course, and the fact that Juanita was always crying about her hyperactive son—as if a girl her age should have a son at all.

The first two bags contained allergy medicine, which was about as useful to Therese as the rest of the cleaning supplies. The third bag contained exactly what she needed.

Eduardo squinted at the label on the bag. Amphetamine salts, 10 mg. He laughed slightly, shaking his head. *"Very clever, Therese."*

Of course it's clever. She threw the bag in a drawer and shoved the other supplies back in Juanita's bag. *Everything I do is clever.*

"We'll see about that."

Therese ignored him and hollered up the stairs. "Juanita! Could you come down here?"

After a few moments, Juanita came scrambling down the stairs with her arms full of supplies and a look of panic on her face.

Eduardo stared at Therese, jaw set. *"She probably thinks you're going to fire her."*

Then today is her lucky day. "Juanita," she said in her sweetest voice, "I'm really not feeling well today. Would you mind it terribly if I asked you to head home?" *Here comes the kicker.* "I'll pay you for a full day's work, of course."

Juanita blinked as if she'd come face-to-face with an oncoming car. "A-a-are you sure, Ms. DuCannes?"

"Of course I'm sure." Therese held out Juanita's zipped-up purse. "I should be the one to clean up the mess with the wineglass. After all, it was my silly mistake!"

"I...I guess so... You're sure you don't want me to finish cleaning? Do you want me to come back at the same time tomorrow?"

"That won't be necessary. You can just come back at the usual time next week." *Because by then,* she added, staring right at Eduardo, *I'll be rid of both you and your wife entirely.*

Eduardo bared his teeth. *"Don't count on it."*

"Here, Juanita." Therese took out her wallet and started counting out bills. "Here's everything I owe you—plus a little extra for your trouble." She held out the money and winked. "Don't spend it all in one place."

Juanita took the money with trembling hands. "Gracias, señora."

As Juanita gathered her things to leave, her cell phone rang in her pocket and she took the call. Therese could just make out Juanita's side of the conversation as the girl left the house. "*Estoy llegando temprano a casa... Señora DuCannes lo dijo! ... ¡Lo sé! ¡Por lo general ella es una pinche perra!*"

Eduardo threw his head back and burst out laughing. Therese whirled on him the moment Juanita shut the door. "What's so funny, you little shit?"

"*She just called you a fucking bitch!*" He laughed even louder, so loud Therese could swear she heard it echoing throughout the insides of her head. "*Smart girl's got you all figured out!*"

A burst of air shot from Therese's nose. She smacked her hand on the counter, slapping her skin against the puddle of wine. Red drops flew through the air like rain. "I gave that stupid brat an extra week's pay!"

"*And you also stole her child's medicine! You really think you're the good guy here?*"

At the mention of the medicine, Therese's fury vanished into nothingness. "That's right. I did steal her medicine, didn't I?" She smiled and pulled the bag from the drawer. Thankfully, whatever drug company pumped out the stuff had been forced to print the instructions right on the package, so she didn't have to look it up online.

Take one tablet every four to six hours as needed. Do not exceed 40 mg per day. Contains 90 tablets.

Her grin stretched wide enough to make her cheeks ache. "Even if I take double the dose, this should be more than enough to get me through a week with you."

"*Either that or you'll have a heart attack and die.*"

"What do you think I am, an idiot? I'm not going to take double the dose right away." She stared at the bag, then looked down at her hand again. Wine trailed between her fingers, mirroring the red rivers covering Eduardo's chest. She shuddered and closed her eyes.

"*I had a private teacher once.*" Eduardo's voice rumbled in the back of her head, reminding her of a predator's growl. "*A tutor that came to my house when I was thirteen. Things worked out for a while, yeah? But then they didn't, and he said something he shouldn't have. So I made him kill himself.*"

Ice flooded Therese's veins. She popped off the lid and dumped six pills into her hand. "The forty milligram limit was for a child," she said to herself. "I can take much more and survive."

Crossing her eyes, she tossed back the pills and swallowed them down with a chaser from the bottle of wine. The sweet liquid burned her throat and she smiled with satisfaction.

"Try to get in my head now, asshole."

Eduardo flashed an ugly grin. "*See you on the other side.*"

Chapter Sixteen

A TORRENT OF snowflakes smacked Andrew in the face as Ed marched his stolen body down the streets of Chicago. To any of the few onlookers unlucky enough to be outside in the weather, Andrew fit in with every other Midwesterner ducking beneath the wind in silence. Had any of them been able to see inside that head, they would have learned its two occupants were at war.

Where are you taking me, you asshole? Andrew thought as Ed took a sharp turn next to one of the city's billion Irish bars. Without control of his mouth, the only way Andrew could fight Ed was to think at him at the top of his lungs. He wasn't using his lungs to think, granted, but he didn't know how else to describe having his body snatched when he was too busy trying to get it back. *What the hell is wrong with you?*

Ed yanked Andrew's jacket closer to his chest. *"We're going to the hospital."*

And you had to steal my body to do that? Andrew willed his hands to tighten into fists, but he couldn't even move a finger. He could barely control the movements of his own eyeballs, and Ed didn't seem to care where those were looking at all. All that mattered to him was moving forward.

"You stopped listening to reason."

Reason is not giving you control of my body? Reason is forcing me to kill somebody?

"Reason is helping your murdered friend!"

The city passed Andrew by as he watched the streets from his prison cell inside his head. He'd lost count of the number of times he'd walked down the same streets when he had control of his own legs, but having someone else driving made the familiar streets seem foreign and unwelcoming. Restaurants where the waiters knew his name and stores he'd been going to since he was a kid were now as inaccessible as walled-off fortresses. Even if Eduardo walked him into one of them, Andrew wouldn't be any freer than he was on the street. As long as Eduardo had control, he'd be a prisoner no matter where he went.

Let's talk about this, Ed. Without body language to help him seem serious, Andrew had to imagine himself with his hands clasped together and eyes on the verge of crying. He had no idea if Ed could see what Andrew imagined, but it didn't hurt to try when he'd run out of other options.

"*What is there to talk about?*" Ed took Andrew around another corner and braced himself against a blast of wind. Andrew recognized the busy six-way intersection from the countless times he'd been stuck waiting at the red lights there in his car. In a few more blocks, they'd be at the hospital.

You don't need to force me to go to the hospital. If you let me go, I'll keep walking us both there. I promise you. I'm not lying.

"*The same way you weren't lying about being in love with Narcy?*"

Andrew bristled. *So this is your way of punishing me?*

"*This is my way of seeing my wife!*"

You should have asked me! A piece of their earlier conversation popped into his head and he scrunched up his nose—or he tried to anyway, but his nose was no longer his own. *And you shouldn't have taken over my body last night!*

Ed gritted Andrew's teeth. *"If I'd been able to see Narcy last night, I wouldn't have to do this now!"*

As pissed as Andrew was—and he was definitely pissed, maybe more than he'd ever been in his life—the notion that something had derailed Ed last night when he seemed so unstoppable now needed some explaining. *Why weren't you able to see her last night?*

"You wouldn't believe me if I told you!"

A gust of wind blew a crumpled sheet of newspaper into Andrew's face. Andrew swatted it away without thinking. It was only once Ed had carried them another half a block without reacting that Andrew realized he'd managed to take back control, if only for a moment. The fact that Ed hadn't noticed meant he was too distracted by his mission to keep Andrew in check.

Hope swelled in Andrew's stolen heart. If he could keep Ed's focus elsewhere, he could exploit the distraction and take control of his body again. He just had to make an opening.

You know what? Andrew thought at Ed. *Try me. Tell me what happened last night. I know a promise to listen isn't worth anything to you, but I can't exactly stop you if I don't like what I'm hearing.*

Andrew felt his own lips twist into a smirk. *"That is true, isn't it?"* Ed turned another corner and the hospital came into view. His ugly smile dropped into a frown that made Andrew's jaw ache. *"It was that puta cop."*

Puta cop? Wait, you mean the cop from last night—Detective Ramirez? What's she got to do with this?

"When I took your body last night, I left the house to go see Narcy. When I stepped through the door, the cop was waiting for me."

You mean she was waiting for me?

"*No,*" Ed replied. "*She was waiting for* me."

Oh. Andrew paused and reconsidered the conversation. Tapping into Ed's frustration with the police seemed like the perfect way to regain control, but taking back control would make Ed a lot less willing to explain why he was getting visitors when he was supposed to be dead. As much as Andrew wanted his body back, Ed's story had become too important to ignore.

I'm confused. It was probably the most honest thought he'd had all day. *Why would she have been waiting for you? You're supposed to be dead.*

"*I know that. She was waiting for me anyway.*" Ed shoved Andrew's hands into his pockets as the cold bit into his fingers. They'd stepped into the long shadow of the hospital, which dropped the temperature from "somewhat miserable" to "bone-chilling agony." Even the insides of Andrew's nose were starting to freeze. "*She knew I'd be in your body.*"

How could she have possibly known that? I didn't know that! You didn't even know about that—right?

"*No, I didn't. But she did, and she was there to keep me from seeing Narcy.*"

Andrew thought back on his brief interaction with Detective Ramirez in the ambulance. She'd been a little more familiar than most cops he'd known, that was true, but he hadn't known a lot of cops in his life. He definitely didn't know enough to say whether or not they were in the business of keeping body-snatching husbands away from their comatose wives. *Did she say that's why she was there?*

"*She didn't tell me shit.*"

The little bit of optimism Andrew had been shielding died like a snuffed-out flame. Even with a limited understanding of Spanish, he'd recalled enough of Ed's previous attempt at body-jacking to know he'd had a full-blown conversation with Detective Ramirez. She might not have been forthcoming when she first met him at the door, but she'd been willing to talk long enough for somebody to polish off half a beer. Considering how short Ed's temper had been since he moved into Andrew's head, the odds that he'd let Detective Ramirez talk for that long without telling him anything were impossibly slim. The odds were a lot higher that Ed was lying.

Andrew forced his stolen eyes toward the hospital doors. If Ed refused to be honest with him, waiting to get his body back until after the hospital trip was no longer an option. If he wanted to get his body back without making a scene, he had to make an opportunity before they got to the front door. Out in the snow, no one would be lingering long enough to stare at a person having a mental duel with himself. Inside a hospital, that kind of move would land Andrew in a bed right next to Narcy.

An ugly idea popped into Andrew's head. It involved invading Narcy's privacy, but it had the best chance of getting Ed to loosen his grip. It also had a good chance of getting Ed to go completely insane, so Andrew would have to move extremely fast.

You know something, Ed? he thought as they approached the last crosswalk before the doors. *I don't appreciate you lying to me—and I definitely don't appreciate you taking over my body. How about I do the same thing to your head?*

Ed froze midstride. *"What?"*

You were a mind reader once, right? You must have spent a lot of time sneaking around in people's minds. But nobody ever did it to you before, did they? I'll bet there's a whole lot of interesting stuff in there that I could dig up if you don't give me my body back. Stuff with you—and stuff with Narcy.

Andrew's brow furrowed under Ed's command. *"You wouldn't dare."*

Oh no? You don't think so? A part of Andrew wanted to make a grab for his body right then so he could laugh in Ed's imaginary face. *I did have a real thing for her, after all. Why wouldn't I want to see what she looks like during sex?*

"You'll regret it."

What are you going to do, huh? Steal my body? Read my mind? You've already taken everything from me; what more do you have to threaten me with? Unless you're willing to give me my body back, I have no reason to stop.

"You're a real piece of shit, you know that?"

Hey, I'm not the one walking around with somebody else's legs. So how about it, Ed? Will you give me my body back, or should I go ahead and look at your memories of Narcy instead?

Ed lifted Andrew's gaze toward the hospital, then looked down at his body. One of his feet stuck out in front of the other, hitting the crosswalk beyond the curb. *"¡Venga, culero!"*

Andrew's fingers twitched and he forced his lips into a grin. *Watch me.*

Dropping what little control he had, Andrew gave up on paying attention to his hijacked senses and sank back into his memories. They weren't just his memories anymore, however; they were both his and Ed's, all mixed together as if the two men had led a single life. With the separate pieces of their past coming together so naturally, finding the right memory of Narcy was as easy for Andrew as remembering his own home.

Moonlight peeked through the curtains of the bedroom window, illuminating the pale skin of Narcy's back. Her copper hair spilled over her shoulders as she bent over the bed. With her breasts flat against the sheets, she looked over her shoulder and lifted her hips with a smile.

"Come on, Ed—fuck me like one of your boys."

The memory burst around Andrew like a pinpricked balloon. Andrew stumbled forward, simultaneously taking and losing control. *Oh, what the hell!*

"*I told you you would regret it,*" said Ed.

Andrew imagined himself speaking in a tone that appropriately conveyed his horror. *Jesus Christ, Ed—what did she mean by boys?*

"*Well, she doesn't mean kids if that's what you're asking—and to be honest,*" he added with knitted brows, "*I'm a little pissed that you'd think that.*"

Then what the hell does it mean! mean...boys...like...?

"*Like the new college grads, the ones fresh out of business school, who think they know everything because they passed Finance 101 and they got their first job, and all they want to do is tell everyone how smart they are—until I show them they don't know shit. Those are my kind of boys.*"

The logical part of Andrew's brain raced to keep up with his gut reactions. *Wait, hold on... Does that mean you're gay?*

"*What else would I be, you idiot!*"

Andrew's nostrils flared out from under Ed's control. *Then why the hell are you with Narcy?*

A clear set of automatic doors reflected Andrew's scowl as Ed came to a halt at the front of the hospital. "*We're here.*"

After having two bombs dropped on him at once, Andrew had almost forgotten about regaining control of his limbs. Seeing his reflection forced him back to reality. If he wanted his body back, he had to act now.

Using all of the strength he had, Andrew threw his energy into his legs. A shout flew from his mouth as his lower half rocked off balance and crumpled to the ground. Before Ed could recover, Andrew commanded his arms to grab the railing jutting out from the door. The freezing metal stung his skin and he snatched his burning hands back to his chest.

"Damn it, that's cold!" he said. A half second later, he realized he'd spoken out loud and let out a whoop of triumph. "I'm back!"

Ed appeared in front of the doors, lips curled and eyes narrowed down to slits. *"You son of a bitch."*

"You can call me whatever you want, buddy." Andrew stuck out his tongue, not caring that he must have seemed crazy for making faces in front of the doors. "I don't care, because I'm back in charge."

"And so what? You're going to drag me back home now? You want to keep me from my wife that much longer?"

"The wife you're cheating on? No, I'm not going to keep her from you—because unlike you, I'm not an asshole." The polite part of Andrew had a feeling he was taking things too far, but he felt entitled to give Ed a good amount of grief after what they'd just been through. "We'll go in there and ask about her again, because believe it or not, I care about making sure she's okay too."

"Yeah, I'm sure you would have wanted to do that, and not just spend all day digging more ass grooves into your couch the way you usually do."

"Oh, don't you worry. I'll have plenty of time to do that when I take my body home once we're done."

Ed crossed his arms. *"We're not leaving here until I see her."*

"No, actually, we're leaving if they say we can't see her and security throws us out."

"They'll have a good reason to do that if they see you out here talking to yourself."

Andrew's triumphant smile collapsed into a tight-lipped frown. Frustrating as it was to admit, Ed had a point. *Fine. We'll go inside. But don't give me any crap if they tell us we can't see her."*

"And you say you're in love with her."

A surge of shame raced through Andrew's body, burning worse than the frozen rail. Though he had a couple of comebacks ready, none of them would do anything to make him feel better about himself, so instead, he tugged his jacket close and stepped into the range of the automatic doors.

Warm air flooded the chilly street as the doors opened for Andrew and Ed. Andrew had never been much for physical activity, but he thoroughly enjoyed being able to walk his own limbs up to the front desk. He even enjoyed being able to talk to the woman sitting there, and talking to people was never high on his enjoyment list.

"Excuse me," he said, leaning an elbow on the counter. "I'm looking to see a patient here. Her name is Narcissa Lynch."

The woman behind the counter peered over the rims of her rectangular glasses as she clacked away at her keyboard. After a series of alternating keyboard commands and frowns, the woman raised her eyebrows and cocked her head at Andrew.

"She's upstairs in room 404. Take the elevator down the hall and to your left, and her room should be on the right side by the stairs."

"Don't I need to register or anything?"

"*Are you crazy?*" said Ed. "*What are you wasting time with procedure for? She just told you where Narcy is. Now take me to her!*"

Andrew shot Ed the quickest glance he could without drawing too much attention to his imaginary friend. *You don't think it's weird she's just letting us up there?*

"*Take me to her, or I'm taking us myself!*"

All right, fine! "Thanks for your help," he said to the woman. *Now come on,* he thought at Ed. *Let's go before she remembers the point of a check-in desk is to make people check in.*

They sped down the hall without looking back, with Ed leading the charge and Andrew two steps behind him. After a quick ride on the elevator, they emerged on the fourth floor and located Narcy's room.

"*Here she is.*" Ed chewed his lip and stepped back from the door. "*Do you think they've told her I'm dead yet?*"

"I don't know," Andrew murmured. He also didn't know why Narcy's name wasn't on the door, or why the pale blue hallway seemed to be missing both security and the kind of medical staff that helped someone who'd recently been stabbed. "But something doesn't feel right here..."

The muscles in Andrew's hand curled his fingers into a fist. Before Andrew could stop himself, his knuckles rapped against the door.

A woman called out from inside the room. Her familiar voice sent a chill down Andrew's back. "You can come in."

Before Andrew could say "*Wait, don't!*" Ed grabbed both of his arms and opened the door. On the other side, they found a room no larger than a closet, containing nothing but a desk, two chairs, and Detective Caroline Ramirez.

She clicked her tongue at Andrew and folded her arms. "I thought I told you two to stay home."

Chapter Seventeen

ORANGE TRAFFIC CONES jutted from the side of the road like neon stalagmites, lining the barren stretch of road Gillen could only identify as "mile marker thirteen." About two miles back, a fly had found its way into the car through the open window, and it had since dedicated its life to buzzing directly in Gillen's ear. Even on a good day, the incessant noise would have pissed him off eventually. Adding in Eduardo's endless chatter had Gillen's patience frayed down to the last thread.

"Are we there yet?"

The fly landed on Gillen's shoulder. Every vein in Gillen's neck tensed in unison as he smacked the insect away. "For the last time, we're not there!"

"Why not?"

"Because we're not! Jesus God! Why won't you leave me alone?"

"Hey, I'm not here by choice. I had reservations for dinner with Narcy tonight. Can't exactly do that now, though, what with the two of us being dead." He shook his head with the kind of disappointment that would make a parent proud. *"I still can't decide if you feel guilty about that."*

"About killing you? I'm feeling better and better about that by the minute."

"No, not about me—about Narcy."

The fly did another circuit by Gillen's ear. He jerked his arm upright without letting go of the wheel. The car lurched to the right, skidding toward the edge of the road.

Gillen clenched the wheel with both hands and whipped back into his lane. "I didn't kill Narcy!"

"*Oh sure, you just conspired to kill me with the woman who ended up killing her. That's much better.*"

"I had no idea she would do that."

"*Yeah, and the people who own pit bulls are always shocked when they rip a child's face off.*" Eduardo emitted a sound that was somewhere between a sigh and a snort. "*You knew exactly what she was capable of.*"

"That doesn't mean I wanted Narcy to die!"

"*And yet she's dead anyway. Guess what you wanted doesn't matter, now does it?*"

The setting sun cast a red haze across Eduardo's ugly smile. Gillen's knuckles turned white on the edge of the wheel. *If he pushes me one more time, I swear to God I'm going to fucking lose it!*

The fly chose that moment to dive-bomb straight into his ear.

Gillen screamed and jerked away from the fly. The steering wheel went with his hands. It, the car, and its occupants all went hurtling toward the edge of the road, where a sharp dip promised their inevitable flip. Gillen's stomach twisted and he shut his eyes tight. *I'm not ready to die!*

His hands seized around the wheel and yanked it to the left. With no input from their owner, his feet betrayed him in kind. They worked the brakes and accelerator in tandem with the speed of someone who was present in the moment, rather than someone who was watching their own body in numb horror from the sidelines.

The wheels locked up beneath his legs and the car came to a halt with an ugly screech. Gillen's seat belt cut across the thin skin on his neck as he rocketed forward in his seat. A thousand spots flashed in front of his eyes, mimicking the brilliant circle of the sun.

"My legs..." he murmured. "You took over my legs..."

With his focus forward and his head aching, he could only see the edge of the dark smile that crossed Eduardo's lips. Gillen didn't have long to think about it, though, as a cacophony of sirens fired up behind him.

Red and blue lights reflected around the car. Waves of hot panic and chilling fear ran through Gillen's body as though someone was pushing him back and forth between a freezer and a stove.

"The police..."

Eduardo smiled wider. *"Looks like they finally caught up with you."*

"Maybe he's trying to pull over someone else."

"There is no one else, pendejo. You're on this road alone."

The gleaming cruiser crawled to a stop behind Gillen's car. Sunlight bounced off the door as the officer stepped out. With his sunglasses covering his eyes, Gillen could only guess at the man's mood from the tight line of his lipless mouth.

"He looks pissed," said Eduardo. *"I bet he's near the end of his shift."* He ran his fingers through his hair with the wide-eyed smile of someone who'd just dodged an oncoming train. *"I sure am glad I'm not the one who has to deal with him."*

As the officer approached Gillen's window, Gillen's heart thudded against his ribs. *This can't be happening! All I needed was one day! Just one day, then I'll be gone!*

"You'd better roll down your window before he gets here. Cops don't appreciate it when you don't play by their rules."

For a fleeting moment, Gillen considered flooring it and trying for an escape. Then he remembered he was driving a beat-up sedan that could barely get above eighty without drifting with the wind. Even with a head start, he wouldn't make it more than a mile before the police cruiser ran him down.

Eduardo nudged the peeling dashboard and snickered. *"Bet you wish you'd taken Therese's Porsche now, don't you?"*

The officer appeared at Gillen's door. The wide brim of his hat cast a shadow over his sunglasses, obscuring the already scant details of his face. For all Gillen could make out, the man might have had no face at all.

Three sharp clicks resonated around the car as the officer tapped on the window. Gillen swallowed hard and lowered it. The dry skin inside his mouth stuck to his gums as he mustered up a greeting.

"Good evening, officer. Is there a problem?"

"You're wanted for multiple murders," said Eduardo.

"You were doing a lot of swerving back there," said the officer.

Gillen flinched. *Stupid fly!* "A fly got in through the window." Even as he said it, he realized how incredibly lame it sounded, but he couldn't think of a better lie than the truth. "It kept getting in my ear and distracting me."

"Mmhmm." The officer peered at the passenger's seat. Eduardo flipped up his middle finger with a childish grin. Gillen's breath hitched in his throat, but the officer didn't react. Instead, he looked back at Gillen and studied him from behind the lenses of his glasses. "You been doing any drinking tonight?"

"What, and driving? No, God no!" Tremors ran through his arms. He clenched his jaw and tightened his hold on the wheel. "I'm just jittery because that fly almost made me wreck my car."

"Mind if I see your license and registration?"

Gillen's stomach dropped as if he'd looked down through the glass floor at the top of the Sears Tower. "What?"

"License and registration."

Eduardo knocked against the glove compartment with his heel. *"Registration's right in here—or it would be, if your car were registered."*

"J-j-just a second," Gillen stammered to the officer. "I just need to get my wallet."

His mind raced as he leaned over for the glove compartment with the speed of a dying snail. "I'm not sure if it's in here," he said, talking one step ahead of his thoughts. "It's my friend's car. I'm just borrowing it while he's out of town."

"Then let's start with your driver's license," the officer replied.

Gillen's hand froze above the console. "You want my license?"

"That's what I said."

"You idiot," said Eduardo. *"Just give him your damn license and accept the inevitable."*

All the air went out of Gillen's lungs at once. *He's right. I'm not fooling anyone except myself.* He sank into his chair and pulled his wallet out of his pocket. "Sure thing, Officer."

Eduardo smirked in satisfaction as Gillen withdrew the plastic rectangle bearing his name. His redheaded portrait stared up at him, taunting him with proof of his discarded past.

"Here it is."

The officer grabbed the card from between Gillen's fingers before Gillen had a chance to reconsider. "You keep looking for that registration." His eyebrows disappeared beneath the lenses of his glasses, reflecting the way Eduardo's brows moved each time he narrowed his eyes. "Meanwhile, I'll go run this and your plates."

"Sounds great."

The officer walked away, leaving Gillen alone to stare into empty space. "I didn't make it..."

Eduardo peered at Gillen with a mixture of amusement and disbelief. *"Come on. You didn't actually think you'd get away with it, did you?"*

"All I needed was one day. Just one day, that was it." He buried his head in his hands and choked back a strangled sigh. "I just needed enough time to destroy it."

"Destroy what?"

A fleeting memory of Gillen's childhood jumped to the front of his mind. It was one of the many memories he'd worked hard to beat down, so hard that he'd started to wonder if it had ever happened at all.

The wooden floorboards cracked beneath Gillen as his mother hugged him to her chest. "We just need to sit here and stay quiet together," she whispered. "If we don't make any noise, your dad won't have a reason to get mad at us."

Gillen held his mother's hand. "Did I do something wrong?"

"Shh. Don't think about that." She ran her fingers through his hair and made shushing sounds with her lips. "Just stay quiet with me."

"Okay, I'll stay quiet." He lowered his gaze to the blue and purple bruises ringing his mother's arm. She'd gotten hurt really badly the last time he was too loud. "I'm sorry."

Outside the bedroom, his father's footsteps echoed like thunderclaps as the towering man raged down the hall. "Why the fuck do you always move the remote? Just put it on the goddamned coffee table when you're done with it and stop leaving it wherever you forget about it! Jesus Christ, can't you do anything right?"

Gillen's mother lowered her forehead into the crook of Gillen's neck. "I'm sorry, too, sweetie."

Sadness pooled in Gillen's heart, filling and filling until his chest felt ready to burst. He squeezed his mom's hand and bit his cheek. Lately he'd been thinking of asking his mom for a brother or sister to keep him company, but his father would probably be mean to them, too. Having a sibling meant, Gillen would have to work twice as hard to make sure nobody could hurt them.

"I'm scared..." he murmured into her chest.

"Shh, don't be scared."

"How?"

"We can play a game." She brushed his hair off his forehead and smiled as wide as she could without hurting the big cut on her lip. "Remember your favorite story, about the gambler who could use magic? He used to spend lots of time staring at a candle and trying to think about nothing, but he had to practice lots and lots because thinking about nothing is hard. Do you want to try thinking about nothing with me?"

Gillen chewed his cheek and nodded. Thinking about nothing felt a lot better than thinking about what would happen if his dad got mad enough to put his foot through the bedroom door. "Okay."

"Good, we'll do it together. Now just close your eyes and picture the very center of a candle flame, and don't think about anything else, and everything that scares you will go away."

The ragged sound of heavy breathing yanked Gillen back to the present. He spun toward the sound, imagining the ghost of his father, and sighed with sweet relief when it was only the officer who had come back to arrest him for murder.

"Here's your license back. Looks like you're all clean." The lenses of the officer's sunglasses reflected Gillen's slack jaw as he handed over the card. "I'd write you up for failing to provide proper documentation of registration, but I just got a call telling me there's somewhere else I've got to be, so it's your lucky day. Just keep your eyes on the road and don't let your car get away from you again."

Gillen's hand shook as he took back his license. "I... okay..."

The officer pulled away from the window and straightened his glasses. "And clear the damn bugs out of your car."

"You got it, Officer."

From his invisible vantage point in the passenger's seat, Eduardo watched the policeman with unblinking eyes and a slack jaw as the officer got into his car and pulled away. *"No mames..."*

Gillen didn't need a Spanish dictionary to understand what that meant. He could figure it out from the tone, in addition to the fact that Eduardo's look of disbelief no doubt matched his own completely. "He must not have bothered to run my license..."

"Cops always run that shit! What? You think he went back to the cruiser just to chug his coffee? He checked you, cabrón! He just didn't find anything!"

"But that's impossible! I left a house with two bodies in it! And I left it with Therese! There's no way she didn't turn me in to them!" He combed his hands through his hair and tugged at the roots, hoping the pain would shock some sense into his brain. "This is insane!"

Eduardo stared at him as if he'd sprouted a unicorn horn on his forehead. *"Are you pissed right now or something? How are you not down on your knees thanking Jesus for saving your ass?"*

"Because it doesn't make sense!"

"Why do you care?"

"They're supposed to catch up with me!"

"What?"

Gillen clutched his forehead and groaned. "Just stop talking to me!"

"Not until you tell me why you want the police to get you!"

"Why do you think I want them to get me, you idiot?" He smacked the steering wheel and spun on him. "Because they have to find me after I die!"

Eduardo's lips parted, but no sound emerged. He simply sat there, blinking like he'd accidentally stepped in front of an oncoming train.

"What do you look so surprised for?" Gillen snapped. "You're the one living in my brain! None of this should be a revelation!"

"I can't believe it..." Eduardo said at last. *"You're going to kill me all over again."*

A horrible chill ran down Gillen's back. He'd never felt anything similar before, but his first guess was that it was shame. "I didn't think you'd be coming with me."

"But your goal hasn't changed, has it? Is that why you tried to drive us off the road!"

"I'm not planning to die just yet."

"Oh what, you want to give it a few days, maybe take some time to make peace with committing triple homicide?"

Gillen dropped his hands to his lap. He sank into his chair and let his head fall to the side, just far enough for him to make eye contact with Eduardo. "You found out about Bernardo."

For the second time in as many minutes, Eduardo's mouth fell open as he blinked in unmistakable shock. This time, he found his voice a lot faster. "Hijo de puta, you killed my therapist."

Gillen closed his eyes. In the darkness, he didn't have to see the way Eduardo was staring at him. He didn't have to think about anything at all. "Yeah. I did."

"How many people have you killed?"

It was a serious question, but Gillen couldn't help but laugh. "Why do you think I want to die?"

Chapter Eighteen

THE DOOR CLICKED shut behind Andrew and Ed. Andrew whirled around and grabbed the handle. It didn't budge.

"It locks from the outside." Caroline grinned as she held up a set of silver keys. "The only way out is through me."

Ed slammed his hands against the little table. They stopped against the surface as if they'd made a physical connection, but the motion did nothing to create a sound or disturb the table. For all of Ed's fury, there was nothing he could do to affect anything—or anyone—in the room.

Without a pounding headache and ambulance sirens distracting him, Andrew had a chance to consider Caroline in a whole new light. He hadn't been able to tell how tall she was before, but the small portion of her chest sticking up above the desk meant she had to be more than a foot under Andrew's height. Her small stature didn't seem to be holding her back, not when she could twirl her wavy hair around her fingers and smile like she owned the room.

Caroline tilted her head at the empty space at Andrew's side. "Is that where he is?"

Andrew raised his eyebrows. He didn't know what surprised him more—that she knew Ed was there or that she knew that yet couldn't see him. "Yeah, he's there."

"Well, tell him he's going to be here for a while, so he might as well settle down." She smirked at the space where Ed stood fuming. "I'm guessing he's not happy right now."

"*Puta cop!*" Ed snapped.

While part of Andrew appreciated not having to apologize for Ed's outburst, he was about thirty seconds away from having an outburst of his own. "I'm not happy either, you know, and I'd love to know why we're here in a broom closet with you when we're supposed to be visiting Narcy."

Caroline folded her arms across the tabletop. "Narcy's not taking visitors right now."

"*What are you doing to her?*" Ed shouted.

After an awkward pause, Andrew realized Caroline couldn't hear Ed any more than she could see him. "Why can't we see her?"

"Because she got stabbed in the neck less than twelve hours ago, and believe it or not, doctors are still working on keeping her alive."

"*Why the hell can't we talk to those doctors ourselves?*" said Ed.

While Andrew wanted an answer to that, too, he had quite a few other questions that took priority over Ed's. "How do you know about Ed?"

One side of Caroline's mouth quirked above the other. "What? Ed didn't tell you?"

"He told me you spoke." Andrew cast Ed a quick look out of the side of his eye. Fighting now wouldn't get them anywhere, but Ed still deserved some grief for lying. "He didn't say anything else."

Ed snarled at Caroline. "*None of her lies are worth repeating.*"

"Oh, she's the liar now?" Andrew said. "Gee, and here I thought it was the body thief!"

Caroline started laughing. "Trouble in paradise?"

Andrew's cheeks lit up when he realized his mistake. Even though she knew he was talking to someone else, he still probably looked insane. "He keeps taking over my body."

"Yes, I know. I told him not to do that. Still, some of that responsibility lies with you. If he's able to take you over with that little effort, well…" She rocked her hands back and forth like she was searching for the right thing to say. When she finally settled on something, she laughed and pointed at Andrew's chest. "It means you're kind of a pussy."

"Hey!"

"What? It's not a bad thing. Well, not really. It's not great when you're trying to keep your ensemble away from your body."

Andrew wrinkled his nose. "My ensemble?"

"The people living in your head—or in this case, the person. With you in control of the body, that means you're in an ensemble of two."

"How do you know all of this? Are you a mind reader?" Andrew asked. Ed's sneer stayed fixed on his face, but his gaze drifted away from Caroline. He already knew the answer.

"No, I'm not a mind reader," she said. "But the people I work for are, and they're pretty pissed about the mess you two are in."

Ed smacked the table again. *"This isn't our fault."*

Now that Andrew could agree with. "This isn't our fault," he repeated to her.

"Maybe not yours," she said, "but it's hard to turn a blind eye to an Oyente who gets himself killed."

"Oyente?"

"It means Listener," said Ed. *"It's their word for what I was. A mind reader."*

"Their word? Who are *they*?" He glanced down at Caroline's chest and noticed the conspicuous lack of a badge. "Are you not really a cop?"

"What are you, crazy?" Caroline rolled her eyes. "You think a cop could set up a private office in a hospital?"

"How should I know what cops can do? I've never been arrested!"

"Yeah, but you do have common sense, and you must have noticed by now that this case isn't being handled in the usual manner."

"If that isn't the understatement of the century," said Ed.

Andrew furrowed his brow at Caroline. "So if you're not with the police, then who are you with?"

"Is that really what you want to know right now?" she said. "The way I see it, you should care less about who we are and what we're going to do with you."

Cold dread crawled up Andrew's neck. "What are you going to do with us?"

"If you touch Narcy, I swear to God—"

"Relax," said Caroline. "We're not going to hurt you. We're just going to send you home and make sure you stay there until we find Gillen ourselves."

"You stay away from him!" Ed clenched his fists. *"Gillen is mine!"*

Andrew's eyes snapped open. "Are you crazy? These people are going to handle it."

Caroline glanced from Andrew to her best guess at Ed's position in space. "What did he say?"

"He thinks we should be the ones to kill Gillen, which is *insane.*"

"Absolutely not." Caroline's hair swirled around her shoulders as she shook her head. "You two are absolutely not allowed to go after Gillen, under any circumstances."

"You don't control me, puta!"

"No, but I do," Andrew said. He could have shared the retort with Ed mentally, but he had a feeling Caroline could understand Ed's half of the conversation from context. He also wanted her to know at least one half of his ensemble was sane. "And I say we're not going after him when there's people who are better equipped to deal with him than us."

"What makes you think they're better equipped than we are? We don't know a thing about these people, Andy! Why should we trust that they're any more capable of finding Gillen than we are? They haven't found him yet. What makes you think they can find him at all?"

Caroline raised her eyebrows at the empty space. "Care to tell me what he said?"

"He says he doesn't believe you'll be able to handle Gillen any better than we can, which is ridiculous, because I'm about as capable of handling a violent situation as I am of socializing without my keyboard."

She covered her mouth with her hand to hide a short laugh. "You shouldn't be so self-deprecating. I'm sure you can handle socializing. You can't handle Gillen, though." Her smile fell and she laced her fingers together. "He was smart enough to kill an Oyente without giving himself away, and his intelligence is about to become the least terrifying thing about him once he inherits Eduardo's abilities."

Both Andrew and Ed looked at each other with wide eyes and open mouths. "Did she tell you about that?" Andrew murmured.

"She didn't say shit to me about that!"

Andrew turned back on Caroline. "Why would Gillen inherit Eduardo's abilities?"

"For the same reason you're going to inherit Ed's abilities: because you both took on a copy of Eduardo when he died."

All the feeling drained from Andrew's face. "Oh my God… I'm going to become a mind reader."

Eduardo gaped at Caroline, mirroring Andrew's expression. *"Hijo de puta…there's a second version of me."*

"Mmhmm," said Caroline. "Both you and Gillen were close to Ed when he died, which means both of you took on copies of his mind when he died. As a consequence of that, both you and Gillen are also going to gain Ed's ability to read people's thoughts once he gets permanently settled in your minds."

"And when is that going to be?"

"From the number of times we've seen it happen, we've got it pinned down to forty-eight hours from initial transmission." She took out her phone and held up the glowing screen. The time flashed 10:31 a.m. "Which means that, based on Eduardo's time of death, we've got about thirty hours until Gillen will have the power to see his pursuers coming—and the ability to jump into a nearby body if he dies."

A thousand emotions wrestled in Andrew's stomach, forcing his breakfast up through his throat. He bit back the urge to puke and asked, "Is that the same for me?"

"It is. But you're staying home. *Both* of you," she added for Ed. "We know how to handle Gillen without letting him jump again. You two just found out you're getting Ed's powers again. So for your safety and my sanity, you two are staying on the sidelines until we bring Gillen in."

"And after that?"

"After that?" She shrugged and offered a smile that didn't meet her eyes. "Welcome to the Oyentes."

Whatever energy Andrew had left after a poor night's sleep and a fight for his own body abandoned him in a wave of fatigue. He sank into his chair with a sigh that emptied his lungs and dragged his hand down his face. "I think I want to go home…"

Caroline pressed her hands against her hips. "Good. That's what you should do. Go home, get some rest. Leave Gillen to us, and we'll call you when we have news on Narcy. Okay?"

"Okay."

Ed narrowed his eyes. "*I don't think so.*"

An agonizing stiffness shot through Andrew's shins. He gasped and tried to stand, but his legs wouldn't move under his command. Everything below his knees had been locked into position, gluing his feet to the floor.

Without his legs to help him, he could only turn his torso and gape at the dead stare on Ed's face. "*We're not going anywhere.*"

Chapter Nineteen

GILLEN AND EDUARDO didn't speak for half an hour after their run-in with the highway patrol. That was just fine with Gillen since he had two big problems to solve before he could clean up the mess that was his life.

Problem number one: the police didn't have a warrant out for his arrest. Given the disaster of a crime scene he'd left, this didn't make any sense. Even if Therese hadn't called the police on him—an impossibility in and of itself—someone would have noticed by now that Eduardo was dead. The only way they didn't was if Therese had not only *not* called the police, but also gone out of her way to cover Gillen's tracks. Not only did that require a kind of altruism Therese didn't possess, but it also required her to do more manual labor than she'd ever done in her life. Just the thought of her cleaning up a bloodstain stretched the limits of plausibility; the thought of her actually moving a corpse defied reality itself. Unfortunately, Therese pulling off a cover-up was the only logical explanation for why no one was looking for him, so he could either choose to believe she'd helped him or accept the fact that he had no idea what was going on.

Problem number two, the larger problem on the list: back when Gillen lost control over the car, Eduardo had taken control of Gillen's limbs. Gillen hadn't been free to consider the ramifications at the time, what with the police and all, but he had plenty to think about now that he was alone. He wasn't alone, though—that was the problem. His body was no longer his own. If Eduardo had been able to take control once, there was nothing stopping him from doing it again. Considering Gillen had been planning to kill himself once he reached his destination, losing control over his body would ruin everything.

Gillen drummed his fingertips against the steering wheel as the last slivers of sunlight disappeared below the horizon. He'd spent countless hours deciding on how he wanted to end his life after Eduardo's death. He had no intention of throwing that away to become a prisoner in his own head. Unfortunately, his end goal of suicide didn't leave much room for him to negotiate.

"What do you want from me?" he said, glancing at Eduardo out of the corner of his eye.

"I don't want you to kill me." Eduardo stared out over the road ahead. *"But I also want to know why you killed my therapist."*

"Why do you need me to tell you that? Can't you just look through my memories?"

"I could." Eduardo shot him a quick look that he couldn't interpret. *"But it won't answer my question."*

"Why not?"

"Because I don't care about what happened. I know what happened. I saw it in the papers. What I want to know is why you did it."

"And you don't see that in my memories?"

"It's easier if you just tell me."

Gillen sighed and shifted his attention back to the road. The last thing he wanted to do was talk about the untimely demise of Bernardo Reyes, but there were far worse discussions they could be having. Hell, it wasn't even the worst of the crimes he'd committed. Compared to his other kills, Bernardo had been a lot less bloody.

"Set the scene for me," he said at last. "I can tell you why I did it, but it's been a few years. If you've got a movie theater running inside my head, you might as well use it to remind me of the details."

Eduardo laughed softly. *"Now that I can do."*

Stretching out his hands, he traced an invisible rectangle in the air in the shape of a giant screen. *"It was ten years ago, right after you dropped out of college. Remember so far?"*

"Yes, I remember dropping out of college." His mother and Gary had both been furious, but he stopped giving a damn about their opinions long before then. They'd spent his whole adolescence telling him to forget about the first seven years of his life, so they had no room to complain when he decided to forget about his education.

"Anyway, you've left home and you're living above a bar. You don't have to pay rent, you just have to clean up after-hours and keep an eye on the place when it's closed down. Remember that?"

"I remember my twenties, Ed."

Eduardo raised his eyebrows. *"Am I Ed to you now?"*

The veins in Gillen's neck throbbed as he clenched his teeth. "Just skip to the night I killed Reyes."

"Hey, you asked me to set the scene."

"Fine, keep going."

"So it's the middle of winter and you're cleaning up the bar. It's not quite closing time, but most of the regulars are gone. There's only three people left in the bar: you, the bartender, and a mutual friend of ours: my old therapist, Bernardo Reyes. Now, at the time, you probably didn't know Bernardo from Adam, but I'd known him forever. He was one of my father's best friends—someone my father trusted with his life. He trusted Bernardo so much, in fact,

that when I came to my father and told him I could read minds, his first thought was that he could use Bernardo to teach me to control myself."

Gillen narrowed his eyes. He could still smell the spilled beer on the pinewood floor of that broken-down bar. He could still see the neon lights flicking in the corner of his eye, just on the edge of his memory. He couldn't remember everything, but he didn't need to think hard to recall the details. What he recalled said something wasn't right with the story.

"Reyes wasn't a mind reader."

"You're right, he wasn't. He was, however, a very good child psychologist—but he wasn't without his flaws." Eduardo licked the edges of his teeth. Something about remembering Reyes must have been affecting his mood because he'd been growing increasingly animated as he recreated Gillen's memory. If Gillen hadn't known better, he almost would have thought Eduardo was enjoying himself.

"When he first started helping me understand my powers, he thought I could only see what was on the surface—and for a while, that was true. But eventually, I got better, so much better that I could dig through Bernardo's memory. And when I was in there, I saw something he'd been hiding from everyone else."

The more Eduardo spoke, the more Gillen could recall from that night. He'd seen a balding, wiry man slumped over the counter, gnashing his teeth and wailing into his beer. "You were going to ruin his career."

"In truth, I hadn't planned on it, but the situation escalated too fast for me to tell him that. Within one day of realizing what I'd seen, he was already in the wind. At the time, I assumed he'd disappeared. But he didn't, did he? He just went to cry at the bar." Eduardo let out a slight laugh.

"And of all the gin joints in all the world, he walks into yours."

At the time, Gillen had been as shocked by the coincidence as Eduardo. He'd thought nothing of the crying man at first—they got a lot of criers around last call—but Reyes had been ranting and raving about a young man who could read his mind. He'd said he had evidence to prove it too—audio and video, enough to bring the whole secret to light. Gillen had been listening with half an ear by then, as the crying man's ramblings had gotten too interesting to completely ignore, but it wasn't until he gave his pupil's name that he got Gillen's full attention.

"Your whole life changed when you heard my name, didn't it?" Eduardo asked. *"You'd been sleeping in a rat's nest, living from one bottle to the next, but all you needed to turn it around was one thing to focus your anger on."* He beamed and pointed at his chest. *"And that thing was me."*

Gillen focused his gaze on the road ahead. With Sioux Falls less than thirty miles up the road, they were coming up on the South Dakota border. He hadn't enjoyed one good minute of his life in that state, and yet he'd spent seven years living there. If he could endure returning there long enough to say goodbye, he could endure anything from Eduardo.

"I couldn't let Reyes leave there alone."

"You couldn't, could you? Not because you were a good samaritan, though. You couldn't let him leave by himself because you believed him. And that's what I can't figure out here—why?"

"Why what?"

"Why did you believe him? He was blind drunk and rambling about a skinny Mexican kid having psychic powers. Even if he said he had proof, why would you buy any of that for a second?"

There were a lot of answers Gillen could have given to that question. Some of them might have even been true. There was only one he felt ready to give. "When I was younger, my mother always read to me at bedtime. My favorite story was the one about a rich man who discovered the power to see through the backs of playing cards. I never cared much about the parts of the story that involved the casinos, but I was always interested in the part where he first developed his powers. He did it by learning to keep a clear head—by emptying out his mind and focusing on absolute nothingness."

"You believed I could read minds because you remembered it from a story?"

Gillen shook his head. "It wasn't because of the story." He hadn't intended to say so much, but once he started talking, he didn't want to stop. "It was because of what I did with it later. Ever since I heard that story, I wanted to learn to clear my mind the way he did—to silence everything inside me, to get rid of all the misery. I used to sit in my room for hours practicing, just like the man in the book. I even talked about it once or twice with Narcy. She always thought it was stupid, though, so I stopped sharing it with her when she made fun of me. That's why it surprised me when she came to me years later and asked me how I'd done it."

The hint of a smile played across Eduardo's lips. *"I'm going to guess she was about nine when she did that."*

"Nine or ten, maybe. By then, I was about sixteen or seventeen. I'd never stopped practicing clearing my head, but I hadn't spoken to anyone about it in ages. I figured she'd completely forgotten. She seemed to remember a lot of it, though, and she had a couple of specific questions— namely, whether emptying out her head meant no one else could see inside it."

"Is that right?" Eduardo chuckled softly. *"And what did you say?"*

"I told her it didn't matter because no one could see inside your head."

"And did you believe that then?"

Gillen drummed his fingertips along the edge of the steering wheel. "No."

"I didn't think so."

"I figured she was just being a pest when she asked me about clearing her head, and she never said anything about it again." The muscles in his neck tensed as he stiffened his shoulders. "She got closer and closer to you, though, so it wasn't as if she and I were talking much anymore."

"Our dads worked together. What else were we going to do when they were talking about business?"

Gillen's upper lip twitched into a snarl. "You know that man wasn't our father."

"You may not have seen him that way, but he raised Narcy from the day she was born. She never cared about the biology of it. Neither did he."

"She and I are different people." A second passed and he remembered the previous night with a shudder. "Were different people."

"So Narcy asked you about clearing your head, and then she became better friends with me. Years down the road, you hear a friend of my family bring up my name, and he happens to mention mind reading. That's when you put two and two together, isn't it? But that's not where it ended."

Goose bumps rippled down Gillen's arms as his memory shifted forward in time. The wind from that distant winter bit at his skin, working against him with every step as he followed Bernardo out of that bar. Before Bernardo came in, Gillen had wanted nothing more than to crawl into bed and never wake up. Once he got a glimpse of the real Eduardo, sleep was the last thing he cared about.

"You were there for him when no one else believed him. You said you'd help him get home—you wanted to lend him a supportive ear. And you did, didn't you? For a while." Eduardo tilted his head. *"I'm curious how you chose what to ask him first. You must have had so many questions for him. How did you know where to start?"*

"I didn't," Gillen admitted. "So I asked him to start at the top."

"You two must have had quite a long talk if he had to start at the beginning."

"We did."

There'd been a full moon that night, one Gillen could still picture reflecting off the Chicago River. His fingers had gone numb from the cold, but he hardly noticed the loss of feeling. He'd been transfixed by Bernardo's story, a nightmarish chronicle of power and deceit that had stretched out for years.

"I'm guessing he left out why he thought I was going to destroy his career," Eduardo said.

Gillen couldn't hide his smirk as he thought back on Bernardo's panicked expression. "He said he'd had a crisis of conscience. Said he couldn't cover up your lies anymore, and people had to know the truth."

"Did you believe him?"

"Not for a second."

Eduardo let out a short laugh. *"You really are sharper than I thought."*

"I killed you, didn't I?"

That earned another laugh. *"Don't flatter yourself, pendejo. That says more about me and less about you."*

"Says you."

A trailing truck crept toward Gillen's bumper. He glanced in the rearview mirror to switch lanes and realized with horror that he was actually smiling. Furrowing his brows, he faced forward and set his jaw.

"I can see your memories in front of me, but I can't see your thoughts from every second. It's not all there, you know—nobody's memories are perfect. That's why I can't say for certain of the exact point where you decided to kill me. I know you were committed to it by the end of the night, though, because you'd already realized Bernardo had to go first."

The world around Gillen turned dark as his memory pulled him to the edge of the river on that same freezing night. He and Bernardo had been talking for almost an hour, but Bernardo was still so drunk he could barely walk. He'd been leaning on Gillen for support, trusting that Gillen would guide him home.

"You might have run into people if the riverwalk had been open by then, but there was construction everywhere in those days, wasn't there? The kind of construction where the workers went home and left empty sites without many lights on—right at the edge of the river." Eduardo clicked his tongue, shaking his head in mock disappointment. *"It must have been so easy to get rid of him."*

A low grumble escaped Gillen's throat. It really had been easy. One minute, Bernardo had been leaning against Gillen's shoulder; the next, he was tumbling into the water. He hadn't even screamed. For years, Gillen had wondered if it was the cold or the water that took him. He'd never been able to decide which was worse.

"They found his body in the river the next morning. They always investigate those kinds of things, but between

the alcohol in his system and the lack of any bruises, they decided pretty quickly his death had been an accident. It certainly wouldn't have been the first accident around the water. Drunks end up in the river or the harbor every year. As far as the police knew, that was all Bernardo was. I knew differently, though—but I'd always thought he killed himself."

"Because of you."

"Because of me. And do you want to know something, Gillen?" Eduardo's lips curved into a wicked crescent. *"I was glad."*

Gillen fought to keep his face neutral, but he couldn't keep one of his eyebrows from popping above the other. "You were?"

"I'd seen a side of Bernardo no one else had; I knew what kind of man he was, deep down. And I also knew he wanted to get rid of me. Whether he'd died by accident or taken himself out, the world was better off without him in it."

"Your world in particular."

"My world in particular. Still," he added, his voice softening, *"he'd been a friend of my father's for years. He'd also been willing to help me develop my powers, even though my powers were what ended up doing him in. Or that's what I thought, anyway. Turns out, it was you."*

Gillen didn't say anything for a while after that. Even at the time, he'd been vaguely aware that killing Bernardo Reyes helped Eduardo more than anything else. Bernardo couldn't be allowed to expose Eduardo, though, since doing so would have ruined Gillen's opportunity to handle Eduardo himself. Still, in killing Bernardo, he'd given Eduardo back more than ten good years that he otherwise wouldn't have had. In a way, it was the most loyal thing Gillen could have ever done—but that wasn't why he did it.

"I always wondered," Gillen said, as much to himself as Eduardo. "What was it that you saw in Bernardo's head that made him turn on you?"

Eduardo flashed a brilliant grin. *"Why not keep us alive a little longer and dig it out of my mind yourself?"*

Gillen laughed slightly. "I'm not interested in tearing through your head."

"Oh, you say that now, but you might change your mind when you realize how interesting I am." His eyes flashed with a wicked glint. *"You might even want to see some of the things I've done with other men."*

A shudder ran through Gillen's limbs. He clenched his jaw and shook his head. "I wouldn't count on it."

"You really are in denial, aren't you?"

"Shut up."

"Have it your way." He glanced out the window, but turning his head did nothing to hide his smirk. *"We can enjoy a moment of silence as we cross into South Dakota."*

Gillen's face fell as his focus locked onto the sun-bleached sign reading—South Dakota: Great Faces, Great Places. The goldenrod outlines of four presidents stared at him, daring him to return to his childhood home.

He grabbed the wheel with both hands and hit the accelerator.

Chapter Twenty

FLAMES LICKED AT Therese's nerves, sending shivers up her spine. Blurred outlines danced across her vision. Her heart thrummed in her chest, beating like the wings of a hummingbird.

She crouched in a circle of papers, eyes darting from side to side. The white sheets, full of information, mocked her at every turn. They knew things they didn't want to tell her—things about Gillen, things he'd been keeping from her. She flipped them over one at a time, then threw them into the air when she couldn't focus long enough to read.

"I have to find out how he did this to me!"

The distorted image of Eduardo sat across from her on the bed. His body shifted in and out of reality, breaking and reforming as if he'd been filmed on a strip full of holes. *"I think you took too many amphetamines..."*

"I'm perfectly fine! I took exactly what I needed!" Something snapped outside and she jerked her head up. The red curtains on the far wall fluttered with the breeze from the open window. She was freezing. It was freezing outside, but she'd been sweating so much that she had to open the windows since it was so hot that she might have died.

"You don't need those papers to tell you why Gillen abandoned you. You already know."

Therese ignored him. She knew the secret was in those papers. She *knew* it, no matter what Eduardo said. If he thought she didn't need the papers to find out why Gillen abandoned her, he was either a liar or an idiot. Hell, he was probably both. Gillen had been both; most people were both. She was surrounded by idiots, beset by them on all sides. Once she got rid of Narcissa and the police and Gillen and Eduardo, she'd get rid of the rest of them, too, and finally, finally she could have some peace.

Blood dripped from Therese's hands as she sorted through the papers. She'd need to put in some real effort to get those files out of Gillen's cabinet. He'd locked it and taken the key, thinking he was so clever, but what good did his locks do when she could break them apart with a sledgehammer? Sure, the clerk at the hardware store had looked at her like she was insane when she'd stood in the checkout line with her arms full of knives and hammers, but she'd laughed in his face and told him he'd never understand. Of course he wouldn't understand, he worked at a hardware store. He was an idiot, the same as the rest of them.

Hammering the cabinet apart had taken a lot of effort, but she'd gotten what she wanted, bloody hands and all. She'd started sweating, too, but the sweat didn't bother her because it helped clean the blood from her hands. Sweating was efficient that way. Eduardo said she really captured the aesthetic of an axe murderer, but he had a bias because he'd just been axe-murdered. Or knife-murdered, rather, but the difference didn't matter.

"What are you expecting to find in there?" Eduardo leaned off the bed. His expression flickered like the channels on a television, jumping from amused to horrified to concerned. *"A map to his secret lair?"*

"Maybe he did leave me a map! You don't know! You don't know anything! You're not even real!"

"You didn't really know him, did you?"

Therese's eyes snapped open. "What did you say?"

"I said—"

"I heard what you said, moron! It's the accusation I resent! Of course I knew him! Why would I marry someone without knowing him? What kind of person do you think I am?"

Without saying a word, Eduardo raised a cool eyebrow at the bloodied pile of papers.

Twin jets of air burst from her nose, and she slammed her fists against the ground. "You have no right to judge me!"

Anger swirled around her, shredding her from all sides. She closed her eyes and imagined the bloody knife she'd seen in Gillen's hand. He'd gotten Eduardo with that knife, driving into his paper-thin skin over and over until there was nothing left of him except gristle and bone. God, she wished she could have seen it—to watch the destruction of the man who kept taunting her, mocking her, picking at the seams of her dreams. She should have done the job herself. If she'd been the one to handle it, she would have done it right. It would have looked like a break-in, the way it was supposed to. She would have even taken a few prizes for herself. Only idiots kept trophies, but she wasn't stupid, she wouldn't put them on display. She'd just take a few choice items to enjoy on her own—a pair of Narcy's shoes, or the flayed skin from Eduardo's face.

She opened her eyes again at the sound of Eduardo speaking. *"I remember something Gillen told me, back when you and him were first engaged."* He sat back on the bed, legs stretched out like he owned the place when he damn well didn't. *"We'd been having a few drinks, and he told me that you once confessed to him that you used to imagine murdering every person you saw. He said it scared him, but he couldn't fault you if it was just a coping mechanism for something terrible you might have gone through. Looking back on it now, it was pretty clever."*

"How the hell is that clever?"

"He must have realized that involving you in the murder meant you'd blow the whole thing if I looked in your mind. Maybe he accounted for that all along, or maybe he saw his mistake too late and realized he had to get in front of it. Either way, he figured out just what to say to keep you off my radar. You may think he's an idiot, puta, but he was a lot smarter than you're giving him credit for. A hell of a lot smarter than you, for sure."

Red spots flashed in front of Therese's vision. She hooked her shaking fingertips into the carpet and anchored herself to the ground. "How dare you... How dare you!"

"You don't even know why he murdered me, do you?"

"He told me it was about the money!"

"Uh-huh, sure it was. And what do those files tell you, exactly?"

Even with her mind moving a mile a minute, Therese knew what Eduardo was driving at. The files told the same story too. Gillen had been hiding money from her, more money than she had ever thought possible. Stocks, bonds, investment properties, even that goddamned house he'd inherited in South Dakota that he'd told her he'd sold. He'd been renting it or leasing it or whatever people who moved houses around did to make money, and he'd flipped a dozen other places, too, and made himself disgustingly, brilliantly rich in the process.

"It's funny that he told you he wanted to kill me for the money." Eduardo pointed a distorted finger at the pile. It clipped in and out of existence, shorting out in a rapid pattern that matched her heaving breaths. *"Because if those*

documents say what I think they're saying, he was hiding more money than I could have made in a lifetime. A full lifetime," he added. *"One where I didn't get murdered."*

Therese ripped one of the papers off the ground. The keen edge sliced through her finger, drawing yet more blood from her hands. "How could he have hidden this from me?"

"He was the CFO of a successful commercial real estate business. He did this for a living."

"I don't mean how, you bastard, I mean why! Why did he keep this from me? Why didn't he share it when we could have had everything? Why did he waste his time worrying about you when he had enough to give to me?"

Eduardo shrugged his hands. *"Maybe he didn't like you."*

"Then why the hell did he marry me?"

"Maybe because he didn't like you."

"That doesn't make any sense!"

"Think about it, puta. Think back to the way he looked at you yesterday before he smacked you across the face. He'd been waiting to do that for a long time, hadn't he? He probably enjoyed that as much as he enjoyed killing me." He lowered his chin, obscuring his shifting eyes. *"I'll bet last night was as much about destroying you as it was about destroying me."*

"I am not destroyed!"

"You're screaming at yourself in the middle of the night. You've got a sledgehammer at your feet and your hands are covered in blood. Even if you weren't already destroyed now—which you are—you'll be ruined the second that Narcy wakes up. Gillen may have murdered me, but at the end of the day, the one he punished the most is you."

"He would never do that to me!"

"Why not?"

"Because I didn't do anything wrong!"

She crushed her hands over her ears and folded her head between her knees. Her heart pounded against her thighs as she sucked in air through her clenched teeth and tried not to scream.

Gillen had betrayed her from the start. She'd thought he was so simple in the beginning, but he had ambition and didn't waste time on affection and love. He was goal-oriented and gave her everything she wanted, and always had a vision for their future. So what if the vision turned out to be real? What good was it if it didn't include her?

"You know, a normal wife might have thought it was strange that Gillen had no interest in her as a person. After all, why would he marry someone he didn't even like? But that's what you did, isn't it? You married someone you didn't care about, and that's why you got stabbed in the back. You never knew him at all—and that's exactly why he married you."

She stared at her cut-up hands with wide, watering eyes. "He used me!"

"He did. The same way you thought you were using him."

A tear slipped from her eyelid when she blinked. Her nostrils flared and she flicked the drop away with a howl of rage. "I won't let him win!"

The heavy thump of someone pounding on the front door echoed up the steps. "Mrs. DuCannes? Are you okay in there? I heard noises!"

Therese whirled around, searching the shadows for signs of betrayal. "Shit! Why is he here?"

"I don't know, maybe because you woke up the whole damn neighborhood with your sledgehammer?"

"That was ages ago!"

"Therese, that was less than a minute ago."

A dark chill rippled beneath Therese's skin. *No, that's impossible...* She'd been staring at the files for what must have been hours. Surely she'd used the sledgehammer more than a minute ago. She'd been talking to Eduardo for at least five minutes, and probably longer because his rambling never ended even when she thought she was going to dig her fingernails into her scalp and tear out her hair.

"You remember those pills you took, right?" said Eduardo. *"You've lost all sense of time. You don't know where you are anymore or what you're doing, and you're terrified because you know I'm right."*

"You're lying again! You're always lying!" She clutched the sides of her head and screamed. "I'm not losing my mind!"

"Mrs. DuCannes!" yelled the detective. "I'm coming in, just hold on!"

Therese jumped to her feet. "Wait!" Tossing her papers aside, she sprinted to the open window and stuck her head out as far as she could go without falling and splitting her head open on the concrete steps below. "Detective, I'm fine!"

Detective Olson craned his neck back and shaded his eyes from the streetlights with the top of his hand. "You sure you're all right in there? I just heard a whole boatload of banging!"

Her burning eyes darted from side to side. "How long ago did you hear it?"

"Excuse me?"

"The banging! How long ago did you hear it?"

"He's just going to lie to you." Eduardo appeared at her side, crossing his arms as he clicked his tongue. *"That's what the police do to you. They lie."*

Detective Olson tilted his head like a stupid dog who needed to move his neck around just to understand a simple concept. "About ninety seconds ago, maybe less."

Eduardo blinked. "*Would you look at that?*" he said at last. "*An honest cop.*"

Therese's pulse pounded in her ears. *Beat, beat, beat,* each beat stretching out over three or four seconds. She grabbed her wrist and felt for her veins, but she couldn't keep her grip with all the sweat on her hands. *I'm dying, I'm dying! Jesus God, I need someone to save me!*

"*No one can save you,*" said Eduardo. "*You brought this all on yourself.*"

A gust of cold air whipped past the window. Detective Olson cupped his hands around his mouth, yelling over the wind, "Are you sure everything's all right?"

Therese bit her lip. *The detective will save me!* He had to save her, saving people was his job. He'd understand how scared she was, her husband was a serial killer on the loose and he was coming to get her at any second. That explained why she was covered in blood. She'd needed to get to his files—she wanted to help the investigation! Breaking open his file cabinet with a sledgehammer made sense. It all made sense. The detective would understand. He had to understand. Detective Olson would be the one to save her.

"Stay where you are!" she shouted. "I'm going to come let you in!"

She didn't waste time wiping the blood off her hands— she needed the blood to make her look helpless. Men loved helpless women because helpless women reminded them of dolls. Dolls didn't talk back, they just sat there looking pretty and doing whatever men wanted them to do. Dolls weren't always covered with blood, yes, but dolls weren't smart and Therese was smart and that's why she needed to improvise.

Her heart raced as she darted down the steps and threw open the door. Detective Olsen gaped at her, openmouthed and wide-eyed. "Mother of mercy. What happened to you?"

She threw herself against him, bursting into tears. "I'm so scared! You have to help me, please!"

Eduardo flickered into existence in the corner by the stairs. Therese could just see him out of the corner of her eye as he shook his head and said, *"You know you look like a crazy person."*

Therese cried that much harder, burying herself in the detective's chest. "I'm so scared he's going to hurt me!"

"Who's going to hurt you? Gillen?" Detective Olson stepped back and took hold of Therese's hands. His thumbs traced across the scratches in her palms, long lines that mirrored the ridges in his furrowed brow. "Did he have something to do with this?"

If she'd had the time to think, she could have used Gillen as an out and said he'd staged an attack on her, but with her mind racing and her hands sweating, she could barely keep track of the details that made up the truth.

"I wanted to help you find him and I knew he kept lots of important files he didn't want me to see in his file cabinet, so I tried to open it up, but I cut my hands on the metal and I'm just so scared he's going to come back for me and Narcy!" She added a wail at the end, stretching out Narcy's name until it had less in common with human speech and more with the cries of a dying animal. *He'll love that. He'll think I really care.*

"Hey now, hey, it's all right. You don't need to be scared. I'm watching over your house, remember?" Detective Olson offered a smile of encouragement, as if a smile would do something beyond taxing the muscles in his face. "You've got Chicago's finest looking out for you."

"Hijo de puta," Eduardo muttered. *"If this guy is Chicago's finest, I'd hate to see Chicago's worst."*

Therese ignored him and ramped up the intensity of her cries. "Please don't let him hurt me, I never want to see him again."

"And you won't have to, Therese. I promise you."

Beneath the fear and the panic and the drugs coursing through her veins, the thrill of triumph made its way to her brain. She pressed her head into his shirt to hide her victorious grin. *He called me Therese.*

"Thank you, Jeremy," she whispered. "I don't know how I'll ever repay you."

"I'm not in this for the pay," he said with a chuckle. "Now let's both you and I go inside and see what we can do about bandaging those hands."

Chapter Twenty-One

GLITTERING STARS FORMED a web of light over the Badlands, illuminating Gillen's path. He could see the edge of the Milky Way out of the corner of his eye, but the looming specters of his childhood memories ensured he couldn't pay attention to the show.

"*Madre de Dios...*" Eduardo craned forward, staring through the windshield. "*I've never seen so many stars.*"

While Gillen didn't much feel like talking to anyone, focusing on Eduardo helped keep the dark thoughts out of his head. It also helped to know Eduardo had dark thoughts of his own. Gillen had expected Eduardo to rip him a new one for murdering Bernardo Reyes, but he hadn't seemed angry at all. Hell, he'd been happy when he believed he was the reason for Reyes's death. That didn't make him as terrible as Gillen, but it certainly stripped away some of his innocence. And, in a strange way, it also made Gillen hate him less. Not much less, just a little. Still, considering how they were stuck together, that little bit went a long way toward making Gillen's last road trip tolerable.

"You've really never seen the sky like this?" he said to Eduardo. "What? You've never driven through the country before?"

"*No, never. I've never been west of Springfield.*"

Gillen raised an eyebrow. "Wait, really?"

"*Really. I went to Springfield once and thought, Well, if this is what the rest of the west has to offer I think I'll have to pass.*"

Laughter bubbled up from Gillen's chest, escaping his mouth before he could stop it. "Believe it or not, there's a whole country beyond Springfield."

"*I wouldn't have believed it before, but looking at those stars, I can't deny it now.*"

Late as it was, there weren't any other cars on the road for Gillen to worry about. That was the only reason he let himself slow down enough to take a better look above.

"*If I'd known we'd be sightseeing on this road trip, I would have told you to buy a car with a moonroof.*" Eduardo's smile soured at the edges. "*Not that I knew I'd be coming along.*"

And just like that, Gillen's brief moment of peace ended and he fixed his eyes on the endless road. The concrete didn't have the beauty of the night sky, but at least it didn't come with the guilt trip about Eduardo's murder.

They sat in silence for a time, with Gillen focused on the road and Eduardo staring out the window. While Gillen welcomed the quiet at first, soon the darkness in his head began to crawl out from the abyss and take hold of him.

I shouldn't have come back here.

This won't make things better.

I won't be better.

I should have never left home.

Eduardo leaned closer to the windshield. "*It really is pretty up there...*" he murmured. "*I wish I could see it better.*"

"I could put the window down and you could stick your head out like a dog."

"*No, that wouldn't work.*" His sardonic smile did nothing to disguise the misery in his eyes. "*I can only see from your perspective.*"

"Really?"

"I'm in your head, remember?" He gestured at himself, waving down his torso with the same flair a waiter would use to show off a piece of meat. *"This is something we've made so we don't go crazy."*

Eduardo's words echoed in Gillen's head. *We,* he'd said; not *I.* Whether Gillen liked it or not, there was no escaping the fact that they were sharing a body. There was also no escaping the fact that Eduardo could take control. If Gillen wanted to stay at the helm, he needed to give his uninvited guest some reasons to stand down.

A yellow light fanned out in the darkness as Gillen flipped on his blinker and pulled off to the side of the road.

Eduardo cocked his head. *"What are you doing?"*

"I'm getting out to stretch my legs," he said. "I'm tired of being cooped up in that damn car, and there's no rush when the police aren't looking for me. We might as well enjoy the scenery."

The night air settled on Gillen's skin, cooling him better than any air conditioner. While it was the middle of winter in South Dakota, a full day in a heated car with a jacket on had given Gillen new appreciation for the cold. He sucked in a deep breath, savoring the open air.

Black shadows jutted up from the ground, forming the outline of peaks and valleys against the glowing horizon. A brilliant band of stars stretched overhead. Bright colors bled in every direction, forming clouds made of light and air. Gillen had seen those lights before as a child, but only in passing, and never on his own terms. As long as he'd known those lights, he'd been kept from them by the whims of someone else. For the first time in his life, he could admire them for himself.

Eduardo appeared at his side, emerging from the darkness like a living cluster of stars. *"They're beautiful..."*

"They are."

The two men stood in silence, basking in the brilliant display. Every so often, Gillen glanced over to see if Eduardo was up to something, but he seemed content to kick back and enjoy the view. He'd always been that way: able to let stress roll off his back. It was no wonder Narcy wanted to be with him. With all the stress in her life, she'd needed someone who knew how to relax.

It had been over a decade since Narcy found out she was bipolar, but Gillen could still remember the sinking feeling in his stomach when she told him the news. He'd seen the signs for years—the constant fights with their mother, the carousel of boyfriends, the weeks she'd spend without leaving her room—but he'd always hoped they were simply hallmarks of being a teenager. He didn't want to face the truth: that she'd been tainted by her family just as he'd been. All he'd wanted was for her to have a better life than he'd had. For her to struggle with that kind of sickness meant he'd failed as a brother. If he'd looked out for her more, she would have had a better chance. If he'd stayed out of her life, she would never have died.

"Can I ask you something?" said Gillen.

"*If you promise not to commit suicide,*" he replied. *Gillen shot him a sidelong glance and he shrugged his hands. "Hey, never hurts to try. So what's your question?"*

"After what you told me earlier, about some of your... relationships...why did you marry Narcy?"

One of Eduardo's eyebrows lifted above the other. "*You really want to know?*"

"Do you think I would have asked if I didn't?"

"*Probably not, no—but if you want me to answer it, you'll probably want to sit down.*" He pointed to the hood of Gillen's car, the one spot that was guaranteed to be warm. "*It's not a question I can answer in a minute.*"

Considering Gillen had been expecting Eduardo to call him a pendejo or otherwise tell him to eat shit in Spanish, being told to sit down didn't faze him in the slightest. He did as Eduardo asked and sat back so his feet just brushed the dirt, giving him the freedom to lean back and stare up at the stars.

"I was thirteen years old when I started hearing what people were thinking." Eduardo stretched back on the other half of the hood, mirroring Gillen's position. *"I didn't know if I wanted to tell anyone at first, but our fathers started working together more and I ended up spending more time with Narcy."*

"She was five years younger than you." Gillen glanced away. "I was closer to your age."

"You were, but you were always up in your room when we came over, so I ended up getting stuck entertaining her. Turned out she was pretty smart. Curious as hell too. Always asking questions, trying to figure out how the world worked. I'd try to answer her questions as best I could, but I was an idiot so I was usually wrong. She knew that, too, but she never judged me. I knew she didn't; I could see it in her mind. And I felt guilty about it. She told me everything about herself—as much as an eight-year-old had to tell, anyway—but I hadn't told her everything about me. And so I did."

"Was she the only person you ever told?" said Gillen. "I mean, aside from Bernardo."

"I told my father too. Narcy said I should. He was the one who suggested I work with Bernardo in the first place. Narcy never bought into that idea, since she thought she was smarter than any psychologist—"

Gillen bit back a laugh. "That does sound like Narcy."

"But I went through with it anyway and ended up regretting it. Once everything with Bernardo fell apart, I was left with no one else to rely on but her."

"What about your father?"

"He was already dying then. I swear, no matter how many times he beat cancer, it just..." Eduardo shook his head. *"I couldn't rely on him anymore. I didn't want to. I wanted to start a new life with someone I could trust. Unfortunately,"* he added, lips curling at the edges, *"the dating pool for gay Mexican mind readers is very small. I needed someone who was gay, single, not racist, and open-minded about having someone rooting around in his brain. Plus, he also had to be good-looking. I mean, I'm only human, right?"*

"Human enough," said Gillen.

"Human enough." Eduardo looked like he wanted to laugh, but he lacked the conviction to make the sound. *"I knew I'd never find what I was looking for, so I realized I had to focus on the most important thing: being with someone I could trust. Someone I could be my whole self with, powers and flaws and all. And that someone was Narcy."*

"Back then, when you wanted to marry her, did she know you were..." Gillen circled his hands, trying to get the words out.

"Gay?" Eduardo supplied. *"Obviously. She knew everything about me. I also knew everything about her, which included some of the uglier issues that had cropped up as she became an adult. For some reason or another, she'd gotten it into her head that the only way to feel desirable was to be with men who thought she was with someone else—pretending she was stolen goods or someone else's property. For Narcy, it wasn't good enough to just be*

with someone; she needed to be with someone who risked everything for her. But that's a dangerous game because the people who will risk anything to be with you are the people who will do anything if you leave them."

"Not to mention most husbands wouldn't be fine with their wives fucking around behind their backs," Gillen muttered.

"Oh, you'd be surprised—but for the most part, you're right. Point is, Narcy had a need for something in life that was only going to end up hurting her, and I knew if I married her, I could help give her what she wanted while maybe guiding her in the right direction." He sighed and ran his fingers through his hair. *"Sometimes, I worried I was holding her back from finding happiness with someone else, but I was too scared to let her go."*

"Scared for her or for you?"

"Both."

Gillen closed his eyes, shutting out the stars. "She got it from our mother."

"Hmm?"

"Our mother did the same thing. She jumped from one relationship to the other, always forgetting that she was still in the first one. Gary, the man who raised us—"

"I know my own father-in-law."

Of course he did. He'd known the man almost as long as Gillen had, probably even longer. In spite of what Gillen imagined as a child, Gary Lynch had been his own man before Gillen and his pregnant mother had wandered into his life.

"My mother cheated on him compulsively. She couldn't stop herself. I wanted to say something to somebody—I'd known since I was a kid—but I knew if word got back to Gary, we'd all end up on the curb. So I never told my mother

I knew, and I never told Narcy." He opened his eyes again, taking in the light with a blink. "But I guess she found out."

"I never knew about that."

It took a moment for Gillen to see the problem with that statement. "How is that possible?" he said, turning to face Eduardo head-on. "You were a mind reader. You should have seen everything."

"She figured out how to block me."

Gillen's lips parted. "She learned how to clear her head."

"No, actually." Eduardo laughed again, this time with a wistful grin. *"She tried that for a while, but she gave up because it was too damn hard. In the end, she figured out another way: music."*

"Music?"

"Mmhmm. You ever get a song stuck in your head, the kind of shitty jingle that worms its way in and won't leave for days?"

"I once had 'I'd Like to Buy the World a Coke' in my head for a week."

"Hah! Exactly. But see, here's the funny thing about catchy tunes and jingles—I actually can't read past them."

"How do you mean?"

"You know how it is when you've got a song in your head—it keeps going and going, but the rest of your mind works just fine. You've still got all your regular thoughts going in there, you've just got the Coke song running in there in the background. When I try to get in there, though, the Coke jingle doesn't just stay in the background—it shoves its way right up to the front, and I can't read anything deeper."

"Really?"

"Really."

Gillen gazed at the stars, openmouthed. "So all that time I spent on learning to think about nonsense...all that time, and I could have just listened to 'MMMBop' instead?"

"Yes, but I might have killed you on principle."

Wind whistled across the road, drowning out their laughter. When the gust died down, Eduardo searched Gillen's face with furrowed brows. The way he stared, Gillen could almost believe Eduardo could actually see what he was looking at.

"What?" said Gillen. "I have a bug on my face or something?"

"You really want to kill yourself, don't you?"

Gillen's shoulders tensed. He looked away, avoiding Eduardo's blind gaze. "I do."

"And you need to drive to South Dakota to do it."

"That's where my past is."

"Seems like a funny thing to do when you want to escape your past."

In spite of the subject matter, Gillen let himself enjoy another smile. He'd given a lifetime of thought to how he'd spend his last days, and there was something enjoyable about the bizarre simplicity of his final revenge. "You've never lived in a small town, have you?"

"Cicero wasn't exactly Chicago, but somehow I don't think that's what you're talking about."

"Not quite, no." For one thing, Cicero had a damn airport. Hill City's most famous piece of transportation was an antique train. "Small town people love to gossip as much as people from cities do, but when it comes to topics they can't handle, they always try to sweep things under the rug. How well do you think those people that can handle a killer fleeing the police to shoot himself in their town?"

"Not that well."

"And what do you think they'll do to the house where the killer shoots himself?"

Eduardo made a sound between a laugh and a snort. *"I'd rather raze a murder house than try to flip it myself."*

"You and anyone else who knows real estate. For all the trouble that house will cause, the town will want it gone as fast as possible."

"So you're going to kill yourself where you used to live, and your old neighbors will get to erase your past for you."

"Mmhmm."

"Clever."

"I don't know that I'd go that far. Still, better than burning the place down. With all the trees around, I'd be lucky if I didn't destroy the town."

"Somehow I don't think you'd be too bent out of shape about that."

"I've killed enough people already."

"I hope you don't think committing suicide will make up for it."

"That's not why I'm doing it," he murmured.

"I know it's not."

"I killed my father."

"I know you did."

"And you think I should get to live after that? After everything else?"

"This isn't just about you anymore, Gillen. This is about me too. And I'm not going down without a fight."

Gillen chewed his lip. The wind picked up again, reminding him of the winter cold. "Let's get back in the car. Nobody's dying until I make it home."

Chapter Twenty-Two

ED LEANED AGAINST the gray walls of room 404, arms crossed and eyes focused on the door. Andrew sat in a nearby plastic chair in uncomfortable silence. The clock on the wall behind Ed ticked past two, reminding Andrew of how long it had been since Ed stuck his feet to the floor.

"It's been four hours, Ed. If you don't let go of my legs soon, I'm going to end up with a blood clot."

"We're not going anywhere until they let us see Narcy."

Andrew dragged his palms down his cheeks. At first, he'd thought Caroline would be able to help him free his legs, but when he told her what Ed did, she just laughed.

"I don't get involved in ensemble squabbles," she'd said. "You're the conductor; you should be able to take your body back without my help." Maybe she'd meant her words to be encouraging, but they sure hadn't felt that way at the time. At least she left the door unlocked when she left them to fight it out. In a world with little kindness, even the smallest gesture had to count for something.

"They're not going to let us see her," Andrew said. "She's still in critical condition."

"She won't be critical forever."

"No, but it doesn't have to be forever for it to be a very long time. I know it's hard to accept, but...she got stabbed in the neck, man. She lost a lot of blood. It hasn't even been twenty-four hours. Wouldn't you rather go home and wait for her there?"

"We're waiting here."

Andrew slumped forward against the table. His stomach rumbled and he muffled it with his hand. The last thing he needed was for Ed to think Andrew only wanted to leave so he could get food.

In truth, there were a whole lot of reasons Andrew wanted to go home. He wanted to check on Hester. He wanted to get out of the plastic chair. He really wanted to pee. Beyond all those things, he wanted to be somewhere safe while he came to terms with the fact that he was about to inherit Ed's mind-reading powers.

Even with a decade of experience in human resources, being around other people had never been Andrew's forte. He didn't have anything against other people; he just didn't know how to talk to them without wondering if they thought he was an idiot. Now he was going to be able to see for certain if they did. A smarter person might have found that kind of power vindicating, but to Andrew, it was a death sentence. He had enough trouble getting to sleep at night when he could only wonder how worthless other people thought he was. Pretty soon, he wouldn't have to wonder anymore.

"Did you know there were other mind readers?" Andrew hadn't meant to ask the question out loud, but then it wouldn't have made a difference if he'd kept it in his head.

"You mean before the puta cop told me?" Ed drummed his fingertips against his forearm, frowning as if he were having a mental debate about how to answer. In the end, he sighed and shook his head. *"No."*

"You thought you were the only one?"

"I did."

"Are you happy that you're not?"

"I'd be happier if I'd stayed dead."

Even the ticking of the clock couldn't fill the awkward silence after that. The only thing Andrew could think to say was "Jesus, Ed..."

"If I were dead, I wouldn't have to see any of this," Ed continued. *"I would have died thinking Narcy was safe at dinner with Therese, and I wouldn't have to learn that my supposed best friend is too chickenshit to avenge my death."*

"Oh come on, that's not fair! Didn't you listen to the detective?"

"She's not a detective!"

"Well, whoever she is, she knows more about this than we do, which means she's equipped to handle this and we're not."

"How do we know that? We don't know anything about these people! We don't even know who 'they' are!" He dragged his hand down his face and shuddered. *"Hijo de puta, I didn't even know there was another me."*

"You didn't?"

"No! You think I want two of me running around out there? The world didn't even need the first me!" He tugged at his hair with an animal groan. *"And I don't even know which me is me! How am I supposed to know if I'm real?"*

The full weight of Ed's situation settled on Andrew's chest with the force of an iron weight. He sank back into the sofa, blinking as he searched for something to say. "I...uh...I mean, I think you're real."

"Great. That and three dollars won't even buy me a cup of coffee."

"Hey, I'm just trying to help!"

Andrew figured Ed would have another snappy comeback for that, but instead, he massaged his face again and groaned into his hands. *"I just want my old life back."*

Now that was something Andrew could understand. "I'm really sorry this happened to you, Ed."

"Thanks." His tone made him sound sarcastic, but there was a hopelessness in his slumped stance that made Andrew realize he was being sincere.

The uncomfortable silence that followed gave Andrew a moment to recall another one of the thousand questions that had been rattling around in his head. "Can I ask you something else?"

"Sure, go ahead," Ed replied. *"What am I going to do, stop you?"*

"Um, okay… are you really gay?"

One of Ed's eyebrows arched. *"Are you serious?"*

"Are you? You never said anything about it before, and we've been friends for an eternity. If you really are gay, how come you never said anything to me?"

"Because I didn't want Narcy to get hurt."

"Wait, so she really didn't know? You were cheating on her?" Andrew's mouth screwed up into a tight knot. *No wonder he doesn't want to leave without seeing her! He's just feeling guilty!*

"Watch your mouth!"

"But I didn't say anything!"

"You thought it!"

"I can't have my own thoughts anymore?"

"Not ones like that, you can't!" Ed's lip curled, but then he sucked in air through his nose and closed his eyes. *"But for the record, no, I was not cheating on her, because she knew about it and was free to sleep with other people too."*

Andrew's mouth fell open. "Wait, wait, wait." He held up his palms to try and slow the verbal traffic. "She was with other people too?"

"Well I wasn't going to make her stay celibate for the rest of our marriage!"

Ed's answer came so close to making sense, but Andrew couldn't accept it when it didn't cover his biggest question. "Then why the hell did you get so mad at me for falling in love with her!"

"Because you're not in love with her, you stupid asshole!"

Andrew lurched out of his chair, but his legs didn't come with him. All he succeeded in doing was rocking forward in his chair. "You're the stupid asshole for trying to tell me who I care about!"

"Oh yeah?" Ed slammed his hands on the table. *"Well, if you really cared about her, you'd want to kill Gillen yourself!"*

And there it was: the low blow Andrew had been waiting for since the second Ed first decided his judgment of Gillen. Part of Andrew couldn't believe Ed had the guts to say something so horrific, but another part of him couldn't believe it had taken him so long.

"That's not fair and you know it," said Andrew. "Asking me to kill someone goes way beyond the call of what love should be."

"What if someone killed your mother?"

A deep pit opened up inside Andrew's stomach. He closed his eyes, wishing the darkness would swallow him whole. "It would probably be a mercy."

Ed made a *tch* noise with his tongue; a good move, since it was about the only response Andrew wouldn't have tried to punch him for. *"What about your old fiancée then? You said you loved her once, before she emptied your bank account. How would you have felt if someone killed her?"*

"I would have been heartbroken, but I wouldn't have wanted to kill anyone—"

"Which means you didn't really love her either!"

Andrew curled his fingers into fists. "You know how I felt about her!"

"Really? Because if you'd loved her, this wouldn't even be a question! When you love someone and they get hurt, you hurt too! When someone you love dies, a part of you dies too! That's why I want to kill Gillen—because when he tried to kill Narcy, he tried to rip out my heart!"

"Oh come on! You couldn't have loved her that much! She was just your beard!"

"What, because I wasn't having sex with her, I'm not supposed to care about her? Jesus, Andy, no wonder you're so bad at friendships!"

"I am not bad at friendships!"

"Then how come you didn't tell me you had feelings for Narcy? Why did I have to pull it out of your head? Why weren't you willing to put your faith in me?"

"Because I..." Andrew blinked. After the most confusing day in his life, one thing finally made sense. "Oh."

"You get it now, don't you?" Ed peered at Andrew through wide eyes. *"You finally understand?"*

"You're not mad that I was in love with Narcy... You're mad that I didn't trust you enough to talk to you about it."

"Yes! Exactly! You say I'm your friend, but friends are supposed to share things with each other—the good and the bad!"

Andrew furrowed his brow. "You never told me you were gay."

"You never told me you had to put your mother in a home!"

The darkness in Andrew's gut roiled up, splashing his throat with a mix of anger and acid. "I didn't tell anybody about that! I don't even want to think about that!" He ran his hand down his face, hiding his eyes behind his fingertips.

"She's only sixty, Ed! You think I enjoy being reminded that she can't even remember who her own son is at her age? You think I want to sit here and wonder if the same thing's going to hit me?"

"But you'd rather sit here and wonder about it than share any of that with me!"

"Because I don't want to share it with anybody!"

"And that's exactly your problem! You want to have friends, but you don't want to do any of the work that comes with it! You don't want to rely on other people because you're too much of a pussy to open yourself up! Who are you to call yourself my friend when you're too afraid to share anything with me? Who are you to say you're in love with Narcy when you don't know a thing about her?"

"How can you say I don't know her? I know everything about her! Her favorite color, her favorite movie, her favorite song." He ticked his fingers down one at a time as he ran through the list, then balled up his hand at the end. "She told me everything!"

"Oh yeah? Let's test that, then, smart guy. Tell me her favorite color."

"Easy, it's purple."

"Why?"

"Excuse me?"

"Why is her favorite color purple?"

"Because I don't know why—she though it was better than the others!"

"Because when she was little, she had a storybook about a lady who lived on a hill in a house surrounded by lots of purple lupines, and Narcy always wanted to grow up and live in a house just like that." Ed leaned in closer, defiance in his eyes. *"Now tell me her favorite movie."*

Andrew shifted under Ed's unflinching gaze. "*The Sound of Music.*"

"*Why?*"

"Because she loved musicals...?"

"*Because when she was nine years old, she was cast as Lisle in a school production of the play, and it was the proudest moment of her life at the end of the play when she looked out into the audience and saw her mom, dad, and Gillen all holding flowers.*"

"Gillen brought her flowers?"

"*Yes, he did, but I'm guessing it's because the little prick had them shoved into his hand right before they walked into the auditorium, so let's not give him any credit for it!*" The muscles in Ed's neck tensed, forcing his veins to bulge under his skin. "*Now do you need to tell me her favorite song, too, or have I gotten through to you?*"

Andrew screwed his lips into a tight knot. "You made your point."

"*I sure hope so, because maybe now that I have, you can understand how incredibly stupid you are for thinking you can fall in love with someone you don't even know!*"

"Well, excuse me for not being able to learn every little detail about people by going through their heads!"

"*It's not about reading people's minds, you idiot! It's about taking some fucking risks and opening yourself up to people so they don't have to do all the work!*"

"Why should I even bother opening up to people? Every time I make an effort to connect with people, it blows up in my face!" He slammed both fists on the tabletop. "My dad walked out on us, Julie left once I told her I was tired of being a walking wallet, and now my mom can't even remember who I am anymore because her brain is turning into Swiss cheese! Once I lost them, you and Narcy were the only friends I had left, and now she's dying and you're dead!"

When Andrew finally calmed himself down enough to take a breath, he looked up to see Ed staring at him with an open mouth. Even his normally suspicious eyes were narrowed in genuine shock.

A wave of guilt washed over Andrew and he lowered his head. "I shouldn't have said that. I'm sorry."

"I'm the one who should be sorry."

"Because I got mad at you?"

"No, not about that." He let out a slight laugh. *"But you shouldn't get worked up about losing everybody. Narcy hasn't left you yet—and I haven't either."*

"You haven't?"

"I literally can't. Now come on. Let's go home." He held out his hand and smiled, and the tension seeped out of Andrew's legs at long last.

But Andrew didn't stand.

"Let's not go home just yet." He smiled back and phased his palm through Ed's hand. "First, let's see Narcy again."

Chapter Twenty-Three

THERESE AWOKE TO an empty stomach, bandaged hands, and the horrific realization that she had no idea where she was or how she'd gotten there.

She jolted from the pillow and whipped her head from side to side. The familiar walls of her bedroom surrounded her, protecting her in a rose-colored cocoon. They could only protect her from outsiders, though; they couldn't protect her from the voice inside her head.

"Where are you, you bastard?" she shrieked.

"Right here, Sleeping Beauty."

Eduardo sat on the windowsill by Therese's nightstand, grinning from cheek to cheek. Therese yanked the blankets over her torso and shrank against the headboard. "What did you do to me?"

"Not a single thing."

"You're lying!"

"How could I? I'm just a figment of your imagination, remember? Your imagination can't lie to you." His smile twisted into a snarl, exposing his gums above his teeth. *"But even if I could, I didn't have a chance with that detective around."*

Therese's heart swelled. *The detective—of course!* She jumped from the bed and bolted for the window. The sky had turned the same shade of pink as her bedroom walls, suggesting that several hours had passed. Thankfully, it couldn't have been too long since she fell asleep, since

Detective Olson's car was still parked outside her door. The detective himself—her personal savior—sat in the driver's seat, munching on a pastry while balancing a cup of coffee between his legs.

"You went a little crazy on the drugs, puta," Eduardo said from her side. *"And when they wore off, you passed out. Thank goodness he was nice enough to tuck you into bed."*

Therese pursed her lips as she stared at the police cruiser. If Eduardo really had been able to take over her body when she slept, he would have known what the detective did with certainty. The fact that he'd only speculated on what the detective did proved that he hadn't been able to take over her body after all—either that, or he'd chosen not to. Either way, it was good news. If he hadn't been able to steal her body, it meant he was weaker than he'd been saying. If he had been able to steal her body but chose against it, it meant he was a coward who didn't have the balls to take them both out.

"I can't believe Detective Olson stayed to make sure I got to sleep." Therese licked her lips, moistening the cracks in the corners. "He must really want me."

"Either that or he's just doing his job."

"How does putting me to bed protect me from Gillen any better than watching me from the street?"

"It doesn't," he said. *"It keeps you from charging down the street with a sledgehammer."*

"Please, as if I'd do that. What am I, insane?"

"Yes. You are absolutely, completely one hundred percent insane."

She scoffed and turned away. "Go occupy yourself elsewhere, delusion. I've got to take a shower if I want to look good enough to thank the detective properly."

AFTER SHOWERING AND changing into her most flattering dress, Therese went to work with her cosmetics bag. Detective Olson didn't strike her as the type of man to want a woman who plastered on makeup like a trollop, but he did seem simple enough to be drawn in by pouty lips and big lashes. With a little help from Chanel and Givenchy, Therese had both of those in spades.

"You're crazy if you think he's going to fall for this," Eduardo said as she descended the stairs. *"Only an idiot would be stupid enough to sleep with you."*

"Gillen slept with me and he was smart enough to kill you."

"It didn't take intelligence to kill me. All it took was a steak knife."

"And I wish I had another one," she replied in a singsong voice, "because if I did, I would kill you twice. Now let's go meet the good detective so we can see about killing your wife too."

"You're a monster."

She passed a mirror and beamed at her reflection. "Takes one to know one!"

With her dress zipped up, her makeup accentuating her features, and the coffeepot on its way to manufacturing its next "cup of joe," Therese threw open the front door and strode up to the detective's car. She caught him in the middle of a call with Christ-knew-who on his earpiece and forced her teeth into a smile as she rapped her knuckles on the door.

He looked up from his conversation with a look of bemusement, then rolled down the window and hit her with a dopey grin. "There you are, Therese! How are you feeling?"

How am I feeling? she wanted to ask. *Like I escaped from a goddamned nightmare is how I'm feeling!* Instead, she bit her tongue and smiled twice as wide. "Much better, thanks to you. You have to let me make it up to you."

Detective Olson laughed and shook his head. "I'm telling you, your thanks is enough."

Therese gritted her teeth beneath her frozen lips. *I don't know how it could be on your salary.* "You sure I couldn't tempt you with a fresh pot of coffee?"

He glanced down at his cupholder, which held the now-empty styrofoam cup she'd seen from the window. "I guess I am running low..."

She leaned in, folding her forearms in the window just enough to push up her breasts. "Then I've got exactly what you need inside."

ONCE DETECTIVE OLSON entered the house, Therese wasted no time in turning on the waterworks. Her clear mascara held its own in the battle to maintain her appearance as she broke down and hurled herself into the detective's arms.

"Thank you so much for taking care of me," she sobbed as she pressed her forehead to his chest. "I'm so scared and you're the only person I can trust."

Eduardo materialized on the staircase beside her. *"Hasn't anyone ever told you about subtlety?"*

She cried twice as loud to drown him out. "I just don't understand how Gillen could do this to me! What did I do wrong?"

A warm, steady hand settled on Therese's back as the detective made a kind of shushing noise that would've been better for a terrified dog. "You've got nothing to be upset about. It wasn't your fault."

Her blood boiled under her skin. The last of her pride demanded she point out that it wasn't her fault, she hadn't done a damn thing to bring this on herself, but she'd opened that door in the name of appearing vulnerable and had to endure whatever walked through it.

"I just feel so ashamed," she went on. "I did everything I could to be a good wife. I cooked for him. I cleaned for him. I did anything he asked of me..." On that last line, she lifted her head and met the detective's eye as she chewed her cherry-red lips. "Sometimes, I think he didn't even want me."

"Smart guy," Eduardo said. *"Who would?"*

Detective Olson patted his hand between her shoulders. "I wouldn't worry too much about what Gillen thought." A simpler woman might have mistaken his movements as friendly, but Therese made note of the way his palm drifted imperceptibly lower with each touch. "Somebody that far out of his gourd can't be a good judge."

"But how am I going to find someone to be with me now? I'm all alone, the wife of a murderer." She bit her lip again, hard enough to make the flesh numb. "No one will want me anymore."

The detective's hand twitched on her spine. Therese pressed her face to his chest, concealing her smile. *Now for the kicker.* "I'd do anything to feel wanted again..."

She lifted her chin and met Detective Olson's eye. He stared down at her, lips parted and eyes wide. His hand slid down her back. She shuddered and let out an "accidental" moan.

"Madre de Dios," said Eduardo. *"He's actually going to go for it."*

Detective Olson lowered his mouth to hers. She dove at it with the speed of a viper, crushing her lips against his. *I've got you now, you hillbilly bastard.*

She led him upstairs with vulnerable whimpers and whispered desires. Eduardo followed a few steps behind, close enough to keep his prying eyes on her but not close enough to get in the way.

They staggered into the bedroom, all moaning and frenzied hands, and she fell back on the bed and gasped like she couldn't believe any of it was happening. Part of her really couldn't believe it—the part of her that still retained some pride and couldn't fathom sinking low enough to fuck an idiot cop—but fucking him gave her power over him, and that power would get her into the hospital to yank the plug out from Narcissa's life support.

The detective slid his fingers down her back and unzipped her dress. She bucked her hips against his and whispered his name. "Oh, Jeremy..."

Eduardo rolled his eyes from his vantage point at the windowsill. *"Give me a break."*

Therese shot him a nasty glare over the detective's shoulders. *If you're going to watch,* she thought at him, *then shut up and maybe you'll learn something.*

He curled his lip, narrowing his eyes. *"Go ahead and teach me."*

That invitation was all the motivation Therese needed to bring her A game. She shimmied out of her dress and pulled the detective on top of her, aligning her hips with his. "Please..." she whispered, voice throaty and low. "I need you so badly."

It had been a long time since Therese actually had to try during sex, as Gillen had made it clear from the beginning that any effort on his part would be entirely perfunctory. She'd never given it much thought before, as she had little interest in sex herself, but in hindsight, she'd clearly missed one of the signs that he was a lunatic. Obviously, because only a lunatic wouldn't want to have sex with her. Even the podunk detective knew that and he barely had two brain cells to rub together.

She ran her hands over his back and dug her nails into his skin as he passed his fingertips over one of her nipples.

Eduardo sucked in a breath. *"Dios mio, woman, easy on the nails."*

Don't be such a prude, she snapped at him, and to prove her point, she clenched her hands even harder and jammed her fingers into the detective's back. He gasped into her neck, writhing in what she could only interpret as enjoyment. *See?*

She slid her hands down to the detective's waistband and undid his zipper. While she didn't have too much of an interest in seeing his cock—it was a cock, they were all the same—she at least thought it prudent to wrap a hand around it and get a sense of the incoming size.

"Not bad," Eduardo said. *"But mine was bigger."*

And you can go down to the morgue and suck it when I'm done. She tightened her hold on the detective's shaft and gasped. "You're so big…"

He must have enjoyed that because he growled into her neck and dragged his teeth over her flesh. She gasped as much out of annoyance as feigned pleasure.

With her dress gone and his pants down, she didn't waste any more time getting him inside her. She wasn't as wet as she could have been, but she doubted he noticed or cared. *That's why the good Lord gave us the ability to spit: so we have the tools to work through this misery when the other parts of our body refuse to cooperate with us.*

"That's beautiful," said Eduardo. *"I had no idea you were religious."*

I'll believe in anything if it gets this over with faster.

Once Detective Olson was inside her, he was mercifully quick to finish. Apparently, he cared as little about her pleasure as she did his. Under a different set of circumstances, she might have been annoyed by his selfishness—after all, he came and she didn't—but she hadn't gone into the affair in search of an orgasm and would have been twice as irate if she'd had to fake it while he fumbled through trying to give her one.

When he pulled himself off of her, he rolled to the side and flopped his head against the pillow with the exhausted grunt of a man who'd just completed a marathon. "That was wonderful, Therese."

Wonderful wouldn't have been her chosen description, but she'd come too far to stop playing along. "You were fantastic."

"As were you." He opened his mouth, then apparently thought better of whatever he'd planned to say and rolled to the side for his shirt. She thought he was going to get dressed to leave, but when he leaned back onto the bed, he'd procured a pack of cigarettes instead.

Before she could say *Don't you dare smoke that cigarette in my house,* he whipped out a lighter, held it to the end of the cigarette, and then glanced at her out of the side of his eye and said, "But all things being equal, Narcissa was better."

Therese's blood froze in her veins. Two terrors raced through her mind at once. One, the fact that Detective Olson had just compared her sexual performance to that of her dying sister-in-law, and two, the fact that his midwestern accent had dropped away and been replaced by something unmistakably British.

"What?" she whispered.

Eduardo leaned forward from the windowsill with wide eyes. *"Yeah, what?"*

The detective took a long drag on his cigarette and stared at the ceiling. "You know, Therese, normally I apologize when I'm asked to deceive people, but given the fact that I find you detestable, I'll say in this case that it was warranted."

"What the hell are you talking about?" She scooted against the backboard. "Who are you?"

"That, my dear, is actually a very complicated question. The simplest answer is that you're currently speaking with Thomas Bristol."

"Jesus Christ! You gave me a fake name?" Her eyes darted back and forth wildly as she tried to make sense of the situation. "Are you even a cop?"

"No, I am not—but for the record, Jeremy Olson is not a fake name. It's the name of the original owner of this body, and one of the members of our ensemble. No introductions necessary; you've been primarily dealing with Jeremy since the six of us met."

She whipped her head around and scanned the room. "What do you mean, six?"

"Myself, the other three members of my ensemble, yourself, and Eduardo. Oh, and you were right about the nails, Ed—they were a bit unnecessary."

All the blood drained from Therese's face as Eduardo's jaw hit the floor. "*Hijo de puta, you can see me?*"

Detective Olson—or Thomas Bristol, or whoever he was—lowered his head and looked Eduardo dead in the eye. "Indeed I can, though I'm afraid I don't speak a lick of Spanish. If you want to engage in that sort of discourse, you'll have to run it through Caroline."

"Who the hell is Caroline?" Therese screeched.

"Caroline is my partner."

"You said you weren't a cop!"

"I'm not."

She dug her fingers into her scalp and yanked at her roots. "What is happening to me?"

"Did you say you slept with Narcy?" said Eduardo.

The detective who was not a detective took another inhale from his cigarette. "Ah yes, I did mention that, didn't I?" He chuckled slightly and blew out a puff of smoke. The acrid cloud swirled around the room, infecting every fiber with its impermeable stench. "I had no intentions of seducing her when I was assigned to her surveillance detail, I'll have you know, but then I got a look in her head and figured out the racket you two were running. Under those circumstances, I deemed the affair to be permissable—open season, if you will."

"Dios mio," Eduardo said. *"You're a mind reader."*

A sly grin split the detective's lips. "Correct."

Up until then, Therese had been listening to the conversation unfold with the vague horror of someone freezing in front of an oncoming train. With the words "mind reader", the vague portion of her horror converted to a real and immediate fear for her life. "You can read my mind..."

"I can, and I'm truly wounded by how little you thought of me in executing this ridiculous charade. Really, a few crocodile tears and you expect me to hurl myself at you like an enamored schoolboy?" He wagged his finger with a condescending *tsk-tsk*. "You really oughtn't think so little of men. It will inevitably come back to bite you—but then again, it already has. Honestly," he added, "I don't know how Gillen stood you as long as he did."

"How dare you!" Therese said.

"Yes, how dare I—and not how dare you, the wretched harpy who tried to murder her husband's sister and attempted to seduce an officer of the law in order to finish the job. You're a dreadful woman, do you know that?"

"*I think she might be the devil,*" Eduardo added.

"It's entirely possible," the detective replied. "Though I imagine the devil might have been a better lay. Really, you disappointed me, Therese. I'd at least hoped you would stoop to oral sex out of desperation."

Therese's nostrils flared. "You're disgusting!"

"Perhaps I am, but I'm quite a bit older than I look, so I get to be. It also goes a long way toward helping me deal with people like you." He took an idle puff on his cigarette and knocked some of the ash from the tip onto her bedspread. "Fortunately, my dealings with you are just about to come to an end."

"What? Are you going to—arrest me?"

"Why would I arrest you? I'm not a real cop, remember?" He shook his head with another *tut-tut*. "No, my dear, I'm here to execute you."

Therese's stomach dropped as if the mattress had fallen three stories through the floor. "What?"

"It's true." He flicked his cigarette, knocking yet more ash onto the bed. "I was asked to determine whether or not you're a threat to society at large, and I'm quite certain you are. Henceforth, I've been authorized to kill you."

"You're not serious!"

"I am indeed, I'm afraid. The order comes straight from the Quartet themselves."

"Is that supposed to mean something to me?"

"No, but it means a great deal to me, and I'm the one who was given the mission. Having said that," he added, tapping his chin, "yours is a particularly interesting case—interesting enough that I'm willing to break the rules."

Hope lifted the weight on Therese's chest. "You're going to let me go?"

"What? Good Lord, no. I can't let you live. You're monstrous." He blinked as if in a daze, apparently so unmoved by her plight that he couldn't comprehend it at all. "Even still, I'd rather not be the one to kill you. Based on the events that have transpired, I believe that honor belongs to Eduardo."

An odd, unwelcome smile crawled across Eduardo's face. He leaned in close, obscuring his eyes in the shadows cast by the overhead lights. "*Go on...*"

Therese twisted to meet Eduardo's stare and clasped her hands over her chest. "Please, Ed, you can't kill me! Not after everything we've been through!"

"She has a point, you know," the detective said. "Not the second part, granted, but the first has some merit to it."

"*I don't care if I die with her.*"

"But Narcy is in the hospital!" said Therese. "If you kill me, you won't be able to see her again!"

"*You think I want to see her like this? Hiding away in your body, like some kind of stowaway soul?*" Eduardo waved his hand at her, lip curled over his teeth. "*I'd rather kill us both and die knowing she'll never have to worry about you again.*"

"A noble ambition, to be sure, but not quite the point I was trying to make." With the last of his cigarette burning down, Detective Olson dragged out what remained and jabbed the dying tube against the side of the nightstand. The heady aroma of burning wood mixed with the scent of the cigarette. "Now, correct me if I'm wrong, Eduardo, but you attempted to take control of her body yesterday and put a wine stem through her neck, yes?"

"*I almost had her.*"

"And a poetic death it would have been. Unfortunately, *almost* isn't quite good enough, and in your attempt to kill her, you lost the element of surprise. This sort of thing doesn't much matter when you're trying to overwhelm a more conflicted mind, but Therese here is not a conflicted woman."

"Sorry if you people forgot to give me the textbook outlining all this shit!" Eduardo said.

"It's quite all right. Believe me, most of us made the same mistake. I'm not saying you won't be able to kill her," he added, "I'm simply saying it won't be easy. You've also got time working against you, as I've got orders to have this one in a body bag before tomorrow evening at seven sharp. That leaves you..." He glanced at his watch. "A little under twenty-four hours to kill her yourself. If you fail to do that, then I'll have to do it. Not something I have a problem with, to be sure, but after what this woman has done to you, I'd like to give you a chance to handle her yourself."

"I appreciate the opportunity."

"I'd appreciate it if you two would go to hell!" Therese screamed. "I'm not going to let either of you kill me, no matter who ordered you to do what!"

The detective flicked the remains of his cigarette away and scooped his shirt off the floor. "Yes, well, it's not as if you have a choice in the matter, is it?" he said as he began putting on his clothes. "You can try to resist it, if you like, but it's no easy task to pull one over on a mind reader. As a matter of fact, the only person I've seen do it is your husband, Gillen. So unless you know where he is and you're willing to bury the hatchet—so to speak—you'll have to figure out a way to handle things by yourself." He stood up from the bed and straightened out his shirt. "I'd wish you luck, but it's my job to ensure you fail. Anyhow, I should really get going. Jeremy's grown rather tired of having me in the driver's seat, and he's very insistent that we get home and shower."

"That won't be a problem," said Eduardo. *"I can handle things from here."*

The detective laughed. "I'm sure you can."

Therese glanced back at Eduardo. He grinned at her with skeletal menace. She shrieked and scrambled off the bed, hurling herself at the detective's feet. "You can't do this to me! Please don't leave me with him!"

With a long sigh, Detective Olson knelt down and met Therese's eye. "You know something, Ms. DuCannes?" His upper-class accent had once again vanished, paving the way for the return of his midwestern drawl. "I'm not much for violence, but me and Ruby were all set to shoot you ourselves. Heck, I was ready to do it right in the interrogation room. If it weren't for Hermann and Tom voting us down, you'd have been dead by dawn. It's thanks to those two that you got to enjoy two extra days."

"You say it like I should be grateful!"

"Hey, I can't tell you how to feel. I'm just giving you the facts. The only reason you're still alive is because those two thought Ed over there should get to do you in himself." He frowned, tilting his head. "Though I'm thinking Tom wouldn't have been so keen on helping Ed out if he didn't think he could trick you into sex. Honestly, guy thinks he's James Bond or something." He laughed and stood up straight. "Anyway, I've got to go. That shower's sounding good right about now, and I don't want to keep Ed from killing you any longer. Until then, Ms. DuCannes, I hope you make the most of your time."

"What am I supposed to do?" she said. "Wait here to die?"

"If that's what makes you happy."

Therese clasped her hands over her face and screamed into her scarred palms as Detective Olson walked out the door.

"Looks like it's just you and me, puta," Eduardo said from behind. *"And if things go my way, we'll be taking that trip to the morgue together after all."*

Her heart thudded in her chest and she slammed her hands against the rug. "I am not going to die!"

Chapter Twenty-Four

FLUORESCENT LIGHTS BEAT down on Andrew's head as he tracked Caroline to the nurse's station to the end of the hall. He choked back the urge to gag at the overpowering aroma of the cleanser used to disguise the scents of the sick.

After turning the corner, he found Caroline standing in front of another unmarked door. She had her phone to her ear and her mouth was twisted into an unhappy crescent, but she didn't hesitate to put it aside when she saw Andrew making his approach.

"You're up." She raised her eyebrows at his feet. "You work things out with your ensemble?"

Ed appeared beside Andrew and crossed his arms. Ed's body language couldn't say much when Caroline couldn't see him, however, so Andrew had to translate the gesture into a frosty stare.

"Yeah, we worked things out. And now we want to see Narcy."

Caroline took a long breath through her nose and looked Andrew in the eye. She had to crane her head back to do it, but she didn't seem intimidated by the height difference— though judging by the way she pressed her lips together, something else was bothering her.

"Okay," she said at last. "You can see her."

Andrew blinked, not sure he'd heard her right. "Wait, we can?"

"Yeah. You can." She tilted her head toward the door behind her. "She's right in here."

Ed phased through Andrew and shoved himself in Caroline's path. *"Tell her to get out of the way,"* he said through clenched teeth.

"Can we go in now?" said Andrew.

"Wait," said Caroline. "I need to tell you something first."

"Push her aside and go in!"

Andrew tensed his fingers at his sides. "We want to go in now. Whatever you want to tell us, you can tell us in there."

Caroline took another deep breath. Both Andrew and Ed stared at her, waiting for her answer. When she finally exhaled, she nodded and stepped aside. "All right. You can go in."

Fragments of memories from the night in the ambulance came back to Andrew as he entered Narcy's room. Complicated machinery littered every square inch of space, filling the room with the same chorus of *beeps* and *boops* he'd heard after his embarrassing brush with unconsciousness. The main difference was that he'd woken up. Narcy still hadn't.

She lay in the center of a nest of wires, as pale as the snow covering the rooftops visible from her window. Her coppery hair fanned out over her pillow like a halo of fire around her head. Clear tubes weaved through her nose, funneling precious oxygen to her lungs. She looked as fragile as one of Andrew's mother's angel dolls, all porcelain hidden under glass.

Ed skipped through space, reforming at Narcy's side. He bent over the bed and stared down at her with tears in his eyes. *"It's going to be okay, Narcy... Everything's going to be okay."*

"She looks like she's sleeping," Andrew murmured.

"She's not." Caroline swallowed hard. "She's brain-dead."

Andrew froze. His heart pounded out his ears, drowning out his voice as Ed seized control of his jaw. *"What?"*

"She lost too much blood." Though Caroline's expression remained stoic, her voice wobbled more with each word. "Her brain went too long without oxygen."

Ed's fingers trembled over Narcy's face. *"No..."*

"Are you sure?" said Andrew. "Did the doctors—"

"Two doctors confirmed it. We had someone come in from our office to check her too. An Oyente, like Ed. It's why we took so long to let you see her in the first place," she added. "We wanted to be sure."

"And?"

"And she's not in there anymore. I'm sorry."

Andrew clasped his hands together and searched Caroline's eyes, praying he would find some proof of deception. There was none.

"How long have they known?" Ed spoke so softly Andrew had to strain to hear him, even with the words coming from his own mind. For a moment, he wondered why Ed hadn't just hijacked his mouth and asked the question himself, but watching him come apart over Narcy made the answer all too obvious: he didn't have the strength.

Andrew looked back at Caroline. "How long have you known?"

"We started to suspect it this morning."

"You've known she's been gone a whole day?"

"Don't say that!" said Ed. *"She's not gone! She's right here, same as me!"*

"Ed..."

Caroline glanced where Andrew was looking. "What did he say?"

He checked to see if Ed had an answer to that, but Ed wasn't looking at him anymore. He had his head bowed over Narcy's chest as tears streamed freely down his face.

"He said I shouldn't say she's gone," Andrew replied. "He said she's right here, the same way he is."

Caroline shut her eyes tight. "He's not wrong."

The way her voice strained set off alarm bells in Andrew's head. "What do you mean?"

"Andrew, Ed...when I said Narcy wasn't in there, what I was trying to say was—"

Narcy lurched forward. Tubes and wires went flying and the metal bars on the side of the bed rattled with the sudden force. Her pale eyes darted from side to side as she clawed at the mattress and screamed at the wall, spit flying from her mouth. "Kill me!"

Andrew's lips parted, but he couldn't make a sound. He didn't have the words. But he understood.

"She's not in there anymore," Caroline said. "But Eduardo is."

Ed rose from the bed, mouth open and eyes blank. His legs held him up just long enough for him to get his back against the wall, and then he slid down and hid his face in his hands.

"Is there...is there something you can do?" said Andrew. "To get him out of there, I mean?"

Caroline shook her head. "We can't separate him from her any more than we can separate him from you."

"Oh..." An ugly feeling dropped to the bottom of Andrew's gut. While he hadn't asked about his situation with Ed, getting such a stark answer didn't do anything to help his outlook for the future. "But there must be something we can do...?"

"There aren't a lot of options." She rubbed her forehead, barely concealing a grimace behind her arm. "Things aren't going to get better from this."

"Andy?"

Andrew looked up to see Ed staring at him from the floor. *Yeah?*

"Can I talk to Caroline?"

It had taken Eduardo long enough, but he'd finally learned how to ask. Had the circumstances been different, Andrew might have laughed. After what he'd seen, he couldn't imagine ever laughing again.

Yeah, buddy, he thought at Ed. *Go ahead.*

Closing his eyes, Andrew relaxed his jaw and relinquished control of his muscles. An awkward moment passed as he wondered if Ed had changed his mind, but then Andrew's mouth began to move on its own.

"Is she in pain?" said Ed.

Caroline shook her head. "She can't feel anything anymore."

"Am I in pain?"

She blinked and pursed her lips, searching his face. A response like that only made sense once he realized they hadn't told her about the switch. She must have figured it out, too, as the confusion faded from her face and gave way to a tight-lipped frown.

"Not physically, no."

"But mentally."

"Look, it's... You saw what happened a minute ago. You heard yourself. There's not much you can do to control a brain that's already dead, but there's enough of you still alive in there that you know you're trapped and can't get out."

"But why am I alive in there and not her? Why did she die in the body she owned, when I just infested it and got to live? How does that make sense?"

"There's a lot we still don't know about how Oyentes work."

"Aren't you supposed to be the experts?"

"Even experts run into problems they can't solve. Just look at all of us." She waved her hands in a circle over her head, indicating all the people around them. "Humans have been reading and writing and researching for thousands of years, and we still can't answer the basics questions of 'how did we get here?' and 'why are we here?' You can't expect us to know everything. Nobody does."

"Somebody should!"

"Maybe you can go ahead and make that your goal for your next lifetime, then. But for now, you need to decide how you want to handle her."

Andrew swallowed a lump of air, inadvertently stealing back control. "What do you mean, handle?"

Caroline glanced back at Narcy, who'd flopped back against the bed with the limp posture of a forgotten toy. "She can't stay this way forever. Neither of you can."

"What are we supposed to do? You said we can't separate them! What other option is left?"

Though she hadn't noticed the switch at first, Andrew's use of the word *them* must have been enough to tip her off. "Andrew..." She stared at him, imploring him with her eyes. "You know what option is left."

Ed's ethereal voice floated up from his spot on the floor. *"She wants us to pull the plug."*

A wave of bile splashed the back of Andrew's throat. He doubled over and clutched his stomach to hold back the pain. "Oh my God."

"You can't leave them like this. She's gone and he's in agony. Letting this go on is just prolonging the inevitable."

"How can you talk that way about this? Wanting to keep them alive isn't *prolonging the inevitable*—it's wanting to save my friends!"

"*You can't save us anymore,*" said Ed. "*We're already dead.*"

"That's not true! We can still save you!"

"*Me or her?*"

"I... uh..." Something Caroline mentioned earlier popped into his head and he snapped his fingers. "Caroline, can't Ed jump bodies again? You said earlier that Gillen could do it, so why can't Ed do it again? I know you said there's nothing left of Narcy..." He flinched and swallowed hard, then tried again. "I know she's passed on, but what about him?"

Caroline winced, closing her eyes and sucking air through her teeth. "That's not going to work."

"Why not?"

"Because if we did that... It takes time for Oyentes to be able to jump again, yeah? We'd have to wait until they were together long enough to do it, but every second we leave Ed in there is agony for him. The kind of thing that would drive a man insane. Do you know what I'm saying?"

Andrew bit his lip. He'd read enough studies of what happened to prisoners who spent time in solitary confinement to know what solitude did to people. He also had a fair amount of experience with loneliness himself. Being alone while trapped inside someone else's dying body took the experience to a whole new level. Nobody could endure that and come out okay.

A lump formed in his throat as he gazed at Narcy. Her chest rose and fell with each one of her shallow breaths. The Oyentes might not've been able to find anything left of her mind, but she was still alive. Caroline had said herself that there was still a lot they didn't know. If there was even the chance that they'd gotten this wrong...

"Could you leave us for a minute?" he said to Caroline at last.

She nodded all too quickly, proving how happy she was to get out. Once she left them behind, he drew in a breath and found his voice. "We can't do this to her."

"Do what to her? Leave her like this? I agree."

"No, not leave her, kill her!"

In the span of a blink, Ed vanished from the floor and reappeared at Narcy's side. *"There's no her to kill anymore."* He looked down into her eyes, but it wasn't for his benefit. He couldn't see her from where he stood. Staring at her served no purpose except to make Andrew feel worse.

The beginnings of tears clung to Andrew's lashes. He pinched the bridge of his nose and turned away. "How can you be so blasé about this? She's your wife, goddamn it! She's supposed to be your friend!"

"She is my friend!"

"So that's why you want to kill her? Because she's your friend?" He clenched his fists so hard that his forearms started to shake. "If that's your definition of friendship, then you're no better than Gillen!"

Ed bared his teeth. *"Fuck you."*

"No, fuck you! This is all your fault, all of it! Narcy was a sweet person with a big heart who only cared about making other people happy, and you took advantage of that! You didn't even want her, but you married her anyway, all so you could keep her from being happy with anybody else! You think she wanted to spend the rest of her life having sex with random guys because it helped you keep your stupid cover?"

"Don't you dare throw that back in my face! You have no idea what she wanted!"

"And you did? You don't know everything about everybody because you can look in their heads, Ed! Even if you can read everything about them, you're only looking at the things you choose to see! You had everything about Gillen in front of you and you missed it because you thought you understood him, but you were wrong and it got you killed! And now, because of you—not Gillen, *you*—the woman you claim to love is lying here in a hospital bed, and all you want to do is get rid of her because you're scared of what might be happening to you inside her head!"

With his mind and his lungs both emptied into the air, Andrew's body ached like he'd taken a wrong step off an unseen flight of stairs. Had Ed still been alive, he would have been entirely in the right to sock Andrew in the face. As it stood, Andrew still expected a verbal beatdown that would rip him straight down the middle. What he didn't expect was for Ed to shut his eyes tight and let out a strangled sob.

"You're right." His mouth contorted into a grimace as he sniffled and bowed his head. *"I am scared."*

Andrew stepped back from the bed. "Oh…"

"I just want to be there for her and do what's right, but I can't stop thinking about what it's like being trapped in the darkness. Can I see in there? Can I hear in there? Or is it all empty except for my silent screaming? Do I even know I'm dead?"

A discarded sliver of one of Andrew's childhood memories stuck out in the back of his mind. He'd locked himself in the broom closet while playing hide-and-seek with his mother once, and to conceal himself, he'd turned off the lights. At first, he'd thought he was so smart, hiding in the dark like that, but as minutes turned into hours and the darkness around him grew, he started to wonder if she'd ever find him or if he'd have to stay in the closet forever.

When she finally found him in the end, he asked her why it had taken her so long to find him. She laughed and pointed to the clock, saying it had only been ten minutes. He couldn't argue with the clock, but he still had trouble believing her. In the darkness of that closet, those ten minutes had been eternal.

"I'm sorry, Ed. I shouldn't have snapped at you. This is...this is messed up."

"It is."

Andrew ran his fingertips over one of Narcy's hands. The skin felt warm to the touch, but there was no life beneath it. Before, those hands had moved at a mile a minute, changing gestures with every word they spoke. Now they lay on the bed, as lifeless as the woman who owned them.

"She's really gone, isn't she?"

Ed bit his lip and nodded. *"She is."*

"Do you know what she would have wanted us to do now?"

"You mean aside from demanding we put makeup under her eyes because she hated when people could see the dark circles?" He attempted to laugh, but it rang as hollow as his joke. *"Yeah, I do know."*

"Because you talked about it."

"Mmhmm." Ed lifted his head, standing up straight. *"She never wanted it to end this way. She always said people who wanted their relatives to keep them on life support were people too vain to notice they were corpses."* He laughed again, but his eyes were hard. *"I guess that's what's going on with me now."*

Andrew glanced over his shoulder at the closed door. "Should we get someone?"

"No. I should do it."

"What—you mean *pull the plug*?" His eyes darted back and forth as he searched the outlets along the walls. "Is there even one plug?"

"I don't know. I just don't...I just don't want it to be so mechanical, you know? For it all to end just because some doctor turns off some machine...it feels wrong."

"It does feel wrong."

Ed rested his palm overtop Narcy's hand. His ethereal skin merged with hers, passing straight down to the bed. He turned away and whimpered like an injured dog.

A funny feeling came over Andrew as he watched Ed try to pull himself together. Had the feeling been driving him toward something good, he might have called it courage, but there was no good in his suggestion. It was darkness pushing him forward; a compulsion to do something so horrific it could never be described in positive terms.

"Do you want me to help?"

"What do you mean?"

Andrew took a long, slow breath. *God forgive me.* He pointed to one of the pillows behind Narcy's head. "Do you want me to help?"

The inference clicked in Ed's mind and his eyes went wide. For a moment, Andrew sincerely thought Ed was going to hijack his body and slaughter them both, but then Ed ran his hand down his face and nodded. *"Yeah."*

The muscles in Andrew's fingers twitched. *Damn.*

"Andy, wait." Ed reached out to him, as if his touch could make a difference. *"You don't have to do this if you don't want to."*

"Neither of you deserve to be trapped, but neither of you can fix it. I can."

"You don't know what you're saying."

"I'm supposed to love her, aren't I? And I'm supposed to be your friend. I haven't been good enough to either of you. I never really opened myself up to you. The least I can do to help you is this."

Ed's voice shook as he responded. *"Thank you."*

Opening the door a crack, Andrew glanced down the hall to check for Caroline. She'd walked a few paces away and had her cell phone pressed to her ear. The deadly stillness in the corridor carried her voice right to his ear, allowing him to hear her side of the conversation.

"South Dakota?" she was murmuring. "Are you sure about that? ... The patrol caught up with him on that road, yeah, but we had them leave him alone. If we kept the cops off of him, why would he stop? And in South Dakota, of all places? There's nothing in South Dakota. It doesn't make sense!"

Andrew's heart pounded as he closed the door before she could notice him. Without both sides of the conversation, he couldn't be certain who Caroline was talking about, but he had a funny feeling it was Gillen. South Dakota was a big state, though, and Andrew couldn't guess why Gillen would choose to go there any more than Caroline could.

The intermittent beeping of Narcy's life support system reminded Andrew of his task. With a stiff swallow, he returned to Narcy's bedside and took the pillow from behind her head. The stiff, sterile cotton rubbed against his skin, reminding him more of something from a hotel than a potential murder weapon.

He removed the oxygen tubes from her nose and took one last look at her face. Her too-big eyes, her too-small mouth, her freckled cheeks and the dark circles she'd always kept hidden: they were all a part of who she was, but none of them came close to defining her. Nothing he knew about her did. Nothing anyone knew did. The only one who could define her was her, and she was dead.

Andrew lowered the pillow over her face and pressed. She stiffened beneath him, though it could have just as easily been Ed reacting as what was left of Narcy's brain. Whoever it was with the power left to struggle, Andrew fought them with his every muscle, pressing all of his weight into the cotton crushing her head.

As Narcy's body twitched beneath the pillow, a vision floated up from Andrew's memory. It wasn't one of his memories, though; it was from a place he'd never been. A foul-smelling room, one with a barking dog and a urine-stained issue of the *Hill City Prevailer*. Somewhere in the distance, a train whistled while driving past, and a gravelly voice whispered in his ear, *"You wouldn't lie to me, would you, Gillen?"*

The pillow stopped shaking in Andrew's hands and the beeping equipment went dead. As Narcy's body fell still, Andrew let out a breath he hadn't known he'd been holding in. "She's gone."

Ed choked back a cry. *"She's gone."*

"We should go before Caroline gets back."

"Are we going home?"

"Yeah, we are. But just to pick up Hester. After that, we're getting in the car and going to Hill City, South Dakota." Blood pounded in Andrew's ears as he tightened his fists. "Because that's where Gillen's hiding, and we're going to kill him."

Chapter Twenty-Five

THIRTY YEARS OF self-loathing coalesced into a pool of acid in Gillen's gut as they rumbled up the driveway to the little tan house.

"This wasn't where you lived as a child, was it?" Eduardo said from the passenger's seat.

Gillen's knuckles were white against the wheel as he shook his head. "This was my grandmother's house. Ours was around the block."

"Is it still there?"

"No. Already torn down."

"They couldn't sell it after your father died, could they?"

"Where do you think I got the idea for this house?"

"Cute." His sardonic smile shifted slightly, mirroring the furrow in his brow. *"I guess that's going to happen to my house, too."*

Roiling hatred bubbled up Gillen's throat, mocking him from within. *I deserve every second of this.*

"What was that?" said Eduardo.

Gillen hit the brakes and threw the car into park. "We're here. Let's go inside."

Had Eduardo been capable of carrying anything, Gillen would have asked him for help unloading the car. Unfortunately, Eduardo's imaginary body hadn't been designed with doing chores in mind, so Gillen had to unpack alone while Eduardo watched.

"You didn't bring a lot, did you?" he said as Gillen hefted his few bags out of the trunk.

"I don't believe in overpacking." With the last suitcase out, Gillen slammed the trunk and locked the car. "And considering I didn't intend to stay here long, I'd say I overdid it."

"If you really wanted to kill yourself, you'd be overdoing it if you brought anything more than a piece of rope." Eduardo narrowed his eyes at the bags. *"So what's the point of all of this?"*

"There's still a few things I need to do here before I'm ready to go."

"Such as?"

Gillen snatched one of the bags off the ground. "Let's just go inside."

His free hand shook as he dug through his pockets for his house key. *Everything is fine,* he reminded himself, ignoring his chattering teeth. *It's just a front door.*

"What are you shaking for?"

"I'm cold. It's winter." Sharp, lancing pain jabbed between his ribs. He shut his eyes tight and pawed through his pocket that much faster.

"You're not cold. You're having a panic attack."

"It'll pass."

"Not if you keep trying to ignore it."

"It'll pass!"

Eduardo rolled his eyes. *"All right, all right. I'm just trying to help. Remember what I told you before: I've had a few of these myself."*

A growl rumbled in the back of Gillen's throat. "What would you ever have to panic about? Your life was perfect!"

"How was my life perfect?" He let out a hollow laugh. *"You think I enjoyed spending every waking moment*

listening to the fucked-up, terrible shit people think about? Do you know how racist everyone is? How stupid and scared? Do you know how many people hated me without even knowing me? How perfect do you think my life felt then?"

Gillen backed up a pace. "Wait a minute, I didn't mean—"

"And don't even get me started on the shit I've heard about being gay!" He pitched up his voice and wiggled his fingers, impersonating some chatty stranger. *"'It's the twenty-first century, Ed! Why don't you come out?' Because I can hear what people are thinking! I know how many people think putting another man's cock in your mouth should be a capital crime! Want to know how many? I'll give you a hint: it's a lot more than who will admit to it out loud!"*

"I'm sorry!"

"Sorry for what?"

Both men stilled. The ache of two days in a car and a lifetime of guilt settled between Gillen's shoulder blades. He hung his head and stared at the ground. *For everything.*

With his eyes on the dirt, he couldn't see Eduardo's expression. He could only hear the terrible pause that lingered for a moment shy of eternity, only stopping when Eduardo cleared his throat and stepped backward. *"You're right. Let's go inside."*

THE FIRST THING Gillen noticed upon entering the home was that the previous tenants had painted the living room blue. They were allowed to do that, according to the lease, but knowing the language in the contract didn't prepare him for the reality of the change.

Eduardo's eyebrows lifted as he looked around the room. *"Why is there furniture in here? I thought this place was supposed to be empty?"*

"I rented it out furnished." He ran his fingertips along the sunny paint and frowned. "The walls were yellow when I was a kid…"

"Does it matter?"

Gillen chewed his cheek. The house had changed from how it looked in his memories, but his memories would not be so easily denied. They pushed and shoved their way to the front of his mind, grasping him and dragging him into the past.

His mother cowered by the windowsill, ragged braid coming apart in pieces over her shoulder. "Please stop, he didn't do anything!"

"It's not what he did. It's what he is!" His father pointed a meaty finger at Gillen, who crouched beneath the Christmas tree, shaking against the torn-up wrapping paper. "He's an ungrateful, spoiled brat!"

"He just wanted to open one of his presents on Christmas Eve! Didn't you ever do that in your family?"

"No, because my family isn't made up of savages who can't wait twelve hours to celebrate on the fucking holiday!"

Gillen shrank against the metal stand. Pine needles scraped his face, coating him with the scent of sap. He peered between the branches, hoping his grandmother would see him, but she was in the kitchen with her eyes on the stove and she kept humming to herself so she couldn't hear the fight. Every time his father raised his voice, Gillen prayed she would finally help him, but she would hum that much louder until she couldn't hear them at all.

"I worked all year to buy him that gift!" Gillen's father threw his arms out, grazing his mother's face. "And now, because of you, he's got nothing to open on Christmas!"

"You're right. It's all my fault! Please, just don't hurt him!"

Danger flashed in his father's eyes and he drew back his hand. "Don't you tell me how to discipline my son!"

The blue room closed in, crushing Gillen from every side. His heart raced within his heaving chest. He backed against the wall and pressed his hands to the paint, desperate to anchor himself, but his memories tightened their hold and flattened him to the ground.

"Get up, Gillen!"

He crouched in the corner, shaking his head. Tears ran down his burning cheeks as he hugged his knees against his chest. He clutched them close, embracing them as if they were his only friends.

"They're not here, Gillen! You have to get up!"

"I can't get up..." he stammered. "It's all my fault!"

"Get up!"

"I can't!"

Every muscle in Gillen's body snapped taut at once. He jerked upright in a single motion, flying from the wall. His feet carried him forward and down the hall as his hands groped for the doors, opening and slamming them until at last one satisfied them and his legs walked him over the threshold.

Light flooded the room, brought about by his fingers flipping a switch. An old bed rested in the center of the space, covered by a variety of blankets and pillows.

"There's a bed here. Good. Now get in it and get under the blanket."

"What?"

"Dios mio, move!"

Gillen's body tumbled forward through space. His shins collided with the bed and pain shot through his legs. He fell face-first into the bed, colliding with the quilt-covered mattress.

"Now get under the covers!"

One at a time, Gillen pulled himself forward until he reached the headboard and accompanying pillows. One of his arms shot in front of the other and yanked the blankets to the side. With an inelegant roll, he flipped onto his back, tugged back the covers, and shut his eyes tight.

"There. You made it. You're alive. Now stop thinking about whatever the fuck you're thinking about and breathe. You think you can do that, pendejo?"

His chest rose and fell as he stared around the room, eyes darting fast enough to tug at his exhausted nerves. "Breathe?"

"Yeah, breathe. Come on, like this. Inhale?"

Gillen drew in a breath.

"Exhale."

He let the breath go.

"Good. Do it again. Inhale?"

He inhaled.

"Exhale."

He exhaled.

"There. You breathed. Easy, right? Now keep doing that and maybe do whatever it is you do when you want to clear your mind."

"Clear my mind..."

A candle flickered to life inside his head. He'd always used a candle to clear his mind, ever since he'd read about it in that storybook as a boy. *Focus on the darkest part of the flame: the emptiness in the center.*

His heart rate slowed as he imagined the dark halo contained within the flames orange edge. He'd been so excited to discover the different parts of the fire when he first started studying the candle; it was a secret only he and the glowing light shared. Everyone else saw the brilliance on the outside, but he'd looked beyond and seen the darkness within.

"Wow, you really did practice with a candle."

Gillen blinked. "Huh?"

"Back when Narcy first wanted to learn how to block me, she came to me one day and told me that you said she could empty her mind with a candle. You didn't exactly give her context, though, so after she spent a whole afternoon almost lighting her head on fire, I told her you were just being a dick and you didn't know what you were talking about."

The idea of a young Narcy waving a lit candle around her head was so absurd that Gillen couldn't help but laugh. He couldn't keep it up for long, though, since remembering Narcy brought that train of thought to its inevitable end.

"She's dead..." he whispered, clutching the blankets close to his chest. "She's dead because of me."

Eduardo materialized next to him on the bed. Between his panicked haze and the limited light, Gillen could barely make out the expression on his face. *"You're right."*

His thoughts raced ahead of his mouth, running through a battery of his greatest regrets. *I should have never come back into her life. I should have stayed away after I left school. I should have killed myself instead of killing Reyes.*

"Probably," said Eduardo. *"But you didn't. You're alive now, and you have to deal with that."*

He hid his face in his hands and choked back a sob. "I just wanted her to have a better chance than I had..."

A faint memory from his high school years floated through his head. He'd just turned sixteen and wanted to spend his birthday by himself so no one could bother him, but his parents insisted that he come with them to Narcy's first play that night. He hated the thought of going to a stupid elementary school musical, especially on his birthday, but then Narcy had found out he was going and got so excited that he couldn't bring himself to break her heart. He even snuck out of school halfway through the day so he could find a flower shop that sold the lupines she loved. It had taken him three different shops to find the damn things, but it had all been worth it to see the look on her face when he handed her the flowers at the end of the play. His parents had never been more proud of him. It was one of the few nights where he didn't want to run away.

"She loved those flowers," said Eduardo. *"She never stopped talking about them."*

Gillen looked up, unsure if he'd heard correctly. "The flowers from the play? That was fifteen years ago."

"You think time matters with stuff like that? You did something to show you cared about her. She couldn't forget that."

"And look how I repaid her..." He hugged his knees against his chest. Focusing on the softness of the blankets helped him ground himself, which gave him room to reflect on what had just happened. "Why did you help me out there?"

"I couldn't let you sit there forever."

"You could have killed me! You should have killed me!"

"I wouldn't burn down my house just because you were in it, pendejo." Though Eduardo had always used pendejo as an insult before, the softness of his voice took some of the bite out of the phrase. *"If you die, I die."*

"But you still didn't have to help me! You could have found a way to let me suffer without letting me die!"

"Why?"

"Because I murdered you!" Gillen clenched his fists around the sheets, pulling them from the bed. "Now Narcy's dead and you're here and I took everything that mattered to you, so why won't you stop helping me and hate me?"

"I do hate you," he said. *"But Narcy loved you—and I think you loved her too."*

"But I killed her..."

He blinked back tears, trying to clear his vision. If he had his sight back, he'd be able to see Eduardo's expression, and then it would be obvious Eduardo was joking because what he'd said didn't make sense.

"I've seen the way you remember her, Gillen. You never wanted anything bad to happen to her. Maybe you are the reason she died, but there was a point where you wanted better for her. How am I supposed to give up on you when I can see how much you wanted to care about her?" His voice cracked and he looked away. *"And how am I supposed to keep hating you when your memories of her are all I have left?"*

Without mind-reading experience of his own, Gillen had no frame of reference for what it would be like to live in another person's mind. What he understood was how it felt to live on the edge of his own life. He'd designed new lives for himself three times. None of them had given him the freedom he wanted, though—not even his latest life, the fiction he'd created to take him back to his childhood home so he could finally give up and die.

He spoke without thinking, emptying the crowded corners of his mind. "My mom was pregnant with Narcy when my father died. Then she met Gary and we moved to Minnesota, and all everyone wanted was for me to start over. All I wanted to do was talk about it...but I didn't want Narcy to worry about any of it. I just wanted her to have the childhood I didn't."

"So you kept everything locked away in your own head, instead."

"Mom didn't want to remember any of it either, so she never talked to me about it. Because she didn't talk about it, Gary didn't talk about it. No one in the house talked about it, so I thought I could make myself forget it. I wanted to start with a clean slate...but my slate wouldn't come clean, and I started to get angry."

"Your parents thought they could fix you, didn't they?"

"They would have liked that, I'm sure," Gillen scoffed. "But they never wanted to talk about what happened, so they couldn't make things better. School couldn't help me either. So I gave up on trying to make other people happy and I left. I wanted to stay gone, too, so I could be broken without anybody trying to change me, and for a while, it was working and I could hate myself while I was alone. Then I heard about you, and what you could do, and I realized you could see the real me... and I couldn't let you do that. If you knew the real me, you'd know about everything I was hanging onto, and you'd want me to get better the way everybody else did. But I didn't want that. I just wanted it to go away."

"You didn't really want that, though, did you? You wanted someone to tell you it was real."

Gillen shivered under the blanket. "You're just saying that because you don't want me to kill myself."

"You're right, I don't want you to kill yourself—but that's not why I'm saying it." Eduardo leaned forward, lifting his head from the shadows so that Gillen could finally make out his expression. He didn't look furious or sarcastic or amused; for once, he looked sincere. *"You waited a long time to kill me after you learned I was a mind reader. You've always been a thorough guy, but vetting me shouldn't have taken you years."*

A slight chuckle escaped Gillen's throat. "Therese used to nag me about it constantly."

"Bet she wouldn't have nagged you if she'd known how much money you actually had."

"I never cared about the money."

"I know you didn't. But you kept making it anyway. More than you needed to keep Therese happy, more than you needed to run away. You kept making money because making money was normal, just like the life you were leading." The mattress held steady under Eduardo's ghostly form as he rolled onto his side, looking Gillen dead in the eye. *"You may have told yourself that you set that life up as cover, but you kept it going because you wanted it to be real."*

Gillen let out a breath through his nose. "I never wanted that life with Therese."

"No, and that's why you married her. You asked me why I married Narcy, remember?" Eduardo shook his head. *"I don't need to ask to know why you married Therese. You picked her because you figured out she only cares about herself, which means she'd never expect someone else to care about her. You would never have to worry about where you stood with her. You didn't have to pretend with her, and she couldn't hurt you. She gave you everything you needed, and all you had to do was put on a show."*

Silence settled between them as Gillen made sense of the thirty-second summary of his entire marriage. "You make it sound so simple," he said at last.

"*I never said it was simple. I just said it was low risk.*" Eduardo ran his fingers through his hair. The gesture made him look surprisingly vulnerable, given how confident he'd been in dissecting Gillen's life. "*But that's got me stuck on one of the last questions about you I can't answer.*"

"You've got the rest of me figured out, huh?"

"*No, I don't. But I've decided to stop prying into most of it.*"

"You have? Why?"

"*Because we've got a long time to get to know each other, and I'd rather do things right with the last person I'll ever meet.*"

A long creak resonated through the walls as the house settled under a gust of wind. Gillen curled deeper into his blanket, covering his hands. "What was the last question you wanted answered?"

"*You really want me to ask?*"

"Yeah." He bit his lip and nodded. "Go ahead."

"*If you spent so long trying to make your life work before you killed me, what finally made you snap?*"

It was the question Gillen had been asking himself since the moment he plunged his knife into Eduardo's neck. That one question had been nagging at him, jabbing at him from his subconscious like a splinter jutting out of a piece of wood. He hadn't dared to ask it aloud, though, not when the answer came with so much risk.

"We should sleep," Gillen said. "When we wake up in the morning, I'll tell you everything. I promise."

Chapter Twenty-Six

THERESE RIFLED THROUGH Gillen's papers, wrinkling her nose at the bloodstained sheets. "Look at this mess!" She howled and tossed a pile of documents aside. "Why did he have to be so disorganized?"

"You're the one who took a sledgehammer to his file cabinet," Eduardo said from the bed.

She looked up from the pile just long enough to shoot him a dirty look. "I wouldn't have needed a sledgehammer if he hadn't felt the need to hide his entire life."

"I don't know why you're doing this a second time. You're not going to find anything in there."

Her gaze settled on a blood-spattered utility bill sticking out from the bottom of the pile. "Oh, yes, I am!" She snatched the document and thrust it toward Eduardo's face. "See?"

He shot her a withering stare over the top of the paper. *"I can't read that."*

"Of course you can't, you're an uneducated immigrant."

"You know I was born in Cicero, right?"

She made a *tch* noise with her mouth and yanked the paper back. "Fine, I'll read it to you out loud." Clearing her throat, she began reading off the top. "From the Black Hills Electric Company, addressed to one Gillen Lynch—"

"Yeah, I can read it now—and believe it or not, I've seen a power bill before."

"For a property Gillen was supposed to have sold?"

Eduardo shrugged. *"I don't know, maybe it was sent to him by accident?"*

"Why would he keep it if it was sent to him by accident?"

"Why would he keep it if he didn't want you to know about it?"

"Because he was just so stupid that he thought a lock would be enough to keep me out of his cabinets!"

"No one would be that stupid—not even someone who married you."

"Very funny, dead man. I bet you're the highlight of the comedy bars in hell." She sneered at him and went back to tearing through the pile. "South Dakota, South Dakota—all of those papers are for South Dakota!"

Eduardo leaned over and peered down from the edge of the bed. *"That does seem strange that he'd keep all those..."*

"It's because he's an idiot! I told you!"

"I'm not so sure about that..."

She grabbed an armful of papers and jumped up from the floor. A few documents slipped from her hands, fluttering to the ground. "This is all I need to go on. We're going to South Dakota *now*."

"You can't be sure he's there."

"Where the hell else would he go? He's got no family and no friends. Nobody cares about him." She waved the papers in Eduardo's face. "As far as I'm concerned, the only place he's got any connection to is the address listed in these papers."

"And what good will that do? Even if you get to Gillen, how do you think he'll stop me from killing you?"

"He got rid of you once!"

"Clearly he didn't since I'm sitting right here."

"No, you're not, because you're dead!"

Eduardo gave her a flat look. *"You know he's not going to want to help you."*

"He'll have to help me if I threaten to turn him over to the cops!"

"*And what about the cop who's coming to execute you?*"

"That man was not a cop!"

"*Well, whoever he was, he seems pretty confident that he can bump you off—and considering how well he played you, I'm thinking he shouldn't have any trouble. That is, if you're even alive when he comes for you.*"

She exhaled through her nose and glared at him. "You heard what the *detective* said: you don't have what it takes to kill me."

"*If that's what he thinks, then he's underestimating me.*"

"Maybe you're the one who's overestimating yourself. But it doesn't matter," she added. "He'll never be able to find me. No one knows about this South Dakota house but me, and I'm leaving town."

"*Olson will follow you.*"

Therese tightened her fists. "Not if he's too busy with his shower to know I'm gone." Of all the things that freak had said to her, his little shower quip might have been the worst. Really, as if *he* was the one who needed a shower after that ordeal! She'd been the one defiled by some sort of mutant; she was the one who should have been sobbing in the shower, scrubbing and scouring to cleanse the filth from her skin. But she didn't have time for that. She had to leave.

"*You think he won't be able to figure out where you're going? If Gillen was sloppy enough to leave his paperwork where someone as crazy as you could find it, it won't take Olson ten minutes to find out exactly where you went.*"

"Not if I don't leave behind any evidence!"

"*And how are you going to be sure not to do that?*"

Therese's eyes narrowed as she gazed around the room. Loath as she was to admit it, the dead man had a point. Obviously, there were no limits to Gillen's idiocy, given everything he'd done in the past several days, so it stood to reason that even someone as thorough as her couldn't dispose of all the evidence of his crimes. *Christ, for as little effort as he put into cleaning up after himself, the only way I can be sure everything's gone is if I burn down the house.*

Eduardo's face fell. *"You wouldn't."*

Her fingers twitched around her files as she reconsidered what she'd thought. She'd only considered arson sarcastically, clearly—what was she, a pyromaniac?—but the more she turned the idea around in her head, the more she came around.

"It could work..." she muttered to herself. "And even if it doesn't, I can't come back here with Olson on my tail."

"Are you insane? There's houses jammed against yours on both sides. If you burn this place down, you'll take out half the block!"

"Oh please, it's the middle of a Saturday. People will be awake to see the signs of fire and escape."

"Not everybody! But even if you could guarantee that—which you can't—you're still going to destroy their homes!"

Therese rolled her eyes. "This is Lakeview, Eduardo. I guarantee you everyone on this block has homeowner's insurance—and if they don't, they deserve to lose everything."

Eduardo gaped at her, blinking like the world's dumbest owl. *"Are you out of your mind?"*

"You seem to think so. I personally consider myself quite sane," she added, fluttering her hand across her chest, "but you've told me otherwise enough times that I might as well play the part. How mad can you really be? Disasters happen every day. This will be just one of them." Her lips tightened into a painful smile. "Unless you think you're able to stop me."

And with that single comment, Therese played her ultimate card: challenging Eduardo's control. If he wanted to keep her from potentially killing innocent people—or burning down their homes, as if he really gave a damn about that—then he would have to sacrifice his ability to catch her off guard and steal control. If that bastard Olson had been telling the truth, Eduardo would be lucky to get one more shot at her before the deadline; blowing it now would mean giving up what was probably going to be his one chance to kill her himself. While that wouldn't solve her Olson problem, it would give her an advantage over Eduardo, and that advantage would last her long enough to find Gillen and make him fix his mess.

The color drained from Eduardo's cheeks as Therese's smile spread. "You're getting it now, aren't you? You see the predicament you've put yourself in. If you want to save those poor, innocent people that you care so much about, you're going to have to stop me yourself. Do you think you can?"

Eduardo tensed his fingers around the corners of the bed. *"You're bluffing."*

"Am I? Why don't we go ahead and see?"

Without any further preamble, she snatched up the rest of the papers and strode down the steps to the kitchen. Setting the papers aside, she pulled out the utility drawer and riffled through Gillen's collection of matches and candlesticks.

"Really, I don't know why you think I'm the arsonist," she muttered as she pulled a candle out. "Gillen's the nutcase who always keeps a million candles around." *Honestly, it's like the man was perpetually preparing for a blackout.*

Eduardo popped into existence on the opposite side of the island as Therese set up her candle on the countertop. She made a great show of positioning the candle as if she actually wanted to use it, setting it next to a pile of napkins and lighting the wick, and then flicked her hand to the side and knocked the candle down. "Whoops! Some foolish person must have let this candle fall over—and it's right next to this pile of napkins!"

The flame jumped to the corner of the closest napkin. An orange line danced along the edge of the paper as darkness consumed the white square, turning it into ash.

"Think about what you're doing," Eduardo hissed through clenched teeth.

Therese grabbed a bottle of vodka from the opposite counter. "Oh no, there's alcohol on the counter too! And such high proof!" She rarely drank the aggressive alcohol she kept around for her hard-drinking family's visits, but she couldn't complain about their issues now that they were going to help her out. With a dramatic flourish, she unscrewed the top and poured the booze on the opposite side of the napkin pile. The pale liquid spread out in a wide circle, forming a lake of flammable fluid.

"You need to put that fire out! People are going to get hurt!"

"I'm not doing a damn thing to that fire." She stuck her hands on her hips and looked him dead in the eye as the glowing flame spread across the napkin. "If you want to stop it, you'll have to do it yourself. So what's it going to be? Will you give up your best shot at me to protect the lives of strangers, or will you let fate decide what happens to them so you can get your revenge?"

He stared back and forth between Therese and the fire, brow furrowed and nostrils flared. She could see his fear and his hatred fighting for control of his face, reflecting the struggle in his head.

When he finally looked back at her, the brilliant flames reflected off the dark pits of his eyes. "*Is this the best fire you can make, puta? Show me what a real killer looks like!*"

She cackled and grabbed a fistful of matches. "Watch and learn, Eduardo!"

Chapter Twenty-Seven

HESTER'S GIANT PAWS padded down the motel hallway as Andrew approached the door to his room. Scratches marred the thick layers of white paint over the wood, highlighting the motel's state of disrepair. Andrew would have preferred somewhere nicer to stay, but there were only so many hotels on the interstate that allowed dogs. Add in the fact that Ed hadn't wanted them to stop at all and Andrew was more than happy to take what he could get.

"We're not staying here any longer than we have to," Ed said as Andrew took out his key. *"You get four hours of sleep and then we're back on the road."*

"Four hours? But we've been driving forever! If I don't get enough sleep, I'm going to pass out behind the wheel!"

"And if we don't get to Hill City before Gillen gets my powers, we're going to lose our best chance to kill him ourselves!"

"We're not going to get a chance if I fall asleep at the wheel and wreck the car!"

Ed muttered a less-than-friendly comeback as Andrew opened the ragged door. A part of him had hoped the inside of the room looked better than its entrance, but one look at the stained carpet and the antenna television proved that part of him extremely wrong.

"Could be worse," Ed said. *"The stains could be on the bed."*

The dirty mirrors on the closet reflected Andrew's face as it collapsed into the world's saddest expression. "Eww, gross."

Andrew's phone vibrated in his pocket, just as it had been doing nonstop since they left. Apparently, it hadn't taken Caroline long to discover they'd left town, and she'd been calling them repeatedly ever since. He'd listened to the first two or three furious messages, but he'd stopped bothering to check them at all when it became clear they were all more or less the same. The wording changed each time, along with the tone, but the message was consistent: I don't know what you think you're doing, but if you think you can handle Gillen yourself, you're wrong.

Ed scowled as Andrew took out his phone. *"I thought you turned that thing off?"*

"I turned it back on about an hour ago." Andrew frowned and put the phone on the desk. "I don't want to miss any important calls."

"Who else could possibly call?"

"I don't know, my mother's home? Something could happen to her while we're out."

"Yeah, something you're not in the position to do anything about."

"You don't know that."

"What, you'd be willing to turn around now?"

"If something was happening to my mom? Yeah, I'd turn around." He put down his sole suitcase and slid it behind the nightstand. In an ideal world, his suitcase would have been holding a toothbrush and some spare clothes, but the only thing he had time to grab was the shotgun from under his bed. "But that doesn't mean I'd be giving up on this. We'd turn back, deal with her, and then get going all over again. I promise"

During the hours he'd spent behind the wheel, Andrew had given a lot of thought to how his life was going to go from here on out. He couldn't count on his job anymore, since the business owners were either dead or on the run for murder respectively. Luckily, he wouldn't have to worry about income for much longer, as Ed had been kind of enough to point out how gaining the power to read minds would make money troubles a thing of the past. Whenever they needed a few thousand dollars, they could hit up the nearest casino and clean out the card tables. Andrew didn't know the rules for any card games outside of Fifty-two Pickup and War, but Ed had assured him that being able to see into people's heads would more than make up for the skill deficit. Unfortunately, it wouldn't help them with their main goal of killing Gillen, since he'd have the same powers as them.

"You really think he's out here?" said Andrew. They'd had the same conversation at least twice before, but the more time passed, the more he wanted reassurance that they were making the right move. He no longer had any doubts about killing Gillen—not after what they'd seen in the hospital—but betting everything on an intercepted memory made Andrew more than a little nervous. Unfortunately, that memory was all either of them had.

"He wouldn't have hurled himself at me if he hadn't had something to hide," said Ed. *"He didn't want me knowing anything about that location, even if all I saw was a newspaper and a train."*

"What I don't get is why Narcy never mentioned anything about living in South Dakota to you."

"She didn't. She was born in Illinois, same as me."

"But Gillen was born in South Dakota?"

Ed shook his head. *"Minnesota."*

Andrew took one hand off the wheel to scratch his chin. He did seem to recall having seen that info on Gillen's paychecks, and there was no way the IRS would have left him alone if the info they gave him was fake. "So does that mean he moved to South Dakota after he was born?"

"I think so, yeah—but I'm not surprised they never talk about it. It's where their biological father died, so I can't imagine wanting to bring it up."

"He fell off a roof or something, right?"

"Slipped off a ladder while cleaning the gutters. It's why Narcy never lets me get on the top part of the ladder that says 'Don't Step On This Beam'." He pressed his lips together and looked away. *"I guess I don't have to worry about that anymore."*

Andrew's phone buzzed across the top of the dresser. He glanced at it just long enough to read the screen, but the second he was able to make out the message, his cheeks lit up and Ed caught his expression.

"I saw that!" said Ed. *"It's that María girl from the internet!"*

"She's not *from the internet*, she's a real human being!"

"Yeah, and she said she misses you and hopes you're doing okay! What is she, trying to get money from you or something?"

"What? No, she's worried about me because she's my friend!"

"How can she be your friend? You don't even know her!"

Twenty-four hours ago, Andrew would have countered by saying all the things he knew about María, like her favorite songs and colors and games. He'd already lost that fight once, so he wasn't excited to have it again—even if María really was his friend.

"Can I at least say hello to her?" Andrew said instead. "There's nothing else for us to do in here."

"We're supposed to be sleeping!"

"I can't take five minutes to check my phone before I go to bed?"

Ed snorted and plopped into a dusty chair. "Do what you want. It's coming out of your sleep time."

Andrew scowled at Ed as he snatched his phone off the desk. Blue_María's old message sat at the top of the window. He read it again and frowned as he briefly considered putting it aside, then shook his head and decided to answer it anyway. Even if he couldn't tell her why he hadn't been around, she still deserved to know he was alive.

Blue_María: *im worried about you Brood*

are you ok?

Broodlord: *you dont need to worry, im fine*

well not fine fine, but im ok

Andrew had been expecting to wait a minute or two for a reply, but he got one not ten seconds later.

Blue_María: *there you are! You had me freaking out, cuate*

Ed scoffed over Andrew's shoulder. *"Cuate! What is she, pretending to speak Spanish?"*

"Oh come on!" Andrew swatted his hand in Ed's face. "You think you've got the market cornered on speaking Spanish?"

"I think I'm more qualified to judge people about it than you are!"

"Well, maybe you should try not judging people at all!"

Before Ed could squeeze in another retort, Andrew snatched the phone to his chest and typed in a reply.

>Broodlord: *sorry to make you worry*
>
>*just needed to take some time offline*
>
>Blue_María: *after what you've been through? makes sense to me*
>
>*you hanging out at home now? I was thinking we could get in a couple games if you're around*
>
>*I know youre probably not feeling up to it, but right now our only healer is Android and hes terrible*
>
>Broodlord: *sorry, cant make it on tonight.*
>
>*not gonna be around for a while, actually*
>
>*Got some stuff to take care of*
>
>Blue_María: *what, in a world with no internet?*
>
>*Come on, brood. you need to give yourself a break*
>
>*I know youre going through a rough time, and you probably dont want to talk to anybody, but hanging out with people is good for you. even if its just in some stupid shooting game online*

Andrew pursed his lips at the phone. He really wanted to tell María more about what was going on—not *everything,* but something—but he couldn't think of a way to begin that didn't make him sound like a nutcase or a criminal. *But on the other hand, Ed keeps telling me to open up to people...*

He tapped his fingers on the keyboard, pounding out an answer about has fast as he could construct it in his head. The problem was, putting together an answer in his head meant that he wasn't the only one privy to it, and Ed didn't seem too thrilled at the direction the answer was taking.

"What do you think you're doing?" He craned his neck forward, as if doing so would actually help him see.

"Quiet," Andrew murmured. "I can't think with you bothering me."

Broodlord: *I do want to talk to you guys, but I'm taking a vacation*

Well, not really a vacation, but I guess it's kind of a trip

Blue_María: *well that's good! Where are you going?*

Broodlord: *nowhere exciting, I promise you*

Just a long drive across the midwest

Ed smacked the air in front of Andrew's head. *"Are you crazy? Why would you tell her that?"*

"You told me to open up to people, remember?" he said. "Well, I'm taking your advice."

"I didn't mean about committing a felony! And I didn't mean you should open up to strangers!"

"But she's not a stranger!"

"Yes, she is!"

Blue_María: *that doesn't sound so bad*

Where in the midwest?

"Don't answer that!" Ed snapped.

Hester let out a wild bark as Andrew jabbed a finger in Ed's face. "Don't tell me what to do with my life!"

"It's my life too!"

"Well, it was my life first, so you're going to have to let me live it!"

"No, I'm not!"

Andrew's hands seized around his phone. Pain shot through his fingers as they moved beyond his control, *tap-tap-tapping* away at the keyboard before he could stop them.

"What are you doing?" he said.

Ed's voice reverberated inside his head. *"I'm fixing your mess!"*

> Broodlord: *im not staying in the midwest, im just passing through to go to the west coast 4 som sunshine*
>
> *o and maybe ill get a little exercise while im there, i sure do need it hahahahaha*

Andrew wrenched back control of his jaw. "You asshole! You have no right to hijack my body that way—and stop calling me fat!"

> Blue_María: *oh come on, dont be so hard on yourself*
>
> *its not like youre a walking milkshake*

The blood in Andrew's veins ran colder than the air leaking through the windows. His hands went limp around the phone as he looked into Ed's widening eyes.

"Hey, Ed?" he murmured. "Where have I been called that before?"

"I called you that when I first took over your body."

"I don't like milkshakes that much…"

"I know, I know, I'm sorry. Still, it wasn't exactly my finest hour. I just wanted to go see Narcy, but I was stuck in your body…"

"Talking to Caroline."

Every last one of Andrew's conversations with Blue_María took on new meaning in light of the past days' events. She'd joined his gaming community about a year ago, but Andrew hadn't thought anything of her arrival because people came and went all the time. She'd taken an immediate interest in him, though, and not just because of her supposed desire to make a friend who knew how to play a healing class. She also seemed to be genuinely interested in his life—or, more specifically, his career. She couched it in terms of being interested in HR—which should have been a red flag in and of itself—but she always found a way to ask about Ed. At the time, he'd let it slide, since people loved trading horror stories about their jobs online. She wasn't interested in his job, though; she was interested in Ed.

"But that doesn't make sense..." Andrew murmured. "Why would Caroline's people have had any interest in you before yesterday?"

"Because they're liars? Because they're crazy people?" Ed's eyes flashed as he hovered in front of Andrew's face. *"She's been lying to us since the moment we met her! Why does it surprise you to find out she could lie before?"*

"But how could María be Caroline? How does it make sense?"

"How does it not make sense, pendejo? Think back on your memories of her! You've heard her voice in your games! You tell me what makes sense!"

The feeling drained from Andrew's face as he recalled the dozens of games he'd played with Blue_María over the last year. From her accent to her expressions, she sounded exactly like Caroline. He'd just been too stupid and too trusting to notice it.

"But it doesn't make sense... she was supposed to be my friend!" The gravity of what he'd done set in and his stomach dropped to his feet. "Oh my God, Ed, I'm so sorry!"

"You can apologize to me later. For now, I'm calling that bitch!"

All the muscles in Andrew's hands tensed in unison. He wanted to be furious, to be ready to scream at Ed for taking over again, but all he could do was sit there in the back of his own head and stare as Ed pulled up Caroline's number from the list of recent calls and punched it in.

She picked up after three rings. "Andrew, thank God!"

Some small part of Andrew's brain recognized his own voice coming out in Spanish, but he'd gotten so accustomed to the rapid translation that he could make perfect sense of Ed screaming.

"Who do you think you are, you fucking whore?"

"Goddammit," she muttered on the other end, "I knew I screwed myself with that milkshake comment."

"You screwed yourself the second you started messing with my friend!"

Without control over his face, Andrew couldn't raise his eyebrows, but the instinct to do so remained. *Wait, why is he bringing me into this? I thought he was mad that she lied to him!*

"I had a job to do!" said Caroline. "Some of us can't rely on our powers to make a paycheck, you know!"

"So you use people for money instead? Andrew thought he could trust you, but you manipulated him to pay your rent!"

"The only reason I did that was so I could figure out if you were a threat to the millions of people surrounding you—and judging by what I've seen of you, I'm not convinced you're not!"

"You don't know one thing about me!"

"I know you killed Bernardo Reyes!"

"You don't know what happened with Reyes!"

Andrew yanked back control of his hand and waved it for attention. *Who's Bernardo Reyes?*

"I know what you told me to my face!" said Caroline. "And I know how you tried to steal Andrew's body and run with it! How dare you call me a bad friend to him after that! I may have lied to him, but I've never hijacked his body!"

"I was scared and confused!"

"Which time?"

Andrew's teeth ground together of their own accord. Harnessing all his anger and frustration at once, he wrenched the muscles apart and took his mouth back for himself. "You lied to me, Caroline!"

The transition to English must have given him away because she immediately changed her tone. "Listen, Brood—"

"Don't call me that!" he said. "Don't pretend we're still video game buddies when you were lying to me the whole time!"

"It wasn't all lies!"

"What part of it wasn't?"

"The part where I said I was worried about you!"

Andrew blew through his lips. "Worried because you lost track of me?"

"Worried because Gillen's going to tear you apart!"

"Not if I do it to him first!"

"Listen to yourself, Andrew! You're not you anymore! Eduardo's infected you. He's too deep in your head! You've got too much of him in you now—you're not making your own decisions!"

"That's not true!" He said it so loud and with such conviction that he caught himself off guard and needed a second to collect himself. Fortunately, Caroline or María or whoever she was must have been caught off guard, too, because she stayed quiet long enough for him to calm himself down and try again. "That's not true. I know who I am now, and I know what's important to me."

"Getting yourself killed?"

"No. Helping my friends."

"Eduardo isn't your friend!"

Having lost control of Andrew's body, Ed had been listening to the phone call in furious silence from his position in the passenger's seat. He couldn't keep quiet after that comment, though, and Andrew felt the familiar tension in his neck as Ed tried to grab control.

He didn't grab it fast enough.

"How can you say that when you don't even know him?" Andrew fought through the pain in his jaw, speaking with all the strength he had. "You don't know how it feels to actually be friends with him. You don't see how many times he's tried to help me be better than I am, even when it made me hate him. You have no idea how many times I've tried to push him away so that I didn't have to worry about screwing up our friendship!"

"Andrew, please—"

The pain in his jaw was long gone, but Andrew kept pushing, no longer willing to stop. "You think I should be mad because he took over my body so he could see his dying wife? You think I'd trust someone who wouldn't do that for someone they loved? He lost everything because of Gillen, but all he wanted to do when he got a second chance was make sure Narcy was okay! We're not out here hunting Gillen down because he wants it; we're out here because of me! And if you think that I couldn't possibly make that decision myself—that I'm too gullible or stupid or weak to think it through—then you know even less about me than you do about him."

He pulled the phone from his ear and ended the call with a defiant jab of his finger, cutting off Caroline's muffled protests.

As soon as the line went dead, all his energy left him at once and he sank into his chair. "Oh geez."

"Dios mio…" Ed gaped at him, openmouthed and wide-eyed. *"I've never seen you lay into somebody before."*

"I dunno if I really *laid into her*," Andrew mumbled. "I just told her how I felt."

"Still, you stood up for what you believed in. You stood up for me."

"I guess I did."

"Did you mean all that?"

Andrew cocked his head. He hadn't given anything he'd said much thought—it had come out all at once, like he'd been vomiting on the phone—but after a moment to breathe and some consideration, he smiled at Ed and nodded.

"Yeah, I did."

"So you're not upset with me for everything I've done to you?"

"No, but maybe stop stealing my body to yell at people in angry Spanish."

"Yeah, okay, I guess I can do that."

"You guess, huh?" Andrew laughed, shaking his head. "Well, I guess I'll take what I can get."

"I guess having a copilot isn't such a bad thing." The remnants of his smile fell away, leaving behind a tight-lipped frown. *"Do you want me to take over when we get to Gillen?"*

An ugly feeling settled in Andrew's stomach. He chewed his lip and pushed it down. "No. I'll handle it myself."

Chapter Twenty-Eight

GILLEN WOKE TO the sugary scent of chocolate and pancakes, fresh off the griddle. He smiled, imagining how good they would taste with maple syrup, and then he remembered he was supposed to be living alone in the middle of the woods and he launched himself out of bed.

He followed the smell into the kitchen, where he found a stack of chocolate chip pancakes on the little blue table across from the stove. At the stove itself stood Eduardo, offering Gillen a gentle smile.

"Morning, sunshine."

"You made pancakes?" Gillen blinked at the pile of food, then at the dirtied stove. Eduardo didn't have any tools in his hands, but the signs of cooking were all over the place. "How?"

"I woke up about an hour ago and I couldn't get back to sleep, so I figured I'd make us breakfast."

"Wait, wait, wait. Are you saying you woke up in control of my body...and you used it to make pancakes?"

"What else was I going to do? I was hungry and all you had was instant mix."

"That's not what I mean!"

"I already told you I'm not interested in messing with you anymore."

"Did you?"

"If I didn't, then I'm telling you now."

Words failed Gillen as the smell of fresh food wound his way around his nose. He sank into one of the rickety chairs and stared at the steaming tower. From overtop the layers of pancakes, he could just make out Eduardo's smile across the room.

All of the self-loathing, anger, and misery he'd been fighting to hold back burst through in a torrent of fury. He slammed his fists on the counter and shouted, "Fuck!"

Eduardo's eyebrows shot up. *"Should I not have added the chocolate chips?"*

"Shut up about the goddamned pancakes!"

Days of hunger and fatigue took their toll at last, stealing the energy that had been propelling his anger. All his rage fled at one growl from his stomach. Then, in what might have been the most pathetic and least masculine moment of his life, he thunked his forehead against the table and burst into tears.

"Jesus, Gillen, what's wrong?"

"What's wrong? What's wrong?" Gillen whipped his head up and glared at Eduardo. "I murdered you and you're repaying me by making me pancakes! What the hell is wrong with you?"

Eduardo's shoulders tensed. *"I told you, I was hungry."*

"If you were hungry, you would have eaten the pancakes while you were in control and then tossed me back in bed! This isn't hungry!" Gillen waved his hands at the pancakes. "This is nice!"

"So? What if it is?"

"I already feel bad enough about killing you the first time, goddammit! Now I can't even fix things by committing suicide!"

The air between them stilled as Eduardo stared at him and tilted his head. *"Did you really think that killing yourself would fix things?"*

"What the hell else am I supposed to do to make things right?"

Eduardo sighed and ran his fingers through his hair. Gillen had only seen him do that a few times before, but those few times had been enough to establish a pattern. He did it when he was at his weakest, without an idea of what to say or how to proceed. He touched his hair when he had nothing else anchoring him. Without his own body, he was lost.

"*I don't know,*" he said at last. "*But you can start by saying thank you for the pancakes.*"

Gillen let out something between a snort and a laugh. "A thank-you isn't much of a penance."

"*No, but I'd appreciate it anyway.*"

"Fine. If it makes you happy, then thank you for the pancakes." He nudged one of the chairs out with his foot. "If you want to sit and watch me eat them, I guess you can."

A smile crept across Eduardo's lips. "*It wouldn't kill you.*"

"Ha-ha."

As Eduardo repositioned himself at the table, Gillen topped off the stack of pancakes with the syrup Eduardo had been nice enough to set beside them. The pancakes were delicious—though it was hard to screw up instant—and even the canned coffee he'd brought with him hit the spot when paired with the chocolate and maple. Neither of them made him feel much better, though, as no amount of food could overpower the bitter memories creeping out of his mind.

"Last night, you asked me when I finally decided to kill you." He set his fork aside. "Do you still want to know?"

"*I do.*"

Gillen took another sip of coffee and cleared his throat. "Narcy came over to talk to me a couple of months ago. Did you know that?"

Eduardo shook his head. *"What did she have to say?"*

"She told me how proud she was of me, and how I'd changed so much from the angry boy she knew when she was younger—like I'd become somebody different. She was glad I'd been able to put all that behind me." He picked up his knife and stared at his distorted reflection in the blade. "She said she was happy we could finally forget about it."

Though Gillen couldn't see Eduardo's face, he could guess at the expression that accompanied his haggard sigh. *"She always knew how to put her foot in her mouth."*

"She always did." He turned the knife so he couldn't see his face anymore and moved it away. "But she didn't deserve to die for it."

"But she did. So why?"

Gillen furrowed his brows. "What do you mean? You know why. You were there. I was there."

"No, I'm not asking about her. I'm asking why that comment was what pushed you to kill me?"

"Oh." He'd had a feeling that was what Eduardo had been asking, but he'd been hoping it wasn't. He knew the answer, but he knew he'd never be able to articulate it.

"I don't need the perfect answer, Gillen. I'm just asking how you feel."

"Sorry... I don't get asked that a lot."

"I know."

"Right. Duh." It came out more sarcastic than he'd meant it to sound, but he didn't bother to clarify it. From inside his head, Eduardo could see the meaning beneath what was being spoken.

Gillen pushed his plate away and rested his chin on his folded hands. "All my life, people have told me to put my past behind me. And I wanted to do it for them." He wanted so badly to look Eduardo in the eye, as it was the least the man deserved, but he couldn't keep his gaze steady without wanting to break down. "I wanted it so badly, even when I hated them for asking me to do it. I thought if I was just better or smarter or more well-adjusted, I could forget about what happened and live the life they imagined for me. I was never able to give them what they wanted, though—not until I had you to motivate me."

Eduardo raised his eyebrows. *"You mean killing me?"*

"I had to kill you. It was the only way to be who they wanted me to be. Before I knew you were a mind reader, I thought if I faked being happy for them long enough, eventually they'd believe it was for real. But you—what you could do—you'd see right through me, even when no one else could. So I had to become such a good fake that even you'd believe my perfect life was real... and in the end, I did it so long that I'd started to believe it myself."

"Until Narcy."

"Until Narcy." He rolled his lips together, fighting back the urge to cry again. He couldn't keep crying; crying was a sign of unhappiness.

A stiff breeze rattled the screen door, stealing Gillen's attention. When he came back to the conversation, Eduardo was staring at him with folded lips and a wrinkled brow.

Gillen shrank back against his chair. "What are you looking at me for?"

"I want to know what you're going to do now."

"You mean right now?"

"You know that's not what I mean."

Gillen's shoulders sank. "I know."

"Killing yourself won't fix anything. You know that, right?"

"What else am I supposed to do? Wait for the police to come get me? I'd been counting on them finding my body, but they don't even know that I exist." He blew through his lips. "If I didn't know any better, I'd say that was some kind of irony."

"*So the only option you considered was suicide?*"

"What other option is there?"

"*Turn yourself in.*"

The idea was both so obvious and so ludicrous at the same time that Gillen didn't know where to begin. He could only sit back, blinking and staring at Eduardo like he'd sprouted a second head.

"*It wouldn't be so bad, you know. You were lucky enough to kill me in Illinois, so you won't have to worry about the death penalty. Beyond that, it's just a question of getting a good lawyer and having him strike a deal.*" He shrugged his hands with the kind of nonchalance that a normal person would have used for suggesting wine instead of beer. "*Sure, you'll do some jail time—a lot of jail time— but you won't be in there alone. I'll be with you the whole time.*"

"You say that like it's a good thing."

"*Hey, I know a lot about prison!*"

Gillen cocked an eyebrow. "You do?"

"*I know how to have sex with men, so I think that covers at least half of it.*"

Eduardo delivered the line with such straight-faced confidence that Gillen couldn't help but laugh. It had been a long time since he had sincerely laughed at one of Eduardo's jokes, but he couldn't deny that it felt good.

"You're insane, you know that?"

"*Hey, what can I say?*" He flicked the air in front of Gillen's head and grinned. "*You don't have to be crazy to live in here, but it helps.*"

Gillen's laughter devolved into a sardonic chuckle. "Yeah, I'll bet it does."

"So what do you want to do? You must have had some idea of how this was going to go down once you got here, assuming I wasn't along for the ride. I know you were going to kill yourself, but you had to have had something in mind before that. I can't believe you were going to drive fourteen hours just to hang yourself on the front step of the house."

"I'd rather do it inside, thanks."

"So you are going to hang yourself." He breathed out through his nose, venting extra air. *"Guess I shouldn't be surprised you picked the most maudlin way to go."*

"I can't say the rest of my plans were any better."

"Tell me about it," said Eduardo.

Gillen flicked a stray chocolate chip at Eduardo's chest. "Oh, shut up."

The chocolate chip sailed through Eduardo's body and collided with the adjacent wall, eliciting another one of Eduardo's brilliant smiles. *"No, really,"* he said. *"Tell me about it. You said you've got this all figured out, right? What was supposed to happen now? Were you going to go right for the rope, or did you have something else in mind first?"*

"Honestly?" He'd been planning to use an extension cord, but going into the mechanics of his own death seemed impossibly depressing now. By comparison, the preamble wasn't nearly as disturbing. "I was going to visit the place where my father died. Just... I don't know why. To give some finality to things."

"You wanted closure."

"It sounds trite when you say it like that."

"Everybody's life sounds trite when someone else is summarizing it. What matters is whether it's important to you."

"It is important," he replied, as much to Eduardo as to himself. "Or at least, it was."

"Has something changed?"

Gillen snorted. "Everything's changed."

"But has something changed with this?"

"How do you mean?"

Eduardo gestured to the window, as if he could tear down the walls with a hand motion and expose the other side. *"Whether I'm here or not, you still want to put an end to things with your father. I mean, you can't kill him twice—"*

"No, he's not as lucky as you."

That earned him a laugh. *"No, he's not. But you've still got unfinished business with him; otherwise you wouldn't have come all the way to Hill City to die. I mean, come on. Why would anybody choose to spend the last day of their life out here? I'm not saying there's something wrong with South Dakota, but you're a rich guy with nothing to lose. Most guys in your situation would spend their last days in Vegas or Monte Carlo or something."*

"I always hated Vegas, and I doubt I could find Monte Carlo on a map."

"Then we can add that to the list of things to do in the prison library. Now what do you say—do you still want to visit what's left of your father's house?"

He sighed and stared at the ceiling. "I don't know. I do, but—"

"You do, full stop. So let's do it."

Even if Gillen had still been on the fence, Eduardo's insistence would have made arguing impossible. He really did want to see where his father died, though, if for no other reason than to prove to himself that it had been real.

He pushed his chair away from the table and started to stand up when Eduardo held up a hand. *"Wait."*

"Why?" said Gillen.

"Last night, when I helped you during your panic attack...that took a lot out of me, taking control. It's one thing for me to do it while you're asleep, but when you're actively fighting me..." His brows knitted together as he ran his fingers through his hair again. *"I don't want you to kill yourself, but I won't be able to stop you if you're dead set on doing it."*

Gillen's eyes opened wide. "Why are you telling me this?"

"Because I need you to understand that what happens to me next is your choice, and not mine." Eduardo bit his lip. He looked like he had a lot more to say, but in the end, he stuffed his hands in his pockets and said, *"Just don't rush into anything, okay?"*

Gillen's mouth twisted to the side. "It took me a while to kill you last time. I guess I can wait until we get to my father's house before I decide what to do with you the second time."

Chapter Twenty-Nine

THE SMELL OF burning wood followed Therese all the way to South Dakota, lingering long after the clouds of smoke had died. She savored the smell with every inhale. Not only did it remind her of her triumph over Eduardo, but it also covered up the stench of sweat resulting from spending thirteen hours crammed into a two-seater.

She popped another one of Juanita's pills and blinked to clear the rainbow spots from her eyes. She'd been seeing them for hours, but she'd gotten as good at ignoring them as she had at ignoring Eduardo. Oh, he was trying his best to bother her—blathering nonstop, blinking in and out of existence, dripping blood from the wounds on his neck—but fake words couldn't hurt her and fake blood couldn't stain. Even if it could, though, that was precisely why she'd gotten leather seats. Cleaning body fluids out of fabric would have been a nightmare. Leather, on the other hand, was perfect for hauling the remains of the dead.

Little chips of polish sloughed off her nails as she clicked her fingertips against the steering wheel. The last of the sunlight reflected off the remaining lacquer, highlighting the places where it had broken.

"We're so close I can taste it," she said, though she could also taste metal from when she'd bitten her cheek outside Kadoka. The damn thing had swelled on her and she'd bitten it a dozen more times since, which had her mouth filling up with as much blood as Eduardo's side of the car.

The outline of Eduardo filled in with color, twisting and converging to form the loose approximation of his form. Red lights flashed in the black pits of his eye sockets, reminding her of the Cartier ruby earrings she'd wanted and Gillen had refused to buy for her. Cheap bastard could have afforded a dozen pairs, but no, he'd been selfish and cruel and hoarded everything for himself! Clearly, murder was the least of his crimes compared to his bottomless greed.

"I always told myself I'd get to ride in this car before I died," Eduardo said.

Her lip curled as blood spilled out of his mouth and dripped onto his shirt. "Too bad you didn't make it."

"You're not going to make it either, puta."

"Yes I will. We're only an hour away. What are you going to do in an hour, kill me?" She laughed until her throat burned, and then the blood from her mouth ran down her throat and soothed the pain and she went right back to laughing.

"If I can't, Detective Olson will."

"Please, he's never going to be able to find me. I burned down half of Lakeview to keep him off my tracks." A good thing too. She'd always loathed Lakeview. Too many young mothers with their oh-so-sweet infants in their double-wide strollers, all running down the street in their yoga pants while they waited for their handsome husbands to come home. Therese wasn't like *those* women. Therese had a mind. A brilliant mind too—not the kind to be wasted on shallow thoughts about pilates and carbs. She had the kind of mind that would let her outwit anyone who came after her. She didn't need to be scared of Olson or Eduardo or Gillen or anybody. They were nothing compared to her. Next to them, she was a god.

"I can hear him."

"Hear who?"

"Detective Olson."

She glanced in her rearview mirror. There was no one else on the road, no one except the birds who'd been following her for a hundred miles and were clearly waiting for her to stop so they could scratch up the paint job on her car. She'd paid damn good money for that shade of teal, yet those terrible birds wanted to punish her for her success—as if they had the right! No one had the right to punish her, not the birds or Olson or anyone else.

"I'm not worried about him," she said.

"Yesterday, I wouldn't have been worried about him, either. But now? Even when I could read minds, I couldn't push my voice into someone else's head. I also couldn't read someone at this range. Him, though?" The solid pieces of Eduardo's face flickered between amusement and fear and wonderment. *"He's more powerful than I ever was."*

"Oh please, you're just trying to scare me. You want to get me off my guard." She clenched her teeth, biting into the tender flesh of her cheek once again. "That's it, isn't it? Is this how you break me, you bastard?"

"Don't be stupid. You wouldn't break because of me. You wouldn't break because of anybody. That's why I don't know what to do with you."

"What the hell does that mean?"

"I always knew you didn't care about anybody but yourself, but I never realized how damning that was until I got stuck inside of you." He started laughing, but he didn't look like he was having a good time. He looked like someone who'd had a knife shoved through his chest and couldn't figure out how he'd survived. *"I thought if I was in here long enough, I'd find some memory I could use to get leverage over you. Some time you embarrassed yourself or someone*

who hurt you or some moment where you did something so bad all you wanted to do was die. But you don't have those moments, because you don't have a life."

"How dare you! I have a perfect life!"

"How can it be perfect when you're the only one in it? I keep looking through your memories, trying to find someone who meant something to you, but all your memories are of you. You! For all that other people mean to you, you might as well not have a past at all! You've spent thirty-five years living your life, but you haven't shared it with anyone. How is another person supposed to break you when you don't know other people exist?"

"Other people are idiots. Why would I need them when they have nothing to offer me?"

"Because when I finally figure out how to kill you, you're going to die wondering why no one is coming to help you out."

"The only person's help I need right now is Gillen, and that son of a bitch owes me one. Once he's gotten rid of you for good, I won't need anyone else."

"Go ahead and keep telling yourself that. See how it helps you when you're standing in front of the gates of Hell."

Her lip curled and she leaned into the accelerator. "If I'm going to Hell, you're coming with me—so you'd better pray Gillen is where I think he is; otherwise, both of us are going to die."

"Perfect," said Eduardo. *"I can't wait."*

Chapter Thirty

THE FAUX-WOOD alarm clock on the nightstand was flashing 11:05 a.m. when Andrew heard Hester crying from the side of the bed. "Eleven oh five?" Andrew murmured. Then his stomach dropped and he lurched upright. "Eleven oh five!"

Ed popped into existence in front of the bedroom window. The midday sunlight illuminating his back, transforming his face into a series of shadows. Andrew didn't need to see his face to know what he was thinking, though, because his scream echoed inside Andrew's head like fireworks on the fourth of July. *"Eleven oh five!"*

Andrew hurled himself out of bed and scrambled for his socks. "We can still make it! We still have time!"

"We're less than eight hours away from the deadline!"

"We're only six hours away from Hill City if we stay at the speed limit the whole time!"

"The hell with the speed limit! Pack your shit. We're getting there in five!"

BETWEEN PACKING THEIR few things and taking Hester to pee, Andrew and Ed lost another twenty minutes before they got on the road. Once they made it to the highway, Ed made good on his promise to set speed limit laws aside. Every time Andrew tried to throttle the car back to a reasonable pace, Ed shoved his foot down onto the accelerator to throw him forward. It didn't take more than four or five rounds of the nauseating game for Andrew to realize they'd both end up dead if they kept fighting for control of the vehicle, so he threw up his hands and agreed to set the laws of the road aside.

By the time they made it past Rapid City, the sun had already started to dip below the hills. Hester had been enjoying himself the entire time—even though Andrew refused to let him stick his head out the window—but the two humans in the car weren't nearly so happy to be on the ride.

"Are you ready for this?" said Ed.

Andrew let out a long breath. "I don't know."

Ed tilted his head toward the cupholder, where Andrew's phone lay facing the floor. Caroline hadn't given up on messaging them, but they'd both agreed she no longer deserved a response.

"She says she's not far behind us," said Ed.

"Yeah, well, she's still behind, so that means we have time."

Neither of them had much to say after that, so they drove together in uncomfortable silence for the last leg of the journey. A passing driver might have seen his gritted teeth and stony stare and read it as determination, but on the inside, Andrew was a terrified child. The thought of actually pulling a shotgun on another human being had him so jittery that when they passed a sign for a nearby reptile zoo, he seriously considered stopping and putting his head in between the biggest gator's teeth. Since dying via gator bite seemed a lot worse than anything Gillen could do to him, shooting him ended up beating out suicide by reptile on the priority list.

When they reached a sign that indicated four miles until Hill City, Andrew clenched his fists and looked over at Ed. "Are you sure you'll be able to find his house once we get there?"

Ed nodded without taking his eyes off the road. *"I could see the train through the window in his memory. A tree, too, but the train should be enough."*

"There could be a lot of houses that look out on the train..."

"Then we're going to be visiting a lot of houses."

Andrew glanced at the clock and frowned. They had less than two hours to spare. "We don't have time to visit the whole city. We need to find him now."

Ed's mouth formed a hard line. Clearly, he didn't need Andrew to stress how much more difficult things would get for them if they couldn't find Gillen in time. While both sides becoming mind readers would maintain an even playing field, whoever had that power could potentially jump to a new body if they died. If Gillen got himself killed by a stranger, they'd lose track of him forever. If Andrew killed him the wrong way, they'd be stuck with a murderer in their mind. Caroline seemed to know how to avoid that, but she'd neglected to tell how. All they knew was that they couldn't be nearby when he died. Beyond that, they'd have to figure out the rules on the fly.

As Andrew reached the top of the two-lane road, the first traces of the train from Gillen's memory came into view. When Ed had first mentioned a train station, Andrew had pictured something like the stations in Chicago: run-down and dirty, but more or less modern. Hill City's 1880 train did not meet that definition. Andrew didn't know much about railroad history, but even he could tell the black machine coming into view in front of him was insanely old—

so old that for all he knew, it might have actually been from 1880.

"Look at that thing," Andrew murmured. "It's a giant toy set."

"I'll bet toy sets don't cost nearly so much to maintain."

"Yeah, no kidding…" His gaze traveled up the opposite hill, where dozens of houses stuck up between the towering trees. "How are we going to find him up there?"

"Simple: we ask one of the locals."

Andrew's eyebrows shot up. "What are you, crazy? If he's even here, he would have just gotten here yesterday. There's no way anyone will be able to tell us anything."

"Are you kidding? I bet everybody here knows everybody." Ed knocked on the window, though his knuckles didn't make a sound. *"Just look at this place, Andy. It looks like Twin Peaks."*

"I've never watched that show."

"Then you need to expand your horizons beyond your Japanese titty comedies."

What little good humor Andrew had to spare abandoned him as he scowled at Ed through the mirror. "Expand my horizons…" he muttered to himself. "I'll show you who needs to expand their horizons."

A streak of blue whizzed past Andrew's window. He screamed and slammed on the brakes. The blue blur raced ahead of him, zipping between lanes with all the care of someone on a six-lane highway in the middle of the night.

"Jesus!" Andrew said. "What's wrong with that guy?"

Ed's eyes snapped open as the offending car disappeared down the hill. *"I'll tell you what's wrong with that guy. It's Therese."*

"Therese? Wait, you mean Gillen's Therese?" He did a double-take, hoping for another glimpse at the car, but it had already vanished into the valley. "How did you see her that fast?"

"I didn't. I saw her car."

"Are you sure it was hers? I thought the detective—Caroline—said Therese was one of the witnesses. If she didn't leave with Gillen, why would she be here?"

"I don't know why she's here, Andy, but there aren't a lot of people driving around in that type of car."

"What? That's crazy! It's just a teal convertible, there's probably a million other people out there with that same exact car!"

Ed cocked an eyebrow. *"You know that car costs over a hundred grand, right?"*

A dry, clicking noise popped in Andrew's throat. He blinked and tried to conceptualize a world in which he had a spare six figures to drop on a car, but he couldn't do it. "Are you...are you sure that's what it was?"

"Andy, I've been ogling that car since the day that bitch drove it off the lot. Now hit the gas and try to follow her, because she just became our best chance of finding Gillen before our time runs out."

Andrew's stomach churned as he stared down at the pedals beneath his feet. While he had fond feelings for the hatchback he'd inherited from his mom, he also knew its limitations. "I don't think I can catch up to a car like that in this thing..."

"You're definitely not going to catch up to her by sitting still, so move your ass!"

"Okay, okay, sheesh!"

He hit the gas and the car lurched forward with a horrific squeal. Hester let out a chorus of barks as Ed threw back his head and laughed. *"We're coming for you, Gillen!"*

Chapter Thirty-One

A LIGHT LAYER of snow had fallen in the night, covering the woods in a patchwork of white. The last remnants of moonlight highlighted the pristine landscape through the cracks in the branches. The only sounds Gillen could hear were the crunch of his boots in the snow and his breath as it formed clouds of steam in front of his face.

When Gillen had first left the house with Eduardo, he'd assumed they would go straight to the lot where his father died. Yet once they got moving, he couldn't bring himself to head that direction, as visiting that lot was the last thing he had left to do before he could die. Two days ago, he'd been counting down the minutes until he could put an extension cord around his neck. Now, he found himself stalling for time.

Instead of heading to the lot right away, Gillen ended up taking Eduardo on a walking tour of the town. He'd expected to spend the entire tour reliving bitter memories from his past, but he didn't have much room to wallow with Eduardo cracking jokes at every turn. While part of Gillen appreciated the levity, deep down, he understood that Eduardo wanted to stretch out the day as badly as he did.

Had Hill City been a larger town, Gillen might have been able to make the tour last long enough to buy them both another day. Unfortunately, what the town had in charm, it lacked in size, which put them on a direct path to Gillen's childhood home by nightfall. In a way, watching the sun set on the city had been oddly fitting—a way of turning the final page in the book of his life.

As they walked through the woods toward his old house, Gillen had to deal with both his bulky jacket and his giant snow boots impeding his mobility. Eduardo wasn't limited by the same protections. He walked five paces ahead, studying every branch as if he were a child running through a new school on the first day.

"It's amazing out here," he said. *"There's nothing like this in Chicago!"*

"I'm pretty certain there's snow in Chicago."

"Not the snow, pendejo, this!" Eduardo waved his hands over his head, gesturing at the staggering trees. *"Nature! Not some manicured park with beer and hot dog vendors down the block—the real stuff!"*

Gillen craned back his head and looked up at the treetops. It really had been a long time since he'd spent any length of time in the woods. If memory served, he hadn't been in a forest since his mother moved them back to Chicago when Narcy was born. At the time, he'd been too upset by everything to care about the change in location one way or the other. Now that he was here, he actually found himself missing the time he'd lost.

Eduardo stopped dead in a clearing between the trees. He knelt down and placed his palms in the snow, but his hands didn't make any more of a mark than his feet. *"It was here, wasn't it?"*

Gillen stiffened in place. He held his breath as he scanned the horizon, studying the lines formed by the hillside and the train tracks below. The cold air on his cheeks burned, sharply contrasting the way his blood chilled in his veins as his memory filled in the pieces of the picture that had gone.

"It was."

The snow lay undisturbed beneath Eduardo's shoes as he stood up and stepped back from the clearing. *"Do you want to tell me about it?"*

Something fuzzy played along the edges of Gillen's perception, buzzing the way a radio did as it went in and out of tune. He stuck his finger in his ear and wiggled it around, but it didn't clear.

"That's odd..." Another chill rippled down his back and he rubbed his hand against his forehead.

Eduardo cocked his head. *"Everything okay?"*

Gillen waved him off. "Yeah, it's just...just a headache from the cold, maybe."

"Maybe you shouldn't be thinking about this." He held out his hand. *"Let's head back. We can try again later."*

"Let's stay."

Eduardo hesitated. *"Are you sure?"*

"I am."

"So...you want to talk about what happened?"

"No." Gillen swallowed against a lump in his throat and tried his best to smile. "I can show you if I remember it."

He closed his eyes and focused on breathing through his nose. In the darkness of his mind, he could see a distant candle flame flickering to guide his path. He didn't go forward into the emptiness, though; instead, he followed the smell of decay to his final memory of his father.

Sunlight bounced off the silver ladder as Gillen's dad propped it against the gutters. "These fucking things are worthless," he muttered as he climbed the rungs. "I swear to God, I'm out here cleaning them twice as often as it rains."

A few yards away, Gillen sat in the grass and watched his father work. He hated being alone with his dad, but his mom said her stomach hurt and she needed to lie down. She'd been doing that a lot lately too. At first, Gillen hadn't thought much of it, since his stomach hurt every time he ate too much ice cream, but his mom didn't eat dessert as much as he did. If she kept having stomach aches, it meant something was wrong.

"Hey, Dad?" Gillen said.

Gillen's father let out a long, haggard sigh. "What do you want?"

The tone of his dad's voice should have been warning enough for Gillen to shut his mouth, but he figured his mom being sick was important, so he decided to take the risk. "How come Mom doesn't feel well?"

"Because she's a woman, and women never 'feel well.'" His father scooped a handful of decaying leaves out of the gutter and hurled them to the ground. They made a sickening splat when they hit the driveway, reminding Gillen of when the ducks flew over their house to poop. "They're always making some dumb shit up about how their head hurts or their feet hurt or their period hurts, and it's never ever true."

"Oh." Gillen fiddled with a blade of grass for a moment, then looked up at his father again. "Why would she say she's hurting if it's not true?"

"Because she wants attention. That's all they want, all the time. Attention and money." He pitched another chunk of dead leaf at the earth. This one hit harder than the first, exploding on contact with the asphalt. "Why the hell else would she get pregnant again?"

The grass fell from Gillen's hands. "She's sick because she's pregnant?"

Gillen's dad smacked his gloved palm against the gutter. "Jesus, don't you know anything? Why haven't you learned this shit in school?" He tilted his head back and groaned. As he shifted his hips, the old ladder pressed against the roof, wedging the two sides closer together. He kicked one of the rungs and swore under his breath, but it didn't seem to make the ladder any more stable.

"Would you come help me out with this thing?" Gillen's father shouted to him. "Your mother hasn't gotten us a new one like I told her to, so I'm stuck using this piece of crap."

Gillen leaped from the ground and sprinted to his father's side. The last time he'd taken too long to help his father, he'd been forced to stay home from school and sit on the bathroom floor for the entire day. He kept himself busy for most of the time with a pile of his mom's old magazines, but not eating for a whole day made his stomach burn.

"There, about time." His father pointed down to the side of the ladder closest to the wall. The ladder was supposed to fold out into an A shape, but one of the feet had gotten all bent out of shape, so Gillen's dad kept the ladder leaned against the roof instead. "Stand over here so I've got a clear shot at the driveway. Once I've got all this crap down there, you can go ahead and clean it up."

"Yes, sir."

As Gillen's father continued lobbing leaves at the ground, Gillen gripped the side of the ladder and imagined life with a little brother or sister. He'd have to help take care of them when Mom was hurt, which wouldn't be fun, but he'd also have a friend to keep him company for things like sitting on the bathroom floor. A boy would probably be better than a girl for that, since if his dad was right, a girl would just spend the whole time complaining that she was in pain.

"Hey, Dad?" Gillen said. "Is it a boy or a girl?"

"They don't know yet."

"Why not?"

"Because they don't know yet!"

"Oh." He frowned at the piles of leaves and dirt on the other side of the ladder. He would feel bad about throwing chunks of dirt at a little sister, but he'd definitely be okay with throwing dirt at a little brother. "Do you know when they'll know?"

"Christ, what is this, an interrogation?" He peered down at Gillen and scowled. "The kid's barely even alive in there. They don't know its asshole from its eyeballs. You think they can tell what gender it is?"

"Um..."

"It'll take months before the thing's anything more than a grain of rice. And hell, as clumsy as your mother is, the damn thing probably won't make it 'til the end of the week."

Gillen's hands went numb around the ladder. "What?"

"You're lucky your mom didn't notice you existed until she was the size of a goddamned watermelon. If she'd known about you earlier, I'm sure she would have done some stupid thing to get you killed. She's the worst when it comes to that shit, you know? Give her something unbreakable and she's fine, but give her a carton of eggs and she'll find a way to smash it in a second. With her luck, you would have ended up as just another smashed egg." He peered down at Gillen through narrowed eyes. "Now don't you feel lucky you've got me looking out for you?"

Gillen gulped. "Yes, sir..."

"Kid, for the shit I put up with to raise you, you should be on your knees thanking Christ every night." He blew through his lips. "I wouldn't have picked you out at the pet store, that's for sure. But that's your mother for you, too *dumb to know she's pregnant until she's ready to pop! Maybe if she'd been a little more on the ball, we could have done things differently. This time, though..."*

Blood raced through Gillen's ears, carrying the violent beat of his heart around his skull. "This time what?"

"This time, I can put a stop to things before they go too far."

"What do you mean?"

The sunlight reflected off the bald spot on the back of his father's head as he turned back to comb through the gutters. "Lemme give you a piece of advice, kid—from one man to another. When you get to be an adult, women are going to try to trap you by getting pregnant. But they don't have to stay pregnant if you don't want 'em to."

"They don't?"

"Nope. It's legal now too; they've got procedures for it and everything. Even if it wasn't, though, it's still your child. You're the father. You made it. You get to decide if it stays or goes."

A gust of wind passed under the ladder, shaking the sides against Gillen's palms. He tightened his grip so hard his nails dug into the metal. "What happens if you want it to go?"

"You tell the woman to deal with it herself. And if she won't, you do it for her." He laughed and shook his head. "It's like my father always said. It's why the good Lord gave us stairs."

Gillen gazed up the rungs of the ladder at his father's feet. From down below on the driveway, the distance to the roof seemed impossibly high. "What do the stairs do?"

"Come on, kid, you need me to spell out everything for you?" His father wiped the back of his hand across his forehead. "If a pregnant lady falls down the stairs, she's not gonna be pregnant when she hits the bottom."

"Wouldn't that hurt a lot?"

Gillen's father grabbed a big handful of leaves. "You tell me." Whipping back his arm like a baseball pitcher, he hurled the leaves against the driveway. The wet lump exploded in a shower of debris, sending flecks of grime in every direction.

A drop of mud struck Gillen's cheek and he clapped his hand over his face. "That's horrible..." he whispered.

"No, that's life, and the sooner you sack up and realize that, the happier you'll be." He turned back to the roof, still muttering to himself as he wiped yet more grime from his head. "Your mother could stand to learn that too. Bitch must be out of her mind if she thinks I'm gonna put up with another nine months of her crying again. I swear to God, I'd be better off if the stairs went bad and I killed two birds with one stone."

The world beyond the ladder blurred, leaving Gillen with nothing but the metal beams and his hands. They shook against his skin, daring the wind to carry them. They didn't need the wind to help them, though. Not when Gillen was right there.

He threw his weight into his arms and pushed with all his might. The wind came right along with him. Together, they rattled the silver stairs, and Gillen's father cried out as he tried to grab the roof, but the grime on his hands broke his grip and he fell to the asphalt in a heap of flesh and bloodied mud.

Gillen stood over his father, numb from his toes to his head. No one had seen him except the wind. He felt he should cry, but he couldn't bring himself to do it. Instead, he turned on his heel and ran.

The first rays of sunlight flickered behind Gillen's eyelids as he emerged from his memory. He opened his eyes to see Eduardo staring at him, tight lips forming a snow-white line. Gillen flinched and averted his gaze.

"I used to think he was a mind reader," he mumbled. "He always knew when we'd done something bad." A gust of wind whipped past and he rubbed his hands together to keep them warm. "That's why I believed the story from Reyes."

Eduardo let out a hollow laugh. *"Your father couldn't have been a mind reader."*

"Why not?"

"Because if he had been, he would have known your mom found out she was pregnant with you even sooner than she did with Narcy."

Gillen blinked. "How do you know that?"

"Because I was a mind reader, and she was my mother-in-law." A beat passed and Eduardo grinned. *"And also because she told me."*

"When?"

"Long time ago, back when I was still dating Narcy." He chuckled to himself again, though the flat look on his face made it clear he didn't think it was funny. *"She said it was the smartest thing she ever did."*

"My God... I had no idea." Gillen swept his hand through his hair. "She knew she was pregnant all that time, but she never told him... She risked everything to protect me."

"And that's what you did for her when you pushed your father off that ladder."

"That's not true!"

Eduardo raised his eyebrows. *"How is that not true?"*

"Because I did something bad!" He threw up his hands, exposing them to the wind. "I murdered him!"

"You were seven, pendejo. A seven-year-old can't murder someone! They don't have the brainpower to know what they're doing is wrong!"

"I knew exactly what I was doing was wrong!" His breath formed bursts of steam as he shouted into the winter air. "I knew if I pushed him, I would hurt him. That's exactly why I did it!"

"And in doing it, you spared your mother, your sister, and yourself from having to live with him for one more minute."

"That doesn't make it okay!"

"How does it not?"

"Because it wasn't okay when I killed Reyes either! It wasn't okay when I killed you!"

A distant branch cracked under the weight of the snow, reverberating in the silence that descended on them. Gillen covered his eyes with his hands and gritted his teeth to fight back another scream.

"You saved your family when you killed your father. When you killed Bernardo, you saved me."

"Saved you from what? Some idle threats he probably never would have followed up with? He was an innocent man!"

Eduardo dragged his hand down his face with a long sigh. *"Remember when I said I'd seen inside his memories?"*

"Yeah, but I don't see what—"

"He had a patient before me—a thirteen-year-old girl. She was young and impressionable, and all she wanted was for someone to show some interest in her. Dr. Reyes was the first person who did, but she didn't understand that he only listened to her because someone was paying him. Instead, she thought he loved her, and she fell in love with him. So she kissed him."

The winter air turned to ice in Gillen's lungs. "Did he—"

"Sleep with her? No, he didn't. He freaked out and told her she could never do that again and then decided they would both just forget it had ever happened and they would put it in the past. She was okay with that for a little while, but then she wised up and decided she had to tell her parents what she'd done. Reyes didn't like that, though; he didn't want to put his reputation at risk." Eduardo narrowed his eyes. *"So he gave her a choice: either she could keep her mouth shut and live with the memory in silence, or she could try to tell someone and he'd use everything he had on her to make her the villain—and then he'd have her committed."*

"What did she do?"

"She killed herself."

Gillen swallowed against the lump that had formed in his throat. Bernardo Reyes might not have killed his patient with his own hands, but through his actions, he'd killed her all the same. Not for any reason he could justify, either; he'd done it simply because he was afraid.

The fuzzy headache he'd felt before returned in force, dulling the edges of his vision. He shook his head to rattle it away, but the sensation remained no matter how hard he fought it. *But maybe that's the problem.*

He stared at the tree-lined earth where his father had once lay dead and sighed. He'd been waiting his whole life to come home and die, but dying wouldn't do anything but bury the guilt with him. If he wanted to get rid of his guilt, he needed to stop fighting it.

"I can't kill myself here," he said.

Eduardo searched Gillen's face with his brows furrowed together. *"You want to do it somewhere else?"*

"I do, maybe—but I can't. Not now that you're with me."

The barest hint of a smile flickered across Eduardo's lips. *"You don't want to kill me."*

Gillen glanced at Eduardo out of the corner of his eye, not daring to meet him head-on. "I can't do that to Narcy, or to you."

"So you'll turn yourself in?"

"As long as you don't mind joining me in prison."

Eduardo's echoless laughter carried through the woods. *"What else am I gonna do, run off on my own?"*

"I know you can't leave me. That's why I'm asking." He looked down at his empty palms. "I need to turn myself in—to atone for this, if I even can—but I won't do it if you're not okay with it." At long last, he dared to meet Eduardo's eyes, even though doing so made him want to hurl himself to the ground and die where his father had. "I already took your freedom once. I won't take what's left of it."

After a moment of silence, a sly grin crept across Eduardo's cheeks. *"You know, prison won't be so bad if you're still questioning things."*

"You mean if I'm gay?" He let out a long breath, ridding himself of both the air and the fear he'd been holding in. Not once in his entire life had he ever dared to apply that word to himself out loud. Now that he'd done it, it felt better than he expected.

"Aww, look at you, opening up to yourself." Eduardo leaned in, smiling wider than before. *"Now imagine how much fun you'll have with this new insight in prison. Just think about it, Gillen: you and me, surrounded by sweaty cholos, all looking good as they peel out of their bright orange jumpers—"*

"All right, all right!" Gillen waved his hands frantically. "Jesus, it's not going to be a porno!"

"Life is what you make of it, amigo. If we want to make it a prison porno, then that's a dream we can achieve together. Oh, and don't think I've forgotten the fact that you're attracted to me, so don't go acting like you're not as ready for this as I am."

Gillen pinched the bridge of his nose to hide the color rising in his face. "I'm actually starting to regret not killing you in a death penalty state."

"There's the sassy guy I know! Now come on, let's have some fun. We don't have to run anymore, so there's nothing to be afraid of. As long as you've got me with you, there's nothing you can't handle. So what do you say, amigo?" Eduardo stuck out his hand. *"Ready to go to prison with me?"*

With the wind in his hair and his only friend smiling at him, Gillen couldn't help but laugh. "Sure, amigo. Let's go to prison."

Chapter Thirty-Two

THERESE PULLED UP to Gillen's house just after sundown. Her tires kicked up a storm of gravel as she sped into the driveway and slammed on the brakes.

She threw open the car door and screamed at the top of her lungs. "Gillen!" A cloud of birds stormed out of the treetops at the sound of her cry. Gillen was not among them.

With a howl of fury, she kicked the car door shut and pounded up the driveway. Eduardo hovered at her side, blood cascading from his gaping wounds. He'd been getting paler and paler since they left the house; over half a day later, he resembled a walking corpse. *Walking* wasn't the right word for it, though, since his feet were no longer touching the ground.

She stopped just long enough to sneer at his floating shoes. "Nice trick, Casper. You think you can scare me with that?"

He stared at her through empty black eyes. *"What kind of a friendly ghost would I be if I wanted to scare you?"*

"A mediocre one, which is exactly what you are." She shook her wrist at him, drawing attention to her diamond-encrusted rose-gold watch. "You've had almost a whole day to kill me, yet you haven't finished the job. Do you have any idea how pathetic that makes you look?"

"Maybe I'm trying to lull you into having a false sense of security."

"Maybe you're so weak that you need a schizophrenic farmer to do what's supposed to be your job."

Eduardo's cracked lips split into a skeletal grin. *"That schizophrenic farmer must be thinking along the same lines as you are, because he's here now."*

"What?"

Detective Olson's familiar midwestern inflection rose above the cawing from the trees. "Time's up, Therese!"

A whip crack ricocheted by Therese's ear. Gray siding exploded a foot from her head. Therese screamed and hurled herself behind her car, covering herself with her hands.

Eduardo appeared at her side in a mist of shadow and blood. *"I think that was a warning shot, puta."* He grinned like he'd just presented her with an oversized check. *"You'd better get to cover inside."*

As much as she hated agreeing with Eduardo, she wasn't going to let herself get shot just to spite him. With both terror and amphetamines fueling her, she dove out from behind her cover and dashed to the front door. A second shot rang out over her head as she grabbed the knob. Fortunately, whoever had been there last forgot to lock it behind them, which gave Therese enough time to whip the door open and hurl herself inside.

The dull yellow of cheap lightbulbs stung her eyes as she slammed the door shut and grabbed the closest piece of furniture to make a barricade. Had the cabinet she found been any kind of quality, she never would have been able to move it, but the pressed wood abomination in her arms proved just light enough for her to shove in her path. Unfortunately, pressed wood wouldn't stand up to gunfire for long, so she needed to think fast.

"He's early!" she hissed as she searched the room for something that would help her. "I'm supposed to have another hour!"

Shadows pooled under Eduardo's eyes as he reformed beneath the hideous lighting. *"I can kill you now if you want to go that way. Just sit back and let me take control. I promise I'll give you a quick death."*

She bared her teeth. "Even if I was stupid enough to believe you, I wouldn't give you the satisfaction." That was what she said, anyway, but continued scanning of the empty room made it clear that someone was going to get the satisfaction of killing her unless a miracle happened. Her teeth clacked together as she rubbed her itching hands. *Where the hell is Gillen?*

The insides of Therese's skull buzzed as Detective Olson's voice reverberated around the room. *"He's gone, Therese."*

Therese and Eduardo snapped to attention in unison. "You!" She spun around, searching for the voice's source. "Show yourself!"

Eduardo's low chuckle scraped through her ears. *"You know he's not in here."*

"He's got to be! How else could I hear him inside?"

"Because he's not inside the house. He's inside your mind."

The sides of Therese's face ached as her eyes darted back and forth in their sockets. "That's not possible..."

"I told you he was more powerful than me. It's no use trying to escape. No matter what you're thinking, he'll be able to hear it."

As if to highlight Eduardo's point, Detective Olson inserted himself in their conversation. *"There's a lot of windows on this place, Mrs. Lynch. I don't need to dump a whole magazine into a cheap shelf to pick you off."*

She shrieked and threw herself to the floor. Her heart raced against the Berber carpet as she clenched her fists and tried to calm herself down. "Come on," she muttered, "think, think!"

"*Yes, puta, think.*" Eduardo reformed in front of her, squatting the way a coach would while giving a pep talk. "*That's exactly what he wants you to do.*"

"Shut up, shut up, shut up!"

Blood dripped down from Eduardo's chest, splattering on her fists. She tried to wipe it off on the carpet, but the ghostly liquid clung to her, seeping through her bandages and into her skin. "Goddammit!" she said. "Why do you have so much blood in you?"

Detective Olson's voice returned, though his midwestern accent didn't come with it. This time, he spoke with that blood-curdling British. "*You really should surrender, old girl. I won't make any false promises about going easy on you, but I'd prefer to get this done quickly so I can sort out the aftermath of your fire. A lovely mess you made, by the way. I hope you can appreciate the fact that we're liable to be written up for that. Not to mention the unenviable browbeating I've been receiving from Ruby. So you'd better come out now, bitch*"—and here his accent switched again, reverting to something Therese could only categorize as urban—"*because I've got better things to do than watch your size-ten feet try to run off in those size-nine shoes!*"

Red fury dripped over Therese's eyes, mirroring the blood cascading from Eduardo's wounds. "How dare you..." Her fingernails bent against the hard floor as she dug her hands into the rug. "Pinche puta!"

Eduardo threw back his head and cackled. "*That's the spirit, Therese! Defend your honor and your boat feet!*

Show them what you're made of, even if it's the last thing you do!"

With a howl of rage, Therese sprang from the ground and bolted for the hall. Eduardo flew along beside her, dragging blood and black fog in his wake.

"He's just a man!" she said as she ran. "It doesn't matter if he can read my mind! He can die as easily as I can!"

"He won't die so easily." Eduardo's voice crackled in and out, as if someone had a hand around his throat. *"I didn't."*

"You're nothing! Just like him! Just like all of them!"

She skidded to a halt in the kitchen and snatched a dirty knife from the sink. Eduardo hovered past her and laughed. *"What are you going to do, stab him? He's shooting you from outside! How are you going to get close?"*

Therese screamed and clenched her fist around the knife. The blade bit into her palm, tearing through her bandage and ripping into her skin. Her blood mixed with Eduardo's in a horrific union of black and red.

"You really need to be more careful with your hands, Therese." Eduardo held up his corpse-white palms and grinned at the syrupy liquid trailing between his fingers. *"Keep cutting yourself and you're going to die."*

She hurled the knife to the ground and jumped back. Her legs shook and her chest heaved and the blood from her hands went *drip, drip, drip* as it splashed against the kitchen floor.

"You've lost your mind, DuCannes!" The British one called out to her again, worming his way around her mind. *"Let me put you out of your misery!"*

"I won't let you!" she screamed.

The heels of her shoes dug into her ankles as she whirled around and bolted for the only door she hadn't checked: a thick, unpainted slab of wood with dents in the rusted knob. She threw it open and slammed it behind her.

Darkness wrapped itself around her, choking the air from her lungs. She gasped for air as she fiddled with the bolt on the door. "Come on, come on!"

The lock slid into place with a satisfying *click*. She threw her back against the door and stared into the darkness. Her erratic breaths heated the cool air around her face as she struggled to get her bearings.

"It's dark in here, isn't it?" said Eduardo.

She couldn't see him in the blackness. He'd merged with it completely, sinking into it with the ease of a stretching shadow. Her burning hands trembled against the door.

"Eduardo?" she whispered. "Eduardo, where are you?"

"Aww, puta, I didn't know you cared."

"Where are you?"

"I'm just ahead of you, Therese. Come join me."

"Join you where?"

His voice coiled inside her ears, like tendrils of smoke inside her brain. *"Just step forward."*

She stuck out a hesitant leg and discovered empty air. *Stairs, I'm standing on stairs.*

With one foot hovering in the air and the other shaking on the stairs, she only had one ankle holding her up straight. All she needed to do to lose her balance was shift her weight.

A hole opened up in Therese's gut. Her lips parted, releasing her breath into the darkness. "Oh no."

"Adios, Therese."

He didn't need to move her much; he only shifted her ankle the slightest bit. That bit was enough to send her tumbling down the stairs, falling into the shadows and Eduardo's deadly embrace.

Chapter Thirty-Three

WHEN ANDREW AND Ed finally caught up to Therese's car, they found it parked in the driveway of the last house on the edge of town. Countless trees jutted up from the surrounding land, blocking out the already fading light and drowning the hillside in darkness.

The engine of Andrew's car rumbled to a stop as he parked at the bottom of the drive. While they could have driven right up to the house, Andrew wasn't crazy about getting that close without taking a second to consider the situation.

Ed's breath left no fog on the glass as he peered through the window at Therese's empty car. *"We took too long to find her,"* he muttered. *"She must already be in the house."*

"It didn't take me that long to find her." Andrew scrunched up his nose. "And I think I did pretty well, considering the difference in our cars."

"You can pat yourself on the back later. We need to find them now."

The dashboard clock flashed 7:24. If Detective Ramirez's story was true, then they had less than twenty minutes to go before both Gillen and Andrew's powers switched on.

"Will I know when I can start hearing people's thoughts?"

"I don't know," said Ed. *"I only know how it felt for me."*

"How was it?"

"You ever been in a room where you can hear there's a television on, but you can't see it?"

"What, like you can hear people talking from a distance?"

"Eventually, yeah. I couldn't hear words at first, though. I could only hear the hum. You know what I mean?"

Andrew nodded. He knew the exact sound, even if he couldn't describe it. Considering what a strange phenomenon mind reading was, that was probably how Eduardo felt about explaining it to someone else.

"I know what you mean, but I don't hear it."

"Not yet you don't," said Ed, *"but it won't be long now, so let's go."*

"Right."

Without taking his eyes off the house, Andrew leaned back and grabbed his shotgun from the back seat of the car. He would have preferred to arrive with it loaded, but he couldn't risk a bump in the road or a curious Hester accidentally setting it off. Compared to those nightmare scenarios, wasting a few seconds on loading in the driveway was a risk Andrew was willing to take.

The shells rattled in his hand as he popped them in the gun. Some distant part of his memory told him there were more technical terms for what he was doing, but he'd always been too scared of looking stupid to ask his mom to explain things again when she was showing him how to fire the gun on her parents' farm. One thing he did remember was that she'd told him never to turn a gun on another person unless his life was in immediate danger. He hated the thought of breaking one of her rules so flagrantly, but he imagined that, if her mind had still been there, she would have understood. After all, she'd been the one to say he could turn the gun on his dad if "the dumb bastard ever came back looking for some quick cash." At the time, Andrew had been so upset about the comment he'd nearly cried, but looking back, he could see how his mom was using dark humor to cope with a bad situation. Considering what he was about to walk into, that skill meant as much to him as knowing how to fire a gun.

Andrew hefted the shotgun over the steering wheel and looked over at the clock. They still had an hour left, which gave them plenty of time to find Gillen in a house the size of a postage stamp.

"We're going to knock on the front door. If he doesn't open up, we'll find a way to break in. If he does open up, I'll fire on him right there."

"Sounds good to me."

"You still okay to back me up?"

"Absolutely."

"Good. Then let's go."

He pushed open the door and stepped out of the car. Crisp air swirled around him as the fresh snow crunched beneath his shoes. If he hadn't been there to kill someone, he would've taken a moment to enjoy the view. With time running out, he had better things to do first.

A streak of gold flew past his shoulder with a bark and a flurry of fur. Andrew's stomach dropped to his shoes. "Hester, no!"

Ed popped into existence at Andrew's side. *"¡Pinche perro! He's going to give us away!"*

All the blood drained from Andrew's face as he imagined Gillen greeting Hester with a knife through the chest. "Gillen wouldn't know it's Hester, right? And he wouldn't just murder a dog?"

"He murdered a human, idiot! You think he'll think

twice about killing a dog? We have to get Hester back before he gets to the house!"

"Do we have time?"

"Not if you keep talking!"

He grabbed his gun and took off after Hester. Unfortunately, Hester took that as a sign that Andrew wanted to play a game. His tail whipped from side to side as he barked in triumph and bolted for the woods.

"Damn it!" Andrew said.

"Quit cursing and keep running!"

Andrew gritted his teeth and continued following Hester's tracks. He stopped dead when the trail merged with a second set of prints. They weren't prints like Hester's, or any other animal he'd seen. They were unmistakably human.

He spun around and traced the human's tracks with his gaze. They led back the way he'd come, only diverging slightly from their path. With so few houses around the property, there could only be one place they went.

Ed narrowed his eyes at the shoe prints. *"Gillen was here."*

"Are you sure it was him? What if it's Therese?"

"If Therese was here, these prints would be twice as big."

"Huh?"

"Have you ever seen that bitch's feet? They're enormous!"

Andrew's sweating palms slid down the shotgun. He set his shoulders back and tightened his grip. "How long ago do you think he made them?"

"It couldn't have been too long. The snow only just stopped; if he'd made them earlier, it would have covered them up." He glanced over his shoulder. *"There isn't a second trail going back."*

"So you're saying he's still out here."

"Maybe he is."

The dull ache in Andrew's stomach cranked up to a crippling nausea. He shut his eyes tight to force down the fear. "I can do this..."

"We both can."

"Right." He opened his eyes again and took a deep breath. "We've got this."

They followed Hester's path together, with Andrew running as fast as he could and Ed jogging at his side to meet his speed. They both knew Ed would have been able to run twice as fast if he'd still been alive, but Ed was kind enough not to point that out under the circumstances. Even still, the burning sensation in Andrew's lungs and the fear of running out of time before getting to Gillen formed giant neon signs pointing toward a future filled with exercise.

A triumphant woof echoed from a clearing up ahead. The reddish-gold of Hester's fur stuck out against the white snow, highlighting his location. Andrew sucked in another breath and bolted forward with the last of his energy.

The moonlight bounced off the melting snow as he emerged in the clearing. Hester stood in the center, tail wagging and ears lifted high off his head. Andrew had seen that goofy expression on Hester before: it was the face he made when he'd made a new friend.

A gaunt shadow of a man stood at Hester's back. In the low light, Andrew could barely make out the stranger's face, but there was no mistaking his lanky frame or his apprehensive stance.

Hester had found Gillen Lynch.

The slick grip of the shotgun shifted in Andrew's hand as Gillen's dark outline taunted him from the edge of the clearing. The shadows threatened to swallow him whole, just as they had on the night he'd killed Ed. The bright lights from Ed's hallway had cast a halo on him then, but he had no halo surrounding him in the blackness of the woods; only an obscene darkness cloaking him from death.

Andrew gritted his teeth and hefted his shotgun, pointing it at Gillen's chest. Hester dashed to the side at the resounding *snap* of the pump forcing the ammo into place. Andrew's finger twitched on the trigger, ready and aching to pull all the way back.

A jolt of pain lanced through Andrew's hand. The air rippled in front of him as if a fire had started in the heart of the snow. Ed reformed in the center, blocking the line of Andrew's shot. He threw his hands forward.

"Wait, don't!"

Ed's plea fell like a single snowflake in the raging storm of Andrew's mind. A thousand other flakes flew in front of it, each carrying the memories of his fallen friends. The largest flake brought back the cry of a brain-dead Narcy, lurching from the mattress and screaming *"Kill me!"* with all the strength she had.

The violent crack of the shotgun resonated around the clearing. Ed burst into a puff of mist and the shot took Gillen through the chest. As Hester bolted from the sound, a circle of blood bloomed from Gillen's shirt. Gillen looked down, blinking at the holes in his heart, and then he dropped to his knees and fell into a puddle of red.

Chapter Thirty-Four

ANDREW'S WHOLE BODY shook as the adrenaline fled his system. He dropped his gun and gaped at Gillen's remains. "Oh my God…"

Even in the cold, sweat clung to the band of his watch, reminding him of its place on his wrist. He sucked in a breath through his nose and dared to check the time.

7:35 p.m. They'd made it.

A long howl was all the warning got before Hester bounded over to him, wild-eyed and panting. Andrew dropped to his knees and threw his arms around the dog. The softness of his fur warmed Andrew's freezing hands and proved he could still feel after shooting another human in the chest.

"I'm sorry, buddy," he whispered into the dog's neck. "I'm sorry."

A strained voice crackled at Andrew's back. *"I'm sorry too."*

Andrew whipped around to find a pale, shaking Ed hunched over the roots of a nearby tree. His body rocked back and forth in time with the wind passing through the trees as he hugged his knees to his chest.

"Ed!" Andrew scrambled over to Ed's side and knelt next to him. The snow soaked through his pants, but he didn't care. "Ed, are you okay?"

Ed's teeth clacked together as he lifted his head to meet Andrew's gaze. He looked like he'd just seen straight into Hell. *"Hey… Andy…"*

Hester padded up next to him and cocked his head at the empty space where Ed sat. Ed held out a trembling hand. For a moment, his fingertips rested atop Hester's muzzle, as if they were physically there, but then flesh sank through fur and Ed's hand fell to the snow.

Andrew placed his palm on the ground next to his friend's. "What happened back there?"

"I..." Ed lowered his head and stared at his open hands. He moved them back and forth, manipulating them as if using them for the first time. *"I'm sorry..."*

"Ed, why did you tell me not to shoot him?"

"I don't know... I think I was scared."

The worry lines digging through Andrew's forehead softened as the tension went out of his back. "It's okay that you were scared. I was scared too. But it's okay now. We're both okay. And hey, Hester's okay too! See?" His breath hitched in his throat as he rubbed the dog's head. "Everybody's okay..."

A deafening *crunch* echoed around the woods. Hester let out a bark and darted forward as Andrew shot upright, weapon in hand. "What was that?"

A woman's voice split through the clearing. "Andrew!"

Andrew hefted his shotgun and searched for the source. With his last shot still ringing in his ears and the wind playing tricks with the sound, he couldn't pin down the voice's source. Unfortunately, there was only one woman who had a reason to be in those woods, and that woman was the kind who'd kill him the second she laid eyes on him.

Tears burned his eyes as he peered through the endless trees. "Don't come any closer, Therese! I've got a gun!"

"I'm not Therese, idiota! I'm Caroline!"

Andrew lowered his shotgun an inch. "Wait, what?"

A short blur raced toward him from the edge of the woods. He barely had time to confirm it was Caroline before she dove on him and wrapped her arms around him in a giant hug.

"Andrew!" she said. "*¡Gracias al cielo!* You're all right!"

Even on his best day, Andrew wouldn't have known how to react if a good-looking woman threw herself at him. After everything he'd been through, the best he could do was blink and try to talk.

"H-h-hi...Caroline..."

Her eyes narrowed and she pushed off of his chest. "Don't hi-Caroline me, culero! You're lucky to be alive! What would you have done if Gillen attacked you, huh? What would you do if he'd known you were coming here?"

Andrew glanced back at Gillen's bleeding corpse. "Um, I think the point is probably moot."

Caroline looked over his shoulder and sucked in a breath through her teeth. Before she could start yelling again, he stuck out his arm and tapped the face of his watch. "I made it in time, see? I even had a few minutes to spare!"

"This isn't an exact science, pendejo!" She smacked the back of her hand against his forearm. "The rules don't hold up in every situation!"

"Wait, they don't?" Andrew drew in another breath and searched Caroline's face for a sign she was telling a joke. She sure didn't seem to be joking, but he had no way of knowing short of reading her mind.

His eyes opened wide and he pumped his fists. "Wait, I can't read your mind! That means I'm right about the time!"

"That doesn't mean you'd be the same as Gillen! This process is different for everybody! There can be aberrations or extenuating circumstances or..." Her gaze drifted back to Gillen's body and all the air went out of her like she'd been stuck with a blunted pin. "Oh, forget it." She swept a hand through her hair and sighed. "I'm just glad you're okay."

He frowned at her, scrunching up his nose. "I didn't think you cared."

"Oh shut up, Brood." She swatted him on the arm. "You know I care. I've been friends with you for over a year."

"No, you've been lying to me for over a year. Remember what you said to Ed—about how you have to work to make a paycheck? I know what I am to you. I haven't forgotten that."

The corners of her mouth turned down, matching her lowered brows. For a liar and a spy, she sure knew how to look ashamed. "Look, I shouldn't have said it that way. I was just pissed at Ed for taking your body. I really am sorry for spying on you, Andrew. Honestly."

"If you're so sorry, then why didn't you tell me the truth in the first place?"

"Technically, I told you the truth a couple days ago."

Andrew raised his eyebrows. "What? When?"

"Give me your phone and I'll show you."

As much as he hated the idea of handing over his phone, there wasn't much she could do with it to ruin his life more than he already had. Even still, he made sure to stand where he could see the screen as he handed it over and watched her pull up his chat program.

She scrolled through his messages until she found what she was looking for and tapped the screen. "Look, see? It's right here."

He leaned forward and muttered to himself as he read the message from the log.

> Blue_María: *Fine, you caught me. I admit it, Brood: I'm a member of an elite, top-secret organization that uses limitless wealth and power to cover up*

mysterious crimes. Because of my skill with video games, I was assigned to pretend to be your friend, all on the one in a million chance that you might be involved in a high profile case I'd need to sweep under the rug

and also im gay

Andrew's face fell. "I thought you were joking..."

"Nope."

"But then the others started saying *same* and *plus one!*"

Caroline rolled her eyes. "They say that to everything. Remember when Android said *same* after Mundy told the story of how he threw up on that girl's face the first time he had sex? You think that really happened to both of them?"

"I'm not convinced it happened to either of them..." Narrowing his eyes, he read the message several times over again. "What about this video game prowess part? That's clearly fake."

"No, that's actually true too."

His eyebrows rose twice as high as they had before. "Wait, really?"

"You must have noticed that I'm almost as good as you are at most of the games we play, right?"

"Well, I..." He rubbed the back of his head, well aware that he was probably blushing. "Maybe I'm not that great at video games, huh? Maybe I'm lousy, which means you are too!"

She shot him a skeptical glance. "Andrew, you're one of the best players on our server. I've seen you kill an entire enemy team with nothing but a bone saw."

"Yeah, well...so what?"

"So when my company said they had two people they wanted us to study as part of our assessment of Eduardo

Sanchez, I saw your file and turned down an easy case with better pay because you and I actually enjoy a lot of the same things. You know what I'm stuck doing most of the time? Pretending to be friendly with stupid housewives so I can figure out if their husbands are using their powers on boring shit like insider trading. Working with you was the first assignment I've enjoyed since I left Mexico."

"Yeah, but—"

"And also, I knew that if any of the other idiots in my department tried to pretend to know their way around a computer game to be your friend, you would have been smart enough to see through them in five minutes."

By that point, Andrew's cheeks were hot enough to burn up the snow around his shoes. "I don't know that I would have. Apparently I'm not so great at getting to know people."

"Well, you won't have that problem for much longer." She looked back at Gillen and winced. "How's Ed holding up?"

Andrew glanced back at Ed's spot on the ground. He was staring into space again, still hugging his knees to his chest and rocking back and forth. "He's not doing great."

The crack of breaking wood echoed around the clearing. An unfamiliar voice cried out, *"Scheisse!"*

Andrew grabbed his gun and pointed it through the trees. Caroline darted in front of the barrel before he could fire. "Stop, it's okay! He's with me!"

The gun slipped in Andrew's hand. "Who's with you?"

A few broken branches and a few more moments later, a middle-aged man with sharp eyes stepped into the clearing. In one of his hands, he held the narrow end of a long, black bag with a zipper down the center. He dropped the bag with a dispassionate thud and looked around. His large forehead creased, matching the line of his frown as he offered a curt wave to Caroline.

"I see you found him."

"Yeah, I did." She cocked an eyebrow at his zip-up bag. "You run into some trouble back there?"

Andrew could barely make out the man's reply through his thick German accent. "Trouble with Tom! You know what he says to me when we have to move the body, Caroline? 'I fuck; you lift.'" He stabbed his foot against the dirt, launching a stone across the ground. "English dog!"

"Did you say body?" Andrew gaped at the bag, then back at Gillen. "Hold on—if I killed Gillen, then—"

The man held up a shining set of keys. "Then I'm the owner of a brand new Porsche."

Caroline didn't seem nearly as alarmed by the body bag as Andrew. She also didn't seem alarmed by the fact that the German man's accent had completely switched to become British.

Instead, all she did was roll her eyes and stick out her hand. "Give me the keys, Tom."

The man who either was or wasn't Tom sighed and tossed Caroline the keys to Therese's car. "I swear, Caroline, you have absolutely no sense of humor."

Andrew sighed and gave up on paying attention. Whatever was going on with their mystery body and Therese, he officially didn't have the energy for it. What little energy he had left in him needed to go to Ed.

Ignoring Caroline for the moment, he knelt back down next to Ed. "Hey." He plastered on a hopeful smile. "We're okay. It's all okay."

Ed didn't look at him. *"Is it...?"*

Caroline must have noticed something was wrong because she dropped down next to Eduardo and waved over her companion. "Hey, can you put Jeremy back in charge for a second? These two have dealt with enough today. The least you can do is properly introduce yourself."

"You know, I would love to, darling," said her companion, "but the others are all very put out about your theft of our new car, so I don't know how amenable they are to conversation."

"The others?" Andrew's eyes went wide as he understood the stranger's meaning. "Do you have people in your head too?"

The man's accent switched back to the sharp German from his entrance. "If you can even call them people when they check out at the first sign of a job requiring effort!"

"*You can check out whenever you like, huh?*" A bitter laugh passed through Ed's lips. "*But you can never leave.*"

Andrew raised his eyebrows and looked back at Ed. Some of the color had come back to Ed's face, but his eyes were still unfocused and he wouldn't lift his head. "What's that mean?"

"*It's nothing, just... just something I heard.*"

A faint wind swirled through the clearing, sending a bitter chill up Andrew's back. He stood and stared down at his soaking pants. He didn't mind kneeling in the dirt to help Eduardo, but it wouldn't help either of them if he froze to death.

As he turned back to Caroline, his gaze passed over what was left of Gillen and his stomach churned. "So what happens now?"

Caroline opened her mouth, but the newcomer spoke first. "Actually," he said, now inexplicably with a midwestern accent, "We just got a call from the office while Hermann was cleaning up the garbage." He nudged his black bag with the side of his foot. "The Quartet wants to see all of us over in Athens."

Something between a gasp and a honk exploded out of Caroline's mouth. "The Quartet wants to see us?"

"Yup, sure do."

"Hijo de puta!"

"Who's the Quartet?" said Andrew. "And wait, does us include me?"

"It includes your whole ensemble. Mine too. Oh, I'm Jeremy Olson, by the by." He stuck out his hand for Andrew to shake. "I'm Caroline's partner."

Andrew took Jeremy's hand and gave it an awkward shake. "Uh, hello." He glanced down at his bag, figuring now was about as good as any time to ask about its contents, but before he could answer, Jeremy shook his head.

"You don't wanna know," he said.

"Oh wow, can you read minds?"

"Yeah, but you see a guy looking at a body bag making that kind of face, you don't need to be a Listener to know what's going on in his head."

Andrew ran his fingers through his hair. "I guess that makes sense." Something warm brushed against his leg and he looked down to see Hester seated at his side. Apparently, Hester wasn't nearly as bothered by the melted snow as humans were.

"So your bosses want to see me in Athens?" He hesitated, remembering that he'd just committed a major crime. "Is that bad, or...?"

"They don't call you up because they want to bullshit, if that's what you're asking." Caroline stuffed her hands in her pockets and stared up at the sky. "But if I had to hope for a best-case scenario, I'd say they're going to offer you a job."

"Me? A job? Why?"

"Because your powers are due to manifest at any minute now, and you can't exactly go back to Sanchez Commercial Real Estate when both Sanchez and his partner are dead. The least we could do after getting you mixed up in all of this is give you a chance to make a living again."

"Doing what?"

Jeremy started laughing. "Oh, I'm sure the Quartet's thought up a whole bunch of good ideas."

Caroline wrinkled her nose at him. "Don't be creepy, Jeremy."

The wind rustled the black bag at Jeremy's feet. Behind them, the second corpse was still bleeding out into the snow. Andrew's mouth twisted to the side and looked back and forth, as if the space between them held some answer to a question he couldn't even begin to form.

"I don't know how I'm supposed to trust you people," he said at last. "I don't even understand why all of this happened. I mean, I know what Gillen did, and what Ed's told me, but..." He glanced back at Caroline and gestured over his head. "But with you spying on me, and how quickly you got involved—there's so much that I want to know before I can believe in you."

Caroline stuck her hands in her pockets. "I'm sorry, but we can't tell you anything unless you agree to work with us."

"How can I agree to work with you if you won't tell me anything about you?"

"How else are we going to find out what these people are hiding?"

Andrew glanced down to see Ed looking up at him, no longer wearing his earlier thousand-yard stare. He hadn't gotten up, though, which meant he must still have been feeling unsteady on his imaginary legs.

"I'm sorry. Can I have a minute to talk to him?" Andrew said to the others.

Caroline nodded. "Take all the time you need."

Unsure of what else to do, Andrew knelt down next to Ed. He would've preferred to talk to Ed privately, but the nature of the situation made that a little difficult.

Fortunately, there was still a way for the two men to talk without being heard.

Andrew cleared his throat and looked Ed in the eye. *Listen, I know you're upset that they were spying on you—and I am too—but you're not seriously saying we should go with these people just to...revenge-spy on them, right?*

"This isn't about revenge; this is about self-defense." He scowled in Caroline's direction. *"As long as these people are out there, they're always going to be monitoring people like us. The only way we can protect ourselves is to figure out how they work."*

I'm really not sure that's a good idea...

A flicker of Ed's old self returned as he narrowed his eyes. *"And that's exactly why I know it is one."*

Jeremy—or Tom or whoever was behind the wheel—let out a short laugh. "Your logic's not too bad, Ed, but you're gonna need a heck of a lot more than two guys if you want to take down Seikilos from the inside."

Andrew's shoulders sank into his aching back. *Damn it, I forgot about him.* He couldn't bring himself to look over at Jeremy, even though his expression couldn't give away anything that wasn't in his head. "You heard all of that, didn't you?"

"You betcha."

Ed frowned at Jeremy from his seat in the roots. *"Seikilos,"* he repeated, sounding out the word. *"That's who you people are?"*

"Sure is," said Jeremy. "If I'm bein' honest, it's not such a bad gig. Can't complain about the pay, and you get to work with folks who can see your whole ensemble. Sure would be nice for you, wouldn't it?"

"I don't know if there's anything about this situation I would call *nice*," Andrew murmured.

Caroline stuck her hands on her hips. "We're not evil, you know. Yes, we were spying on you, but we really are trying to help."

"Help with what? Getting people killed?"

"That's exactly the opposite of what we're trying to do."

"And what are you trying to do?"

"I'm trying to help you too."

"Why should I believe you?"

"Because back when I was a kid, my sister was an Oyente like you, and I'm the idiot who got her killed."

A light breeze rustled the trees overhead, filling the silence that fell over the clearing. Andrew cleared his throat and tried to look anywhere but at Caroline's face. He didn't have the guts to call her a liar on the off chance she was telling the truth, but he couldn't trust someone who would tell such a terrible story for her own benefit. He couldn't ignore her forever, though, since he had to make a decision.

Andrew glanced down at Hester and Ed. Both stared up at him with the same expectant expression. Both of them were relying on him to decide their fate.

A light tingle prickled at the base of Andrew's skull. *"Come on, Brood. Just trust me, please."*

Andrew opened his mouth to speak, but Ed stopped him with a shake of his head. *"She didn't say that out loud, Andy. You read it."*

With two bodies beside him and his best friend's ghost at his feet, Andrew had thought he'd reached the limit of how much could shake him. The faint crackling in the back of his mind proved him wrong. His hands shaking at his sides, he closed his eyes and tried to tune out everything around him, hoping the silence would help him decide what to do next.

The silence didn't help him. The voice of an older woman did. *"Welcome to the Listeners."*

Andrew looked over his shoulder to see Jeremy smiling at him through the shade.

"You'll be all right," he said. Though he kept his natural tone, the same stranger spoke overtop of him in Andrew's head. Her words lined up with Jeremy's, creating a harmony like the voices in a choir. *"No matter what you choose, you'll be all right."*

The rising moon passed over the trees, illuminating the clearing. A few of the beams fell across Ed's face. He still looked awful, but there was life in his smile that Andrew hadn't seen since the night he died.

"Okay," Andrew said. "We'll go."

Epilogue

A CHORUS OF birds chirped on the branch outside the bedroom, rousing its occupants from sleep. The morning light shot a spotlight through the window as Gillen rolled over in his bed.

After seven years of sleeping in a separate bed from Therese, he'd grown accustomed to waking up alone. That was why he was so surprised to get an eyeful of oversized plastic breasts.

He blinked awake and jolted up from the bed. The offending orbs came into focus, proving themselves to be part of a scantily clad figure on the adjacent nightstand. At the sight of the grinning girl's dead eyes, the shock of being blasted with a shotgun came back to him and he clapped his hands over his chest.

"Oh my God!" he said. "Warner sent me to Hell!"

"You know, I've never been partial to breasts myself, but I don't think being forced to look at a pair of them means you're in Hell."

Gillen whipped around. Eduardo stood against the opposite wall, leering at him with a lecherous grin. *"Morning, amigo."*

"Eduardo! You're still here!" He glanced back and forth as he tried to make sense of his surroundings. With the exception of the computer in front of him, all he could see was action figures and dolls. "Where are we?"

"*You're in the same place I've been for days, apparently.*" He spread his arms wide, still wearing a grin. "*A lovely place you can call Hotel Andrew.*"

"I'm in Andrew's house? Why am I in Andrew's house? Why would he bring me home after shooting me?"

"*Because he didn't mean to—and because you're not in his house. You're in his mind.*"

Reality crumbled to dust around Gillen as he looked down at his giant hands. "Oh my God."

"*Oh my God is right. You're living north of Irving Park now.*"

"Irving Park – Irving Park?" Gillen threw back the covers and gaped at the unfamiliar limbs jutting out from his hips. "I've got to get out of here!"

"*Sorry, amigo, but we're here for life.*" Eduardo shrugged his hands. "*Still, not a bad upgrade from prison, wouldn't you say?*"

"How is this an upgrade?" Gillen shouted. "I'm inside the person who shot me!"

"*Yeah, and I'll give you about a second to really get a taste of that irony.*"

Just as Eduardo suggested, it only took Gillen about a second to understand that his current situation was indeed brutally ironic. "I deserve this, don't I?"

"*It goes a long way toward making us even. Still, it really won't be so bad. I've had a few days head start in here—no pun intended—and it's given me some time to get things set up real nice. Nice enough that Andrew doesn't ever have to know you're in here.*"

Gillen raised his eyebrows. "He doesn't know what happened?"

"*Not a clue.*"

"So how do you?"

Eduardo flashed another smile. *"Stay here with me and I'll show you."*

"What, can I go somewhere else?"

"You can't," he said, *"but we've got a lot to do here."*

"What do you mean?"

The distance between the two men narrowed as Eduardo leaned in toward the bed. *"How would you like to know why you were never targeted by the police?"*

"Andrew knows that?"

"He certainly does, amigo—and he also knows that Therese is dead."

Just when Gillen had thought his eyebrows couldn't go any higher, he searched Eduardo's face and realized he was serious. "What the hell happened?"

"That's a very good question. Want to help me get the answers?"

Gillen hesitated and looked around. His body felt disgusting, his room looked awful, and he had a dark feeling his diet was going to include about three-thousand percent more chicken fingers than ever before. Yet in the middle of all of that stood Eduardo, grinning and asking for Gillen's help.

"Definitely," he said.

"Perfect," Ed replied. *"But first, we need to find you a place to hide."*

Acknowledgements

Thank you to everyone who made this book possible. My friends, my family, my co-workers, my fellow writers: I could not have done this without your support. I definitely could not have done without the help of my beta readers, including my husband, my parents, Kerry, Sinead, Lori, and Jo. I owe you the world for giving me your feedback and I will always be grateful.

Thanks to the entire team at NineStar Press for taking a chance on Listener's Remains, and to Raevyn for putting up with my infinite questions. You have the patience of a saint!

Last, but never least, a special thanks to my husband: you never gave up on me and you always pushed me to be the best writer – and the best person – I could be. There's no one else I'd rather have at my side. I love you.

About the Author

L. Julia earned a bachelor's degree in English at the University of Pittsburgh and a master's degree in business administration at DePaul. She is currently employed as the CFO of a very cool video game merchandise company, although she was not the CFO when she wrote a novel about a CFO murdering his boss. That was an unfortunate coincidence and her real-life boss is actually a very nice guy.

L. Julia currently lives in California with her husband and their two terrible corgis. In her spare time, she enjoys reading, gaming, and posting poorly on every forum she visits.

Email: ljuliawrites@gmail.com

Twitter: @ljuliawrites

Website: l-julia.com

Also Available from NineStar Press

Connect with NineStar Press

Website: NineStarPress.com

Facebook: NineStarPress

Facebook Reader Group: NineStarNiche

Twitter: @ninestarpress

Tumblr: NineStarPress

www.ingramcontent.com/pod-product-compliance
Lightning Source LLC
Chambersburg PA
CBHW030553170726
48283CB00002B/307

Gillen Lynch has a complicated relationship with his brother-in-law, Eduardo Sanchez. Gillen hasn't mentioned his attraction to Eduardo; Eduardo hasn't mentioned he's a mind reader. Betrayed by the deception and mortified by his attraction to his sister's spouse, Gillen decides to take it out on Eduardo by killing him.

Murdering a mind reader is no easy task, but this isn't the first time Gillen has killed. His other victims didn't mean anything to him, and they definitely didn't use their dying breaths to copy their minds into Gillen's head. Now, with no barriers between them, Gillen can't stop Eduardo from digging up the secrets he'd hoped to take to his grave. He's scared, powerless, and unprepared to face the fallout of his actions as he flees from both the cops and a group of mysterious pursuers who are as connected to Eduardo as he is.

With his pursuers closing in on him and Eduardo threatening to tear him apart from the inside, Gillen must overcome his self-hatred and take back his mind. If he can't, he'll be at the mercy of the man who has every right to want him dead.